# The Weavers of Meanchey

A Unit 1 Novel

Allen Kent

The Weavers of Meanchey: A Unit I Novel. Copyright © 2014 by Allen Kent. All rights reserved.
Printed in the United States of America. No part of this book may be used or reproduced in any manner whatsoever without written permission except in the cases of brief quotations imbedded in articles or reviews, with attribution shown. For information address AllenPearce Publishers, 16635 Hickory Drive, Neosho, MO 64850

AllenPearce Publishers © ©

Library of Congress Cataloging-in-Publication Data
Allen Kent
Weavers
Kent, Allen
ISBN 978-0-9898400-3-3
Cover Design: Jillian Farnsworth

Allen Kent © 2014

To my Thai friends,
Tanom Intarakumnerd and Laongtip Mathurasa,
and to Allen Cissell with whom I first
explored the wonders of Southeast Asia

## ACKNOWLEDGMENTS

I am most grateful to my team of reader/editors: my wife Holly, Anne and Richard Clement, Diane Andris, Marilyn Jenson, and Paul and Jim Farnsworth, whose invaluable editorial advice improved this book immeasurably. Special thanks to Stephen Farnsworth for his assistance with descriptions of critical computer security techniques and program construction, and to my Thai friends, Drs. Tanom Intarakumnerd and Laongtip Mathurasa, and Dr. Allen Cissell who first introduced me to Jim Thompson and his legacy. William Warren's book, *Jim Thompson: The Unsolved Mystery* provided much of the detail about Thompson's life and disappearance, and I owe a deep debt of gratitude to my talented daughter-in-law, Jillian Farnsworth, for the wonderful cover idea and artwork that introduce the novel. Thanks, also, to Fran and Eric Pope who hosted us at their beautiful home in St. Kitts where a good part of *Weavers* was written. Without all of you, this book would not have been possible.

# The Weavers of Meanchey

### ...a country home near Ashburn, Virginia

The encrypted message from the Director of Central Intelligence reached Fisher's computer the very morning he had been wondering aloud to Anita if the Weaver affair had amounted to anything. The message was in the Director's terse style: long enough to give the essentials; short enough to be enticing.

> *Re: Weavers memo of five months ago. New chatter coming out of NSA concerning a CIA source who disappeared in Southeast Asia in the late 60s. Name: Jim Thompson. You may remember him. Intel indicates that before disappearing, Thompson sent security-critical info to a CIA contact that was not received, but recently discovered. Advisors here see this as old news – unrelated to current security interests. They advise not to pursue. Don't wish to countermand and may be seeing connections that don't exist. But Han at NSA has asked to see all communication involving Jim Thompson. Coincidence?*
>
> *New chatter involves retired agent, Eric Compton, who you no doubt remember. He and Thompson were friends in Bangkok. Now lives in Remington, VA. Was contacted by a Davis Eckerson, indicating Eckerson has a message for Compton from Thompson. Davis meets with Compton tomorrow. Is now at Comfort Inn in Culpeper, VA. May be a dead end, but worth finding out. Contact if more info needed.*

Fisher transferred the message to Anita's console. "What do you think?" he asked.

She quickly scanned the Director's note. "His advisors may be right," she said, pushing her chair away from the computer. "This looks like old news. But wasn't Han the NSA man mentioned in that Weavers message?"

Fisher pecked quickly at his keyboard, then leaned back and squinted through the bottom of his bifocals. "Here's the last note from the Director. *'Received anonymous message addressed "Director's Eyes Only." Asks that we investigate relationship between Bradley Han at NSA, Marshall Ding at a Dallas firm called FedTegrity, and a group called the Weavers. Advises we do so quickly and with great caution. People here think a hoax. I'm not certain. Please follow up.'* In addition to the people inside thinking this wasn't serious, I suspect the Director wasn't excited about having his people investigate someone inside the NSA. So he asked us to do it."

Anita nodded. "But what makes the Director think this new information might be related?"

"Intuition," Fisher said. "Mention of Han, Jim Thompson, and weavers in the two memos. Thompson was sometimes referred to as the Thai Silk King."

"You knew him?"

"More like, knew *of* him. Everyone in the Agency knew about Jim Thompson. And I knew Eric Compton pretty well. Good man."

"And what does *your* intuition tell you?" Anita asked.

Fisher's aged chuckle rasped like boots on gravel. "Thompson, Compton, Weavers? Gotta be more than coincidence. There's something to this."

Anita wheeled her chair back up to her console. "Then I'd better send this to Adam Zak," she said.

# ONE

The blue ball skipped midway up the front wall, arched high above mid-court where it barely grazed the ceiling, then dropped softly against the glass of the back wall, eighteen inches above the floor. It hit the varnished maple of the court surface with a muted plop that signaled it wasn't going to rebound more than six or seven inches. Adam was ready. He took two quick shuffle steps to his left, reached behind the ball with racquet poised, and snapped his wrist as he swept his arm forward, catching the ball four inches from the wood surface. The blue sphere didn't rise an inch as it traveled the thirty feet into the front left corner, hitting the joint of the front and side walls so perfectly it died instantly, dropping lifeless without so much as a dribble.

Dreu Sason bent forward with hands on knees and glanced sideways at her opponent, a drop of perspiration sliding down her nose and beading for a moment before she brushed it away with the back of her racquet hand, then wiped her forehead with a wristband.

"I don't know what it's going to take," she panted. "That lob was almost perfect – and on your blind side. And you still got it."

Adam forced the knuckles of both hands into the middle of his back, twisting from side to side to relieve the tension in his aching muscles. "Don't know what you're complaining about," he said. "You won the first game with a shot just like that. Everything I know, I learned from you."

"Yeah – right..." she laughed, straightening and walking to the door that opened into the corridor separating the racquetball courts from the fitness center's central gymnasium. Adam followed, admiring from behind the shapely hips outlined so perfectly by her thigh-length Lycra shorts and the sculpted legs that were at least half of her slender, six-foot frame. He swatted her playfully on the butt with his racquet as they walked toward the dressing rooms.

"Time for lunch today?"

"Can't. Some of us have to work. We have people coming in from Washington this morning for meetings that will last most of the day. In fact, I need to head right into the city as soon as I get cleaned up. I'll call you tonight."

In the hallway outside the dressing room doors, he turned her toward him, kissing her lightly and looking for a moment into her hypnotic eyes. They were the color of liquid caramel with bursts of gold radiating from the pupils and had been the first thing he noticed about her when the membership director first introduced them, a meeting that had been at his request.

"I understand you're a racquetball player," he'd said, extending a hand. "I'm Adam Zak and I'm looking for a partner who comes in about six."

"There are a number of guys who play early," she said. "They might be better competition." The beautiful eyes were set under dark, carefully shaped brows into a finely-featured face of uncertain ethnicity: smooth light brown skin with silky black hair, pulled back into a single braid that fell midway down her back. Her mouth was full and wide and, when she smiled, displayed perfect teeth. Not at all what he had expected from the Fisher dossier that had led him to rent the house in McKinney, Texas, and join Lifetime Fitness to arrange this chance introduction.

"I hear the guys come in already paired up – that you're a pretty good player, and usually choose to play whoever's available. I'm available this morning...."

She had shrugged her consent and led him to an empty court. One item in the dossier was right. She was a mean racquetball player. And though Adam had always considered himself pretty decent, they split their first four games.

"Rubber match tomorrow – same time?" he had asked as they left the court that first morning.

She stopped outside the dressing rooms and considered the invitation for a long moment.

"I think I'd like that," she said finally, and they had been seeing each other now for nearly four months.

To the gym's other patrons, they had become the talk of the morning exercise crowd: the polite, distant woman with the striking figure and dark, natural beauty; and the tall, quiet newcomer with the black eye patch who looked like a younger, chestnut-haired version of actor Sam Elliot, complete with mustache. Since joining the center, Adam had been keeping his hair shoulder length and pulled back into a ponytail when he worked the cardio equipment or played racquetball.

Now, as he pushed into the dressing room, he was thinking that he was becoming too fond of Dreu Sason. Definitely not part of the assignment. When he began his investigation of Marshall Ding, she was simply a name on a list of FedTegrity's top-level employees: the senior female programmer and one who, on paper, looked like his best shot at getting information about her boss.

And in its own way, Fisher's profile information had been spot on: thirty-three and single; six feet tall and of mixed Indian and East European ancestry; former model, with a Stanford degree on computer analytics. But the file photo hardly did her justice and looked like a post office mug shot taken on a bad hair day. Not exactly Miss October. And according to the dossier, she had been pretty badly carved up by a stalker who purportedly was intent on disfiguring her. Adam fully anticipated that when they met, she would be trying to hide surgically-softened traces of a brutal knife attack. Plus, he had grown up in central Nebraska, and his corn-fed vision of a woman with a Stanford degree who developed computer security programs subconsciously added twenty pounds to the parts of her body that didn't show in the file photo. When he asked the guy at Lifetime to introduce them, he expected a round-shouldered, slightly over-weight woman with unkempt hair and disfiguring facial scars, who used the morning workout in a vain attempt to tighten a drooping bottom and slim thighs that were getting away from her.

That was not Dreu Sason. And as he veiled his surprise at their first meeting, he gave himself a mental kick in the pants for thinking like his uncle Max. When at age forty his aunt Olivia had shown serious interest in going back to school to become a veterinary technician, Max not only said "no," but "hell, no," and joked about it for the next two weeks until Olivia's resolve crumbled.

"Won't have any wife of mine with her arm shoulder-deep up the south end of a north-bound heifer," he laughed at a family get-together. But he never seemed to object to her driving the combine during the wheat harvest or slaughtering, hanging, and dressing-out a 200-pound hog. That somehow fit his image of how a bright, attractive, Midwestern woman should be spending her time. Adam had never aspired to be like uncle Max, and didn't like the fact that he had allowed the kind of chauvinism Max enjoyed joking about to color his own thinking. Adam liked to call those errant thoughts Maxian Brain Farts.

And now that he and Dreu had been seeing each other two or three times a week for four months, it was much more than her stunning good looks that was chipping away at his resolve to remain detached. The woman had a candor and genuineness that were completely disarming, and as their relationship moved from the racquetball court, to dinner together, toward greater intimacy, she stopped him one evening as he moved his hand under the back of her shirt and began to massage her bare shoulders.

"Time for a little truth talk," she said, backing away.

He also retreated a step, wondering if she had somehow discovered that he was investigating Ding and FedTegrity.

"Sorry if I over-stepped," he said, his smile tight but apologetic. "I must have misread some cues."

"Oh, I know I was tossing out the cues," she said quickly. "I just don't want to have to deal with the *OMG* if you get too much farther into my clothes."

His smile softened and he separated from her by another step, looking her over critically. She was wearing a pair of figure-hugging jeans and a loose denim shirt with the tails hanging over her hips. "Everything I see looks perfect," he said.

Dreu nodded and cocked her head to one side. "It's what you can't see that you may have trouble with. And you're getting there pretty fast."

"Okay.... Then let's have your truth talk. I don't want anything to be uncomfortable – for either of us." They were in the entryway of her apartment and he led her into the living room and eased her onto one end of her olive-colored sofa, taking the other end with a knee propped up on the cushion between them.

She tucked her legs beneath her and looked down at her lap, then directly into his uncovered eye.

"You told me the first day we met at the gym that I had a familiar face, then joked that it wasn't just a lame pick-up line. That you really did feel like you'd seen me before."

He nodded, letting her speak without interruption.

"Well, you've probably seen me a dozen times on the end of the check-out stand at the supermarket. I modeled pretty successfully for six years...."

The modeling wasn't news, but when he saw her the first time, the face did seem uncomfortably familiar for a woman he was planning to turn into an informant. He rarely looked at the magazine racks and knew that if he had seen her there, it would only have been a quick impression. But a face like hers would have made one. Again he remained silent.

"Do you remember reading or hearing about a model who was attacked by a stalker about eighteen months ago?"

Finally – she was getting to the stalker incident. He did vaguely remembered the news item, but none of the details. Adam's media intake consisted of a quick online review each morning of the local paper, the *New York Times* and the *Wall Street Journal*. Practically no TV. But he thought the *Times* had featured a short piece.... He nodded an acknowledgment.

Her mouth twisted into a wry smile. "That was me. The guy believed God told him I was destined to be his wife and have his children. I had to get a restraining order...." She watched Adam's face for any sign he knew where the story was going and, seeing none, leaned back into the arm of the sofa and folded her hands in her lap. "...and when he figured out it wasn't going to happen, he broke into my apartment and attacked me with a knife. Didn't want to kill me. Just punish me for, as he put it, 'putting my body on display.' So he cut me up so no one else would want me."

Though Fisher's dossier had forewarned him, Adam felt his throat tightened and eyes begin to moisten.

"I'm so sorry," he murmured. "How badly?"

She raised her left hand to her right breast and placed her other hand across her stomach. "He slashed my breast almost in half – this way." She drew her index finger from under her right arm over to the middle of her chest. "And he cut across my stomach where he thought my uterus was. Got more intestine than uterus, and some amazing surgeons were able to get everything stitched back together and in place. But he did manage to ruin the uterus and there are some pretty ugly scars."

Adam could think of only one thing to say. He straightened on the couch and moved his own hands to his lap. "May I see?" he asked.

Her quick smile showed relief, and she slowly unbuttoned her shirt and lifted her bra. Her right breast, otherwise beautifully shaped, had a thick-edged crease that ran horizontally just below the dark circle of her nipple, with visible marks where the skin had been stapled together.

She looked down at her chest. "They could have done more cosmetic surgery, but I didn't want it. It is what it is, and I was getting sick of New York anyway. The pressures of schedule, the paparazzi that hovered outside every place I went, and the constant simpering attention of almost everyone. Plus, though most of the women who worked with me were intelligent, interesting people, we were treated as if we never had an original thought of our own and were no more than under-fed, pretty faces who had learned to strut."

Her comment added new odor to his brain fart.

She lowered the bra and buttoned her shirt. "Even if they'd been able to get me back on the runway, I was ready to get out of there."

She pushed her hips forward on the sofa and unzipped her jeans, wriggling her red underwear low enough to reveal another knotted rope that ran from hip bone to hip bone.

"He cut me top and bottom," she said, pulling the jeans back up and giving him a "well, there you have it!" look.

Adam pursed his lips, still looking at the beltline that covered the scar across her belly. When he picked Dreu Sason as a potential avenue to Marshall Ding, he should have asked Fisher for a more comprehensive bio.

"Where is the guy now?" he asked.

Dreu smiled thinly. "Locked away in Bellevue in Manhattan. Should be there a long time."

Adam raised his elbow again to the back of the couch and rubbed his fingers across his chin. "Well, you're in luck," he said, reaching up to lift the black patch that covered his left eye. Beneath it, the prosthetic eye was perfectly matched in color and had a life-like shine that made it almost indistinguishable from the right – but not quite. She looked back and forth between the eyes, then raised a questioningly brow.

"This one," he said, pointing to the prosthesis, "happened to be my judgmental eye. It saw flaws in people that shouldn't have mattered. You've never asked about it – and I guess now I know why. I'll tell you sometime." He lowered the patch and pointed at the other. "This one is my 'thing of beauty' eye. It's all I have left... so when I look at you, and I mean *anywhere* on you, that's all I see."

Her own eyes teared and they sat for another hour, telling more truths. He explained how he had lost the eye in a military flying accident, and she confessed that she hadn't been in a relationship since her attack: partly because of the scars, partly out of fear, but mainly because she found men a little too obsessed – one way or the other – with how she looked.

"You want so badly to be seen as more than a pretty face," she said. "But you also don't want to be defined by a couple of ugly scars."

"All I notice is that you have a great backhand," he teased, and she bent forward and kissed him.

As he held her in the front entryway before saying goodnight, he again gently rubbed her back beneath her shirt.

"If you decide you're comfortable with this going further," he said, "there's nothing about you that will trouble me in the least."

"How about dinner tomorrow night," she said.

From the night of truth-telling, he had added to the information in Fisher's dossier that Dreu was the daughter of two physicists who worked for a private research group in Palo Alto, California. Her mother, a first generation Indian immigrant from Mumbai, met her father, a Sephardic Jew, while both were graduate students at Stanford. Both had shattered family taboos when they married.

As he had listened to her from the other end of the couch, Adam began to understand her dark, multi-ethnic beauty and innate genius. But the genius had come at the price of growing up in a home of continuously unmet expectations. After a year working for Microsoft, a year during which she was constantly reminded by both parents that her career path should be on a steeper trajectory, she fled the West Coast to pursue a modeling career in New York.

"My younger brother rebelled first," she laughed. "He's a professional cyclist, racing with a team in Italy. Drives my parents crazy. But I had a high school friend who had become successful in New York, and she connected me with her agent. It turned out I was pretty good at it.... And I don't think my agent ever really believed I went to Stanford. Even when I told her I was leaving to work for a computer programming firm, I could tell she was skeptical."

Brain farts aren't limited to small-town guys from Nebraska, Adam thought. But said, "And that's what brought you to Texas...?"

She nodded matter-of-factly. "Yup. A position as one of the lead systems designers for a Dallas group called FedTegrity. We provide contracted computer security for departments of the federal government. Mom and dad are *soo* proud..."

"I'm impressed!" Adam said with a convincing smile. And though he had known before he met her exactly what she did, hearing her say it and looking at her curled comfortably at the other end of the sofa did make an impression.

She had chosen to live in a modest condominium on the south edge of the Dallas suburb of McKinney where she spent the 6:00 a.m. hour every weekday morning at the gym – not trimming her flabby thighs, but keeping her lithe figure in enviable condition and working stretch into the fibrous tissue of the scars. Adam had never been so smitten by a woman, and that troubled him more each time he lied to her.

In the gym's locker room, he twirled the numbers into his combination and instinctively checked his iPhone. There was only one text, but he immediately pulled out his clothing and gym bag, closed the locker and, without changing, walked out of the building to his blue Nissan Sentra that sat surrounded by more expensive SUVs. He slipped into the driver's seat, fished a second cell phone from the bag, and punched in a fifteen digit number that encoded the call as it was entered. The "yes" that answered was slow and rasped with age.

"I received your message," Adam said, referring to the text that had simply announced that his dry cleaning was ready for pickup.

"There's an email waiting," the voice said. "It may require immediate attention."

"I'll get right to it. Do you need a reply?"

"Only if you need more information," the aged voice said.

"Very good." Adam pushed the 'end' button and fumbled again for the iPhone, quickly tapping in a brief text to Dreu.

*"Called in for an unexpected work assignment. Will call later. Enjoy your meetings!"*

He dropped both phones onto the seat, started the car, and eased out of the parking lot toward the turn under the Sam Rayburn Tollway that took him back to Stacy Road. At Custer Road he turned north into McKinney and relaxed back into his seat. He had been inching his way toward Marshall Ding and FedTegrity so slowly that it sometimes felt like trying to run in a dream – every step a slog through wet, ankle-deep mud. The message from Fisher might be just what he needed to slap himself awake and put some pace back into this investigation.

# TWO

If the last will and testament of Gladys Eckerson had included only the box of travel stickers with the mysterious letter in it and not the three million dollars, Davis probably would have stayed in college. And he probably wouldn't have ended up in a back room of the *Pussy Cat* lounge, halfway around the world, with two Thai bargirls feeling their way through his pockets. But Aunt Gladys's will *had* included the three million, and even when you've never worked a day in your life and been given pretty much everything you wanted, three million dollars is still a lot of money.

The letter hinted at a mystery that was just enticing enough to pique the interest of an aspiring student of investigative journalism. But as a sophomore living on ramen noodles and sharing a two-room apartment near the University of Missouri campus with a starving Russian, without the money the letter would have been no more than an intriguing curiosity. Davis probably would have spent some Google time finding out about Jim Thompson, worked the letter and Thompson's story into a class assignment, then let it drop. But the settlement of Gladys's estate happened over the Memorial Day weekend when he had about overdosed on noodles and was starting to sneak away from his college friends to grab dinner at some of Columbia's better restaurants. It was also a weekend when Alex Korfy – the starving Russian – wasn't around to keep apartment life lively with a couple of coeds from the International Club.

Alex was a sixth-year junior in the journalism program with a focus on international media, an interest he pursued primarily by bringing as many ethnically diverse coeds as possible to the apartment for what he called "his research." Selection wasn't entirely random. His only criterion, by his own admission, was that they have great bodies. Faces weren't nearly as important. Just bodies. Alex once told Davis with a wink that there was an old Russian saying that "You never look at the mantel when you're poking the fire." Davis suspected there was nothing at all Russian about the expression, and that it was something Alex picked up as a freshman over a couple of beers at Mojo's. But it was as close as Alex came to having a philosophy of life, so Davis didn't argue with him about etymology. Since Davis and the Russian shared the single bedroom of their studio walk-up, Alex always managed to invite his subjects over in pairs: one to occupy Davis on the futon in the combination living room-kitchen, while Alex conducted his special brand of inquiry in the bedroom.

"I'm doing a study of what foreign women enjoy," he told their friends, who seemed constantly amazed at the Russian's ability to attract women. Davis they could understand. He was the picture of the budding evening news anchor: frat boy good looks, dishwater blond hair that always looked perfectly disheveled, and GQ clothes. He humored Alex and his college friends by pretending to be one of the struggling masses, but they all knew he had a money train making regular runs from his father's bank in St. Louis.

Alex, on the other hand, was short and stocky with a rugged face that gave the impression he had just emerged from a coal mine somewhere in the Urals, with a background story to match. He didn't ever seem to have two kopecks to rub together. But women loved him and when asked what he was learning about the tastes of his global bevy of bodies, Alex just laughed and said; "Don't know. But I'm learning what *I* like."

Davis was learning that he enjoyed Alex's research more than he did the rigors of academic life. He guessed his grades this semester might place him on probation – at least with the School of Journalism. It was time to reevaluate, and what the hell! He'd gotten into the J-School because of a legacy gift from his old man, who had really wanted him to go into the College of Business anyway. Davis's application to the J-School was partly to annoy Davis Eckerson III and partly because of *Dateline NBC* and television's weekly menu of real life 'who done it' docudramas.

Davis rarely missed *Dateline* and loved the way it took a mystery – usually a murder – and systematically unfolded it until, *voila*! You suddenly realized that on that fateful day in early May, Reba Jo had *not* been sent home early from her shift at the dog food factory by the night foreman because she was feeling ill. Instead, during the last break before closing, he had lured her into a storage area behind the bagging room where he had raped her, strangled her with three twisted strips of bag-stitching tape, and dumped her body into the dark waters of an abandoned quarry.

Davis was fascinated by the kind of detective work that unfolded during each *Dateline* hour and had fleetingly thought of a career in law enforcement: of becoming a detective. That would *really* piss off Davis III! But then a high school classmate whose father actually was a police officer, told him it took years to become a detective – years of sorting out domestic disputes, responding to gruesome highway fatalities, and doing crowd control detail when some dignitary decided to come into town. Not Davis's idea of a good time. He wanted to be *Dateline* reporter Keith Morrison, sitting cross-legged in an overstuffed chair with a look of puzzled concern creasing his distinguished brow as he interviewed all the players involved in the murder drama, gradually letting the public know how it all came together. And if it could be a mystery Davis had solved himself – something really mind-blowing – well, so much the better. Like the kind of mystery that was wrapped up in the letter he'd found in the box of travel stickers. It was a story that could put him on primetime television, especially with Gladys's three million to carry him through the investigation.

To be honest, showing up in the old girl's will had taken Davis completely by surprise. He'd never really cared much for his father's only sister, but had gone to see her about once a month when he'd been in high school, just because she was such a case. To say Gladys was eccentric was a little like saying that old men have gas – obvious to everyone, but not something you mentioned out loud. She had never married or had a partner, probably because she was just too weird to live with. The old lady spent most of her days in a huge greenhouse she'd had custom built behind her home in the St. Louis suburb of Ladue. In a third of the Plexiglas-covered space she raised heirloom vegetables, turning the rest into a rainforest where she kept an assortment of tropical reptiles. She got the idea, she said, from the tropical dome at the St. Louis Botanical Garden and from a big greenhouse in Faust Park, west of the city.

Gladys loved the humid, musty smell of shiny-leafed rubber trees, banana palms, vines that scaled the walls with tendrilled fingers, and a cascading stream that started high at one end of the double-walled structure and tumbled down mossy, faux rocks to a pool at the other end that teemed with multicolored koi. Her jungle was inhabited by a pair of yard-long iguanas and three Burmese pythons that she fed every other week with a delivery of a half dozen, worn-out hens from an egg-laying operation somewhere near Union, Missouri. The chickens were released live into the jungle, clucking and squawking until they found a place to roost, and were gone by morning. Gladys would stalk down the arched pathways that ran like a maze through her rainforest, an ancient bolt-action .22 rifle tucked under one arm. Most days she wore a long-sleeved linen blouse and divided khaki skirt, patterned after one she had seen Deborah Kerr wear in the 1950's version of *King Solomon's Mine*. If she were feeling casual, it might be bloused riding pants and high leather boots – but always the safari theme, right down to the broad-brimmed Stewart Granger hat. She rarely saw one of the pythons, just scatterings of white feathers on the moss-covered flagstones. But Gladys wasn't looking for snakes. She was after bigger game.

At the end of the greenhouse opposite the headwaters of the cascades, a flight of rough stone steps descended through a thick screen of fern and rubber tree leaves down into a dimly lit tunnel that ran for thirty feet into the basement of her sprawling Victorian home. The walls of the subterranean corridor were painted with murals of an African savannah that were so real and had such deceptive perspective that when Davis entered the tunnel for the first time, he felt like he was walking right out onto the Serengeti in the early light of morning. He found himself feeling for the walls to know where the floor ended and the sides of the tunnel began. Gladys said she had the murals done by a sidewalk artist she saw downtown near the Gateway Arch one afternoon: a man who did those chalk drawings on the pavement that you just can't get yourself to step on, so convinced that you might *really* be stepping onto an escalator that would take you down somewhere beneath the Arch. To add to the illusion in Gladys's basement, a hidden fan wafted a light breeze over the open plain, carrying recorded sounds of animals moving in the distance across the grasslands.

At the end of the corridor was another screen of red, head-high grass that Gladys would cautiously push through into what looked for all the world like a thicket of tropical strangler fig. In front of them, in another wide panorama carpeted with thick artificial grass the color of Gladys's skirt, the African savannah stretched to the horizon. In the distance, probably sixty feet away under what must be the kitchen but looking much farther because of their size, mechanical antelope bound across the room from right to left, disappearing into a painted grove of thorny bushes. They were followed by Cape buffalo, wart hogs, spire-horned bushbucks, hyenas and heavy-maned lions that loped onto the plane, each coming from different directions and at unpredictable intervals like a randomized carnival shooting gallery. The ultimate prize was a white rhino that charged onto the scene, stopped for two quick seconds, then thundered out of sight, complete with snorting and the drum of hoof beats. Gladys never went beyond the screen of strangler fig – just crouched there with her .22 braced with an elbow against one knee and shot big game. There wasn't another show in St. Louis that came close to the one put on by the old lady as she blasted away across the length of her basement with the bolt action .22.

"Remember, Davis," she would instruct. "Don't hold your breath when you shoot. Release it and relax. Then squeeze the trigger smoothly." When she first gave him a turn with the rifle and he fired off a quick shot, she grabbed the .22 in exasperation and quickly dispensed a couple of bushbucks.

"*Squeeeeze!*" she said in a long, breathy exhale. "You kids to-day are so impatient. You've got to learn to relax and *squeeeeze!*"

Under her able tutelage, he had reached the point that he could *pling* a bounding antelope better than the old lady, and she pledged to take him with her if she ever headed for the real savannah.

Playing along with the charade, Davis asked her one afternoon if she planned someday to go in search of the fabled King Solomon's Mine.

"Oh, I found that a long time ago," she said, and left it at that. When the will was read, he learned that King Solomon's Mine for Aunt Gladys was three hundred shares of Walmart stock, purchased when the initial 30,000 public shares were issued in 1970. King Solomon should have been so wise! She left three million of the fortune to him with a brief note:

> *You have shown yourself to be remarkably spoiled and undisciplined, and this might make things worse. But you are my only nephew and for whatever reasons, the only family member who has come to visit me in the last ten years. I know it was usually so you could tell your friends what your crazy old aunt was up to, but at least*

*you came. Your father didn't even have the decency to do that. Now try to do something worthwhile with your life!*

Davis discovered the letter from 'Jim' in the bottom of a box of vintage travel stickers: the kind tourists once collected to cover the sides of their suitcases and adorn pages of their journals. Davis suspected Gladys wasn't even aware the letter was there. Seeming to know that her days were numbered, she had hand-written a brief note and left it with the box.

*Davis:*

*I know you don't share my passion for travel or for collecting stickers, but when it comes to the stickers, neither does anyone else I can think of. As for the travel, you should get out and see the world. Nothing helps a person learn to put his life into perspective better than seeing how others live. And some of these stickers are quite old and quite unique. Maybe they will entice you to visit some of the places they represent. I bought many of them at a sale when I lived in Pennsylvania from the estate of a woman a lot like myself. Her name was Katherine Wood and she traveled broadly and loved to collect. (The poor woman had been murdered in her bed and her family didn't want to keep most of her things. We might be alike in that respect too – aside from being murdered in my bed, I hope!) As you can see, she had stickers from hotels and airlines from as early as the late Thirties: places she had visited, ocean liners from the glory days, and cities and towns from around the globe. Even if you don't decide to pursue this hobby, get out of St. Louis and go see the world!*

*Gladys*

Davis had no interest at all in the old lady's hobby. And that's what it was – an old lady kind of hobby. But he did feel compelled to empty the box to see if there was anything else in it that might be of value. The letter was beneath a pile of over two hundred stickers and had wedged under the box's bottom flap. It was still in a yellowed envelope addressed to Katharine Thompson Wood, postmarked Bangkok,

Thailand, February 7, 1967. When he discovered it, Davis was staying at the Pear Tree Inn across the interstate from the St. Louis airport, waiting for the financial part of the estate to be settled. He saw no reason for his parents to know he was in town and was certain none of their acquaintances would discover him at the Pear Tree. They would be a half mile east at the Hilton. His father, an AT&T exec in the city, didn't seem to care what Davis did as long as it didn't embarrass the family. And this was a man whose sister raised pythons and shot big game in her Ladue basement!

Davis scattered the stickers out over the bedspread to begin to sort them into piles by shape and country so he could check them on eBay. He found the letter under two that had partially stuck to the bottom of the old box. One rectangular specimen was from the Yorkshire and Blackpool Rail Line in England and showed the Blackpool Tower and a woman sitting on a beach sporting a wide-brimmed yellow hat. The other, a round Pan American sticker, displayed an old humpbacked Super Constellation airliner flying over what looked like a village in Spain and had to be peeled away from the end of the envelope. Davis dropped into the room's desk chair and pulled the letter from its brittle casing, expecting to find an exotic decal from someplace like Budapest or Morocco, but finding instead a short, hand-written note.

*Kaa:*

*Hope you're doing well and wish you wouldn't continue to live by yourself that far from the city. Also hope to see you again this Labor Day but may have to drop out of sight for a few months. Looks like I've gotten myself into a bit of a mess and, should anything happen to me before our get-together in September, get this note to Eric Compton at the Asia desk at the CIA. He needs to learn more about a group of Chinese children being trained at the Cambodian village of Paoy Snoul, not far from Siem Reap and Angkor Wat. The villagers call these children the little "Weavers." I asked my friend Pridi about the kids and, after looking into it, he told me to forget about them. Someone doesn't seem to believe I will, and what I think was an attempt to abduct me here in Bangkok last week may be related. Possibly just my imagination which has become vivid of late. It may just be scare tactics by the government to get me to give up my antiquities collection. But should anything happen to me, contact Eric and give him this letter.*

*(Eric, if you're seeing this, they must have gotten to me. Find out about the Weavers of Paoy Snoul!)*

*Jim*

So there Davis was at the Pear Tree Inn, avoiding his own parents who lived no more than a mile away, finding the only satisfaction of college in Alex's collection of global beauties, but thinking it would still be cool to be an investigative journalist. Now he had this enticing letter from "Jim" in hand and within a couple of days, would have Gladys's three million dollars. The old girl wanted him to see the world, and not in the seductive eyes of Alex's two latest friends, Sienna and Boonchop. He thought of sending Alex a text but didn't want to risk being talked out of the scheme that was hatching in his head before it even got off the ground. So he scribbled a quick note to mail at the desk on his way out of town.

*Hey, Man. You know I love ya. And love your research even more. But I don't love Sharifi's College Algebra class and don't understand a thing the guy says. You're the only one in there who does, and that's because you don't speak English either. So I'm outta here! I'll cover the rent through the rest of the semester so you can have the place to yourself and your research. I know you prefer Sienna but give Boonchop a tumble. She's a good time. Have a grand summer! I'm planning to – and will be in touch. I'm off to find the Weavers.*

## THREE

Adam's confession night with Dreu Sason had glossed over a number of details, not the least of which was the fact that it was now nearly three years since Adam had ceased to be Tom Mercomes. As he drove the three miles from the gym to his rented home in Virginia Hills, his mind drifted to the morning when as Mercomes, he had been leaning against the rail of his condominium's second floor balcony in Colorado Springs, gazing across the valley at the jutting spires of the Air Force Academy chapel. Below him, a light breeze lifted spray from a sprinkler head that watered the fifteenth fairway of the Gleneagle Golf Course, painting a faint rainbow across his view. He could still picture the wash of color over the shining parallel ribs of the chapel and how it reminded him of the reason he had entered the service: to fly jets and see the sun gleam off the perfectly aligned wings and tails of silver aircraft flying in formation. When he had finally experienced it, it was a sight he had never forgotten, even after the accident forced him from the cockpit and into a classroom at the Academy.

The memory again drew Adam's hand to the patch over his left eye with a twinge of melancholy. He had been in his second year as a T-38 instructor at Laughlin Air Force Base in Del Rio, Texas, when a sandhill crane, an awkward, long-necked bird the size of a large goose, smashed into the canopy of the jet trainer. The thirty pound mass of meat and bone shattered the Plexiglas at three hundred knots in a blast of bloody tissue and plastic shrapnel. The student in the front seat had been killed instantly, and a pellet-sized piece of canopy shot through Adam's tinted visor into his left eye. With his face streaming blood and the wind battering him in the broken cockpit, he had somehow managed to land the crippled jet. But he had lost the eye and his place as a flight instructor.

His master's from MIT in electrical engineering landed him in Colorado Springs and in a classroom at the Air Force Academy. He loved the Front Range of the Rockies, the solitude of backpacking in the high mountain air, and teaching his students. But he had never fit in. Too much regimentation. Too many meetings, extra duties, and reports when all he really wanted to do was open these kids' minds to what technology could mean to them and to their country. His attitude hadn't escaped the brass. They didn't even like him to wear the patch, asking regularly that he leave his prosthetic eye uncovered. What difference did something like that make? There wasn't a student in his classes who didn't know the story of Captain Tom Mercomes landing the crippled T-38 with only one eye and a dead student in the front seat, when he could have punched out and let the plane crash into the Texas desert. Apparently his reluctance to follow orders made enough difference that he was still a captain after ten years and had been informed that he would probably not make major. They weren't going to force him out of the service. Partly because he was something of a folk hero, and partly because he was too damned good in the classroom. But the message was clear. No reasonable career opportunities ahead. So this time, he was bailing out.

His furniture was already gone – sold with the red '85 Mustang convertible to buy a van. No wife to worry about. Julie had suffered along with him for three years after his accident before becoming overwhelmed by his constant depression, the shadow cast by lost dreams and the moodiness of an uncertain present. And he had been no kind of a husband, spending as many hours as he could in his office and in the classroom so he didn't have to think about where he would rather be and what he would rather be doing. Fortunately, the gods of biology, in all their wisdom, had kept them from having children. All Tom had to show for his life was in the boxes stacked on the living room floor behind him. As soon as the apartment manager came to check the place over, he was history.

Behind him through the open patio doors, the phone buzzed loudly. The apartment manager must have been delayed. Tom walked across the empty room and snatched the phone from the floor.

"Mercomes," he answered.

"Captain Mercomes, I understand you are a person who enjoys interesting assignments and likes to do things your own way."

"Who is this?"

"I represent a group that might have an attractive employment opportunity for you." The voice at the other end was a raspy, smoke-stained baritone.

"What kind of job are we talking about?"

"It has many of the same enticements of your old flying position. I can't say more about it now, other than that it's not Air Force but is involved in maintaining the nation's security. If you're interested, you will find another phone in your mailbox and I'll call you in exactly ten minutes."

"What the ...?"

There was silence at the other end of the line.

Tom tested the connection. "What makes you think I'll be interested?"

"If you're not at least curious, you aren't the person we're looking for," the voice said, and the line went dead.

Mercomes stood with the phone cradled against his shoulder, a puzzled grin etching his face. Now, what the hell was that all about? He looked absently out the windows toward the gates to the estate where the mailboxes lined the entrance wall, then glanced at his watch. Two fifteen. This thing smelled like dog's breath. No one who's up to any good would make a job contact like this... except maybe some branch of the intelligence community. One of his college friends at MIT had gone into the CIA, and they had recruited him through a series of secret meetings that were like something out of an old *Get Smart* episode. Tom stepped again onto the balcony and looked over at the buildings of the Academy gleaming at the base of the mountains, then back at the small pile of boxes on the corner of the carpet. He'd been planning to travel – see the country. Maybe go overseas for a year or two. Vietnam, perhaps. But this call stirred something inside – the feeling he'd had as he looked along that row of perfectly aligned wingtips or pulled up into a barrel roll and watched the world turn beneath him. It was the most alive he'd felt in a long time.

He looked again at his watch. Two twenty. "Why the hell not," he muttered and pulled a pen from his pocket to scribble a note to the manager.

. . .

The man who exited the blue Sentra in the garage on Hunter Chase Drive in McKinney's Virginia Hills would not have been recognized as

Tom Mercomes. The face was essentially the same shape: long and chiseled, with a lop-sided grin that lifted the left side of his mouth more than the right, and the same engaging hazel eyes. But Tom Mercomes had been balding, with only a thin peninsula of brown hair that ran from his crown out to the center of a high forehead. This man had a full head of hair, so expertly grafted that there were no visible rows or patches: just thick brown waves that he combed straight back. Tom Mercomes' nose had been broken as a teenager when he foolishly swung an ax down onto the joint of a V-shaped tree branch that kicked back into his face: a nose that had been allowed to heal with a visible leeward tilt. This man's nose was straight and narrower at the bridge. And his ears were set more tightly against his head. Mercomes had almost always worn the eye patch, finding it less disconcerting to others than his less-than-convincing prosthetic eye. With the new prosthesis, even when standing a few yards from the man who entered the house in Virginia Hills and looking at him directly, it was difficult to tell that one eye was artificial. And though he still often chose to wear the patch, this man's name was Adam Zak.

Adam had chosen the name because he thought that when starting life over, there should be some element of symbolism: a beginning and an end. Alpha and Omega. Adam Zak. He had briefly considered Aaron Zyce to stretch the alphabet to even greater extremes, but thought there was additional symbolism in Adam. And he simply liked the name Zak.

Mercomes' divorce from Julie had been amicable, and she made more money. A successful personal financial advisor with a string of well-healed clients. So there were no financial ties. She remarried eighteen months after the divorce and was living in Memphis with two children from the second marriage. A year after his transformation, Adam tested his new persona by going to Memphis and visiting the church she and her new family attended. When he was introduced, she looked at him with a quizzical smile, furrowed her brow ever so slightly, then shook her head and chuckled. "You reminded me of someone," she said, then didn't give him another look.

Adam now operated in a world that was neither depressing nor unfulfilled. His Control, a man who went by "Fisher," was no more than a ragged voice on the phone or a coded computer message. Their second phone conversation beside the mailboxes in Colorado Springs had been direct and to the point. Fisher informed him that he worked for a small unit that "supported U.S. intelligence interests without being formally attached to the intelligence community."

"We look for people like you, Captain Mercomes. Men and women of talent, but with independent spirits and few connections. We're aware that your father died flying F-4s in combat in Vietnam and your mother passed away from breast cancer while you were in college. You have no siblings, and no one but you really worries about where you go or why. We see your inclination for respectful insubordination as an asset. The people who work for us – and there are very few – are assigned special projects the government can't, or won't, handle through official channels. And our people work entirely by themselves."

"Sounds a bit like Mission Impossible," Mercomes said suspiciously.

"Same idea, but no team. In fact one of the reasons we like you is that you have virtually no connections. If you decide to come with us, we'll give you a new identity, new face, and new life. Tom Mercomes disappears."

"Do you burn off my fingerprints?" Tom asked cynically. "I have an Air Force file an inch thick and must have prints in every national law enforcement database. Maybe international."

"Nothing that crude. We just make those records disappear. There will be no Tom Mercomes."

"How do I know this is legit?"

"Let's try this for a beginning," said the voice. "You graduated from high school in Kearney, Nebraska, in the middle of your class because you were bored with the classes you had to take. You didn't participate in sports during high school and got your BS in math as a part-time student at Kearney State, because you had to help your mother run the family dry cleaning business. After she passed away and the business was sold, you accepted a graduate assistantship at MIT where you got a master's in Electrical Engineering with a 4.00 GPA. You looked into SEAL Training with the Navy but decided you wanted to go Air Force and become a pilot like your father...."

Mercomes interrupted. "There's nothing there that a little research couldn't dig up."

The voice on the phone continued without comment. "You graduated fourth in your pilot training class and initially chose an F-16, but they were pulling units out of the Gulf about that time and reducing the number of fighter slots. Your second pick was an instructor position in T-38s at Laughlin. You currently have five thousand, seven hundred and thirty-eight dollars in your checking account at the Bank of America branch on North Academy Boulevard and another forty-nine thousand three hundred eighty-three dollars in a savings account at the Academy Credit Union. Do you want to know how much is in your two mutual funds?"

"I get the idea," Mercomes muttered. "Do I have any choice about this new assignment?"

"Complete choice. We want you only if you want us."

"And if I decide I do want you?"

"You're headed back to Del Rio to see some old flight instructor buddies. Call and tell them something came up. Go instead to an address in Ft. Bragg, North Carolina, that I'll text to the phone you're using now. We want to start you through Special Forces training."

Tom Mercomes laughed. "At thirty-two? I'm sure with every-thing else you know, you've got my age – and know I only have one eye."

"I also know the one eye isn't a handicap. You've received permission to drive because you've been able to demonstrate that you remain fully aware of what's around you. You don't think you can do the training at thirty-two with one eye?"

"Of course I can."

"Then start driving east and when you get up tomorrow, there will be a text message on this phone with the address of an apartment in Ft. Bragg."

Mercomes had spent the next eighteen months in Special Forces training – basic combat, special operations, army airborne, then thirty-six weeks at the Defense Language Institute in Monterey, California, perfecting the French he'd learned from his Canadian-born mother. During Basic Combat Training, he had generally held his own with the younger troops and seemed to be given a pass when his age made him a step slow, or a few seconds behind going through the obstacle courses. In some cases, he proved to be exceptional. The loss of his left eye had heightened his other senses and he anticipated changes in his surroundings and was able to act more quickly than the other trainees. And the strength he had acquired in his remaining right eye made him an excellent marksman. He had been an avid sky diver before entering the

Air Force and when a few classmates balked at the plane door on their maiden jump, Mercomes threw himself joyfully into the air and was able to guide his chute, tuck and roll, as well as any of his instructors.

The new name and face had come later, avoiding the likelihood that he would run into a commando on some operation and be recognized. Of course the eye didn't help. He had worn the patch through the full year-and-a-half of training and was confident now that with the new prosthetic eye, he could pass any one of his teammates on the street and wouldn't be recognized. He hadn't run into any of the group since leaving Bragg and as far as he knew, no one had ever asked whatever happened to Tom Mercomes.

Adam dropped his clothes and gym bag on a living room chair and went directly into his study. Inserting a remote drive into a USB port on his laptop, he logged into an email account that was innocuously labeled "friendmail" and downloaded the single message to the decrypting software on the remote. The message was two short paragraphs.

*Message from the Director. The NSA has picked up intel that may relate to your assignment. A source who went missing in Southeast Asia in the late 1960s may have sent security-critical information in some form to one of his CIA Asia contacts before disappearing. Most Agency people see this as unrelated to current security interests. They advise the Director not pursue. Director unsure, yet unwilling to countermand his advisors on this one. But he's still troubling over the anonymous Weavers warning you are working on and thinks there could be a connection.*

*Intel involves a retired agent, Eric Compton, now living in Remington, VA., and a college drop-out named Davis Eckerson. Subject of inquiry is one Jim Thompson, an early OSS operative who disappeared in Malaysia in 1967. Eckerson has contacted Compton and indicated he has a message for him from Thompson. Davis meets with Compton tomorrow at his home and is now at the Comfort Inn in Culpeper, VA., scheduled to be there through tomorrow night. Let's see what he has to say to Compton.*

Adam made a few notes on a pad beside the computer, found an online map of western Virginia, then switched to a website for American Airlines to find a flight that would get him into Washington's Dulles Airport by early afternoon. That would put him an hour north of Remington, and when Eckerson met with Eric Compton, Adam planned to be there.

FOUR

Katharine Wood was actually Katharine *Thompson* Wood. Davis's first Google search using "Katharine Wood murder" seemed bent on telling him about the murder of Catherine Woods, a New York dancer who was killed by her estranged boyfriend in 2005. But adding "1967" to the search brought up an item titled "A murder mystery for GOP chairman Terry Strine – Delaware Grapevine," and at least moved the scene of the murder to the right part of the country. The article, about a home purchased by Delaware State GOP Chairman Terry Strine, was not about Katharine Wood at all. But as background, the report noted:

*Terry A. Strine, the Republican state chairman, does not have just any country house across the line in Pennsylvania. It was the scene of a sensational murder mystery that rocked Chateau Country one summer day 37 years ago.*

*The original homeowner there was Katharine Thompson Wood, who was beaten to death in her bed on Aug. 30, 1967, even though two unfriendly guard dogs, a German shepherd named Mr. Magoo and a golden retriever called Rumpus, were in the house with her. She was 74.*

*Wood, who was nicknamed "Kaa" in her upper-crust social circle, was prominent in her own right as one of the founders of the Vicmead Hunt Club, but what really sent interest skyrocketing was the timing of her death, five months after the disappearance of her internationally famous brother.*

*James H.W. Thompson was the "Silk King," a businessman who worked for the Office of Strategic Services, the forerunner of the CIA, during World War II and then struck it rich in the Thai silk trade. On Easter Sunday 1967, Jim Thompson walked into the Malaysian jungle, leaving behind his cigarettes even though he was a heavy smoker, and never came back.*

And there it was, all in one simple package. Katharine (spelled with two 'a's) Wood was *Kaa*, and sister to James H. W. Thompson, formerly of the OSS, who disappeared a few months before Labor Day in 1967. And Jim Thompson was involved in the silk trade.

A Wikipedia entry for Thompson told Davis all he needed to know to reaffirm that dumping the journalism program and leaving the apartment to Alex was the step he needed to be taking to kick-start his career. Davis was sitting on a bigger lead than any of the professors at the MU Journalism School had ever seen: a key to the disappearance of a mysterious silk trader with links to the CIA. The Wiki article explained that the man had never been found! And although there were a dozen theories about what had happened to Jim Thompson, after forty-five years there was no credible trace of the man. A perfect excuse to leave school, give up any future support from Davis III, and become a real-life investigative journalist. That, and Gladys's three million dollars.

Davis put three-quarters of a million into a savings account that he could draw against with a debit card, hired Gladys's financial advisor to manage the rest of his inheritance, and left the university without letting the college know he was dropping. He had no idea why Thompson's sister hadn't turned the letter over to this Eric Compton before her death. Maybe she hadn't had time. From what he was able to learn about her, she was a bit like Gladys and ferociously independent. The reports of the break-in at her home called it a "botched robbery," but nothing of note was taken, and she wasn't found until the next morning by her housekeeper. Davis could almost hear the sonorous voice of Keith Morrison asking: "What caused a robbery to be botched, when the thief had all night – unless he couldn't locate what he really came for? Perhaps the only thing he was looking for was a letter, carefully hidden away beneath the flap at the bottom of a box full of old travel stickers. And who *knew* where the strange lady, the recluse people referred to as Kaa, kept the box?"

Davis had thrown his few belongings into a duffle, loaded them into the back of his red Mini Cooper, and headed for Washington in search of Eric Compton. The first night put him in Lexington, Kentucky, where he checked into a moderately priced hotel along the interstate, thinking fleetingly that he could afford something more expensive, but not certain where this adventure would lead and how far three million dollars was going to take him. His father had set up a bank account for Davis when he was ten and had somehow managed to keep its balance ahead of his son's spending. But once the old man learned he'd quit school, goodbye bank account! Money wasn't something Davis had ever thought much about, until now. And though he knew three million dollars was a helluva lot, he needed a little time to decide how much a helluva lot really was.

During the night in Lexington he did a more extensive web search on Thompson and learned that he graduated from Princeton and studied architecture at the University of Pennsylvania before joining the Delaware National Guard shortly before the Japanese bombing of Pearl Harbor. At the height of the war, he was recruited into the Office of Strategic Services and spent time in North Africa and Europe. When the Germans surrendered, Thompson was sent to Ceylon with the expectation he would make his way into Thailand to support the *Seri Thai*, the Free Thai movement that was planning an uprising against the occupying Japanese army. But the war ended in Asia before he could get involved in operations, and he was assigned to set up an OSS office in Bangkok, working as military attaché for the U.S. consulate in the Thai capital.

Davis took a moment to look up Ceylon, learning that it was now Sri Lanka. He quickly typed in "Sri Lanka" and remembered as soon as he saw the tiny dot off the southeast coast of India that it was the island state that had been devastated by the tsunami in 2004 and was home to the Tamil Tiger insurrection.

"Okay. I'm with ya now…" he muttered and turned back to the article on the Thai silk king.

Thompson left the army in 1946 and returned briefly to the U.S. but following a divorce, went back Asia. Over the next two decades he was credited with revitalizing what was a dying industry, returning silk production to the country and bringing new life and profitability to the silk weaving villages that had gradually begun to disappear. Though he frequently denied it, some claimed he remained an agent of U.S. Intelligence despite his outspoken opposition to American involvement in Vietnam.

Over the years, Jim Thompson became one of the most successful collectors of Thai and Southeast Asian antiquities and applied his architectural talents to building a beautiful traditional Thai home in the center of Bangkok, along one of its famous *"klong"* canals. He furnished his home with his collected treasures, much to the consternation of some who feared he might eventually ship them out of the country. Among his detractors were powerful figures in the Thai government – the government officials to whom Thompson seemed to be referring in his letter to Kaa.

On Easter Sunday in 1967 while vacationing in the jungle of Malaysia's Cameron Highlands, Thompson attended a service at church, then accompanied friends on a picnic outing. After returning to the bungalow where he was staying, while others rested he walked away, leaving his cigarettes, passport, and asthma medication on the table in his room. Several villagers claimed to have seen him walking in the area later in the afternoon, but he failed to return to the bungalow that night and was never seen again. An exhaustive search failed to find any trace of him and his disappearance remains a mystery. Five months later, Katharine Thompson Wood, his older sister, was bludgeoned to death in her bed during a "bungled robbery."

Nothing Davis found in the online information concerning Thompson's mysterious disappearance said anything about a letter to "Kaa." Every reference did note, however, that James Harrison Wilson Thompson was born in 1906. If his associate, Eric Compton, was a contemporary, he was now either one of the oldest men alive or Davis would find his name on a headstone. If, by some chance, Compton were still living, Davis had no real reason to believe he had remained in the Washington area and doubted he could just call CIA headquarters and ask for the address of a retired agent. So he did what any investigative journalist would do under the circumstances: Googled Eric Compton.

There were 2,400,000 entries under the name, and the first hundred had to do with a professional golfer: part American, part Norwegian, who was playing on the PGA tour after his second heart transplant. Davis took a quick glance at his stats, found him to be a pretty credible player, then added "Central Intelligence Agency" to his search.

The CIA may not give out addresses, but they apparently don't prevent former agents from including them in a bio. Up came 'Eric David Compton,' retired from the Central Intelligence Agency and honored as Citizen of the Year by Remington, Virginia, for his role in leading the community drive to restore portions of the Civil War battlefield of Rappahannock Station. At the time of the newspaper article, Compton, age 82, still lived with his wife of fifty-seven years in a refurbished farmhouse that dated from the time of the battle. The article noted that the home was located a few miles south of town on Sumerduck Road.

Davis turned to Mapquest. According to the site, Remington was 477 miles and eight hours from his hotel in Lexington. The article about Compton was a year old but if the man was still living, perhaps at 83, Agent Compton could still cast some light on Jim Thompson's Weavers.

. . .

There are no hotels in Remington, Virginia. When Davis's smart phone didn't even turn up a B & B, he reserved a room at a Comfort Inn in Culpeper, Virginia, twelve miles short of Compton's home town along U.S. 29, and was up and on the road by daybreak the following morning.

As he guided his Mini off the highway into Remington shortly after 7:00 a.m. on a misty Tuesday morning, the sleepy town didn't appear to Davis that it had changed much since it was called Rappahannock Station and was the site of the Civil War battle Compton was trying to memorialize. The town covered about ten square blocks, sandwiched between the highway leading north to the county seat at Warrenton, and the Norfolk Southern Railroad which, Davis had learned from his Wiki search, first came through the community ten years before Union and Confederate soldiers clashed there. Main Street ran northwest to southeast through town and connected the highway with the rail line, becoming Sumerduck Road as it crossed the tracks and exited town to the south.

In the center of the village where Main crossed James Madison Street, an eatery called the Corner Deli faced a service station across the two-lane road. From the row of pickup trucks nosed up against the curb and the men clustered around tables beside the lighted windows, Davis guessed that this was where morning began in Remington, Virginia. He parked beside an aging Chevy and walked self-consciously into the lively chatter of the morning coffee crowd. The room hushed immediately, as if the town pastor had risen to offer prayer. Tables of farmers and local businessmen turned on cue to look at the out-of-towner, dressed conspicuously in his khakis and green North Face pullover.

A fortyish waitress with a friendly smile guided him to a small, two-chair table in a back corner and poured water, setting a plastic laminated menu in front of him.

"Would you like coffee, hon?"

"Yeah, thanks. Regular with cream and sugar."

"You need some time with the menu?"

Davis did, and a few minutes later ordered the sausage and cheese omelet with hash browns. The room had hummed cautious-ly back to life, and the order was at the table in ten minutes. Davis smiled up at the woman as she placed the plate in front of him, turning it slightly on the checkered tablecloth so the omelet was closest, and warning him that the plate might be hot.

"Do you have a minute for a question?" he asked.

"Sure. What can I help you with?"

"Do you happen to know Eric Compton?"

Several of the men at nearby tables glanced over at him.

"Well, of course. Everyone here knows Eric," she said. "Used to come in for breakfast almost every morning." Davis breathed a sigh of relief. The waitress had said *"knows* Eric," indicating the agent – and Davis's chance to make a name for himself – were still breathing. The waitress slid into the opposite chair. Visiting with customers seemed to be a normal part of breakfast service at the Corner Deli.

"But doesn't come in anymore?" Davis asked.

"Doesn't get out much at all. He's pretty well confined to the house."

Davis's relief hiccoughed and he tried to sound casual. "Health problems?"

She leaned secretively across the table. "Parkinson's, I think."

He nodded sympathetically to acknowledge that he appreciated her sharing the secret, but his relief slipped another notch. "You know if he would accept visitors? I mean, can he communicate at all?"

She sat back with her hands folded on the table top. "Well, I haven't seen him in months.... His wife – Naomi – she's gone now, you know. But if he's able to talk, I'd guess he would love company. He's a man who enjoys visiting. You know him?"

Davis smiled and shook his head. "No – we just have a mutual friend."

The waitress glanced at a large jeweled wristwatch with Minnie Mouse peering out through the bottom half of the face.

"I'd be happy to call the house for you – to see if he can have visitors. I know him pretty well. But it's too early. Finish your breakfast and we'll give him a call about eight."

"Thanks. I'd appreciate that."

"Who should I tell him wants to visit?"

"My name is Davis Eckerson. Tell him I have a letter for him with a message from Jim Thompson."

# FIVE

Just before noon, Bradley Han left his office on the second floor of the National Security Agency's mammoth complex in Fort Meade, Maryland, and drove south on the Patuxent Freeway to the exit for state highway 198. He turned west around the Tipton airport, then wound along secondary roads until a gravel drive looped through the trees into a small, but neatly maintained cemetery. Han parked beneath an overhanging maple on the north edge of the open square of ground, climbed from the car, and leaned back against the hood. From a brown lunch sack, he unwrapped a sandwich and spread the cellophane out on the warm metal surface, opened a bag of Fritos, uncapped a bottle of water, and pulled a pre-paid cell phone from the pocket of his jacket. Han had rarely called the number but knew it as well as his own. When a male voice answered, Han said simply; "This is Seven. Can you take a message?"

The man at the other end paused before answering as if the call had taken him by surprise. "I can," he said finally.

"We picked up a communication this morning that mentioned the silk merchant and went to a person of interest: his former associate in the Thai capital who now lives in Remington, Virginia." Bradley had carefully rehearsed what he was going to say to insure that he avoided words or phrases that would trigger just the kind of flagged alert that had drawn his attention to the message in the first place – mention of *Jim Thompson, Eric Compton, CIA* or even *Bangkok*.

"What made the call of interest?" the voice asked.

"The caller was a woman, but asked if the silk merchant's former associate could meet with a man named Davis Eckerson. The woman said Eckerson wanted to talk to the associate about a letter to him from the merchant."

"A letter to the associate from the merchant? How is that possible?"

"It's an old letter that was just discovered – but may have information of interest."

"And they met?"

"The associate is not in good health. He couldn't meet until tomorrow."

"Where is this Eckerson?"

"I found him registered in Culpeper, about 10 minutes west of the associate's home."

"Should we try to intercept and get the letter?"

"My advice would be no. That may create a situation where none exists. We need ears at the associate's house when Eckerson visits."

"You are closest...."

"And the most visible. And that isn't my skill set. We need Four. Where is she?"

"In Atlanta. I'll see if I can get her there by evening. If I can't, I'll call your regular number and let you know we won't be available for dinner this evening."

"Very good," Han said and ended the call. He picked up a club sandwich from the wrapper on the hood and lifted the top slice of wheat bread to see if his wife had remembered mayo, then took a large bite and leaned again against the car. The American public was all up in arms about NSA's monitoring of millions of calls, afraid that their personal conversations were being listened to. But that wasn't how it worked. The system was much more like a search engine into which the NSA entered thousands of key words, phrases, names, and places that were of special interest – or became of interest when links appeared among them. As an Asia specialist, Bradley Han had asked to be notified if Jim Thompson's name came up and was linked to any of several hundred identifiers: among them Thompson's old Bangkok CIA contacts including Eric Compton. Han had come to believe that it would never happen, but had kept Thompson's name in the system. It was his principal reason for being where he was – that, and to act when called upon by others among the ten. It was probably nothing, but he had done his job. It was now in the hands of Nine and Four.

# SIX

The three analysts at the table with Dreu and her boss, Marshall Ding, were from the Federal Aviation Administration and had all been on the job for less than a year – what Ding liked to call "Greenies." The meeting was largely a training session and was Dreu's to run, but Mr. Ding always took the first half hour of these gatherings to show people from the agencies that he knew his business, and that he was passing the training along to one of his subordinates only because he had other, more critical matters to deal with. He was six inches shorter than Dreu, with a slight, agile frame that showed the benefit of the thirty minutes of Tai Chi he completed every morning. To beat Dallas traffic, he made a habit of arriving at the office at 5:30, beginning the day by slow-dancing his way through a Tai Chi routine in the rooftop atrium of the seven-story office building the company occupied a quarter mile from Dallas's Love Field. By the time Dreu arrived at 8:00, Ding had showered in the private bath attached to his office and was an hour and a half into his workday. She found the little man's constant concern about demonstrating his own competence to be amusing, but had to admit he deserved every bit of recognition he drew to himself. He was a genius of the first order when it came to systems architecture, and she had learned more from Marshall Ding during her sixteen months with the company than from her entire six years at Stanford.

"You must always begin by realizing that systems are not impervious," he told the Greenies from the FAA. "They are designed by people for other people to have access to them, so security has a built-in weakness right from the beginning. People. If a single person can access the system, anyone can – if they have the same authentication tools. So security construction is simply a matter of providing access to those who are authorized, insuring that it is denied to everyone who is not, and eliminating the possibilities that those who are not authorized can duplicate authorization in a way that the system cannot detect." He paused and looked at the three young specialists who Dreu determined to be working very hard to disguise their feelings that the little man was stating the obvious.

It's obvious, but so essential to understanding how good security architecture works, she wanted to say aloud, but restrained herself. Mr. Ding was old school and did not like to be interrupted.

"That means," Ding continued, "that the more uniquely discreet a characteristic is to the authorized individual, and the more difficult it is to pass along, the better it serves as an authentication tool. A fingerprint, voice print, or iris scan, for example. Once that authentication device or tool has been created and built into the architecture, creating levels of authorization is relatively simple. The key to your security system is identifying the right authentication tools and designing them into the system in such a way that they cannot be duplicated or by-passed." The trio nodded politely.

Ding studied the young faces with a sternness that bordered on suspicion. "As an added security measure, we do not share with our clients the full details of your system's architecture." The oldest of the FAA analysts leaned forward across the table, raised a timid hand, and did what Dreu was unwilling to do.

"So you people know how the code works that safeguards our system, but the actual owners of the system do not. Isn't there something backward about that?"

"If you had the time and sophistication to develop the architecture, you could have done it," Ding said acidly. "Then we would have the same people creating the programs and designing their security – a weakness in and of itself. But you have neither the time nor the sophistication, and you have asked us to do that for you. Since we are doing the design work, is the system more secure if only one of us fully knows how the code is designed, or if both of us know?"

"You don't seem to put much faith in our internal people," the analyst replied, still failing to see that he was pushing against an immovable object. "We all have top level security clearances."

"Even people with much lower clearances have managed to penetrate federal systems and share classified information," Ding muttered, as if that answered everything. "They had too much access."

The analyst sat back and his colleagues nervously adjusted themselves in their seats.

"Now," Ding continued. "Ms. Sason is going to walk you through the general construction of the system, acquainting you with it to the point that you can request modifications, effectively watch for attempts to breach it, or for what appear to be efforts to gain access in legitimate ways, but from places or equipment that should raise suspicion. She was the primary architect, so knows this system inside and out. Anything you want to know within the limits of your own authorizations, she can tell you."

Ding left the three in Dreu's hands and for the next two hours she walked them through the security system that protected the FAA's giant national flight scheduling and tracking network. As she wrapped up the session and asked if there were other questions, the single woman among the three turned to her.

"If there are parts of this architecture we can't examine and review, it seems to me that there is a level of our own security we can't monitor. Would that be correct?"

Dreu nodded, anticipating where this was going.

The woman looked at her pointedly. "Then who is watching to insure that no one here is tampering with that core level of the protection – the level only you are privy to?"

"I grant you," Dreu admitted, "that at that level we are monitoring ourselves. We design the IVKs I was discussing, and have built in what we internally call 'auto-cams,' after the red light cameras we all love so much. If anyone begins to tamper with the basic code that encrypts the IVKs, in addition to stopping the transaction, these auto-cams take a picture of the offending computer and send an alert to our internal security desk." She realized as she said it, however, that the internal security desk was manned by the person most capable of successfully tampering with the code if he wanted to: her boss, Marshall Ding.

# SEVEN

At the single service station in the middle of Remington, Adam Zak pulled his rental up to the pump and frowned at the display showing that regular was $3.88 a gallon. Prices always seemed higher on the East Coast and even though he didn't have money worries, he liked to see a good deal when he bought gas. And he didn't like this new rental car policy of leaving cars partly full and expecting renters to return them at the same level. The agencies knew drivers would always fudge on the up-side, and companies were constantly getting their cars back with more fuel in them than when they left. And he was about to be complicit.

He prepaid $40 and while he waited for the pump to dispense his 10.31 gallons, began to clean the windshield. As he dipped the squeegee into the blue plastic bucket hanging from the pillar that held the overhead canopy, a plumpish Latina who Adam judged to be close to seventy, struggled from the driver's seat of a car parked at the end of the lot and walked toward him with an open map draped over her hands. She smiled shyly as she approached.

"I wonder if you could give me some help," she said.

Adam had been expecting her and stepped back between the car and the row of pumps.

"I'll do what I can."

She looked down at the map. "The information and equipment you want is in this box," she said softly, sliding a box that might hold legal sized envelopes from beneath the map. "Davis Eckerson has gone back to his hotel in Culpeper, and the home you asked about is only a few miles south of here."

Adam eased beside her so that both were facing the side of the car and slipped the box through the window onto the seat. He leaned over to examine the map more closely.

"Did you learn if anyone lives with Compton?"

"He has a live-in aide. A young woman. And several outside dogs. With the equipment we've provided, you won't have to go inside. But the dogs could be a problem. We brought something for them too. If you decide you need anything else, let Fisher know immediately. He's fairly close and can get it to you tonight."

"If you sent what I asked for, this should do the trick." Adam turned and gestured along James Madison Avenue toward the east.

The woman nodded. "We'll be available," she said, and returned to her car, folding the map as she went.

Adam hung the nozzle back on the pump and drove out of the station, turning southeast on Main until it crossed the tracks and became Sumerduck Road. To his right, a church parking lot stood empty and he pulled in and idled the car while he checked the box. It contained a sheet of paper with a rural address farther south on Sumerduck and a photograph of a white frame house that appeared to be surrounded by open fields. Under the paper was a heavy card displaying what looked like four small suction cups and two black thumb tacks, strapped with a rubber band to a wireless receiver with ear buds. Each cup was attached to the card with a twisty tie, numbered consecutively, 1 through 4, and centered with a hyper-sensitive microphone. When pressed to the outside of a window, the mics picked up even the most muffled conversation inside the room. The thick-headed tacks were numbered 5 and 6 and were also small microphone heads. For the porch, Adam thought, glancing back at the photo.

The other items in the box were not part of the order. An audio player the size of a deck of cards was sealed in a plastic bag with four, thin, eight-inch sticks of what looked and smelled like pepperoni sausage. A tag attached to the player said "Coyote Cries," with a footnote that added; "One stick per dog. Will last about four hours."

Adam eased the rental back onto Sumerduck Road and drove south until he saw the address on a solid metal mailbox on the left side of the road. The house was down a long curved drive, separated from Sumerduck by a screen of tall evergreens. A creek, lined by ancient sycamores bordered the property on the north, and Adam drove past the drive until he could see beyond the house to a thick wood that backed the property on the east. He estimated the house to be fifty yards from the woods - perhaps eighty from the row of cedars in front. Someone had a lot of lawn to mow.

Two hundred yards beyond the house, a paved road turned left into the same woods and Adam steered the rental along the side road until a rusted metal farm gate opened through the fence onto a dirt track that disappeared into the trees. He pulled to the side, checked that he was alone on the road, and quickly walked to the gate. It was secured with only a double-turn of wire wrapped around the post. Adam untwisted the strands and followed the track a hundred yards into the woods. As he had guessed, nothing but the stand of timber separated the road where he was parked from the back of Compton's property. He returned to the car, latching the gate behind him, and drove back toward Remington. On the east side of Culpeper he had seen a place where he could get a drink and a basket of wings, give Dreu a call, and wait for dark.

Shortly after midnight, Adam stood in the darkened woods that faced the front porch of Eric Compton's refurbished, two-story farmhouse. He had watched the house settle in for the night and knew that Compton slept in a room in the back left corner on the main floor, as Adam faced the house. The front door opened toward the woods to the east and was centered on a long covered porch. He guessed that as you entered the house, the living room was to the left and a kitchen to the right. The room Compton now used as a bedroom may once have been a dining area, leaving another unidentified room on the ground floor behind the kitchen in the northwest corner. The aide's bedroom, perhaps – or possibly a study.

Between the house and where he stood in the trees, a small yard extended from the porch to a split rail fence with a gateless opening into a broad meadow that Adam guessed covered about an acre: neatly mowed and also bordered by a rail fence across the tree line a few feet in front of him. The driveway passed through the stand of cedars he had seen from Sumerduck Road and looped up to a pad and separate, two-car garage on the side of the house to Adam's right. A short, covered walk connected the garage to a side door into the kitchen.

Adam had been in the woods since dusk. As twilight fell, Compton and his aide had come out onto the porch: the young woman pushing her charge in a sturdy wheelchair with a head and neck brace that held the retired agent erect. The man must be suffering from a stroke or degenerative muscular disease of some kind. But through Adam's field glasses, Compton's eyes seemed alert, and he was conversing with the aide as she scratched the bellies of two chocolate Labradors. The dogs danced around their master's chair, tails wagging wildly as they nuzzled the blanket across his lap and licked the hands that stayed immobile on the armrests.

The aide was a thick young woman in light green nursing scrubs who looked to Adam like she could easily pick Compton up and carry him back into the house if she felt the need. The right side of her head was shaved to a bristly black, the left half dyed an assortment of colors, none of which were natural to human hair.

They stayed on the porch with the dogs for fifteen minutes, then as the last glimmer of sunset faded behind the house to the west, the aide pushed Compton back inside, leaving the porch light on. The dogs made a circuit of the perimeter of the yard, then settled down on either side of the porch step like a pair of stone lions.

Adam was relieved to see the dogs. He wondered what kind of security a retired CIA agent might have around his home, and watching the dogs move freely about the yard indicated there were no exterior motion detectors. A security light above the garage door blinked on for two minutes as the dogs passed, but otherwise the yard gradually faded into a muted rosy gray as the sun disappeared behind the house. He scanned the area for cameras and saw nothing, but guessed there would be an interior alarm system. Not a problem. He had no intentions of going inside. Compton apparently had decided he was no longer of interest to anyone and relied only on the security common in any rural home: an interior alarm system and two faithful dogs.

The old agent had chosen his dogs more for companionship than security. Labs were protective and territorial but generally good natured and curious, and this pair seemed to match the description. Within minutes of the lights going out on the lower floor, an upper room brightened above the front door where a dormer window faced the woods. Adam watched the aide's shadow move back and forth across the curtained frame for another thirty minutes then disappear, leaving only a warm yellow glow for another hour. Shortly after ten, the room fell dark. He waited two more hours, then moved to the edge of the trees where he crouched beside the rail fence and pushed the play button on his small recorder. Immediately the quiet of the summer night was broken by the yapping cry of a coyote: four short yelps followed by a rising howl that for a few seconds hung in the warm air like a weather siren, then faded into silence. The Labradors sprang to their feet, hackles raised as they rushed to the yard fence, barking in the direction of the cry from the woods. The coyote yapped again and the dogs charged through the gap and sprinted toward the trees. The light flashed on in the aide's upstairs window and the young woman, now dressed in a white, hip-long T-shirt, threw up the bottom pane.

"*Rambo! Sheba!*" she called across the meadow in a sharp whisper. "*Quiet!*"

The dogs stopped fifty feet from where Adam crouched at the edge of the trees, looked silently back at the house, then at the dark line of woods. They sniffed suspiciously, picking up Adam's scent, and sat rigidly eying his hiding place.

The aide looked across the field into the darkness for a few moments until satisfied the dogs were silent, then lowered the window and extinguished the light.

"*Rambo! Sheba!*" Adam said in a sharp whisper, standing and moving into view of the dogs. They jumped to their feet and quickly crossed half the distance between them, again barking loudly.

"*Quiet!*" Adam ordered and threw a piece of the pepperoni stick in front of the pair. The dogs moved to it in unison, sniffing at the bait. Edging sideways to block his mate from the treat, the larger Lab grabbed it in his teeth and with three quick gulps, swallowed it down. The second stick landed in front of the female and before her mate could bully her aside, she snapped the stick up, threw back her head, and it was gone. The Labs sat back on their haunches and watched the shadow in the trees expectantly, heads and eyes alert.

"Good dogs!" Adam whispered. He broke the third stick in half and tossed the pieces in front of the animals. The bait disappeared as quickly as it hit the ground and the Labs licked their chops, waiting for more.

"Come!" Adam said and held his hand forward. The dogs edged toward him cautiously, their tails beginning a relaxed swish. He let them sniff at him, then slipped his fingers under their chins and scratched their necks and behind their ears. They pushed forward, rubbing their heads against his legs, and for the next five minutes Adam sat in the darkness of the trees with Compton's dogs nuzzling against him until the pair began to yawn and stagger. Sheba was the first to go, dropping suddenly onto her front paws into a dazed slumber. Rambo looked at her through bleary eyes, then collapsed beside her.

"Good dogs," Adam said, giving each a final pat. He slipped out of the trees and hunched cautiously across the field to the house. The night smelled of freshly mown grass and to his right along the creek, a pair of frogs began a duet and cicadas droned in the woods behind him. The porch front and sides of the Compton home were lined with thick azaleas and Adam pushed through them onto the porch and thumbed the two pin mics into the railing at either end of the deck. Low near the floor where they were obscured by potted plants. He placed one of the tiny suction mics in the upper corner of the living room window that faced the porch, then skirted the house to the south to get the side window of the room he knew must be Compton's bedroom. With two of the devices remaining, he crouched briefly between two thick crepe myrtle and considered how the mics might best be used. The kitchen, of course. Compton may decide to be homey and invite his visitor to sit at the kitchen table. But the final mic? The other window in Compton's bedroom, or a window in the unidentified room in the house's northwest corner? If it turned out to be a study, it might also serve as a meeting place. He opted to mic each room on the main level and slid along the side of the house toward the back that faced Sumerduck Road.

Adam hadn't been able to study the back of the house from his observation spot in the woods and, out of habit, paused low in the bushes before rounding the corner. He glanced cautiously across the wide expanse of grass that separated the back of the house from the road, pulling back immediately and flattening against the white board siding. A shadow moved silently across the dark lawn between the line of cedars and the house, running in a low crouch. Though Adam had only seen the figure for a brief instant, it registered as a woman and she was headed for the space between the garage and the house's north side. He peeked again around the corner and watched the shadow disappear beyond the other end of the house, then moved quickly away from the wall to the south.

A large clump of lilacs stood midway between his corner and the line of evergreens. Adam moved silently to it and slipped into the deep shadows of the tall bushes. The clump formed a tight circle of thick foliage, with a small spot of bare ground at its center. He sat cross-legged among the branches and drew the control box and ear buds from his pocket. On the face of the control, a small button with a low-light LED represented each mic and glowed pale green when the button was pushed, selecting that listening position. He had started on the porch with mic 6 at the northeast corner, then 5, 4, and 3 as he moved around the house. Mics 1 and 2 remained wired to the card in his shirt pocket: one for the kitchen and one for the unidentified room in the back. He inserted the ear buds, pressing the button for 6, and turning the volume control full on.

Through the tack mic at the far end of the porch, only feet from the outside door into the kitchen, Adam heard the faint scratch of metal on metal, then the sound of an aerosol as the intruder lubricated the hinges. Seconds later, he heard the door being eased open. If the house had an alarm system – which surely it did – things were about to get exciting.

He trapped his breath and waited, deciding that if the alarm sounded he would sprint directly south towards the side road and his car rather than back to the trees. But nothing but the frogs and cicadas disturbed the summer night. Either there was no system, it hadn't been armed, or the intruder had managed to disarm it within the few seconds she was inside.

The number 6 mic fell silent and he switched to 4, probing the living room. For a few seconds there was nothing, then the faint rustle of someone moving into the room. As the sound dis-appeared, he switched to 3 covering the bedroom, hearing only the labored breathing of Eric Compton. For the next five minutes, Adam scanned the house for signs of the intruder but found none, switching back to 6 to listen for the exit. He heard the faint click of the door being closed, then a louder *swish*, followed by the barely discernible patter of feet moving along the porch. The steps paused, then Adam saw the figure slide over the porch railing at the end closest to him and move along the south side of the house. He covered the faint LED display and froze in place, but the figure passed without looking toward him, moving swiftly again in the direction of the screen of cedars. It was indeed a woman – slim and cat-like and silent as a wisp of night mist. She disappeared through the evergreens and, moments later, Adam heard the distant sound of a motorcycle starting somewhere south along Sumerduck Road. As the bike passed the house, its single headlight flashed among the cedars as it raced north toward Remington.

He sat without moving until there was only the chirp of the courting frogs and drone of cicadas. He didn't remember the motorcycle passing on the road while he was watching from the woods. The woman must have been there before him, watching the house from the west but screened from his own surveillance point and his approach to the house. But she surely knew about the dogs. Had she seen him drug them, or simply known they had disappeared into the woods, following the yelping of the coyotes? She had approached the house as if she weren't aware that he was there and must have had her own way to silence the Labs if they returned. Either that, or she knew he was there and didn't care. The thought troubled him even more than her presence.

He eased from the lilac clump and hurriedly made his way around the rest of the house, placing the remaining two micro-phones. He needed to get back into the woods and call Fisher. Someone else was interested in Jim Thompson and his Cambodian Weavers.

# EIGHT

In a low, ranch-style home fifty miles north of where Adam and the woman in black were bugging the Compton house, another aging man sat blanketed in an elaborate wheelchair. A broad, wrap-around display in front of him contained wireless links to an impressive bank of computers that filled one wall of the room in which the man sat: scramblers and descramblers, satellite links to intelligence networks world-wide, and synthesizers that instantly examined a caller's voice signature to determine identity and authorization. He punched a delete key beside the digital display in front of him, blanking out the name of Adam Zak.

Bud "Fisher" Liljigren looked across the room where a plump, pleasant-faced woman was encoding a request to the computers at Langley for information on all Agency or NSA employees who might be tracking communication related to James W. H. Thompson or his former associates.

"Let me know if anyone other than Han is interested, Nita," Fisher said, thumbing a lever on his chair arm to turn more directly toward his partner.

"Not good – if the Director doesn't know someone's poking around," she muttered, leaning back from the console.

Fisher nodded thoughtfully. "What did you think of our man Zak? I know it was breaking all rules for you to meet him, but it seemed the simplest way to get the equipment to him as quickly as he needed it."

"Nice looking man," she said. "And very personable. I'm sure he just thought I was a courier. I don't think I've ever had to take a call from him, so he probably doesn't know I exist."

"Still best that way," Fisher said, realizing as he said it that it wouldn't be much longer before Nita would be taking over his role completely – assuming the Agency continued to support the unit after Fisher was gone. He was now in his mid-nineties and though still very much in command of the people and information that made his operation an indispensable part of the American intelligence network, each morning as he awoke beside Nita, he thanked whatever gods may be for another opportunity to open his eyes. If something were to happen to Nita, their entire operation might simply disappear.

They had been together now for over fifty years: ever since the day in the spring of 1961 when the Agency Director entered Bud's office on the third floor of the headquarters building in Langley and closed the door quietly behind him.

"Bud, I'd like you to resign," he said simply.

Bud wheeled his chair from behind his cluttered desk to face the Director at close range.

"I'm too good for you to ask me to resign. What do you really want?"

The Director's face was stony. "Just as I said. It's time for you to get out. With your military time, you've got your twenty years. Plus, you've got disability pay. You'll do fine."

Bud placed his hands in his lifeless lap and studied the Director's expressionless face.

"There's more to this than you're telling me. Did I cross someone?"

"It appears that way to some around here."

"Who? I think I'd know about something like that."

The Director leaned back loosely against the office wall and crossed one ankle over the other. "How long have we been in this business, Bud? Since '43? I joined the OSS just before we picked you out of Norway. You'd been sending us intel since the Norwegian underground rescued you, after your Glouster went down."

"May of '43," Bud acknowledged.

"You've been one of the best from the beginning. And I've always told people inside that you're the best recruiter we have. Sometimes I've wondered about your bias for ex-flyers, but I have to admit your people last and have talent and grit. Your Baltic sector's the flagship of the agency."

"This doesn't sound like a farewell address. Where's the 'but...'?"

"But...," the Director continued, "things have changed. These are new times. We're having to operate with too many constraints. Too near the surface. That forces an accumulation of errors and somehow our victories, which are never publicized, don't cancel them out." He looked very tired. "Some heads are going to roll, and I want you out before it starts."

"When am I retiring?"

"End of the week."

"Any choice?"

"No."

For a second time since the young aviator from Lindsborg, Kansas, had returned secretly from the war and been absorbed into the fledgling Office of Special Services, Bud Liljigren dis-appeared: this time to a modest rural home hidden down a twisting country lane five miles from Ashburn, Virginia. The house had ramped access at every door, extra wide hallways, and the most sophisticated array of electronic gear Bud had seen. With the elaborate consoles came a partner: a brilliant soft-spoken woman named Anita. No last name. Just Anita. When Bud reached the house she met him in the drive and wheeled him into the study where she presented him with a handwritten letter from the Director.

> *I'm sorry I had to handle things this way,"* it began, *"but I've learned that ignorance is the best cover. Everything you need to know is in the manual in the study and in Anita's head. Read the manual thoroughly, memorize its contents and burn it.*
>
> *I've given each of you the best partner I could find. Take care of each other. You'll find this a lonely assignment. The operation is yours to run, Bud. Anita can handle the electronics. She's a whiz. (By the way, don't let her stories about Cuba convince you she has no heart. She's a pussycat when you get to know her.)*
>
> *I'm going to be resigning within a month. The new Director will know about you. And the President, of course. But they alone. No one will know where you are. You're that deep and it has to stay that way. Your operation is called 'Unit 1.' Not terribly original, but I couldn't think of anything that expressed your mission better. Your ops name is Fisher. Much rests in your hands. Godspeed.*

The Director had been right about Nita. She was bright and intuitive, gentle and at the same time fiercely strong-willed. None of the original electronic gear now remained. She had progressively replaced it with the latest in surveillance and intelligence-gathering equipment. A smaller version was fixed to Fisher's mechanized wheelchair and accompanied him wherever he went.

But Nita's greatest value was her companionship. She refused to cater to his disability, the paralyzing result of having crash-landed a Glouster on a Norwegian ice field early in World War II. But she helped him work his impotent limbs until they responded with new tone and suppleness. He had grown to love her as much as life itself. Even now, he slept wrapped in her warm, ample body. She had taught him that there was intense sexuality in the simple touching together of skin and lips. She and the agents of Unit 1 were Fisher's entire existence. As he now turned to Nita and considered her suggestion that the Director might not be aware of other internal interest in Jim Thompson, he was especially relieved that he wasn't handling this one alone. Internal issues could be so messy – and potentially dangerous to his unit.

"I remember when Thompson disappeared," Fisher said, pulling Nita's attention away from the console. "We'd only been in the buildings at Langley for five or six years. There was a lot of buzz around the place about whether he was still connected operation-ally."

Nita glanced toward him. "And was he?"

"It was never clear. If he was, it was pretty loosely. I think he may have remained an asset for some of our people in Southeast Asia, but not in any official capacity."

"I can't imagine that anyone who cared would still be around. Compton was a very young agent in '67 when Thompson disappeared, and he's been retired for years."

"Maybe this Davis kid has talked to someone else about the letter."

"I'll run a trace on his phone and email for the last ninety days and see what comes up," Nita said, turning back to her computers.

"And we'll see what he has to say to Compton tomorrow," Fisher muttered. "I wonder who else will be listening?"

# NINE

Eric Compton had not been able to see Davis the morning the waitress called from the Corner Deli. According to his aide, he had slept fitfully and wasn't interested in getting out of bed. But the message ignited a spark in the old man's eyes and he had asked that the visitor come by the next day about ten. He would take a sedative and try to be rested.

At nine forty-five the following morning, Davis headed south out of Remington on Highway 651, locally dubbed Sumerduck Road. As the trip odometer in the red Mini showed two miles, he saw the pasture on his left with a creek running through it and a huge, white-barked sycamore standing on the bank in the middle of an open field – just as the waitress described it.

The drive curved through a row of lacy cedars that largely veiled the house. But as Davis passed through them, he could see Compton sitting in a wheelchair on the spacious porch of the old farmhouse that faced away from the road. Though the day was comfortably warm with only a wisp of high horsetail clouds, the old man had a quilt across his lap and was wrapped from waist to neck in a gray blanket. The drive ended in front of a garage with a walk that looped across the front of the house to wide steps, rising to the deck. Compton sat at the top of the steps, his head lulled heavily to one side. As Davis stopped the car and climbed out, the man raised his chin with obvious difficulty and looked at his visitor with gray, curious eyes.

The screen door opened immediately and a stocky woman of about Davis's age in blue medical scrubs stepped out and stood beside the wheelchair, placing a protective hand on Compton's shoulder. Her head was shaved on one side, a rainbow on the other, with a silver stud piercing the middle of her lower lip that pushed forward when she smiled.

"You must be Davis. When I told Mr. Compton what you wanted to talk to him about, I haven't seen him that interested in anything in months. But he was exhausted yesterday. Thanks for waiting...."

Davis stepped forward and hesitantly grasped a hand that Compton was struggling to raise above his lap. "Thanks for seeing me," he said, looking up at the attendant. "I hope I'm not...."

"Talk to Mr. Compton," she said, nodding to her charge. "You're here to see him. Right? I'm Kirstin. Let me get you a chair, and you can visit here on the porch. Mr. Compton likes being out in the sun." She hurried back into the house while Davis stood awkwardly, wondering what good it was to be out in the sun with all those blankets on. Compton's gray eyes smiled and his speech was slow and deliberate, slurred by a tongue that refused to behave as it should, but still clearly understandable.

"Good morning, Mr. Eckerson. Welcome to my home."

Davis squatted on his haunches as Kirstin pushed back through the screen door, a metal folding chair tucked under one arm. "Here – this will be more comfortable. Do you need anything, Mr. Compton?"

"Would you like something to drink, Mr. Eckerson?" the old man asked, each word sounding as if it were forced through his lips with his last ounce of strength. "Tea or lemonade?"

"Some tea would be great. Unsweetened."

Kirstin again went inside and Compton turned immediately to the reason for the visit.

"Jim Thompson. I haven't heard that name in a long time." He spoke so slowly that Davis wanted to tug each word from his lips.

"I'd never heard of Thompson until a few weeks ago," he said. "Then I was given something that I think will interest you. Do you mind if I take some notes while we talk? " He pulled a small note pad from his pocket as he told Compton about inheriting some of Gladys's estate and of finding the letter in the box of travel stickers.

"Read me the letter," Compton said, leaning his head slightly forward.

As Davis unfolded the letter and read, Compton closed his eyes, his brow furrowed and face concentrating on every word. When Davis finished, the old man continued in the same deep thought for several seconds without moving or speaking. Davis wondered if he should call for Kirstin.

"Kaa," Compton muttered finally, and it took Davis a moment to realize he was referring to the letter – not beginning to choke. "I heard Jim refer to his sister by that name once and asked him about it. He said that's what her friends called her, and he just adopted it. She was murdered, you know. I think her name was Katharine." His statement took a full minute, but his eyes gleamed with the recollection, telling his listener that he was relishing every word.

"Yeah, that's right," Davis said. "I looked up the news accounts about her death. It was pretty soon after Thompson disappeared."

Compton's nod was more a forward tremor and he grunted his affirmation. "I was pulled back to Washington from Bangkok just before Jim disappeared, but we all heard about his sister's death. The Agency followed up, but nothing ever came of it. What are you going to do with this letter?"

Davis folded the single page and slipped it into his shirt pocket. "I'm an investigative journalist. My aunt also left me some money, and this mystery intrigues me. I think there might be a big story in it. Thought maybe I should go to the CIA with it and see what they have to say."

Compton made his best effort to laugh. "Thompson is long dead, no matter what happened to him. And this Weaver thing is almost half a century old. No one there will care, if they even remember him at all. They have much bigger fish to fry. Until you find that there's something to this, they won't give a damn."

Davis fingered the letter in his pocket, wondering if he should accept the old man's word for how the CIA might react. "You knew Jim Thompson in Bangkok?" he asked finally.

"Got to know him pretty well. I was a new agent but was assigned to Thailand because I was one of the few people who spoke both Thai and Khmer. I'd been in Mae Sot, over on the Burmese border, in the early days of the Peace Corp... then in a Khmer-speaking area on the eastern border."

"You were a lot younger than Thompson, then..."

Compton's eyes said "dumb question."

"Much younger – and he wasn't officially with the Agency by then. But he knew all the important people – and knew what was going on inside the country." He paused and licked his lips slowly, regaining his breath.

"So I met with him once or twice a month," he continued. "He liked me because I was the only person with the Embassy group at the time who thought we should be staying out of Vietnam." A thin smile crept across Compton's pale lips. "Both of us thought our involvement in Southeast Asia was pretty stupid. I think that's why they finally pulled me out."

"And that's why he asked his sister to contact you?"

"That, and probably because I had traveled with him to Cambodia on some of his buying trips. My cover at the Embassy was that I was with USIA – the Information Agency. So I'd go with him to Cambodia and Laos as a 'goodwill ambassador.'"

"What did he do on those trips?"

Compton again slowly ran his tongue over his lips and closed his eyes, as if deciding if he had the energy for what he knew would be a long response. He continued at an even slower cadence.

"Before Jim took an interest in the Thai silk business…it was almost dead. There were villages where they were still weaving… but silk production had almost died out…. He had to buy raw silk from other countries…and was bringing silkworms and trees… back into eastern Thailand. Some of the villages…where raw silk was still being made…were in Cambodia."

"Did you ever go with him to this place he talks about? This Paoy Snoul?"

Compton slowly shook his head. "No. But I know where it is…. It's in an area where Jim liked me to go along because I knew the history – and he liked to know the history. It was right across the border from where I'd been with the Peace Corp… in an area that had changed hands between Thailand and Cambodia over the centuries. It's called Banteay Meanchey Province…. In Khmer it means "Fortress of Victory.""

"But he mentions Siem Reap and Angkor Wat in the letter."

"Probably because his sister would know where they were…. Angkor Wat's where the old Cambodian temples are. You've probably seen pictures…."

"Lara Croft," Davis said. "I think that's where they filmed *Tomb Raider*."

Again the trace of a smile crept across Compton's face. "Angelina Jolie," he said. "That's the place."

The old man's not dead yet, Davis thought, then asked, "Why do you think he was concerned about these Chinese children?"

Compton paused again for what seemed minutes to Davis.

"Jim was very smart," the old agent said finally. "Observant. There was no reason to bring children…from China to Cambodia to learn about silk…. The Chinese were experts. It sounds like he thought they were being schooled…for something else."

Compton's speech was laboring enough that Davis hated to force the conversation, but he needed more answers. "Do you know this Pridi who's mentioned in the letter?"

This time Compton didn't hesitate. "Oh yes. Pridi Phanamyong. He was one of Thailand's most colorful politicians...and a friend of Thompson's. His family came from China originally.... During World War II, a Thai Field Marshall declared war on the Allies.... Pridi was Foreign Minister and refused to sign the declaration."

The old man paused, his tongue playing over his sticky lips, and drew a long, raspy breath.

"Would you like to take a break?" Davis suggested.

Compton wagged his head enough to say no. "Pridi later helped found *Seri Thai*, the Free Thai movement that resisted the Japanese.... When Jim was still with OSS, Pridi was one of his contacts – Code name *Ruth*, as I remember.... Later, as Prime Minister, he was accused of the assassination of young King Rama the Seventh." Compton again paused and steadied his breathing. "Don't think he was guilty, but Pridi had to flee the country. Ended up in China and later Paris where he died.... He had enough connections in China that Jim would have checked with him...about these children."

"And Pridi told him to forget about them."

"Maybe...or may have been saying; 'You stay out of this, but someone needs to find out what's going on.'"

"Someone like you, Mr. Compton?"

The man again forced a nod. "His letter's just forty-five years too late."

"And what would you have done if you'd received it when he disappeared?"

A smile again twisted the old man's face. "What I would do now...if I were you. I would go to Cambodia. See if there is anything there that might get others interested...."

"Like you say – it's been forty-five years...."

"You have to start somewhere."

"I've only been out of the country once – and that was more like going to Hawaii."

"And you're an investigative journalist?"

"Well, I'm just getting started. But I see this as maybe being my big break...."

"Do you have a cell phone?"

Davis pulled the latest upgrade of his smart phone from his pocket.

"Kirstin bought me one of the kind that fits in your ear," Compton said. "I can still hear – and if you have enough time, I can still talk. Call me. It will give me something to look forward to."

Davis took the old man's trembling hand and gave it a gentle shake. "Wouldn't mind having a partner. Thank you. Where do I start?"

"You have a passport?"

"Yeah. I went to the Dominican with my friend Alex – one of those all-inclusive resorts."

Compton slowly shook his head and looked skeptically at the would-be journalist. "This will be different."

"Yeah, but I think I'm up to it. And I need this," Davis said.

Compton's eyes seemed to narrow but he nodded again and gestured with his fingers toward Davis's Mini.

"Then go find out what Thompson wanted me to know...and what happened to the little weavers of Paoy Snoul."

# TEN

Somewhere over Alaska, Davis decided he was being too frugal with Gladys's money. Cathay Pacific's Boeing 777 was five hours out of Chicago and it was 10:00 p.m. in the eastern U.S. where he had started his day. But his flight to Bangkok was chasing the sun, and the sky beyond the thick, double-paned window in row 36 was still a sharp azure against the snow-covered peaks that rose twenty thousand feet below.

The passenger in 35F, a balding man with a halo of hair that splayed out over his ears like a Franciscan monk, had pushed his seat full back and was almost resting in Davis's lap. The man dozed fitfully, giving a snorting jerk every now and then that shook the tray on which Davis was trying to balance a diet coke against the mild turbulence of the outside air. To his left across the aisle, two Asian women sandwiched a pre-teen boy and girl between them in the four center seats, the children playing some internet-connected video game on their smart phones and chattering back and forth in what was probably a normal tone, but seemed loud in the enclosed cabin. The preschooler in the seat behind him was just able to reach the back of Davis's seat with her feet and gave him a healthy push each time she decided she wasn't comfortable – which seemed to be every few minutes.

"Keep your feet off the seat," her mother hissed each time the girl thrust Davis forward, and the jarring stopped only until the girl braced again for another adjustment. Six more hours to Hong Kong, and the extra two thousand dollars for a business class seat was starting to look like a bargain.

An attractive Asian flight attendant in a crisply pressed red jacket and skirt pushed past him down the aisle, carrying a coffee pot to replenish the cups of passengers who had just finished dinner. He had flown a bit domestically where a lot of the flight attendants seemed to have an attitude, and looked too old to heave open the forty-pound emergency window if their lives depended on it. But every one on this flight was young and cute and as he boarded, he'd seen a real beauty handing out pillows in business class. He'd see if he could upgrade for the leg into Bangkok from Hong Kong.

Getting out of the country had been more complicated than Davis anticipated. When he and Alex had gone to the Dominican Republic, once he had his passport they had just booked a flight and gone. Simple as that. But it had taken almost three weeks to get what he needed for the trip to Southeast Asia.

After his meeting with Compton, Davis had stayed another night in Culpeper deciding what to do next, then driven north to Arlington, Virginia, and found a hotel that rented by the week, a few blocks from the Clarendon Metro Station. The place looked like it had once been a Holiday Inn, but the section of Clarendon along Arlington's Wilson Boulevard had changed over the years, and the nicer hotels had moved elsewhere. His room was decent, but faced the noisy street and he had stayed away until he was ready to go to sleep, leaving early each morning to go into D.C.

Compton had suggested Cambodia, but Davis decided to begin his search for Jim Thompson in Bangkok where the silk merchant spent most of his post-war life until he disappeared. And he'd heard Thailand was a tourist-friendly country: a good place to break in a rookie globetrotter whose international experience hadn't taken him beyond the walls of the all-inclusive resort in the Caribbean. Once he was getting the hang of Bangkok, then on to Cambodia to find the village of Paoy Snoul. From there, he had no plan. If the search for Thompson proved to be a bust, he may as well take advantage of being there. Alex had always talked about getting to Bangkok and trying out Patpong, the city's infamous red light district, and joked about renting a girl in Ho Chi Minh City's Hoc Binh Park for 300,000 dong.

"You get it?" Alex would snort, thumping his fist into Davis's shoulder. "Vietnam money called *dong*, and you get sex in Ho Chi Minh City if you got big dong!" Vietnam might be worth a few days.

An online search told Davis that no visa was needed for Thailand, and he could get one to enter Cambodia at the border. But if he crossed into Vietnam, he'd need to apply for a visa before leaving the States. And he might want to go on into China – maybe to Xian to see the terra cotta warriors. Gladys had wanted him to use her money to travel, so….

While still in Arlington he had placed online orders for travel clothing – pants with zippered double pockets, shirts that weren't supposed to wrinkle, two pair of socks with zippered pouches in the ankles, and a money belt. All to be delivered to his hotel room. He parked the Mini in the hotel's underground lot and rode the metro into the District to work on the visa applications for Vietnam and China.

By Washington standards, the two embassies weren't close, with the Vietnamese Embassy south of DuPont Circle on 20$^{th}$, and the Chinese out near the Naval Observatory on Wisconsin. But both were a short walk from stops on the Red Line, and Davis shuttled back and forth, filling out paperwork and explaining as well as his roughly formed plan allowed, why he would be entering both countries across their western borders – and on the ground. Americans traveling to Vietnam generally flew into Ho Chi Minh City in the south or Hanoi in the north, and entered China via Beijing or Shanghai by air. To do otherwise, with no real reason and without being part of some tour group, seemed to raise suspicion. So Davis began to frame his trip in terms of writing travel articles about less-visited places in both countries and convinced himself he might even do that.

"For what do you write these?" a female Chinese official asked.

"I'm a freelancer," Davis decided on the spot. "I write the articles, then send them to magazines that might be interested when I get back to the States."

"You write anything before?" the woman wanted to know.

"Yes. Several articles."

"What about?"

"An article for *Mother Earth News* on trellising cantaloupes, and one for *Antique Magazine* about a man in Iowa who repairs player pianos." Davis was being truthful, but didn't add that these had been class assignments for a magazine writing class, and that neither had been accepted for publication.

"Humph," she muttered skeptically. "Don't sound like travel articles." But within three weeks he had both visas.

As they passed over the coastline of western Alaska, a flight attendant asked over the intercom for passengers to shutter their windows so the cabin lights could be turned off for those wishing to sleep. Davis pushed his own seat full-back to discourage the toddler and to give him some distance from the snorting Franciscan. Sometime in the next four hours they would cross the International Date Line and by the time he reached Bangkok, it would be just after midnight, day-after-tomorrow. He had tried to work the time thing out in his head, struggling to figure out what happened to the day in between, but finally decided it was "just the way things worked." When he returned to the States, he arrived back about the same time he left Asia – which was even harder to figure out. But he got his day back.

The toddler in the seat behind him leaned forward and began to rhythmically bump her head against the back of his seat. Definitely business class going into Bangkok, he thought.

. . .

Forward in the cabin of Cathay Pacific's flight 807, Adam Zak rose from his aisle seat and made his way toward the restroom in the rear of the aircraft. His hair was now loose over his ears, and he sported a dark, three-week beard with his mature mustache. The black patch covered his left eye, and those who glanced up at him in the dark cabin immediately fixed their gaze on the patch. Adam found that people meeting him for the first time wanted so badly to look elsewhere, but couldn't resist glancing first at the eye covering. If he passed them quickly, they didn't remember the rest of his face at all. To his few acquaintances in Virginia Hills, their lanky neighbor with the occasional eye patch worked in some vaguely defined area of airline security. To his friend Dreu, who saw how frequently and unexpectedly he was called to duty, he was an air marshal.

"I've violated every one of our policies by telling you this," he confided, knowing full well that she would protect his bogus secret. But as he walked down the aisle of the cruising 777, he looked every inch the part.

The air was choppy enough that the captain had turned on the seatbelt sign, and an attendant in a trim red uniform came toward him, smiling politely.

"You should be seated, sir," she said in flawless English.

He returned the smile with a trace of pained urgency. "It's something of an emergency."

"Please hurry then," she said, and he pushed past her toward the rear of the plane. As he neared row 36, he glanced across the center set of seats at the passenger on the far aisle who was trying to stretch his long legs around a small gray duffle that was jammed under the seat in front of him. Adam had watched the passenger board, noting that he was half a head taller than most of the Asians on the flight and dressed like he was headed for the Australian Outback: khaki cargo pants made from some light, water-resistant fabric and decorated front and back with zippered pockets; a lemon yellow short-sleeved shirt with an equal number of pockets; and a bright red St. Louis Cardinals cap with the distinctive StL logo above the bill. During transit in Hong Kong, following him to the Bangkok departure gate would be simple. When they reached the Thai capital, Adam would see if the kid took the monorail into the city or grabbed a taxi. If he took the monorail, he would be harder to follow and remain inconspicuous. But Adam could certainly be just another exhausted tourist.

Davis Eckerson had a kind of spoiled innocence about him that Adam found especially irritating. As the kid transited to his international flight in Chicago, he had shown both the wide-eyed confusion of an inexperienced traveler and a cocky expectation that everyone was there just to take care of him. At check-in, he ignored others in line and walked up to the side of the counter, pushing his passport and boarding pass in front of the gate attendant and asking if he had to check in before boarding. She looked up from the passenger she was serving, glanced quickly at the pass, and patiently pointed at the seat number. "You have what you need," she said. "We will board by rows."

Despite the continuous warnings over the airport's intercom, Eckerson left his duffle in a seat unattended, walked nervously around the gate area studying the departure board and paying little attention to other travelers. When the boarding call came, he pushed to the front and waited anxiously to be the first on when his rows were called.

"What is this kid doing heading off to look for Jim Thompson?" Adam muttered as he watched him start down the wrong aisle, then clamber across a middle row of seats to get to his place at 36F. But he knew the kid was just doing what Eric Compton had advised.

Adam had monitored the conversation with the former CIA agent from a grassy perch twenty feet back into the trees east of the Remington house, wondering where the woman in black was hiding, and who she was working for. As Davis read the Thompson letter to the old man, the two pin mics on the porch fed the conversation directly to Adam's headset and to a standard-looking iPod in his shirt pocket. He guessed the woman was also getting the full story.

His call to Fisher, warning that someone else was monitoring Compton's home, resulted in a short five-line message, delivered in a plain envelope to his hotel room early the next morning in Culpeper. Fisher was favoring paper communication, probably for reasons revealed by his note:

*All electronic communication mentioning Jim Thompson and going to a list of former associates, including Compton, has been requisitioned by NSA analyst, Bradley Han. Han has authorization and is a China specialist. Link connecting Eckerson, Thompson, and Compton was fed to him as well as to the Director. No identified out-going communication from Han that appears to relate.*

Adam already had a photo of analyst Han, a bespectacled Chinese-American with a pleasant round face and thin black hair, who looked to be in his mid-fifties. And the Thompson letter had shown that Fisher and the Director were right. Somehow Han and Dreu's Marshall Ding were connected to these Weavers.

As Adam watched Davis board the Cathay Pacific flight for Hong Kong, he had also watched the throng of passengers for Han or for someone who might have been the shadowy woman in Remington. He didn't really expect to see the man from the NSA, and nearly thirty women boarding the flight could have been the dark figure in the Virginia woods. During the flight he studied movement in the cabin, thinking that a tail would check to see where Davis was seated in the aircraft, just as he had. Again, more than a dozen eligible women made the trek to the rear restrooms. Adam watched them all, wanting each face to trigger recognition, should he see it again.

As the 777 began its descent into Hong Kong International Airport, Adam strapped himself back into his seat and watched the small model of the airplane approach the landing strip on the screen on the seatback in front of him. Eckerson, he guessed, was on a wild goose chase, and Adam was missing his morning racquetball workout with Dreu. He wondered if she was missing him a fraction as much as he missed her – and if that concern meant he might not be in the right business.

# ELEVEN

By the time he cleared customs and retrieved his bags in Thailand, Davis was so exhausted that he just stood stone-still in the middle of the bright reception area of Bangkok's Suvarnabhumi International Airport and struggled to organize his thoughts. A mass of humanity swirled around him: voices chattering in languages he didn't recognize, and people moving in equal numbers in every direction, adding to the confusion. Toward the exits, a row of glass-fronted booths traded currency, and he wondered if he should exchange some money. He had opted for a print guidebook, unsure what kind of wi-fi access he would have. The book said Thai currency was called *baht* and traded at around thirty-three to the dollar, so was worth about three cents. But the guide also said U.S. dollars were accepted as legal currency in most places in Bangkok and that the city was full of kiosks that exchanged money. There was more activity at the airport exchange windows than he wanted to mess with, and he decided to wait.

Passing through the airport in Hong Kong had been easy. As he exited the plane from Chicago to change flights, two sixtyish looking men, one the bald monk who had been seated in front of him and the other a gaunt, wisp of a man dressed like he was still lost in the Sixties, said they were headed for Bangkok. He just fell in behind them. There was another pass through security where two very polite and very thorough young Chinese men in blue uniforms went through every piece of his luggage. He asked about upgrading to business class and learned that it was full. But his seat to Thailand was further forward, without the monk in front of him and no seat-pushing kid behind. He slept a little, but still felt so tired he could drop onto one of the lounge benches and be out in a second.

The travel book said the airport was thirty kilometers from the city – just over twenty miles. Tourists were advised that the best way to get into the city late at night – and it was almost 1:00 a.m. local time – was by taxi from a transportation center he could access via a shuttle.

An American-looking man wearing a neatly tailored combination of dark pants and a light gray sports jacket over a navy, open-collared shirt, passed him heading for the outer doors. He was pulling a black leather roller bag and Davis hurried after him.

"Are you headed for the transportation center?"

The man glanced back over his shoulder, taking Davis in with a quick look.

"No – should be a car waiting. You going into the city?"

"Yes, sir."

"Where you staying?"

"Some place called the LIT Hotel...."

"That's just off Rama I Road – not far from where I'm going. Come on. I'll have my driver drop you off."

"Oh, that would be great! My first time here and I'm just learning my way around."

"Well, you picked a nice place to stay," the man said as they pushed out onto the covered drive that fronted the airport terminal.

The air slapped Davis in the face like a hot towel: thick and humid, assaulting his lungs as if he had stepped into a steaming sauna. He stopped suddenly, gulping for breath.

The man with the roller bag looked back again with an amused smile.

"Welcome to the 'Hot and Wet,'" he said. "It will rain sometime during the night, and that will cool things down a bit – into the high 90s."

The air conditioning of the black Mercedes was cold against Davis's damp skin as he climbed into the car. He wiped his face with a sleeve, gazing out at the row of gilded statues and gigantic lighted billboards that lined the avenue as the car left the airport.

"You come here often, then?" he asked his host, turning to the man who sat comfortably beside him on the dark leather seat.

"Every couple of months. I'm a surgeon at Johns Hopkins and we're involved in a research project with Bumrungrad Hospital here. You might have heard of it. It's one of the premier hospitals in the world and a major destination for medical tourists. People come here from all over for everything from cardiology to cosmetic surgery. It's just off Sukhamvit Road, so your hotel's only a half mile away."

Davis nodded in the darkness of the speeding car. "And what kind of research do you do?"

"I'm an oncologist. We're involved in some gene therapy work that we can't do in the States. Too much regulation. And what brings you to Bangkok?" He glanced at Davis's outfit, appearing to have said as much as he wished to about his work.

"I'm a journalist – doing a story on Jim Thompson. You heard of him?"

The doctor chuckled. "You can't come here more than once and not know about Jim Thompson. That explains why you're at the LIT – over near his house. But I didn't realize there was anything about Thompson that hadn't already been written. What's your story about?"

Davis improvised. "I'm looking at a new angle on his disappearance. That he might have been involved in something over in Cambodia."

Again the doctor smiled. "Didn't know there was any disappearance story that hadn't been worked to death, either. But good luck!" He turned to look out his own window at the dark stretch of open countryside that separated the airport from the outskirts of Bangkok. "You a single guy? You'll probably want to take a little side trip into Patpong while you're here."

"Yeah, I've heard about Patpong."

"That's the reason half the people on the plane were coming to Bangkok," the doctor said, his smile tightening. "All those older men. Too bad, as far as I'm concerned. One of the most fascinating cities in the world, and half the tourists are coming to Patpong."

"Don't know that I'll have time on this trip," Davis lied, not wanting to be one of that half who were just in Thailand for the sex trade.

"Well, if you find time, it's right off one of the Sky Train stops. Anyone at the hotel can tell you how to get there. And it's worth walking through, just to see the place. Sex is big business here – and very open. In fact there's a street near where you're staying called Soi Cowboy. *Soi* means a side street, and you'll see lots of addresses that begin with Soi. Anyway, it's sort of a mini version of Patpong. But watch what you drink and keep your money some place safe."

"Thanks," Davis said. "Right now I feel like I could sleep for a week. And if I can get out tomorrow, I'll be going to the Thompson House."

"Lots to see. You know anyone here?"

"No. I'm on my own. Not even sure anyone at home knows I'm here."

"Best to be very careful, then. As I said, this is a great place to visit with wonderful, friendly people. But just like any big city, you can get yourself into trouble if you're not careful."

"Don't think I'm going to be doing anything crazy," Davis said, not realizing how wrong he could be.

68

. . .

The vaulted honeycomb of the arrival terminal at Suvarnabhumi International Airport was so vast that Adam was able to watch Davis Eckerson without being noticed as the kid collected his bags and stood in confusion in the middle of the concourse. Midnight arrivals from Sydney and Dubai, each carrying more than 300 passengers, crowded the terminal with tourists of every description. Just keeping Eckerson in sight was turning out to be a greater challenge than being inconspicuous.

Adam traveled light – a single carry-on with five changes of socks and underwear, and two complete outfits. Overnight laundry service in Southeast Asia was generally cheap and reliable, and if he stayed in a place long enough to need more clothing, he bought what he needed and left it behind when packing for home.

When Davis turned suddenly and hurried after a man who was headed toward the outer terminal doors, Adam had to move after him more quickly than he liked. He suspected he was not the only person watching the would-be journalist and though he had studied the crowd around Davis, no one seemed to be paying particular attention to the young American.

When Adam reached the drives that passed in front of the arrival terminal, Davis and the man had crossed two of the lanes and were standing expectantly beside a third, apparently waiting for a private car to pick them up. Adam knew that taxis and other ground transportation were not supposed to operate in the arrival lanes and that the men must be waiting for a scheduled pick-up – a development he hadn't anticipated. As a black Mercedes pulled to the curb beside Davis and the stranger, Adam scanned the street for one of the rogue cabs he knew regularly passed by the terminal, hoping to avoid the lines in the transportation center with a quick fare. Two were just entering the arrival lanes and he flagged one to a stop, threw his bag into the back seat, and slid in beside it.

"Do you speak English?"

"Yes. English okay," the driver said, pulling quickly away from the curb.

Adam pointed at the black sedan that was just exiting the drive.

"Follow that car. I want to go where it goes."

"Okay," the driver said, and swung into traffic as an airport security officer ran toward the cab, gesturing that it wasn't authorized to stop.

"You get into big trouble," Adam joked as the driver accelerated.

"Not too much," the man said. "My boss pay his boss. He turn in my number: nothing happen."

Ah, graft at its best, Adam thought, then realized that he was also working for a boss that often paid handsomely so that he could bypass the system.

. . .

The second cab that entered the pick-up lanes in front of the terminal was waved down by a slim, attractive Asian woman who had also flown Cathy Pacific from Chicago to Bangkok. She had not paid much attention to the tall, bearded American who caught the cab ahead of her, noting only that his brown hair was a bit shaggy and he wore a black patch over his left eye. A typical sex tourist headed for Patpong.

When the black Mercedes turned off the tollway onto Sukhamvit Road, the cab carrying the bearded man was still ahead of her and she began to watch both automobiles more closely. Sukhamvit was a street that never slept and though it was well after midnight, street vendors still sold roasted chestnuts and meats, bowls of rice and soups, and sweet, multi-colored crepes from carts along the avenue. Lights shown from small cafes and open-fronted bars where girls in short minis and halter tops sat on stools in animated conversation with foreign men or watched the traffic on the sidewalk for a likely client.

The Mercedes traveled west for over a mile with the cabs trailing, winding under the massive concrete pillars that supported Bangkok's overhead Sky Train. On the right, the brightly lit up-scale storefronts of Siam Square and the MBK Center came into view above the level of the elevated tracks, their walls displaying giant posters of exotic models dressed in haute couture and expensive jewelry. As the cars passed through a main square, the ultra-modern Bangkok Art and Cultural Center filled the skyline in front of them. The square pulsed with the city's nightlife, and traffic seemed as tangled and impatient as at midday.

Once through the square and just beyond the Art Center, the

Mercedes turned right into a narrow side street and the woman ordered the cab to follow. The first cab follow the sedan for a hundred meters, then pull to the curb as the Mercedes stopped in front of a towering glass building, its windowed sides screened by a space-age façade of white, perforated concrete that resembled vintage computer punch cards. She signaled her driver to stop, sat for a moment watching the cars in front of her, then paid and walked quickly between the rows of parked automobiles into one of the shadowy storefronts.

The young American exited the Mercedes, leaned back in to offer his thanks to the man who had given him the lift, then stood and gazed upward at the imposing front of the hotel. He shook his head in apparent disbelief, then disappeared into the brightly lit foyer.

The lane was surprisingly non-descript: simple shops shaded by the occasional tree; tangled spaghetti cabling overhead that crisscrossed the Soi and joined each building like massive umbilical cords; a massage parlor that still buzzed with late-night activity; and small compact automobiles pressed nose-to-nose against one side of the alley. The woman made her way to the dimly lit doorway of a narrow, three-story guest house that advertised rooms in Thai, English and German, and watched the other cab. After a few moments, the bearded man with the eye patch slipped from the car and into the shadows fifty meters in front of her. He stood motionless for five minutes, then crossed the street and entered the hotel. The woman watched the brightly lit glass door for another ten minutes to see if he would return, then entered the guest house and asked the sleepy attendant behind the counter for a room.

# TWELVE

The Jim Thompson House is actually a collection of traditional Thai homes, built or relocated by Thompson to a walled compound beside one of Bangkok's few remaining *klongs*, the system of ancient canals that once served as major travel routes throughout the city and earned it the name "the Venice of Asia." Thompson was an architect by training and found in the classic design of the traditional Thai "stilt house" an artistic expression that needed to be preserved and displayed. Early Thai homes were raised head-high above the ground to afford air movement and protection from flooding during the monsoon season. Most were a collection of separate rooms, clustered about a central open terrace that made up nearly half of the living space. Constructed from a variety of woods, depending on region, the houses were distinctive for their steeply pitched, wood-shingled roofs, ornately decorated with serpent motifs from Buddhist and Hindu mythology. Within the Thompson House compound, narrow pathways wind through lush tropical gardens, connecting homes that represent building styles from across the country and of varying degrees of sophistication.

The street leading to the popular tourist site was a block west of Davis's hotel and he walked the distance in fifteen minutes, again surprised that such a treasure should be hidden along a narrow, nondescript lane. He paid the 700 *baht* entrance fee and descended into a sunken courtyard where a slender young woman in a traditional, form-hugging Thai dress was announcing that the next tour would begin in twenty minutes. Beside the entrance gate, a large house the color of red clay had been converted into a gift shop, and he climbed the steps to the main level and entered the shop. Immediately to his left, a man sat casually on a long wooden bench, his right arm stretched across the back of the seat. Davis glanced quickly over at the figure, turned his attention to the clerk behind the counter, then jerked his head back toward the man as he recognized the distinguished face of Jim Thompson – permanently etched in wax.

"Nice touch," he commented to the woman behind the counter.

"People like to have their picture taken with him," she said.

He studied the still, smiling figure. "Kind of creepy, if you ask me."

"Would you like your picture? I will take it for you?"

Davis shrugged. "Sure. Why not." He slid onto the bench under Thompson's outstretched arm, handed the woman his iPhone, then forwarded the picture to Eric Compton with a note that read; "And you said this was going to be tough!"

When his tour was announced, he followed his graceful guide through the hour-long visit to each of the compound's buildings, taking notes and questioning the young woman about the details of Thompson's resurrection of the silk industry.

"Did he travel much out of the country?" he asked as she described how silk production had almost died in Thailand by the end of the Second World War.

"People were still weaving in small villages," she explained. "But almost all cocoon production was happening elsewhere – primarily in China, Vietnam and Cambodia. As I mentioned before, the worms feed on mulberry trees and there weren't many left in the country. Mr. Thompson made a number of trips abroad to bring back new pattern ideas and import trees and cocoons."

When she described his disappearance, Davis again pushed up beside her as she led the group along a shaded path lined with the sweeping, orange and yellow blossoms of Bird of Paradise.

"Do you know if he'd been in Cambodia close to the time he disappeared?" he asked.

The girl, who looked about seventeen, smiled politely and turned toward him as she walked.

"I don't know about his travels in so much detail," she said. "He traveled very much. No one is here now who knew him when he was alive. Now," she said to the group clustered behind him on the path, "please enjoy these beautiful flowers and the many orchids you will see along the walk...."

Davis backed off with the questions but when the tour was over, returned to the souvenir shop and purchased a copy of William Warren's *Jim Thompson: The Unsolved Mystery*. It was a few minutes before eleven a.m. and as he approached the gate that emptied back onto the narrow Soi, he was suddenly overwhelmed with a fatigue that crushed him like a leaden overcoat. He couldn't remember ever being so tired – and so suddenly! "Watch what you drink," the American physician had said, but Davis hadn't had anything but bottled water since he woke up.

"My God!" he muttered as he passed through the gate beside an older tourist couple wearing matching "Born in the USA" T-shirts. "I'm so tired I can hardly stand up!"

The man laughed. "Jet lag," he said. "You'll feel wide awake about ten tonight. It'll go away in a week, just when you're ready to go home."

Davis looked at him bleary-eyed, trying to make sense of what the man was saying. Too tired to think about it, he turned sluggishly down the street toward his hotel and the welcoming embrace of that luxurious king-sized bed. As he exited the lane onto Sukhamvit Road, he took no notice of the woman who watched from the top of the concrete steps that rose above the street, leading to the Sky Train station.

. . .

Soi Cowboy is a narrow block-long strip of bargirls, blazing neon signs, and throbbing music that parallels Sukhamvit between Soi 23 to Asoke Road. On the wide verandas of clubs named *Midnight*, *Raw Hide*, and *Suzie Wong's*, girls in skin-tight shorts and minis sit on tall stools and wait for customers: some faces seductive, some bored, and some etched with fear. Most of the girls come to the Thai capital from villages in the countryside or from neighboring Cambodia, Laos, or Myanmar, lured by promises of work as waitresses or housekeepers where they can earn enough money to support their families back in the villages. Their travel and lodging are paid by their new employer who is more than willing to invest in getting the girl into the city. Once she learns that her job is not to wait tables or clean kitchens, but to provide sex for the flood of tourists who come to Thailand seeking Bangkok erotic nightlife, her sponsor refuses to let her return home until she has worked off her debt. She is alone in the city, knowing no one but the pimp, without money, and beaten if she refuses her sponsor's demand that she give her body to strangers. By the time she has earned her fare home, she is too ashamed to return to her village and too damaged to expect a respectable future in the city. Though Thai authorities have cracked down hard on sexual exploitation of children, forcing much of the kiddie sex trade across the border into Cambodia, the exploitation of the innocent now simply requires that the victim be sixteen.

Adam followed Davis Eckerson from the lobby of the LIT Hotel down Sukhamvit to Soi 23, then into the press of humanity that converged on Soi Cowboy. The narrow street pulsated with lights and sound, and the smell of beer, cigarette smoke, roasted meat and human bodies oozed from every club: an exotic perfume for those wanting only to experience Bangkok at its seamiest. Men and women of every age and nationality elbowed their way along the street: some alone, but most in pairs or small groups. There were a surprising number of couples, holding hands and gazing from side-to-side at the gaudy display of young, caramel-colored bodies. In front of a club called *The Dollhouse*, a heavy-set German with rumpled gray hair and a grizzled beard, held a hand-painted sign at arm's length as one of the girls snapped his picture.

*Dollhouse*
*20 Gorgeous Girls, Plus a lot of Ugly Girls,*
*and a few fat ones!*

Behind him a cluster of young Asian women in frilly pink skirts that barely covered their hips primped as a backdrop to his souvenir photo, seemingly representing only the twenty. There wasn't an ugly or fat one among them.

Davis had entered the street alone, an immediate invitation to girls from clubs on both sides of the street to call to him: some approaching and attempting to guide him toward their tables along the verandas. Davis shook his head and the girls didn't pressure. It was a general rule in Soi Cowboy that tourists should not be hassled, and the girls let him pass with only a quick invitation to come back if he decided he liked what he saw.

A hundred feet behind, Adam was attracting girls like a human magnet. They seemed to find the tall American with the long wavy hair, short beard and eye-patch especially interesting.

"Hey, Cowboy! You want to party? Cheap beer here. Only sixty *baht!*" Two girls in orange tops and sailor hats, with denim shorts that looked painted onto their hips, pushed beside him and took his arms.

"You want picture? Come inside. You buy me a beer?" He shook them off and they moved back toward their bar. "Come back, Cowboy. This the very best place!" they called after him as he kept his eye on the blond head moving ahead of him through the crowd.

The kid had stopped and was looking through the open doorway of a club called *Coyote* where a row of girls wearing only sequined G-strings gyrated on top of the bar. As he watched, two of the more attractive girls Adam had seen on the strip walked up to Davis and nuzzled against him, one whispering into his ear. Davis looked from one of the women to the other, then shrugged slightly and put his arms around their waists, allowing them to lead him farther into the strip.

A girl in yellow shorts and a loose-fitting halter top that covered only the top of her breasts took Adam's arm and pulled him toward a club called *Cowboy 1*. He eased her gently away, pushing quickly ahead to keep the trio in sight. They turned into a club with *Pussy Cat* blazing in flashing red letters over the veranda and Adam followed, elbowing his way to an empty stool along the bar where dancers in spaghetti G-strings swayed overhead, smiling down at their new guest and thrusting forward to encourage him to slip money under the tiny band around their hips.

The girls led Davis to a table on the far side of the dark room where one nibbled at his neck and stroked his chest while the other went for drinks. A girl in a poured-on black dress that showed there was nothing beneath pressed up against Adam at the bar.

"You buy me a drink?" she whispered. "You American? I like big American men." Adam wondered if she could really be sixteen and began to shoo her away, then decided that to remain inconspicuous, he might need company.

"Sure." He signaled to the man behind the bar to bring them two Singha beers, keeping an eye on Davis and his attentive companions. The girl in the black dress pushed between Adam and a man who was groping another girl on the next stool and pressed her slim body harder against him.

"Maybe we can party," she whispered. "We go to your hotel, or I have room in back."

"Maybe later," he murmured, watching Davis's girl with the beers return to the table with two drinks in one hand and a third in the other, carefully positioning the glasses so that Davis got the single. Watered for the girls, Adam guessed, and suspected from the way Davis drained his, that the kid didn't realize Thai beer had twice the alcohol content of the Bud he was used to guzzling with his college pals.

"You just want to drink?" Adam's girl pouted. "Maybe I go find someone else who wants to party."

"Just enjoy your drink," Adam said, finding a five hundred *baht* note in his pocket and handing it to the girl. "We can party later." He pulled her closer against him and slipped a hand under her short skirt, massaging her naked bottom as he watched the trio across the room. It flashed through his mind that he was glad Dreu didn't know what he really did for a living. In fact, he could probably get arrested in Dallas just for fondling this girl. But the five hundred *baht* seemed to satisfy her and she pushed up onto his knee and didn't seem to be encouraging more as long as she was getting money.

One of Davis's new friends fetched a second round of drinks and as her partner turned Davis toward her and smothered him with a deep, probing kiss, pulled a small vile of clear liquid from between her breasts and poured its contents into Davis's glass. Adam sipped slowly at his Singha and stroked his girl's leg as she rocked gently against his chest and nuzzled her cheek against his beard.

"What happened to your eye?" she whispered in blunt Thai fashion. "It make you very sexy. I like this." She reached up and fingered the patch.

The two women across the room were now working Davis from both sides, one whispering into one ear and the other adding her own suggestions in the other, while both stroked their way up and down his legs. The second round of drinks was gone and Davis's eyelids drooped heavily. He finally nodded in resigned anticipation, and the girls pulled him to his feet and guided him toward a door at the rear of the bar.

"Let's go to your room," Adam said to the girl, who by now had molded herself to his side. He lifted her with him as he rose from the stool. She wrapped around him like a koala hugging a tree, and he looped an arm under her hips and pushed his way across the room after the trio.

In the back of the club a narrow hall went left and right, and Davis and the girls were out of sight, stumbling somewhere around the corner to Adam's left. He turned to follow.

"No! This way!" the girl insisted, tugging at his neck in the other direction. Adam wrapped her more tightly and, with his free hand, pulled her face against his neck to silence her protest, carrying her down the hall and around the corner. The bare hallways formed a rectangle behind the main bar, filled by ten small back-to-back rooms. Davis and his escorts had turned the back corner and were again out of sight. As Adam reached the rear corridor, they disappeared into the middle of the five back rooms. He lowered the girl to her feet and pushed her along the narrow hallway to the door of the second room, where he tried the knob and found it unlocked.

"In here," he said, and the girl shook her head.

"Not my room."

The door pushed open into a small, stuffy chamber with a plain wooden floor, lit by a single red bulb hanging over a queen-sized bed that filled two thirds of the space. The walls and bedspread were a faded pink, the only other furnishings in the room a washstand in the corner with a shelf above it, holding a statuette of a seated Buddha and tube of lubricating jelly.

Adam pushed the door closed behind them and locked it, pointing to the bed.

"Sit," he said, and she silently obeyed, her eyes reflecting a trace of fear. He stood against the wall that separated them from the room that held Davis, listening intently. The muffled voices of the women reached him through the thin plaster, speaking in Thai.

"This not my...," the girl with Adam began again, and he hushed her with a raised hand and withering glare from his single exposed eye. For five minutes he stood in silence, listening to the murmurs in the adjoining room as the confused girl watched from the bed. Then the door of Davis's room opened and the girls moved past them down the hall. When they had turned the corner, Adam stepped to the bed and grasped his escort's arm.

"Come," he said.

She stood in confusion and he pushed her ahead into the corridor and to the next door.

"In here," he said in a loud whisper.

"This not my room," the girl protested, and he lifted her again against his side and pushed through the door.

It was an exact replica of the one beside it with the exception of the lanky, blond-headed body that sprawled face-down across the bed. Adam dropped the girl into the corner beside the washstand where she shrank against the wooden cabinet and stared at the figure on the bed, her eyes widening.

"Ohhh," she whispered. "I go back to bar. This not my room...." She slipped toward the door and Adam grabbed her around the waist and lowered her again to the floor.

"Don't move," he warned in a tone she immediately understood, and he rolled Davis onto his back, leaning over him in the dim light. Under the ruddy glow of the naked bulb, the kid's face was pasty gray and foamy spittle ran from one corner of his mouth. Adam thrust the fingers of his right hand up under Davis's jaw, probing for a pulse, but found none. There seemed to be no movement in his chest. Adam pulled him to the floor in front of the door and straddled him, pumping his back with long rhythmic strokes as he would a drowning man. With the first downward thrust, a throat-full of vomit poured out onto the bare wood. Adam knelt to the side, flipped Davis onto his back, pinching his nose closed and forcing three long breaths into the kid's lungs. When there was no response, he wrestled Davis's long frame up onto his right shoulder.

"Come!" he ordered the girl as he struggled to his feet and, holding her arm tightly in one hand, forced her in front of them back into the hallway.

Immediately opposite the door, an exit opened into an alley that backed the clubs and shops in the adjoining street. Adam pushed the girl into the alley, grimacing as the acrid sting of urine and rotting garbage assailed his nostrils. They picked their way through piled crates and mounds of litter, emerging finally onto Soi 23. A green metered cab unloaded a group of rowdy men a few feet in front of them and Adam pushed the men aside and threw Davis's body into the rear seat, sliding in beside it.

"Bumrungrad Hospital. Go!" he ordered, and as the cab wheeled away from the walk, Adam pulled two more five-hundred *baht* notes from his pocket and tossed them through the window at the feet of the terrified girl.

· · ·

The two women wound their way back through the couples that crowded the front barroom of the *Pussy Cat* and exited onto Soi

Cowboy. They walked side-by-side through the stream of tourists, ignoring the whistles, suggestive calls, and occasional gropes that followed them down the street. At the brightly lit veranda of *Cowboy 1*, they stepped up onto the open porch and approached a slight Chinese woman in tight black leather pants and a black silk blouse who sat alone, sipping at a beer and watching the flow of humanity that passed in front of her on the street.

"Here is what you want," one of the girls said to the woman in English, handing her Davis's wallet, a paper copy of the photo page from his passport, and several tightly folded one hundred dollar bills. "What drug you give him? He look very bad." The girls looked nervously behind them back toward the *Pussy Cat*.

"Maybe he had too much to drink," the Chinese woman said.

"Not too much. I think maybe too much drug. We don't like trouble here."

The woman in black frowned. "This is all you found? No letter or room key? And no passport?"

"Just that," one of the bargirls said. "We check him pretty good. Wallet and money in his pocket. No letter, no card. Maybe in wallet."

"Where did you leave him?" the woman asked, thumbing quickly through the wallet and finding no key card and no letter.

"A room in back. Not our room. But someone find him soon."

"You need to check him again. There must have been a room key or card."

The girls shook their heads in unison. "Not going back now. Someone will go to room and find him. We need be gone from club. Don't like trouble here."

The Chinese woman looked down the street toward the *Pussy Cat* while the girls fidgeted nervously, then drew a small purse from the black handbag she wore on a strap that looped across her shoulder like a bandolier.

"Here is the other five thousand *baht*." She handed the bills to the woman who had not taken the first installment. "Now you two disappear."

The girls looked back in the direction of the *Pussy Cat*, expecting to see one of the bouncers carry the man out into the open air. When they turned again, the woman in black had slipped off the veranda and disappeared into the crowd on Soi Cowboy.

Once back among the early morning throng on Sukhamvit, the woman placed a call to a cell phone in Telluride, Colorado, where she knew it was just after 1:00 p.m. She knew also that somewhere within the giant black box of NSA Headquarters in Maryland, her call and its content would be scanned, recorded, and stored. If she used the wrong words, the message would end up on the desk of an analyst who might eventually tie it to her reason for being in Bangkok. When the male voice answered, she spoke quietly in perfect English with the accent of the American Southeast.

"This is Four. I'm in the Thai capital and calling to let you know I'm taking care of business, but there are a few loose ends. I think I've discouraged our competition. See what you can learn about a tall American in his mid-thirties with a beard and heavy mustache, long brown hair, and a black patch over his left eye. He was on the Cathy Pacific flights from Chicago. The papers I'd hoped to find weren't in the file, so I need to do a little more searching. I'm thinking this other man may be after them as well. I'll check back with you when everything is in order."

"You didn't find the letter, then?" the man asked.

"It wasn't on him. There are other places I can look. It needs to be found and destroyed."

"Agreed," the man said. "And the letter carrier?"

"He's been taken care of."

She disconnected and stood for a moment watching the human circus of Bangkok's nightlife swirl around her. Her target really couldn't have picked an easier place for a search like this that wouldn't attract too much attention, but it troubled her that the girls hadn't found the letter or room key. Once the young American was discovered at the club, it would take some time to figure out who he was and where he was staying. But her training wasn't current enough to pick a lock with an electronic key card. She would need to talk her way in.

# THIRTEEN

The police officer stood in a small conference room near the hospital's admission desk, scratching notes into a thin notebook as he spoke to the cluster of nurses and attendants he had assembled.

"He was left here at 2:00 a.m. by a tall man with a beard and a patch over his left eye," he repeated in Thai.

One of the night attendants nodded and pointed through the room's large window that opened onto the spacious, tastefully furnished reception area.

"He was carrying the man on his shoulder and put him there – on that sofa – and said, 'this man collapsed in Soi Cowboy. He needs help breathing. I think he may have been drugged.' Then, while we were calling for the nurses, he walked out. We don't know who he was."

"What else about the man who brought him?"

"Very tall," another attendant said. "Long hair: brown and wavy. Dressed in a plain gray T-shirt and blue jeans."

"Anything on the T-shirt?"

The staff looked at each other and shook their heads.

"And the man he brought in. It was a drug overdose, taken orally?"

"Our initial tests indicate GHB," a nurse said. "A large ingested dose."

"And no identification?"

"No sir."

"So we don't know the nationality?"

"All of his clothes have American labels but were Asian-made, except his pants. They were made in Mexico."

The officer grunted. "Probably American. And the man who brought him in?"

The same nurse, who seemed to be the senior staffer, answered. "He spoke English, but the receptionist at night does not speak English well. So she was not certain about accent. She thought he did not look British, but could have been American, Canadian or Australian."

"And there was no indication that he knew the man who was drugged?"

"No. He put him on the sofa and left."

"And what was the patient's condition when he arrived?"

"Extremely critical. He was already comatose and his vitals very weak. He was given enough of the drug that with the alcohol, it had completely depressed respiration. Bringing him here may have saved him if we can get him through the night. But I think his chances are not good."

"If he makes it, call me when he is able to speak," the officer said, looking through the room's window at the hospital's entrance. "Now I would like to talk to this man with the eye patch to see if this happened in one of our bars. If I check with the hotels, he shouldn't be hard to identify."

. . .

The man with the shoulder-length brown hair and distinctive eye patch was no longer at the LIT. He knew Davis was in serious trouble when he turned him over in the back room at the *Pussy Cat,* but couldn't leave the kid lying there with no one to look after him. Bumrungard was the only safe place he could think of, and it was close. Adam had once had a physical there while in the Thai capital and the hospital was known for its exceptional medical care.

He knew also that the two B-girls hadn't just drugged the kid to take his money. The clubs along Soi Cowboy didn't stand for that kind of thing. Bad for business. And whatever the pair had given Davis was way too potent to have come from the girls. Someone was paying them a lot of money to take that kind of risk.

As the taxi sped toward the hospital, Adam had checked Davis's pockets and found them empty, then remembered feeling something against the kid's ankle as he carried him down the alley. The room card was secreted in a small pouch in one of Davis's fancy travel socks, still in its paper jacket. Either the B-girls hadn't found it, or they'd been asked specifically to retrieve something else – possibly the letter. But they had taken his wallet, passport, and money. He would be a hard patient to I.D.

In a moment of conscience, Adam considered telling the hospital staff that the victim was American and that his name was Davis Eckerson. But that would tie Adam to the incident in a way he couldn't afford. He had to appear to be just a Good Samaritan, bringing in a man he'd found in distress. After leaving the kid in the hospital's admitting area, Adam had walked to the LIT so that a taxi driver couldn't retrace his steps and had gone directly to the room number shown on Davis's key jacket.

For having hidden the card so carefully, the kid wasn't careful about anything else. His clothes were thrown over the backs of chairs and tossed loosely into the closet, the contents of his shaving kit scattered across the long marble counter that surrounded the sink. An iPad sat plugged into a wall receptacle on the desk beside an open notebook.

Adam donned a thin pair of leather gloves and quickly thumbed through the notebook, finding only a few scratchings about the trip: probably written during the flight to Hong Kong. Nothing revealing. He systematically sorted through the clutter, checking pockets and desk drawers. A small safe with a four digit code was locked in the clothes closet, and Adam decided to search everything else before worrying about the combination. He found the letter tucked into an outside zipper pocket of Davis's carry-on bag.

Adam pushed some of the clothing aside on the bed, straightened the covers, and sat for a moment wondering what about this letter was worth the kid's life. It was just possible the bargirls were after his passport and wallet, but much more likely that whoever had been listening in on the conversation at the Compton house wanted this letter – and wanted Eckerson out of the way. Off the trail. But if whoever hired the girls expected Davis to be carrying the letter, they would know by now that it wasn't on him, and may not be through with their search.

He rose quickly and gathered up the iPad and charger, surveyed what he could see of the hallway through the security port in the door, and listened for any movement outside the room. Hearing nothing, he slipped into the hall and descended three floors to his own room where he hurriedly packed, then went into the bathroom. Using electric clippers from his luggage, Adam trimmed away his hair and beard, finishing by shaving both head and face cue ball smooth, and completing the transformation with a pair of dark, heavy-rimmed glasses. The hair from the sink went into a laundry bag that he pushed into a side pocket of his roller bag, wiping the bathroom clean. The hair would go into a trashcan somewhere far from the hotel.

He had checked into the LIT as Galen Brown with a passport and credit card that supported the identity. The hotel's TV express check-out allowed him to leave without going to the desk and, with the eye patch in a pocket of his baggy shorts, Adam descended to the main floor using the stairwell and walked out a side door into the sultry Bangkok morning. Galen Brown's credit card would be good, but not traceable to any identifiable human being. Adam always paid his bills - but not always as himself.

He walked for nearly a mile along Sukhamvit before signaling a cab, asking the driver to take him to the northern bus station at Mo Chit. The first bus to the Cambodian border would leave sometime around 5:00 a.m., giving him time to get a ticket, make his call to Fisher, and see if he could get into Davis's iPad.

The Mo Chit terminal was a curious combination of bus station and 7-11 store, and Adam took a seat in the empty rows of plastic yellow chairs that faced a green and white storefront that filled half of the interior of the sprawling building. Digital signs in Thai and English stretched across the top of the brightly lit shop, directing passengers to various gates and to restrooms, but he had guessed right about the time for the bus. Five a.m. He had just over an hour to wait and the ticket windows were not yet open. A woman in a green smock poked along between the rows of yellow seats with a long-bristled broom, and half-a-dozen backpackers were stretched out on bedrolls along the walls. Otherwise, the station was quiet.

Fisher answered his call to Virginia with a gravelly "Yes?"

"Things have not gone well here," Adam said, knowing that the old man was not one for chit-chat and that this call would escape NSA's review. "The kid went into Soi Cowboy last night and two bargirls gave him a heavy dose of some drug. My guess would be GHB – gamma hydroxybutyric acid – the stuff they use as a date rape drug. It's clear and tasteless and they slipped it into his drink. If he's still alive, he's comatose in Bumrungrad hospital. The B-girls were probably hired by someone who wanted him to give up on this hunt, and may have been looking for the letter."

"That's tragic," Fisher said. "I don't like innocent people getting caught up in our messes. Have you seen anyone following him?"

"No – which troubles me. I'm usually pretty good at spotting a tail.

But this has to be one of the easiest places in the world to follow someone unnoticed. The main streets here look like a U. N. convention, and you're always running into the same people at different places."

"Did they get the letter?"

"No. I have it. He left it in his room – almost in plain sight. Doesn't seem to have any idea that it's of interest to anyone else. But I suspect whoever's after him knows what it says, or they wouldn't be working so hard to make it disappear."

"There's something we're missing here," Fisher said. "We can't find any electronic trace of Davis telling anyone about the letter until the call to Compton. And kids his age communicate almost entirely electronically. The Compton call didn't even come from Eckerson, but from a waitress in Remington. But someone else knew he was going to talk to Compton, and what about."

"I've been focusing my attention on Marshall Ding, trying to keep NSA out of it until we know how they're involved" Adam said. "But maybe we need to learn more about this Bradley Han. As far as we know, he's the only person who asked for intel on Thompson and past associates."

"Right…as far as we know. But we can't see that Han did anything with the information. And he's had that tracking request in the system since it was set up."

"Has anyone asked him why he wanted it?"

"Yes. But he's China and East Asia. Said it's just been one of those loose ends he's kept an eye on. Makes sense, if you think about it."

"Any communication between Han and Ding that we know about?"

"None."

"If Han were going to do something with the information, no one would be in a better place to keep it invisible," Adam suggested. "And if NSA has a leak inside, I'm sure they'd want to know. Speaking of wanting to know, could you find a way to let the kid's family in St. Louis know he's in a hospital here in Bangkok? I don't think he was on very good terms with them, but if he were my kid, I wouldn't want him to die in some Thai hospital and not know what happened to him. I'll leave it to you to figure out how to do that without raising a lot more questions."

"I'll figure out something," Fisher said, then paused. "Could whoever is after Davis know you were following him?"

"I'd bet on it. They had to know where he was staying to follow him into Soi Cowboy. So they probably came over on the same flights and tracked him from the airport the same way I did. In that case, I would think they saw me follow him into the hotel."

"Are you sure you aren't being followed now?"

Adam chuckled. "Very sure. The man who followed Davis into the hotel doesn't exist anymore."

"Then I assume you need someone new to be leaving the country when you get ready to cross a border."

"The main reason for the call. I'm now Randall Murch. You have the profile and photo. I'll need it to be in the Thai passport system within four hours."

. . .

Although entering rooms secured by electronic keys hadn't been part of the Chinese woman's training, creating new documents in very short order had been – as was being very convincing to a young male hotel receptionist. She prepared the California driver's license in her room at the guest house, waited until the night shift changed at the LIT so she wouldn't run into the person who had initially checked in the young American and at 6:15 a.m. walked briskly to the reception desk.

"I was going out for breakfast and realized I left my key card in my room," she said, giving the young man behind the counter an embarrassed smile. "And I hate to admit it, but I don't remember my room number. It was on the little envelope you gave me, and I didn't pay that much attention." She slid the California license with her picture and the name Davis Eckerson across the desk.

"Do you have your passport?" the receptionist asked, glancing at the license.

"I'm afraid it's in the room too," the woman said. "I had just planned to come down for coffee."

The clerk checked the license against his computer screen and swiped a new card. "This is no problem, Ms. Eckerson. Many people do not remember the room number."

She clasped her hands prayer-like beneath her chin in the Thai gesture of appreciation and thanks. "*Khob khun ka,*" she said gratefully. "I'll be right down and will give this one back to you."

"You may keep it," he smiled. "Put it in your purse."

In the elevator, the woman thought to herself that it was fortunate that Eckerson was named Davis and not John, Tom or William – names a young Thai, who had probably improved his English watching American television, might recognize as male. If asked, she had been prepared to say that it was a female form of David, but the clerk hadn't questioned it.

The card worked perfectly and she slipped into Room 714, taking in the general clutter with a sweeping glance. It took only ten minutes to thoroughly search the room and she found nothing. It was possible, she decided, that Eckerson had destroyed the letter, committing it to memory or scanning it into a document file. But she found no computer either. The wall safe was locked and she toyed briefly with calling the clerk and asking for help getting in. Too much risk. She walked confidently out of the room as if leaving her own, but met no one in the hall. As she passed the desk, walking toward the exit, she caught the receptionist's eye and waved both her key card and passport.

"*Khob khun ka!*" she mouthed again, and the young man nodded brightly.

"No letter and no computer," she thought as she walked the two hundred yards to the guest house, remembering the bearded man with the eye patch who had followed Eckerson into the hotel. Perhaps the letter was in the safe, but no computer? And no cell phone? She climbed the one floor to her room and logged in to her computer, entering "Bangkok to Siem Reap" into the search engine. Taking care of Davis Eckerson may not have solved her problem, and if the man with the patch was a step ahead, he may already be on his way to Paoy Snoul looking for the Weavers.

# FOURTEEN

The only connection Dreu had maintained among the New York fashion crowd was Brio, a statuesque black model whose humble roots in the pine forests of rural South Carolina had so infused her with natural humility and appreciation for the gifts she had been given that Dreu found her a refreshing and lasting friend. Brio had no last name, explaining that her mother wasn't sure who had fathered her and didn't want to assign credit to the wrong irresponsible son-of-a-bitch. The girl had grown up sharing a two-room trailer with five, one-named siblings, a mile from the town of Summerville. Had it not been for a junior high physical education teacher who had taken her to Charleston the summer before her ninth grade year and introduced her to an agent friend, Brio would likely have followed in her mother's reproductive footsteps. But the teacher saw in Brio's young, leggy body and striking, high cheekboned face, the kind of distinctive look her old college roommate was always describing to her.

"We're looking for that face that you can't see, whether man or woman, without wanting a second look – and once you've seen it, can't forget," the agent friend said. Brio had such a face and, between the two ladies, they turned her into a project. The P.E. teacher kept Brio from getting pregnant, and the talent agent convinced her that there were opportunities beyond Summerville and groomed her for them.

Brio was named Brio, she said, because her mother had heard the word in some movie and learned it was Italian, meaning "great energy and confidence." The least she could give her daughter was a name that held promise, even if life didn't seem to offer the girl much. When her face was gracing the cover of *Vogue*, Brio recognized that it was there, not because she had done some great thing to deserve it, but because she was born with genes that made her tall and striking and because of the rescue and life support of her two guardian angels. Though they were from completely different worlds, Dreu found in her a kindred spirit.

Her call reached Dreu at the office just before the noon lunch break.

"How you doing, sister," Brio asked.

"Enjoying the life of the working stiffs," Dreu laughed. "How's the Big Apple?"

"Same. I'd be with you if I knew how to do anything else. But my little Kountry Kids Foundation in Summerville is doing good things. Money has its advantages."

"There's money in other places," Dreu said. "When you've had as much as you can stand, give me a call."

"Your emails are sounding better," Brio said. "I'm glad you've found someone you really seem to care about. Are you healing up, girl? Inside, I mean?"

"He's wonderful, Bri. Gone a little more than I like – like now, for example. But he seems interested in what I do like no one else I've met since I came back here, and he's just… well – wonderful! You need to come out…."

"Got a shoot in South Africa next month. For some reason, they think they need to be flyin' a black girl down to South Africa! But then, maybe I can get out there…."

"It's not like you to call in the middle of the day, Bri," Dreu said. "Something up?"

Brio paused just long enough to make Dreu nervous. "I'm guessin' you haven't been told," her friend said, giving substance to the concern.

"No…. What?"

"Lonnie Marchisio's been released. It was on this morning's news."

Dreu's heart spasmed and she gulped a quick breath, pulling her palm hard against her chest to kick it back into rhythm. "That's not *possible,*" she whispered. "He's only been there a year."

"I don't understand it," Bri said. "They say he's 'better.' That they've been able to stop his psychotic episodes. And since he was sick, further imprisonment would be inhumane."

"*Inhumane!*" Dreu gasped. "That's crazy! The *man* is crazy!"

"I didn't want to upset you," Bri said quietly," but I thought you should know. You need to be careful, girl."

Dreu was silent long enough that Brio asked, "You okay?"

"I'll be okay," she said. "And thanks for letting me know, Bri. I'll call you…."

"Okay. Gotta go. You be safe!" And she was gone.

Dreu walked to the window and looked down over the noon traffic that surged along the North Stemmons Freeway. Lonnie Marchisio was crazy smart. He'd convinced his shrinks that he was safe to turn loose, but she knew better. He was still a psycho, and he would be coming to find her. She wished Adam were here!

# FIFTEEN

The bus ride to the Thai city of Ananyaprathet took just over four hours, passing first through an industrial section of east Bangkok, then out across open rice fields and groves of mangoes, citrus and bananas, and finally through low, rocky, tree-covered hills to the provincial city of Sa Kaeo and on to the Cambodia border. The 5:00 a.m. bus was crowded: sleepy Thais headed for border casinos; the few haggard backpackers mixed in who had spent the night at the station.

The bus disgorged its passengers far enough from the border that Adam signaled a tuk-tuk, the motorized rickshaws that putter-ed by the hundreds around every Thai city.

"Cambodian border," he said.

"You need visa?" the tuk-tuk driver asked, heading east along a broad, tree-lined avenue that bustled with motorbikes, people on foot, and dozens of handcarts loaded to the point that they almost disappeared under a mountain of fruits, vegetables, housewares, and bolts of cloth. An ancient truck rumbled past, piled high with white Styrofoam coolers strapped to the bed in a towering bundle that threatened to topple onto the street every time the truck bounced over one of the potholes that punctuated the roadway.

"I know special agent who can get you visa with no wait. Very quick!"

"No – just get me to the border." Adam knew that these "special agents" could indeed get him a visa, but at a substantial premium that was shared with the driver who brought the unsuspecting tourist.

To their left, a covered market sprawled along the side of the highway, its narrow alleys running back into a labyrinth of stalls that offered the wares that now passed him on the carts and trucks.

"Maybe you want to visit market?" The driver shouted back over his shoulder. Adam had been to the border once before just after his mother died – during the summer between his junior and senior years of college. He and his girlfriend at the time, an adventuresome archeology major from Flagstaff, Arizona, had been traveling like the backpackers on the morning bus, headed for the exotic temple ruins of Angkor Wat. They were making a four-country tour of Malaysia, Thailand, Cambodia, and

Vietnam, and spent two hours wandering through the market at the Thai border. Somewhere in his packed-away treasures, Adam still had a tiger's tooth on a leather thong that he had purchased from one of those stalls, only to discover a few days later when they ventured behind a shop in a Cambodian village that the teeth were carved from buffalo bone and soaked in cattle urine to stain and age them.

"Just to the border," he said, anxious to beat the rush of tourists he knew would soon be arriving by private tour bus from Bangkok.

As they approached the crossing, an imposing gray stone gate arched over the street, crowned by three miniature temples symbolic of those that covered the Cambodian landscape north of the ancient city of Siem Reap. Stone-cut lettering below the crowned top announced that the traveler would soon enter the Kingdom of Cambodia. Adam climbed from the tuk-tuk, gave the driver a generous 100 *baht* note, and joined the line waiting to clear the Thai exit point.

There were no border guards or barricades and as he awaited clearance through the border, carts and trucks seemed to pass through freely without showing paperwork to anyone. He thought it would be a simple matter to slip across the border unchecked. But that meant he would have to leave Cambodia the same way, and he couldn't anticipate the circumstances of his departure. Best to enter officially and leave legally.

The passport he handed the green-uniformed Thai official displayed a picture of the bald, clean-shaven face with hazel green eyes. The officer entered the number and name into his computer, studied the picture for a moment, then looked up at Adam.

"Remove your glasses, please, Mr. Murch," the officer said, holding up the picture. Adam lifted the pair from his face and slipped them into his pocket.

"Just for reading," he said.

"How long are you planning to stay in Cambodia?"

"About a week."

"Will you return through this point of entry?"

"I expect to, but may go into Vietnam first. Will that be a problem?"

"Not for us," the officer said with a thin smile. "But you cannot get a Vietnamese visa at the border."

"Ahhh, then I'll probably be coming back through here."

The man stamped the passport and Adam followed the queue of casino-goers diagonally across the street to the Cambodian entry station where a sign informed him that a visa would cost 1200 *baht* or $40 in US currency. He would also need a photograph, but could have one taken for another $10 or 200 *baht*. Much cheaper in *baht*. None of the fees were in Cambodian *riels*, a grim reminder of the native currency's instability.

The Cambodian portion of the check-through took the better part of an hour, with the processing officers and photographer appearing to be in no particular hurry. Three lines melded into two when an official decided to take a break, then hastily divided again when he returned, only to have another leave his station. With each transition, the order in the lines changed as some hurried to the front as an agent returned to his booth and others, who were almost at the window, were forced to the back as their officer unceremoniously walked away from his post. Since joining Unit 1, Adam had learned the art of infinite patience, knowing that no one is remembered more vividly than the complainer or trouble-maker. He flowed from line to line without reaction, finally reaching a window where an official remained long enough to allow him into Cambodia.

Once on the street in Cambodian territory the crowd quickly dispersed, with most of the Thais hurrying into side streets that housed a gaudy array of gambling establishments. Thailand did not permit casino gambling, and Cambodia was more than willing to accommodate the daily crowd from Bangkok who thought they could strike it rich by beating the house odds at places named *Vegas Star*, *Golden Crown*, *Grand Diamond City* and *Holiday Palace*. Adam smiled cynically as he watched the scurry of gamblers. Each seemed to believe that if he didn't beat the rest of the crowd to the tables or slot machines, someone else might get that big payoff. His cynicism also reflected how incongruous this first quarter mile of Cambodian territory was with the general economic malaise that began a short walk beyond the gray stone arch.

On the Cambodian side, the city was called Poipet and along both shoulders of the chaotic main street, vendors sat under bright canopies of orange and yellow, hawking cell phone cards, knock-off watches, purses, DVDs, and T-shirts emblazoned with the exotic temples of Angkor Wat. During the bus ride to the border, Adam had considered how he could most easily and discreetly travel into the interior and had decided the way would reveal itself once he crossed into Cambodia. Buses to Siem

Reap and the temple ruins ran hourly along the same road he needed to travel, but the village of Paoy Snoul was north of the city of Sisophon, only a third of the way to Angkor Wat. If he took the bus, he would need to get off at Sisophon and somehow make his way the remaining sixty kilometers north into the heart of Banteay Meanchey Province. Taxis meant drivers – and drivers meant someone in Sisophon who knew he had gone north to the village.

Adam started down a packed dirt path that separated a row of open-fronted shops from the carts of the street vendors, working his way toward Poipet's transportation station and the lines of buses and taxis that awaited passengers headed east. In front of a shop that spilled luggage and backpacks of every description out onto the walk, a silver Honda motorcycle blocked the path, a hand-lettered "for sale" sign in English and Khmer taped to its fuel tank. The cycle looked almost new and Adam stopped and walked slowly around the 750 cc Magna.

A young man who looked to be in his mid-twenties called from behind a pile of silver-blue hard-sided Samsonite suitcases. "You like that bike?"

"It looks nice. You the person who's selling it?"

"Yes. Very good price. Got it cheap and need money more than the bike," the man said, smiling broadly. "Two Canadian guys rode it across China and Vietnam. Got here with no money and no gas. Made me a good deal."

"How does it run?"

"Run real good. I give you a ride, okay?"

"What you asking for it?"

"Three thousand dollars, U.S. Worth four thousand."

"How many people come by here with three thousand dollars?" Adam wondered aloud.

"Not many. Bike still here," the young Cambodian laughed.

"Take me for a ride," Adam agreed, knowing that if the bike was in decent shape, it was easily worth what the man was asking. "This a 2003?"

"Ah! You know Hondas. That the last year they make this bike." The luggage merchant called in Khmer to someone in the back of the shop to mind the counter.

With Adam towering over him on the rear seat, the man kicked the cycle to life and bolted out onto the road, almost throwing his passenger backward into the dust. He roared east toward the end of town, weaving in and out of the jam of trucks, buses, and handcarts that filled the street, then spun around a wide roundabout and sprinted down the less busy side of the road back to the shop.

"Full of petrol and has Cambodian license," the man said as Adam dismounted and looked appreciatively at the sleek machine.

"I like it," Adam said, "but I'm among those who isn't carrying three thousand dollars. And I suspect you won't take a credit card, and no bank around here is going to give me that kind of money on my card."

"Yes. Cash for me," the man said, widening his smile. "But you don't need bank. You have good credit card? Go to casino, buy chips, take chips to another window and get dollars. Better than bank. No charges."

"Will you take twenty-five hundred for the bike?" Adam knew the asking price was fair but when in Southeast Asia, became a compulsive bargainer. He enjoyed the game.

The man shook his head dubiously. "Very good deal at three thousand. Maybe take two thousand eight hundred."

"Twenty-seven hundred, throw in a backpack, and we have a deal," Adam offered. "I'll give you my roller bag. All leather. Worth three hundred dollars."

The Cambodian frowned and looked for a long moment at the Honda and at Adam's expensive leather bag. "Okay," he said finally. "But you better hurry. Maybe someone else want it for three thousand before you get back."

"I'll take my chances," Adam said and turned back toward the border crossing and the high arched entrance of the Holiday Palace Casino.

A hundred yards beyond the border on the Thai side, a privately leased car and driver pulled to a halt beside the passport checkpoint. The driver jumped quickly from the black sedan and held the door for his attractive passenger.

"You check your passport and I get permit to cross to Cambodia," the driver said in English. "I meet you here."

The slender Chinese woman nodded without speaking and joined the line waiting for clearance through the border. By leasing the car she had reached the border sooner than all but the earliest buses from Bangkok, and the clerk at the ticket counter at the Mo Chit terminal assured her that no passenger with a dark beard and eye patch had boarded the 5:00 or 6:00 a.m. bus. If he was headed for Paoy Snoul, once she was in Cambodia she could still get some breakfast and would be at the village waiting.

# SIXTEEN

The first five minutes of Dreu's meeting with Marshall Ding went much as she had expected. The rest took a nosedive, then raced steadily downhill. The only thing that kept her in her chair and pressing forwards was hearing Adam's voice playing in the back of her brain. "I'd put my money on you," it said.

She had unloaded some of her work frustrations on him just before his most recent trip out-of-town, sharing the client concerns she was hearing about checks and balances within FedTegrity. They were sitting at the small dinner table in her apartment, leisurely finishing the bottle of Chardonnay Adam had provided when she said she was fixing salmon.

"Sometimes I think they have a pretty valid point," she said, gazing into the pale amber liquid and running a fingertip around the rim of the glass.

"What's at the heart of their concerns?" he asked.

"Well, my boss – Marshall Ding – has this fanatical belief that the fewer people who know how a security system works, the better."

"Sounds reasonable to me," Adam said.

She gave a quick nod and lifted her finger from the glass edge to emphasize a point. "But he extends that even into our development work. I'm the only person who really knows the intricacies of the systems I develop, and he knows his, and our third senior developer – a guy named Anthony – knows his." As she named each person, she moved the finger to a different point in the air to make clear the distinction. "And there's really nothing in our internal checks and balances that would prevent any one of us from manipulating the programs we develop without the others knowing." She lowered the finger to the table beside her glass.

"So, no one reviews another developer's final product before it goes out?"

"Well, Ding does. But mainly to make sure it works as it should. Are you familiar with IVKs?"

Adam shook his head. "Greek to me. Tell me what they are."

He smiled as she leaned forward over the table, her eyes gleaming and her ginger face showing a touch of blush.

"Well, put very simply, we know that one of the best ways to secure an operating program is to construct its security system like you would an old fortress, with guards at intervals all along the perimeter wall. The guards watch the areas between them to make sure no one tries to breach the wall. If there's an attack, they fend off the attackers and immediately repair any damage that's done. We call these sentries IVKs: Integrity Verification Kernels. And that's where the program architect does her best work... or his, as the case may be."

Adam nodded, acknowledging both her enthusiasm and what he was learning about FedTegrity's work.

"These IVK's are *super*-encrypted," she said, bunching her fingers and pressing the fingertips of both hands together, as if squeezing something into a tiny ball. "If you're really good, no one can break open your IVKs."

"Are you that good?" he asked with a teasing smile.

"All three of us are that good," she said, sitting back and narrowing her eyes to tell him this was serious business. "And Ding is probably the best."

"But if you're really going to have a legitimate check and balance system, you need to be able to examine and understand each other's IVKs," Adam concluded.

Dreu sat back and grinned with satisfaction. "Exactly right. But Ding will never do that."

"Have you asked him?"

"You don't just suggest things like that to Mr. Ding. The idea would have to come from him – and it never will."

"Plant the seed," Adam suggested. "You never know...."

"Are you a betting man?"

"I'd put my money on you," he said, and that was enough to get her to call her boss's secretary, ask for thirty minutes, and keep from walking out before ten of the minutes were over.

Ding was always respectful – more than she could say for the other men in the office who seemed to fall into two groups: the guys who had spent their adolescent lives playing computer games in their rooms, and now watched her pass with doe-eyed worship; and those who thought they were God's gift to womanhood. The latter bunch seemed intent on seeing how close they could come to being completely offensive without crossing the legal line, waiting until she passed to mutter something to each other she couldn't quite hear, or moaning in much the same way her younger brother did before he bit into his favorite burger at Barney's Gourmet Hamburgers in San Francisco. A primal "Uuuumm" that resonated with "I can't think of anything I want more than a big bite of that."

Instead, Ding always seemed a bit embarrassed in her company, sitting stiffly with his hands folded in his lap, a polite smile animating his round face.

"I know you are busy," she began apologetically, "but comments by several of our clients have made me think about how we might improve our own internal procedures." She felt a momentary twinge of guilt for putting all of the concern on the backs of their clients, when much of it was her own.

Ding nodded without changing expression, indicating she should continue.

"The three of us who are team leaders – you, myself and Anthony – are each responsible for creating the final level of security for our client's projects: the level that imbeds the IVKs and triggers an alert if someone tries to bypass or alter it."

Again Ding nodded.

"The question I'm being asked, since we keep that deepest level of protection pretty much to ourselves, is 'Who monitors the monitors?' Our clients want to know if there is some kind of check and balance within our own security structure."

Ding's smile remained fixed but his brow furrowed ever so slightly and his eyes became wary.

"They are questioning our integrity?" he asked in a voice that barely reached across the table.

"I think it's more a matter of them responding to our lectures about the system being no more secure than the people who know it best," she said. "And they realize we know it best."

"And what do they suggest?"

"It's not what *they* suggest," Dreu said, trying to deflect his concern by assuming some of the responsibility herself. "It's what we might do to provide them with greater assurances."

Ding's brow dropped another degree. "And what might that be?"

"We could easily create a multiple alert, where two of us – or even all – are notified of an attempted breach while the design work is still largely under our control. Then the integrity of the system doesn't rest wholly on our trust in its principal architect."

Ding lifted his hands, prayer-like, in front of his chin.

"Do you have reason to question the integrity of any of us?"

"No – not at all. But it's like having an internal audit. It's less a question of trust than of assuring clients that we are responsible."

"And if an alert comes to two or three of us – what then?"

"We get with the owner of that code and see what triggered the alert."

"But if only that person understands the specific structure of the IVKs, it is still dependent on him – or her – to recognize if and how an incursion has occurred. So we must still depend on the integrity of the principal architect – unless all three of us understand and have access to the complete code."

Dreu nodded. "One or the other."

Ding rubbed his folded hands up and down against his chin. "You raise an important question, and one that is at the heart of our business. Is a system more secure if several people can check on each other, but all understand the construction of the primary security measures? Or if only one person fully understands it? In the first case, we must have complete trust in all three people."

"But each of us is responsible for highly sensitive systems anyway," Dreu argued.

Ding nodded slightly. "Just so. But just those systems. Should one of us decide to compromise a system, the damage is limited."

"We all know the protocols we use well enough to deconstruct each other's work, given a little time," Dreu said.

"Yes. Given a little time – and given access. And the warnings would have sounded well before that. I would rather trust three of us independently than as a group."

Dreu straightened slightly in her chair. "I'm not sure that is fair to our clients. I'd like to be able to tell them that their security doesn't depend on the integrity of just one of us."

For the first time, Ding's smile disappeared and he became the man who delivered the "I'm in charge" lecture to visiting young analysts.

"If you have questions about the integrity of any one of us, Ms. Sason, now is the time to say so," he said pointedly.

"No sir," She said – beginning for the first time to wonder if she did. "Again, this is not a matter of trust, but a matter of greater assurances to those we serve. If we can trust each of us individually, I see no reason not to trust us collectively."

"Our clients have *my* assurance." Ding's voice had a note of finality. "And that is enough."

"What if something were to happen to one of us?"

"As you said, we could go in and study the code and see how it was constructed. It would only take a few days at the most."

"With your permission," she said, "I would like to modify the systems I am responsible for to show both of you how my IVKs are constructed and send an additional alert – at least to you...."

"*No*," he said, so sharply that it upset even his own sense of decorum. He returned his hands to the desktop and again lowered his voice to a loud whisper. "The weakness of a system multiplies with the number of people who know its secrets. That will not be our practice."

Perhaps not yours, Dreu thought as she rose from her seat, bowed slightly to her boss, and excused herself. During their evening of openness about their pasts, Adam had confessed that while in the service, he had been skipped over for promotion because he had a tendency to be a little insubordinate. Now it was her turn.

. . .

She was no longer modeling. At least he had been able to achieve that much. It was so debasing – displaying her body in sports magazines and strutting up and down in front of crowds, like some fifty-dollar 10$^{th}$ Avenue whore. She left it because he had convinced her it was evil. She had learned that much from him. She would listen to him now, he was certain. Understand that she was destined to be with him. They could still be a family. Through him, God had delivered her from Gomorrah, and God would heal her womb.

He had known that she was intended for him the first time he saw her. She had walked into the sandwich shop in which he worked and when he asked for her order, she smiled at him and said "Good morning." And God had spoken to him as clearly as if He had been the black woman who stood beside her, saying "This is the one. This is the woman I have prepared for you. For neither is the man without the woman, nor the woman without the man, in the Lord."

He was not a sick man. God had chosen to place him on a higher plane: a place of greater communion. But he had been forced to lower himself to the plane of the ungodly to convince the doctors that he was well. "For my thoughts are not your thoughts, neither are your ways my ways, saith the Lord." And they were not prepared to understand his ways: the ways of the Lord. He had convinced them that Lonnie Marchisio had changed. Satisfied them by becoming again one of the sons of Adam. And they had released him to further the Lord's work.

She had not been hard to find. Her phone number was unlisted, but she was still a creature of the world – of this plane – and had joined LinkedIn. She was working for a firm called FedTegrity in Dallas, and he would find her there. Follow her until the moment was right. Then, he thought, she will know that I have been sent, and that she was prepared for me from the beginning.

# SEVENTEEN

When Adam had traveled the road between the Cambodian border town of Poipet and Siem Reap with the archeology major from Flagstaff, it was one of the worst stretches of highway he had ever seen: red dirt ground into smothering dust, deep ruts that tossed vehicles about like skiffs on the Mekong River during the monsoon, and regular detours that took them rumbling across stretches of bare, sunbaked fields. The bus in which they were traveling stopped every hour, as much to let passengers sprint for the cover of a nearby tree to relieve their churning stomachs as to stretch their battered limbs or patronize roadside stands.

The highway was still lined at intervals with buildings that seemed to have been forgotten midway through construction: corrugated metal lean-tos that served as shops, and houses that barely hung together under their red metal roofs. Between these tiny villages were open paddies of young rice, scattered banana groves, and stretches of parched land that had been left fallow for years. But the road had since been paved into a passable two-lane highway with wide shoulders and, in most places, the semblance of a center-line. Occasional signs indicated that he was on National Highway 5, but he saw nothing limiting speed and along open stretches, throttled the Honda up to cruise at 110 kph.

The light traffic was mostly locals on motorbikes, strange-looking carts with powerful motors mounted on a narrow front axle that extended six feet in front of the wagon bed, and tourist vans and buses making the run to Angkor Wat. Adam occasionally passed a heavily-laden ox cart, a peasant on a bicycle carrying a brace of trussed-up hens, or a cluster of school children plodding in their blue and white uniforms through red dust that still defined the edges of the road. But as one of the first to pass through the border, he often rode for five or ten kilometers without passing another vehicle and felt a growing exhilaration as the cycle sped east.

As he neared Sisophon, the groves of trees gave way to more fields of rice and grain: some carefully cultivated and others parched and stubbled. The villages became even smaller collections of a few huts with rangy chickens that flapped out of his way in a squawking flurry as he sped through. He realized he was doing what he would never consider at home – riding too fast, without a helmet, and without enough attention to what was happening around him. He was violating one of the basic rules of flight instruction: keep your head on a swivel and see everything around you. It was a practice that had saved him more times than he could count since he lost his eye, and he was being careless.

He slowed as he crossed the river into Sisophon, the provincial capital of Cambodia's Banteay Meanchey Province. Here, 60,000 residents lived in simple brick and white-plastered homes that clustered around a major crossroad where highways went east to Siem Reap and south to Phnom Penh. At a wide central roundabout, National Highway 5 made the turn south, with the road east to Siem Reap becoming Highway 6. As he approached the city center, Adam recalled that somewhere south of the highway among the red-roofed buildings was one of Cambodia's infamous boneyards: a collection of tall bamboo cages that held the bones and skulls of thousands of local residents who had been executed by Pol Pot's Khmer Rouge in the 1970s for being too well educated or too independent. During the latter part of that decade, the Khmer Rouge executed over a million and a half of the country's six million people in an effort to purge the country of what they called the dangers of subversive intellectualism. These boneyards remained scattered around the Cambodian countryside as memorials to those who died and as reminders of the atrocities that can be committed by the powerfully corrupt. He wondered fleetingly if the Chinese children of Paoy Snoul had been in the country as late as the purge. If they were, they must have been protected by the Chinese allies of Pol Pot, adding to the question of what they were doing in the country in the first place.

He swung the bike around the roundabout, glancing up at the seven meter tall bronze statue of a Cambodian woman who looked out across the litter-strewn circle with a serene smile. At the first right, he turned south for a short distance on a diagonal that cut across the city to join the Phnom Penh road. Although the route to Paoy Snoul would take him another forty kilometers east, he was beginning to feel the effects of a long morning with no food and vaguely remembered that he and the archeologist had stopped at a restaurant south of the town center that served a western-style breakfast.

The Suon Kamsan restaurant was still there beside a single story, red brick elementary school: a long colorfully-decorated row of dusty windows that looked out onto the highway. Adam congratulated himself that after so many years he could find the place and that it was still in business. He parked the Honda beside a collection of wicker chicken cages piled along one end of the low restaurant front. The air smelled of sizzling grease, ginger, and spicy barbeque and as he stepped up onto the rough wooded porch, he fleetingly considered abandoning the western breakfast for more traditional Cambodian cuisine, but remembered he would soon be in open country again where he needed a stable stomach.

A girl he judged to be in her early teens showed him to a table along one wall and laid a menu in front of him, turning it over to show that its choices were displayed in both English and Khmer. He ordered bottled water, a pot of hot green tea, and what was listed as a traditional western breakfast, then sat back to study the room.

A van-full of Europeans who had probably spent the night in Sisophon were seated at a long table against the opposite wall, washing down their breakfasts with the local Angkor Premium beer. The rest of the diners appeared to be Cambodian. At several tables, families clustered around what looked like bundt pans perched atop small gas burners, with a central grill, shaped like an inverted colander, filling the hole in the middle of the pan. Dishes of vegetables, shrimp, and sliced meats surrounded the burner, and diners picked from the side dishes with wooden chopsticks and placed the items on the grill until sizzling hot, then doused them in a steaming broth that filled the circular pan.

His breakfast arrived: dry toast, two links of thin pale sausage, and a vegetable omelet that was almost runny enough to drink. He looked again at the pots of savory soup, dipped his toast into the flow of egg yolk, and decided his stomach may have been safer with native fare.

Twenty minutes later, with the water bottle stuffed into a pocket of his khaki shorts, he was on the bike again heading east out of Sisophon. Almost immediately, the terrain flattened and the houses began to thin again into open fields, many flooded to feed the young green shoots that stretched like artificial turf in every direction. In deep, murky roadside pools, black water buffalo wallowed and snorted, rising to their feet and shaking their sweeping horns as he passed.

He almost missed the small metal sign beside a red dirt road that turned north to Phnom Srok, the district that held the silk-weaving village of Thompson's letter. The side road was every bit as bad as the ones he remembered from his earlier visit to Cambodia and he slowed the cycle to a speed that allowed him to navigate the ruts and fissures without rattling his teeth. Oil-colored canals lined the narrow track, their sides facing the fields punctuated by canvas gates that could be lifted to pour water out across the paddies. Ahead, a plume of red dust rose behind another vehicle, visible only because of the raised roadbed and flat plain of the Cambodian countryside.

He guided the cycle to the edge of the road where the tires of heavier vehicles hadn't rutted its surface and increased his speed. Others must travel this road. But he had seen so few that weren't scooters that it struck him as unusual that one of the few cars or trucks would be moving north ahead of him toward Paoy Snoul.

As he closed on the red plume of dust, his suspicion grew. The vehicle wasn't a battered Japanese pickup, but an expensive black sedan – the kind an owner would keep off a road like this unless paid handsomely to drive it. He dropped back until he could see only the dust cloud and stayed there until the sedan approached the village, then pulled the bike to the side and stopped.

The fields on either side of the road were divided by a patchwork of small paths that allowed farmers on foot and bicycles to get to the outer fields. Adam walked the bike forward until a crude wooden bridge crossed the canal on his right, eased the cycle across, and guided it east along the paths until the road was no more than a flat bar on the horizon behind him.

Another canal paralleled the road and Adam rolled the Honda onto the low dike that kept its water from spilling into the paddies, turning north until the village was directly to his left. At the corner of two fields, a simple four-post shelter with a palm-thatched canopy shielded farmers from the sun during brief breaks. No one was in the fields and Adam left the bike beneath the cover, locked the rear wheel, then donned a pair of sunglasses and slung the backpack over his shoulder. The village was a half-mile away, no more than a hundred simple wooden structures raised on stilts, with corrugated metal or thatched roofs. On one edge to his right, two buildings of whitewashed block suggested a school.

The people of the Paoy Snoul, he hoped, would be curious about their visitor in the expensive automobile and wouldn't notice him slipping between the houses on the village's eastern edge. As he moved along the paddies toward the houses, a pair of tall, awkward birds squawked loudly and launched their black and white bodies into the air from one of the flooded fields, turning instantly into streamlined javelins of bill, neck, and legs as they soared overhead.

Storks, he thought. Supposedly a good omen.

A dog rushed him from beneath one of the raised huts as he reached the edge of the village, sliding to a halt six feet in front of him with black lips curled back over yellow teeth. Adam grabbed a heavy stick that leaned against a rough board wall, put there, he thought, to ward off this particular beast. He waved it at the animal who resentfully backed away, continuing to snarl as Adam eased past it between the huts.

The town center was a small plaza surrounded by the same raised houses and a few open-fronted shops. A crowd of villagers surrounded the black sedan where a young woman, almost a head taller than the Cambodians, leaned against the car's side engaged in lively conversation through an interpreter with the village elders. Adam watched unnoticed from the shadows of the huts, then stepped onto the square and approached the gathering. When he was mid-way across the plaza, a man at the outer edge of the crowd noticed him, nudged his neighbor, and within seconds a hush fell over the group as all turned to study the new stranger.

Adam lifted a hand in greeting and as he approached, the crowd opened a path to the automobile.

"Anyone speak English?" he asked lightly, smiling at those who stood beside the car.

"I do," the visitor said with an American accent, looking at him with open curiosity. "And my driver does."

"Hey, that's great!" Adam said. "But it looks like I'm interrupt-ing something. Go ahead with your conversation."

The woman leaning against the car wasn't more than mid-twenties, a stunning Amer-Asian blend of what Adam guessed to be Anglo and Chinese. She had inherited the jet-black hair of her Asian roots and her dark, almond-shaped eyes retained an exotic trace of the East. But her sharper nose and full lips looked distinctively western. She wore blue jeans that hugged her hips and long shapely legs, and a white silk shirt that was clearly expensive. From the press of her breasts against the fabric, she was wearing nothing beneath it. She studied Adam with an amused smile and nodded toward the village elders.

"I'm, like, doing some genealogy here. My mother may have spent some time in this village when she was young. So I'm trying to learn why she was here."

"She was Cambodian then." It was more a comment than a question.

"No. Mother was *soo* Chinese. That's what makes this so interesting. She was an artist. Not *just* an artist but she, like, painted as a hobby. In some drawings she did of when she was little, she shows herself with a group of other children, with 'at Paoy Snoul' written at the bottom of the pictures. This is, like, the only Paoy Snoul I can find."

Adam wanted to grab the girl and shake the "likes" out of her and wondered how the interpreter was dealing with this, like, American bastardization of the language. He asked instead, "So you came all the way over here to find out?"

"It's pretty hard to get information out of one of these villages without coming," she said. "And to be honest, I wanted to, like, see the place. It seems to have been pretty important to my mom."

Adam glanced at the village elders who were also studying him curiously.

"Are you learning anything?"

"Well, when you came up, they were just telling me that there was, like, a group of Chinese children who were kept here before the time of the Khmer Rouge." Her voice rose at the end of each statement as if it were a question. "There were, like, ten? Who stayed in a building on the edge of the village up that way?" She pointed across the square to Adam's right, toward what would be the north end of the village.

"Ten Chinese children? What were they doing here?"

"Well, ten children and a couple of teachers. The villagers say they were, like, here to learn about silk making. The children helped some with the silk but seemed to spend most of their time in school. The old villagers who can remember them call them the little weavers."

"And you think your mother was one of them?"

"Well, that's what I'm thinking. It, like, fits with her pictures."

"Great story!" Adam said. "Do you mind if I listen in and look around with you?"

The woman gave a slight shrug. "Well, I guess not – but what are *you* doing here?"

Adam stepped forward, extending his hand. "Randall Murch," he said pleasantly. "I go by Rand. I'm a freelance writer and came up here to do a story about the gold silk these villages are famous for.... But I'm intrigued by your mother's story. Sounds like you're from the States...."

"California." She took his hand confidently. "Los Gatos in the south Bay. I'm Angie Robb." She looked past him toward the stilted wooden houses where Adam had emerged onto the square. "But, like...how did you get here?"

Adam turned, following her gaze, and laughed. "I use a motor-cycle. Much cheaper and easier to get around. And out here in the rice growing areas, it's a lot smoother to ride the edges of the canals than the roads. You probably noticed coming up...."

"Oh, for sure!" she said.

He turned back toward her. "But Robb. Obviously not Chinese."

"My dad's a Scot by origin, which makes for an interesting mix. And how mom got to the U.S.? That's partly what I'm here to find out." As Angie became more comfortable and the subject more serious, the "likes" began to fade from her speech.

"What have they been able to tell you?" Adam asked.

"They say the children left, like, forty or fifty years ago? When the Khmer Rouge started to control the area? They assume they went back to China."

"No one knows for sure?"

Angie Robb nodded toward an old woman who stood near the elders. "This lady says I need to find one of their teachers – someone named Phyllis Morin. At least I think that's the name. She says 'Phee-lees Moreen.'" Angie smiled at the old woman who returned the smile with a broad toothless grin and nodded vigorously. "This Phyllis was, like, the children's English teacher and has stayed in the country – somewhere over around Siem Reap. The old woman said she comes back to visit the village every now and then, so is still alive."

"Wonderful story!" Adam said again, wondering if the speech affectations were legit, or just for his benefit. In the Dallas area, "like" had pretty much run its course.

"So – are you headed to Siem Reap?" he asked.

"I was just going up to see the place the children stayed," Angie Robb said. "They still use it as a school. Can come if you want."

"Love to." Adam followed Angie and the elders as they pushed their way through the crowd, heading toward the north edge of the village.

The buildings that had once housed and schooled the Chinese "Weavers" were now a row of classrooms with plank tables and benches and a few bare offices. They told them nothing about their earlier inhabitants, and it was clear the villagers had little more to contribute. Angie was immediately anxious to find Phyllis Morin.

"You rented the car and driver?" Adam asked.

"In Phnom Penh."

"How much luggage do you have?"

"Today? Well, like, just a little carry bag. I thought I might be gone overnight somewhere up here, then back to Phnom Penh."

"If you want to turn the car loose, you can ride with me. I'll take you back to the capital after we find Phyllis Morin."

"*We?*" she said with a skeptical smile.

"I like this story. It's a lot more interesting than a piece about gold silk. Send the car back and I'll take you to Siem Reap. Let's go find the lady."

"And if it takes more than a day? I don't have a lot of clothes."

"Lots of places to buy clothes in Siem Reap. And they're cheap."

"And, like, I should just climb on a bike with a stranger and head off across Cambodia?"

"You climbed into a car with a stranger and headed off across Cambodia."

"But he was a *hired* stranger. They're safe."

"So, hire me. I'll take you to find Phyllis Morin, then back to wherever you're staying."

She looked him over thoughtfully for several minutes, then turned and walked to the car. He watched as she negotiated with the driver and paid the man, then pulled a small plaid carry bag and a cardboard tube about eighteen inches long from the rear seat of the sedan and returned to where he was standing.

"Lead on, Macduff!" she said, waving the tube in the general direction of the motorcycle.

Well educated, despite the vernacular, Adam thought. "I think the quote's actually '*lay* on, Macduff,'" he corrected with a grin. "They were fighting."

"Whatever," she said with a shrug. "But I guess I should be able to trust a guy who knows some Shakespeare."

The question, Adam thought, is whether he should trust an attractive young woman who shows up in Paoy Snoul asking about the Weaver children minutes before he does, sometimes sounds vapid, but knows about MacDuff.

. . .

Nine stood on the deck of his home that edged Telluride's San Miguel River and looked east up the narrow valley to where Bridal Veil Falls plummeted 365 feet to the valley floor. It was early morning and a full moon shimmered off the cascading ribbon of water. This view was part of the reason Nine had chosen to live here: the view, the free-spirited attitude of those who lived year-around in the canyon, and the place's solitude. The residents of Telluride were responsible neighbors, kept their homes and yards in good order, and were people who believed in letting everyone do pretty much their own thing. And what Nine valued more than anything was order and privacy in the middle of an isolated, responsible, hard-working, community. He was a fastidious man: a man who as a child had suffered from severe allergies to the point of always being one misstep away from an emergency run to the hospital. It was important to know what and where things were. To know what you needed to avoid, that your inhaler was always in your jacket pocket, and your shot of epinephrine in the pocket of your pants. The Colorado resort town was relatively allergen-free, and the people here liked things to be peaceful and orderly, but would willingly run you to the Medical Center in the village if you just stopped anyone on the street and said you needed help.

The call from Four awakened him just after 1:00 a.m. and he walked out onto the deck, mostly out of habit. Though he was certain his home was secure, one couldn't be too careful. The constant rushing whisper of the river served as white noise to any listening device, should one be nearby.

"There may have been several people following Eckerson, and they know about the letter," she said without introduction. "One of them went to Paoy Snoul."

"And has already been there? You must have gotten there pretty quickly...."

"He must have been one of the first people through the border, and I was delayed for several hours. No one on the Cambodian side seemed to be in any hurry to check people through."

"There can't be much left in Paoy Snoul," Nine said.

"Nothing. Only the school. It's become run down, but is still a school."

"So there's nothing to worry about."

"Not quite. Phyllis Morin is still living – and in Cambodia."

"Phyllis Morin." Nine repeated the name with a nostalgic trace of amusement. "Does this person know where she is?"

"Near Siem Reap. I think he'll be able to find her."

"Then you need to find her first – or he must be stopped. While still in Cambodia."

"My feeling exactly."

"Then get it done," he said and disconnected the call, continuing to stare up the dark valley at the silver-tinted falls, remembering Phyllis Morin.

Pieces of the plan had been fitting into place now for over twenty years and until this last year, there had been no hitches. He had occasionally allowed himself the thought that there would be no hitches. Then came the defection. Two had decided she could no longer be part of the plan, and there was even suspicion that she had tried to contact federal authorities. They had gotten to her before she dismantled her piece, but losing one of the team had shaken Nine. They had grown up together, tutored by Phyllis Morin and the other young Americans, and were like family. But even within families there can be traitors. A "Benedict Arnold," their teacher Ms. Amanda had taught them. And now other cracks were beginning to appear around the edges. This Thompson letter showing up that mentioned the Weavers, people going to Cambodia, and Phyllis Morin still living in Siem Reap.

He suspected the old English teacher knew very little. But her simply knowing that after six years the Weavers had disappeared, might add to the resolve of those whose curiosity had been piqued by the letter. Nine was their leader. In the early days he had received regular direction from Beijing, but that ended suddenly years ago following a regime change.

He knew that it was now his responsibility to decide if, and when, to execute the plan. Those who were now in positions of leadership in China may have no immediate desire to see the plan carried out – if even aware of its existence. But it had been his life's work, and he knew he would sacrifice his life for it. And if they got close – if he could feel the hounds of hell nipping at his heels – he would execute it before they got to him. It would hasten the time of chaos, but that time would come eventually. It was inevitable. And he wasn't willing to let his beautiful creation go to waste.

Morin had been among those who recognized his early genius as a leader. "I can always count on you to have your work done when I ask for it, Lawrence. And in perfect order," she often told him. As the group began to identify its task and its eventual contribution to the grand design, their contacts in Beijing designated him as "Nine." It was a very propitious number, representing those who have sharp insight and will sacrifice their own interests for the sake of the whole. It is the mystical number embodied in the design of the Forbidden City, home of the emperors. It was a number appropriate to his talents and to his assignment.

"We need your sense of precision," they said. "Your attention to detail." Since he had lost touch with them, he had worked to sharpen that precision and it now governed everything he did. It would carry them through this minor crisis – or he would use it to execute *Seres*.

# EIGHTEEN

They were checked into the Angkor Secret Garden Inn, an eighteen room boutique hotel that Angie's travel guide described as "traditional, yet contemporary, and designed with comfort in mind." More importantly, it cost only twenty dollars a night. There were more expensive places, of course: five star hotels that ran as high as three or four hundred dollars. But he was a freelance writer, and freelance writers didn't have money. Angie agreed begrudgingly until they entered the hotel's comfortable rooms, then decided it was the best twenty dollars she had ever spent.

"This is Cambodia," Adam reminded her. "Good service and warm hospitality are just the way things are – no matter what the price."

The Inn was 200 meters off National Highway 6 on Psanyai Road, shielded from the main street by a thick screen of trees and buffered from the constant drone of traffic by a short, lightly traveled alleyway. They showered and met again in the small foyer in front of a wall-sized wood carving of ancient Khmer warriors, marching beside an elephant bearing their spear-wielding leader. Adam hailed a tuk-tuk, and for the next twenty minutes their driver snaked through the swarm of locals on bicycles and motorbikes, and high-windowed buses with curious tourists pressed against the glass.

At the Old Market they plunged into a labyrinth of covered stalls selling everything from fruits and vegetables to opium pipes carved as elephants. The air was heavy with the fragrance of spices, braised meats, and smoldering incense. Angie moved from stall to stall like a child on a carnival midway, smiling and nodding at the merchants who chattered in pigeon English as she sorted through piles of clothing and tables covered with native crafts. Adam watched her through the clear, dark-rimmed glasses that had replaced his sunglasses, thinking that her joyful fascination with all things Cambodian seemed genuine, but that her curious combination of independence and naiveté didn't mesh. And he was still struggling with her showing up in Paoy Snoul only moments before he reached the village.

They emerged onto Hospital Street at the far end of the market carrying white plastic bags containing a loose T-shirt and flowered blouse, a pair of beige linen shorts, and a brightly patterned, ankle-length Cambodian wrap-around skirt. Evening was beginning to cast dusky shadows across the street, and strings of brightly colored lights appeared suddenly around the trunks of trees that lined the avenue. They turned right to walk along the river promenade where a hundred yards downriver, the terrace restaurant of the Grand Angkor Hotel twinkled like a tropical Christmas wonderland.

"Let me treat you to dinner," she said, taking his arm and pulling him toward the terrace. It was not late enough for the evening dinner crowd and they found a secluded table under one of the glittering trees with a view of the river. Angie ordered wine and, while they waited for the waiter to bring their drinks, leaned back comfortably and gazed across the rooftops at the gilded pagoda of a Buddhist temple that rose just beyond the adjacent buildings.

"It's so nice to be *clean!*" she smiled, stretching her arms and enjoying the breeze that drifted off the river. "When you offered to be my new 'stranger for hire,' you forgot to mention I'd arrive here looking like I'd been sorting through a landfill."

"Part of the adventure package," Adam said, returning the smile and noting that Angie's speech was losing even more of the "likes."

They had taken a back road from the village: a long diagonal dirt track lined by stagnant canals that ran east from Paoy Snoul to meet the highway midway between Sisophon and Siem Reap. The afternoon had sweltered under a white sun that made the flooded paddies shimmer like sheets of hot, emerald glass. She had started by trying to stretch back as much as possible on the rear seat of the bike to let the air stream over her, but when the rutted road jarred her off balance, leaned against his back and pressed her damp shirt into his soaked shoulder blades. Every thirty minutes he pulled to the edge of the canal and they tugged their clothing away from their skin and wiped a thin orange film from their sunglasses. They had walked into the hotel after three hours on the road looking like two soldiers in desert camouflage.

"You clean up well," Adam said, studying the beautifully exotic face of the woman who sat across from him on the Grand Angkor terrace and wondering if this was a case of 'keeping your enemies closer.' She seemed so disarmingly innocent and he was struggling with the urge to believe she was. After showering at the hotel, she had changed again into tight jeans, but now wore a pale blue shirt with three-quarter length sleeves – still bare underneath. A statement of her perpetual independence? A comfort preference? Or was Angie Robb so insecure she needed always to be on display?

To shift his train of thought, he asked; "Any idea how we're going to find Phyllis Morin?"

"You're the travel writer. Like, how would *you* start?" she said.

"With a phone call to the Embassy in Phnom Penh. They should have a record of all American citizens living in the country."

"She's been here a long time – even when there was no embassy. And may have married and have another name." Angie Robb knew enough about recent Cambodian history to realize there had been a period without diplomatic relations with the U.S. during Phyllis Morin's lifetime.

"True. But that's where I'd start. There can't be that many permanent American ex-pats in Siem Reap."

"And if they don't know about her?"

He shrugged. "There's a major hospital here...one that I'd guess foreigners go to if they need medical care. We might ask there."

"And they'd give out patient information?"

She didn't know the country well enough to realize that hospitality was more important in Cambodia than privacy or some international version of HEPA. "If you tell them your story and they know about her, I think they might help," Adam said.

"And if she's, like, some kind of secretive, healthy recluse?"

He laughed. "I've only had the ride from the village to think about this. What are your ideas?"

"That's all the time I've had, and I'm new to this part of the world. I wouldn't have thought of the hospital."

The waiter returned and took their orders: *bai sach chrouk*, a pork and rice dish for Angie; *ang dtray-meuk*, grilled squid for Adam. Now that they were in the city he was willing to be more adventuresome with his meals. While they waited for their food he shifted the conversation.

"Tell me about your mother. She sounds like such an interesting person."

"She grew up in the Bay area and met my father at Berkeley when they were in college. Dad got a job with Intel in the south Bay after they married and we've lived there since. I didn't know about this whole Cambodian connection until she died earlier this year."

"And she was an artist?"

"Yes. Pretty good, but mainly as a hobby. She, like, worked for Pacific Gas and Electricity right up until she died."

"Oh? What did she do for PG&E?"

"Computer programming of some kind. She worked on the systems that control distribution of power throughout the grid."

"Interesting," Adam mused as the waiter brought their meals. He pushed an eight inch gray squid from its skewer and squeezed a twist of lime into a bowl of red dipping sauce. "How did she die, if I'm not being too personal?"

Angie looked absently at a long, brightly lit boat that churned upriver beside the veranda, carrying tourists on an evening dinner cruise. "Dad found her when he came home from work one evening. She worked from the house most of the time and had a heart attack or something. They didn't ever quite come up with a good explanation. When they think it's natural causes and they can't find anything else, it's always a heart attack." Her eyes and voice became distant. "She'd been having bouts of depression for months – seemed to constantly be unhappy but couldn't ever explain why. Sometimes would mutter about being trapped, but wouldn't say in what way...."

Adam said quietly, "I'm sorry. I shouldn't have pried."

"No.... It's alright." She brightened and turned to her plate, stirring some of the pork into a heap of steaming rice. "But to get back to why I'm here, she didn't ever talk much about her early life. Then I found these drawings that, like, showed her with other children 'at Paoy Snoul.' I asked my grandmother about them and she said it was, like, some fantasy she had as a little girl. That she'd been adopted, and had been born somewhere in China. But Paoy Snoul? That didn't sound like something a little girl would make up, and this is the only Paoy Snoul I could find."

"And now you learn about these Weavers," Adam observed.

"Yes," she murmured, gazing again across the river. "Now I learn about these Weavers.... I wonder if it had anything to do with her feeling trapped or exploited or something...? I'd like to know."

"And you were brave enough to just take off on your own and come to Cambodia?"

Angie looked up from her plate with a tight smile. "If I were a guy, would you be asking that?"

Adam thought of Davis Eckerson. "I might," he said.

They ate in silence, then sat for an hour discussing ways to find Phyllis Morin and what they would ask her if they did. Couples walked arm-in-arm along the promenade below the veranda, and the night cooled under a light river breeze.

"Are you, like, attached?" she asked after a long period of silence.

"You mean married? No."

"I mean in a serious relationship."

"One that's getting serious."

"Do you want it to be?"

"I'm thinking so. Yes. You?"

"In and out of several. Currently out."

They had pulled their chairs side-by-side along the edge of the veranda overlooking the river and she reached over and laid a hand on his arm. "You interested in testing the strength of your relationship?"

Adam placed his free hand on hers and squeezed it gently. "I don't think it needs to be tested. How about we just keep it 'stranger for hire.'"

She returned the squeeze against his arm. "Just wanted you to know I'm interested," she said.

. . .

Dreu Sason had begun to sleep over at the office at least every other day. There was a shower in the restroom in the project managers' office suite, and she brought a change of clothes and slept curled up on the sofa in her office with the door locked, a chair wedged under the handle, and the Glock G42 Adam had given her stashed under her pillow. She had asked that the night cleaning crew start with her office, then barricaded herself in and worked at her standing desk until too tired to stay upright.

Adam's daily messages said he might be away for as long as two weeks – not unusual in his line of work – but she just didn't enjoy going out in the evenings without him. Plus, she was becoming obsessed with being able to assure her clients that they had the degree of security protection from FedTegrity they expected and deserved. She knew the obsession was largely hers, but she was in a business where it didn't hurt to be a little obsessive. Plus, her conversation with Ding was scratching at that obsession in all the wrong places.

She had decided, completely without authorization and with every expectation that she might be fired, to do two things: explore the architecture of her colleagues' primary accounts to see if she could do so without being "discovered," and see how easily someone working from inside could penetrate the programs. If she couldn't do it, she seriously doubted anyone else could. Not that she was that much smarter or better trained than a good hacker. But FedTegrity's programmers used C as their coding language and she had inside knowledge of their standard construction protocols. Since C is a binary language and not typically presented in human readable code, the company had designed a modification of a program called Objdump, an interpreter language that converted C into a much more readable version of Assembly. This interpreter program went to the users with the code, allowing them to review the FedTegrity product in understandable language and request adjustments as desired. Having the company's version of Objdump gave Dreu a significant leg up as she tried to penetrate the system. She would love to be able to assure her clients that even as an insider, it couldn't be done.

The most significant security feature of FedTegrity's internal computer network was just that. It was completely internal. None of the design computers were linked in any way to the world beyond the office complex. Every desk had at least two computers: one for design work that was integrated into the internal network to allow developers to exchange and evaluate ideas, and one linked to the outside world and the internet. And never the twain shall meet. By company policy, nothing related to program design was downloaded onto external devices until a product was tested and ready to ship. Even then, it was generally delivered by a highly vetted courier directly to the client, with encrypted access codes and the copy of Objdump sent separately. But Dreu always remembered Marshall Ding's cardinal rule. Any program that can be accessed by one person can be accessed by others, if they have the proper tools.

She re-read Adam's latest text: a two liner that simply said *"Running routes in SEA for the next week. Love you much."* He had just started to use the L word in his messages and she liked to be reminded. She downed the last few swallows of a strawberry Slimfast and returned to her desk. Six months earlier, after reading an article that argued that sitting for long periods of time was as unhealthy as smoking, she ordered the "standing desk," a work surface with a gradual slope that stood four feet above the floor on rollers that could firmly be locked into place, or released to move easily to other parts of the office. She stood at her computer and called up the internal project network, selecting Marshall Ding's log-in screen.

Normally, each programmer used a fingerprint as a primary password, but had a written backup that was kept in the company safe in case something happened to the analyst. Marshall was a stickler for complex, diverse passwords with a mixture of alpha-numerics and symbols. But Dreu knew the little man to be a superstitious creature of habit, a trait that gave order to his personal application of randomized diversity. She had observed that in case after case as he demonstrated password protection, all of his passwords were twenty characters long and all started with two symbols from the upper case number keys. And all ended with three numbers. In between were fifteen letters in upper and lower case. But like every other computer user, Ding didn't want to have to remember fifteen random letters. So he found two words that totaled fifteen characters and combined them, usually putting caps at the beginning of each word.

She had also noticed that, perhaps because of some superstition, he preferred words with six and nine letters in either combination. For example, he might use YellowPineapple, VermillionRabbit or OvermixedSpices. She had once seen him enter #*SpunkyWallabies195 and was surprised that a man in his position would be so predictable, then reasoned that if no one knew this idiosyncrasy, there was nothing predictable about it.

But once she knew about the habit, finding his passwords didn't require her to identify twenty, completely random characters. She simply had to develop an algorithm that tested combinations of twelve symbols in the first two positions with combinations of six and nine letter words in the third through seventeenth positions, and three number combinations at the end. And the computers in the office were remarkably capable of running such an algorithm.

The challenge she faced was that in order to run a password identifier program, she had to be connected to Ding's login screen. And every computer that was part of the internal network at FedTegrity had an intrusion alert built into it: a program that detected efforts to enter a computer with more than three incorrect login attempts. If a third try failed, the program was designed to shut down the computer, monitor the intrusion activity, and trace the attempts to the IP address of the machine that initiated the attack. Dreu's first hurdle was to find a way to run her algorithm in a way that circumvented this login alert.

As one of three senior analysts, she was authorized to put new employees into the network and, using one of the company's backup machines, created a dummy account she affectionately called *Tanvi* after her mother's given name. If the second part of her attack strategy failed, Ding's computer would trace her intrusion back to an IP address that belonged to Tanvi – an employee who didn't exist. And a search of company personnel records wouldn't find a relative named Tanvi. After immigrating, Dreu's mother had changed her name to Julia.

But Dreu had no plans of triggering the login alert, even from a fake account. One of the valuable rules she had learned from Ding during her first few months on the job was "simple is better," and her solution was almost absurdly simple. Since the computers were set to trigger the intrusion alert and lock down after the third unsuccessful login attempt, something had to unlock the machine and put it back into operation, once the reason for the login failures was determined. That something was another code available only to the senior analysts. Dreu's solution was to include in her "password search" algorithm a short piece of code that reset the password delimiter after every entry, convincing the computer that even though the algorithm was testing tens of thousands of combinations per minute, each new password was a first attempt.

She tried it initially on her own account and though the algorithm couldn't tease out her password, multiple wrong attempts didn't trigger the shutdown. Just after midnight, she accessed Ding's log-in screen from the spare computer as Tanvi, activated the password identification program, and watched the algorithm spin through its combinations. She waited breathlessly for the computer to initiate a shutdown and for Ding's machine to hum to life in the next office as it began to track her attack. But the program found Ding's login password without a hiccup and by 3:00 a.m. she knew she could safely enter Ding's computer using +%PresetFacepages417.

The following night she ran passwords to enter the code he had developed for the Social Security Administration and - Bingo! It turned out to be $#JoyfulSixtyfive065. If FedTegrity had an initial point of vulnerability, it was Marshall Ding's sense of order and relationship. And as she identified the passwords and entered each of his programs, no alarms went off.

Tonight she was again scanning the code for the Social Security program using side-by-side screens: one displaying the dizzying array of binary code produced by C, and the other the version in Assembly as interpreted by their customized version of Objdump. The construction followed FedTegrity's standard architectural protocols: limitation of access only to approved user names; requirements for fingerprint scans and elaborate passwords that had to be changed at thirty day intervals; tightened limitations on access as sections became more sensitive and of greater value to hackers. Most importantly, the code imbedded in the operating program the encrypted IVKs – Integrity Verification Kernels. Using a technique developed by David Aucsmith in the late 1990s, these imbedded kernels communicated with each other across the program, identified any attempt at modification, and immediately initiated a repair if attempted changes were detected. As she neared the end of the script, she conceded an appreciative smile. Ding was a master. The code was efficient and concise, the IVKs ingeniously designed to make them virtually tamper-proof, and each did exactly what it was meant....

Dreu's eye had started across a new line of code and realized suddenly that she had reached the end of the Objdump conversion to Assembly. But on the screen presenting Ding's coding, the binary script continued through most of another screen. The designer had apparently encrypted instructions so that Objdump could not see the added code. Dreu matched up the lines to be certain she hadn't misaligned the end of the Assembly language and the binary code. No... she was right. Marshall Ding had what they called in the business "obfuscated,"... imbedded hidden instructions at the end of the program that were invisible to anyone entering without specific passwords – including the client.

For the next two hours, Dreu painstakingly worked her way through the added code, feeling the beginnings of a shiver raise the fine hairs on her arms and work its way up across her shoulders and into her chest. As she struggled through the code, the shiver amplified and spread, tightening her chest until she had to step back from the computer to breathe. Crudely interpreted, the code said "hide all instructions that follow from everyone but those who enter the program using the following passwords." The first listed was Ding's JoyfulSixtyfive password. The second was one that had not appeared earlier in the script, but still followed Ding's habitual formula. The password was #@CommittedWeaver009. What followed were instructions that allowed these two users to enter the operating program and....

Dreu skipped back to the beginning of the obfuscated section to be certain she was interpreting the instructions correctly. She was. They allowed the password owners, with a single command, to send "termination" instructions to encrypted code within each of the IVKs: instructions that were then communicated across the IVK network, turning off the repair functions and ordering the program being protected to delete itself. There was nothing particularly sophisticated about the command. It instructed that, should any backup version be introduced, the machine hosting the program should delete it immediately along with anything held in trash. It was a suicide command, with an order not to resuscitate.

# NINETEEN

It took two days to locate Phyllis Morin. The Embassy in Phnom Penh had no record of her, and she hadn't visited the Royal Angkor International Hospital. As Angie feared, she was a secretive, healthy lady, or went elsewhere when she needed medical attention. They caught a cab back into the heart of the city, stopping at two clinics the Royal Hospital staff had recommended, ending at the sprawling provincial hospital near the market. Still no record of a Phyllis Morin or of an American woman of her age who was a resident of the area.

They re-grouped late in the afternoon, a short walk down Hospital Street toward the river at a French eatery and ice cream parlor called the Blue Pumpkin. Despite the frustrations of the search, Angie squealed with delight as they entered the trendy ultra-white interior, pulling Adam toward a row of yard-deep, pillowed sofas that lined one wall. Some moments, he puzzled, she was a mature young woman. The next, a Valley prom queen. Her ability to move so effortlessly from one to the other troubled him as much as the transformation.

A young waitress dressed in black pants and shirt with a red cap and apron was serving croissant sandwiches and drinks to a couple farther down the sofas on lap trays that straddled the side-by-side diners.

"Oh, I love this place!" Angie exclaimed as they sat back together on an open stretch of the deep sofa. "It's so... *not* Cambodian!"

Adam accepted a menu from the waitress.

"Pretty mixed choices," he said. "Steaks, club sandwiches, and milk shakes. But I think I'll stay local and try this *goi cuon*." He pointed at a picture of a plate of shrimp and vegetable spring rolls, wrapped in rice paper and served with a spicy red sauce.

"Cheddar and walnut salad for me," Angie said, and the waitress nodded and hurried toward a long white bar and ice cream counter at the far end of the parlor. She returned moments later with a wide lap tray, and Angie pushed in closer until their shoulders touched and he could feel the brush of her long legs. She was wearing the linen shorts and smelled faintly of vanilla.

The waitress set two glasses of water in front of them and returned to the bar.

Angie looked skeptically at the water. "Do you think this is safe?"

"In here? Yes. I'm sure it's bottled."

She pressed in more tightly as she reached for her glass.

"We still have some work to do," he said, knowing that it sounded more reproachful than he intended. "We're no closer to finding Phyllis Morin."

She jabbed him with an elbow. "I'm just enjoying the moment, Mr. Hired Stranger. Having a nice dinner doesn't mean we can't do some planning. Relax a little."

"I'm relaxed," he said, leaning back and waggling his feet that stretched beyond the edge of the deep seat. "But I have another idea for tomorrow."

"I'm all ears."

"If you were Phyllis Morin and living in Siem Reap, what would you do to make a living?"

"Maybe she doesn't need to make a living."

"Well – to stay busy then? What would you do to keep life interesting?"

"Be a tour guide at Angkor Wat?"

"She's got to be at least sixty-five. I doubt she's climbing temples with groups of tourists from Omaha."

"Maybe she just does senior groups...."

"Possible, I guess. But I think the Embassy would know about her then."

The waitress brought their meals and Angie stirred her salad, looking like she was counting the walnuts, while Adam dipped a spring roll into the bowl of red sauce.

"So, what are you thinking?" she asked.

He took a bite of the roll, felt the spices bite back, and raised an eyebrow approvingly, lifting a delaying hand until he had savored the bite.

"Teaching English," he said finally. "That's what she did for the children, and my guess is that she enjoys the contact with kids."

"So... we look in the Yellow Pages or online?"

""If she's staying below the Embassy radar, I'd guess she doesn't advertise."

"So, how does she get students?"

"She goes to where they are. To language schools."

They did go online on Angie's phone, looking for language schools in and around Siem Reap. In the morning they took the Honda and began with BELS British English Language School, a mile across the river from the Old Market near Angkor High School.

No, they were told. This is a *British* English language school, and we *do not* employ teachers of *American* English. But it might be worth trying the International School in Wat Damnack Village, a quarter mile back toward the town center. They are a bit more open to linguistic variation.

"She doesn't teach here," a young Australian teacher at the International School told them. "But I may know where she does." She was a tall, heavy-boned girl from Perth with a very pink face, who said she was taking a year off from university to see some of the world.

"I believe I met the woman you're asking about when I visited an orphanage school – just after I came here. They told me she was a volunteer but lives here all the time. I talked to her a bit, and when I asked how she had come to be in Cambodia, she said she'd first taught in a village school somewhere north of Sisophon."

Angie, who Adam thought was showing signs of becoming weary of the hunt, suddenly popped from neutral into overdrive, grasping the woman's arm.

"Can you tell us how to get there? How long ago was this?"

"I can't tell you where the school is. I'd just arrived when I visited it. But our headmaster can. He took all of the new teachers there – to show us, I believe, how fortunate we are to be teaching in this school. Three of us almost stayed."

Following the headmaster's directions, they left the city on National Highway 6, heading for what the man called the Kandok Commune.

"You will see a Toyota sales establishment on the right about twelve kilometers out of town," he said in his own proper British English. "Turn left on the street just opposite, and proceed perhaps three hundred meters. There is a race track on the right and just past on the left, you will see a sign. It's called 'PeopleHelpingPeople School and Orphanage,' and is a privately run establishment by a former government minister and his wife. A genuinely good man...."

The school was as easy to find as the headmaster implied and Adam pulled the bike into a tree-lined drive that led to a collection of open-sided classrooms, grouped around a central house and surrounded by towering coconut palms. He stopped short of the buildings at the end of the drive and Angie leaned forward across his shoulder, watching the collection of children who sat intently at long, gray metal tables that reminded Adam of his grade school cafeteria. The children appeared to range in age from about six to ten and had their own school uniforms: baggy T-shirts bearing messages and logos from across the globe: loose cotton shorts or sweat pants. They were all barefoot. An older girl in the back row of the class nearest to them turned and smiled, waving at them shyly. The back of her blue shirt said "Crowder College Spring Fling, 2010."

Adam parked the bike and he and Angie walked toward a long pillared balcony that extended from the house and held another class of smaller children, seated on the bare tiled floor. The children all stopped what they were doing and turned to watch the strangers approach, and Adam felt the suspenseful breathlessness of an orphanage being visited by a young western couple. In his work he often played the role of pretender, but this felt especially uncomfortable.

A small Cambodian woman in a long-sleeved white blouse that fell to her hips and an ankle-length, wraparound skirt, came down the concrete steps from the balcony, greeting them with a slight bow.

"Welcome to our school," she said in heavily accented English. "I am Mrs. Keo. How may I help you?"

Adam returned the bow. "My friend and I are looking for a teacher named Phyllis Morin. We were told she may teach at this school."

Mrs. Keo smiled and bowed again. "Yes. Miss Phyllis is one of our teachers. But she is not here now. She teaches only two days."

"Do you have an address for her?" he asked.

"Or a phone number?" Angie added, pushing forward. Adam cautioned her enthusiasm with a slight touch on the arm.

"I can tell you how to find her home," Mrs. Keo said. "Go again to National Highway 6 and to the next road, away from Siem Reap. It is Highway 67. Turn to the left and go exactly four kilometers. There is a small stand there where she sells her mangoes. That is her home."

"Thank you so much," Adam said with a slight bow, and they turned back to the bike with sixty pairs of eyes following them.

The drive that left Highway 67 beside the empty fruit stand wandered left through a grove of broad-leafed mango trees, ending beside a small white bungalow with its own tiled veranda with pink, concrete railings. A neatly trimmed lawn separated the house from the drive, and three white geese strutted like orange-legged sentries in front of the raised porch. A black Mercedes, identical to the one Angie had rented to take her to Paoy Snoul, sat in front of the house with the driver dozing at the wheel.

As the motorcycle came to a stop behind the sedan, the door of the bungalow opened and a woman with salty blond hair, pulled tightly into a bun, stepped onto the porch. She was a young sixty-five, dressed in a long-sleeved man's shirt and wide-legged cotton pants, her feet in brown sandals. She looked in amusement at the pair as they climbed from the bike, her arms folded loosely across her chest.

"My," she said as they approached the porch. "So much company in one day!"

# TWENTY

Davis stood as the couple entered and met them midway across the comfortably furnished living room, extending his hand.

"Davis Eckerson," he said, sensing a brief shadow of surprise cross the man's face as he introduced himself.

"Randall Murch," the man said. "Call me Rand." He stepped aside to let the young woman beside him take Davis's hand. "And this is my friend Angie Robb."

The woman was beautiful: the kind his old roommate Alex fantasized about for his dorm studies. And she fit the name. A real angel face. But one that looked way too familiar, and he feared for a moment that she was a hazy memory from Soi Cowboy. Then he realized why he thought he knew her. She looked just like Tia Carrere, the real reason he and Alex had made it a monthly habit to watch the DVD of *Wayne's World*. Same face. Same terrific body. Same perfect smile.... A face the villagers had described as having been in Paoy Snoul the day before his visit. Under one arm, she still carried the brown cardboard tube they had described. Davis wondered if among its contents was the letter from his hotel room.

Phyllis Morin stepped up beside the woman and looked at the three with amused curiosity.

"I can go months without a visitor – and never from America. And here, within ten minutes, I have three. Please.... Find a seat. Can I get you some tea?"

"Thank you, no," the man who called himself 'Rand' said, and his companion shook her head in agreement. "We don't want to interrupt your visit, but were just in the village of Paoy Snoul looking for information about Angie's mother when she was a girl. The villagers thought you might be able to help us."

"Three visitors with the same questions!" Phyllis Morin said, her amusement beginning to turn down at the corners. "Do you know each other?"

Davis shook his head, searching the faces again for something that would connect them to the disaster on Soi Cowboy. He had awakened in a hospital bed in the Thai capital, his nostrils chaffed by plastic tubes that ran through his nose into his throat, his left arm stinging from an IV drip that hung beside the bed on a rolling stand. When he first opened his eyes, a vice behind them was screwed down with such intensity that he clenched them shut again to shutter the little light that filtered into the room from a heavily draped window. His throat burned from his stomach into the back of his mouth and tasted of vomit and the blackened fish he'd eaten the last time he remembered a meal. To his right, another stand held a lighted panel that beeped rhythmically as a reminder he was still living.

He had lain without moving, struggling to push aside the throbbing in his head long enough to reconstruct the events that left him strapped to this bag of liquid and to the LED display. He remembered finding himself wide awake at 10:00 p.m. after the visit to the Thompson House, and the temptation of Soi Cowboy had been too much to resist. The two girls, even harder. One in particular had been gorgeous: the best put together he'd seen on the street. Lying with his eyes clamped tightly shut, he still could visualize her full breasts swelling out of the top of her tight black dress. They had promised him a threesome if he would buy them a few drinks – and that was all he remembered.

The pain behind his eyes extended down into his lower jaw and seemed to pull it back and up into his head, and he feared for a moment that his teeth might break against each other. He forced his mouth open to stretch the cramped muscles and eased his lids open again, forcing his eyes downward to see what he held in the hand that was propped across his stomach. A cable with a blue button taped to his palm – a call button or morphine drip. He didn't care which, just jabbed hard at it with his thumb.

Within seconds a nurse appeared: a thin young Thai woman with a round, chestnut face and wide nose. She glanced quickly at the panel of gauges, then bent over him.

"You are awake," she said in clear English. "How do you feel?"

"My head's killing me," Davis rasped, feeling again the burn in his throat.

"I will give you something. We could not give you pain medicine until you wake up. Can I give you some ice for water?"

Davis nodded slightly and she left for a few moments, returning with a syringe of yellow liquid that she added to his IV and a cup of ice chips.

She raised the head of the bed until he was partially sitting and spooned a few chips into his mouth.

"Where am I?" Davis asked as the water eased the sting in his throat.

"Bumrunsgrad Hospital."

"When did I come in?"

"Last night – very late. You were very sick. We were worried about you."

"So.... how am I now?"

"You are good. Very good. Once you wake up, you are okay."

"How long do I need to stay?"

"Not too long. But now you rest. It is almost night again. We need to get information from you and tomorrow, some people come talk to you. Then maybe you can leave."

The drug was already loosening the vice in his head and he relaxed back against the pillow and drifted back to sleep.

When he awoke, the dim light had faded from the window and the corridor beyond his room was silent. The tubes had been taken from his nose and the throbbing behind his eyes was now only a dull ache. The ice had soothed his throat to the point that he could comfortably swallow. Davis depressed the button and another nurse appeared – this one older and unusually heavy for a Thai.

"I need to go to the bathroom," he said. "Can you unplug me from this stuff?"

"I can take off the monitors now," she said, snapping the connectors loose from three small cups that were taped to his chest. "We were waiting until you woke up. But the IV, you take with you." Her English was perfect and almost without accent. She raised the bed until he was sitting upright, helping him twist to the side until his feet touched the floor. Slowly they shuffled to the small bathroom, the back of his hospital gown flapping open and exposing his bare backside. Davis thought of stopping to tie it more tightly, but really didn't care. They passed an open closet alcove where his clothes hung, cleanly pressed, above his shoes and socks that were neatly arranged beneath them on the floor. He could tell from the neatly folded socks that his room key had been removed.

Davis stopped in front of the bathroom door and looked back at his clothing.

"What happened to my wallet and belt?"

The nurse pointed to a folded paper bag on a shelf above the clothing rod. "Your belt and whatever you had in your pockets will be in there, along with your underwear."

He nodded. "When I'm through in here, can we walk for a few minutes? I need to move around some."

"We need a specimen – to make sure your system is working as it should." She handed him a clear plastic cup.

He partially filled it in the bathroom, taking advantage of the moment of privacy to examine the IV connection, then washed his hands, delivered the cup, and let the nurse lead him on one circuit of the long corridor, rolling the IV drip beside them. Through the doorway of a patient room he could see that it was night beyond the windows and that he was on the third or fourth floor of the building. The hallway smelled of sickness scrubbed away with strong antiseptic, its silence disturbed only by the muted, metronome rhythms of a dozen beeping monitors. At a central nursing station, a second nurse hunched over a patient file and looked up with an obligatory smile as they passed. Two elevator doors opened onto the floor immediately opposite the station, and at each end of the hall, emergency exit signs indicated stairwells.

They returned to the room and Davis swung back onto the bed.

"Thanks for the walk. Think I'll sleep for a while."

She helped him get arranged and left the room, flipping off the light and pulling the door partially closed. Davis waited until he could hear the murmur of the nurses talking at the station, then pulled the IV connection from the stint in his arm, unwrapped the tape, and drew the needle out of his bruised vein. A small box of gauze sat on the bedside table and he folded a square and used a strip of the tape from the stint to press it over the oozing puncture.

"People will come see you tomorrow," the younger nurse had said. He didn't like the sound of that.

He dressed slowly, struggling a little to maintain his balance. The paper bag crinkled as he lifted it from the shelf and he froze for a moment until certain the nurses hadn't heard the noise. He removed his underwear and slipped the belt from the bag, but there was no wallet. The belt's inside zipper compartment still held six folded fifties. The girls at the bar hadn't known to look there. But otherwise the bag was empty. No room key.

Through the gap in the doorway, Davis listened to the quiet conversation of the nurses until confident they were not about to begin rounds. He slipped from the room and walked quickly away from the station, keeping to the side of the hall that shielded him from the nurses' view until he reached the stairs. There was no crash bar on the door and nothing that indicated he would set off an alarm if he pushed through it. Stepping silently across the hall and into the stairwell, he descended until a number beside the door indicated he had reached the main floor. When he exited into the corridor, he was opposite a small gift shop that was closed for the night, and the brightly lighted hallway was empty. To his right he could see an open foyer where an occasional figure hurried to the elevators or main entrance. Davis drew a deep, calming breath and walked confidently down the corridor and across the foyer to the high glass doors that opened onto the hospital's sculpted front gardens. A cab idled along the curb and he slipped in.

"LIT Hotel," he said, and glanced back as the cab pulled away. No one had raised an alarm.

The night clerk at LIT stood for a good twenty seconds without speaking – looking first at Davis, then toward the door to the back office as if he expected someone to come to his rescue.

"You are Davis Eckerson?"

"Yes. I lost my key and need to get into my room."

"Do you have some identification?"

"No. My wallet was stolen – along with my key."

"You cannot be Davis Eckerson. She came last night. That is not you."

"*She?*" he laughed nervously, jabbing his chest with an index finger. "*I* am Davis Eckerson. I was injured and was in the hospital overnight." He held his arm out to show the taped bandage over his IV puncture.

"Wait here," the clerk said and started for the back room.

"No! Wait!" The last thing Davis needed was the police. "I can prove I'm Davis Eckerson. My passport and one of my credit cards are in the safe in my room. It's 714. Take me to the room and I'll show you."

The man hesitated, then continued to the door to the back office. He spoke a few words in Thai and a young woman came out to cover the desk, looking curiously at Davis. The clerk followed him to the seventh floor and opened the door to 714. Davis scanned the room quickly and swore under his breath.

"My iPad's gone – and someone's been through my stuff." He went to the closet and punched a four number combination into the safe, producing his passport and showing the picture page to the clerk.

"See? Davis Eckerson. That's me."

"I'm very sorry, Mr. Eckerson," the man stuttered. "A woman showed me a driver's license with your name and her picture. She said she had lost her key. I will call the police."

"A woman said her name was Davis? Didn't that sound strange to you?"

"My name is Prayote," the clerk said defensively. "Is that a man or woman to you?"

"I get your point," Davis said. "Give me a minute to look around here and I'll come down and we can call the police. I need to be able to tell them what's missing."

The clerk hurried from the room and before he reached the desk, Davis had gathered his clothes into the carry-bag, pulled the remainder of his money and his credit card from the safe, and was in the other elevator. He paused briefly at the desk, signaled the clerk and insisted that he had been able to find everything.

"But I'll be checking out," he said. "Bill my card and don't worry about charging me for tonight."

"I am most sorry about letting someone into your room," the clerk said, showing relief that Davis wasn't asking for senior management. "We will not charge you for tonight or last night."

Davis nodded to indicate it was the least they could do, then pushed through the glass doors and descended the wide steps that fronted the LIT. Three cabs sat across the narrow street, their drivers standing in a small huddle, smoking and keeping each other awake. The driver who had ferried Davis from the hospital was with the lead cab and jumped forward as he approached.

"You need another ride?"

"You want to make some good money tonight?" Davis said.

"Where you want to go?" the cabbie asked.

"Cambodia – Poipet."

"Ohhh...," the man muttered. "That a long trip. Maybe two hundred thirty kilometers."

"I'll give you a hundred dollars."

The cabbie thought for a moment. "I can't go into Poipet. Only Thai side."

"That's okay. I just need to get to the border."

"You can't go across tonight. Seven o'clock tomorrow."

"That's okay. Just take me and I'll wait. One hundred dollars."

The man shrugged. "Okay. I need gasoline. You buy gasoline, and you pay me now."

"I buy gasoline and pay you fifty now. I give you fifty more when we get there."

"Let me see the other fifty" the man said. Davis showed him the bills.

"Okay. Let's go!"


They had reached the border at just after three a.m. and Davis spent the early hours of morning sitting in an all-night bar a hundred yards from the "Welcome to the Kingdom of Cambodia" arch. After his icy rejection of the first three bargirls, word got around, and they left him alone. At seven o'clock he was first in line at Thai passport control, worried that the Bangkok police might have an APB out for Davis Eckerson. But he passed through with no more than a glance at his face and a quick stamp on the passport. He moved just as quickly through the "Already has Visa" line on the Cambodian side and by 7:30, had rented a car and driver to take him to Paoy Snoul.

His arrival at the village caused a minor stir. Through his driver, they questioned him about why, in two days, so many strangers had come to visit them, all interested in the Weavers. He told them the truth. A letter from the famous Jim Thompson had been discovered that talked about the Chinese children, and people wanted to learn what had happened to them.

"Do any of you remember Jim Thompson?" he asked.

An old man stepped forward, brown and wrinkled as worn shoe leather. "I remember him," he said to the driver. "He took cocoons from us and some of our best weavers – to teach the Thais how to weave again."

"Did he meet the children? The Chinese weaver children?"

The old man nodded. "He was interested in the children and talked to all of them – and their teachers."

The villagers took him to the school, showed him where the Weavers had lived and studied, and told him about Phyllis Morin. As he walked back toward the car, a small girl tugged at his pant leg and handed him a book.

"Mees Phee-lis," she said shyly.

The book was in English – a children's classic that Davis recognized called *Goodnight Moon*. He crouched beside the girl and pointed to the words on the cover.

"Good-night Moon," he read slowly as the girl followed his finger. He opened to the first page. Printed across the inside of the cover in neat block letters was PHYLLIS MORIN – and a phone number. It was the number that had taken him to the home of Phyllis Morin before the others found her.

The Tia Carrere look-alike sat with one long leg comfortably folded across the other and explained that she had come to Paoy Snoul from Phnom Penh and hadn't been to Bangkok at all. Her mother had passed away recently, leaving behind some drawings that suggested she may have lived in the Cambodian village when she was young – with other Chinese children.

Phyllis Morin sat opposite her on an uncomfortable-looking settee and listened with rapt attention. Davis decided to let her do the questioning. He hadn't had a chance to get into his own story before the pair arrived and thought he'd like to hear theirs first.

"She left drawings?" the old teacher asked.

Angel Face unwrapped the tanned legs and pulled a rolled sheet of sketch paper from the brown carrying tube.

"This is one of mother's sketches." She knelt on a throw rug beside a low mahogany table that fronted the settee and spread the page in front of Phyllis Morin. The drawing showed four Asian children from the knees up, sitting side-by-side and leaning into each other to see some object one of the girls held in her hand. Though it was done in pencil or charcoal, the sketch was remarkably lifelike, with each black hair appearing to glisten separately and the central girl's lips glowing soft and moist.

"Helen," Phyllis murmured, placing her hand gently against the flattened sheet and pointing at the girl.

"Yes! Mom was Helen. But I thought it was a name she was given after she was adopted."

"They all had English names," Morin said. "And Helen was my little artist. Even then. And this is Marion, Lawrence and Henry." She touched each of the children as she named them. "My... what an amazing memory your mother had! To draw them this well after so many years...."

"Tell me about them," Angel Face said, sitting back on her heels.

"There were ten children and three of us," Phyllis remembered. "All young American teachers. In fact, I hadn't even finished my degree and came to Cambodia to work during the summer. They hired me to teach the children English and I just stayed."

"And the other two?"

"One taught Math and Sciences: that was Jonathan from Spokane. And Amanda taught History and Social Studies. She was from Baton Rouge, as I recall. And I taught music as well since I played the piano. It wasn't really teaching music as much as teaching the children about American music. Common folk songs, popular hits from the sixties: that sort of thing. Everything was taught in English and it was pretty much like being in a grade school in the U.S. In fact, they weren't allowed to speak Chinese."

"And the children helped with some of the silk processing?" the man called Rand asked.

"Only for a few hours in the morning. From about six to eight. They helped unravel cocoons and did a little spinning. But the villagers like to call them their little weavers since that was the more important job. Mainly, though, they were in school. Five days a week with us, and Saturdays with their Chinese guardian. We weren't part of that day, but it was all about China and its history and was sort of an indoctrination day. Even Sunday morning was exercise and personal study. Every week, all year. They were there to learn."

"And they were at the village until the Khmer Rouge gained control?"

"Yes – but I think their leaving really didn't have much to do with that. They seemed to have completed their studies."

Rand nodded. "And you stayed here since – for all these years?"

Phyllis Morin smiled. "It's been an unusual arrangement but one I've been very happy with. The people who hired me said that as long as I stayed here, they would reward me with a very comfortable pension – and I was twenty-six! I had no ties in the U.S. and loved Siem Reap and the people here. So I stayed. The checks come to me each month."

Rand raised a surprised brow. "The Chinese have supported you here all this time...?"

"Not the Chinese, really. Mr. Hsieh. He hired me and was grateful that I stayed with the children until they completed their education. I think his son has taken over his company now, but still supports me. I really loved the children...."

"But why here in Cambodia?" Angel Face wondered. "And why in Paoy Snoul? And why, after they went back to China, were they all adopted?"

"Oh, they didn't go back to China," Phyllis said. "One day in the spring of 1969 – probably the saddest day of my life – we took them all to Phnom Penh. At a very nice old hotel there – I think it was called the Hotel Le Royal – they met their new families. The parents were all Chinese but living in the U.S. The children went directly from here to live in America."

"No way!" Angel Face exclaimed. "I'm staying at Le Royal! So...that's where my mother met her family!" She shook her head with obvious delight, but Rand turned to look at her as if he were seeing her for the first time.

. . .

The same compulsion for order that had allowed Dreu to tease out Marshall Ding's passwords took her into each of his other major accounts with the same ease and to the sections of code she was looking for. She had started with the program that protected the Social Security System, then moved to the NPB – the National Payroll Branch of the federal General Services Administration. NPB processed all transactions affecting a federal employee's service life, from initial hiring to separation, and FedTegrity – specifically Marshall Ding – had developed its network security program. The coding architecture was again clean and efficient, almost elegant, and Dreu was again struck by the man's genius. But in the same place in the script, she found the backdoor. It was again encrypted to be invisible to Objdump and began with a command that anything beyond those specific lines of code could not be accessed without one of two passwords. In this case, Ding's password was &^MiserableStiffs442 – one of the first indications she had seen that Ding had a sense of humor. The second had been the same password that opened the backdoor to the Social Security system: #@Committed-Weaver009. The code that followed contained an identical suicide command that sent messages between the IVKs, deleting the programming that was supposedly being protected, and preventing back-up language from being installed.

Tonight Dreu was working her way through Ding's copy of the FAA's security program that he had been lecturing the federal agency analysts about. It was her program, but she guessed he must be modifying everyone's work once it reached his computer. She had slept on the office sofa until just after 2:00 a.m. when a brief text from Adam beeped her awake. He loved her and was still flying Delta routes somewhere in Asia. Couldn't tell her more, other than it would probably be another week. She stretched herself fully awake and did a dozen squat thrusts in the middle of the office to get blood pumping through her system, then moved to the computer on the standing desk beside the window, but kept the office dark.

Her algorithmic search the night before for Ding's password to the FAA's security programming had yielded ^+Monitored-Skyway747. She again entered the system as Tanvi without setting off any alarms and ran quickly through the code to what would normally be the end of the security protocols. There again was the cloaked suicide code: no one beyond this point but Ding and whoever entered the system using the CommittedWeaver password. As she scrolled down the page looking for the familiar termination code language, a small icon on the toolbar at the bottom of her screen, shaped like the "all-seeing eye" on the dollar bill, suddenly blinked red and her heart skipped a beat, then began to race. It was an icon Dreu had installed herself. It told her someone had entered her computer and was watching what she was doing.

# TWENTY-ONE

Phyllis Morin had insisted that her guests stay for what she referred to as afternoon tea and the three spent the first half hour sparring with each other about what brought them together around her mahogany coffee table within fifteen minutes of each other. Phyllis provided Adam with an opening when she announced that Davis had just been asking about the children of Paoy Snoul when they arrived.

"So... what's your interest in the Chinese kids," he asked. "Angie here is looking for her mother...."

"I'm a writer. Looking for a story. What about you?"

"Looks like we might be competitors," Adam smiled. "I went there planning to write about the gold silk that's unique to the village. For some reason, the worms they raise in the region produce a rich gold silk that's pretty rare. But then I ran into Angie, and her mother's story sounded better. So I'm following up on it with her. But how did you learn the kids were even here?"

Davis looked from Adam to Angie and back again, seeming to debate what he wanted them to know.

"I'm a freelance journalist," he said finally. "Mainly magazines. I found an old letter in some stuff I inherited from my aunt – from a guy named Jim Thompson. The letter talked about the kids being at the village. You ever heard of him?"

Davis's eyes again moved quickly from Adam to Angie Robb, watching for a reaction.

"Sure. You can't research silk in Southeast Asia without his name coming up," Adam said. "He was an American guy living in Thailand who did a lot to get the silk industry back on its feet after the Second World War. But how was he tied to the village?"

Davis seemed to relax a little. "He visited Paoy Snoul while he was looking for sources of weavers to move back into Thailand, and found these Chinese kids there. He just thought it a bit unusual. And as you probably know, Thompson had been involved with American intelligence during the war and disappeared in the late 1960s. Hasn't been heard from since." He turned to Phyllis Morin. "Do you remember Thompson coming to the village?"

"Oh, yes," she said. "He was intrigued by the gold silk you just mentioned and took some of the weavers with him. They were away for almost a year."

"Did Thompson show any special interest in the Chinese children?"

"He came to the school and talked to all of us," Phyllis said. "He was especially interested in knowing how the children were helping with the silk production."

"Seems like a long way to come for a story, this many years after the children were here," Rand said. "Where were you thinking of going with it?"

Davis shrugged. "I really hadn't decided. Thought I'd let the story develop itself. I got some money from my aunt at the same time I got the letter and hadn't ever been to this part of the world. Seemed like it would be kind of fun to come here, go to Angkor Wat, and see if I could find out what happened to the kids. Make it a business expense."

"Oh, yeah, I'm, like, really hoping to go to Angkor Wat too," Angie piped in. Now that she had solved the puzzle of her mother's Paoy Snoul drawings, she was suddenly in no hurry to get back to the States and the "like" was creeping back into her vocabulary. She seemed to be performing for Davis.

Adam turned his attention to his traveling companion. "Now that you know where your mother went, don't you want to get back home and find out what happened to the other nine?"

"Well, I want to see the temples before we go back to Phnom Penh. That was, like, part of my reason for coming. Let's take a couple of days and look around."

"You're not curious as to why ten Chinese children were educated as if they were American kids – in some little village in Cambodia?" he pressed.

"For sure. But not so curious it can't wait a few days. That was, like, fifty years ago. So what difference is a couple of days going to make? Have you seen them yet?" she asked, turning to Davis. "The temples, I mean."

"No – I just came straight here when I got to Siem Reap. But if you're going...."

So they had gone to the temples. While Davis and Angie were

working to impress each other across Phyllis Morin's mahogany table, Adam had excused himself to look at her mango grove and place a quick call to Fisher.

"Don't worry about getting help to the Eckerson kid," he said when the old man answered. "He's here in Cambodia – and very much alive. But there were *ten* Chinese children educated in the village called Paoy Snoul: American curriculum, and all in English. And the children were all given English names. In Sixty-nine, they were taken to Phnom Penh and adopted by Chinese-American parents. One was named Helen Robb and lived in Los Gatos, California. See if you can find out who the others are and what happened to them."

"The parents picked the kids up in Phnom Penh during the height of the Vietnam War?"

"Yes. At a hotel called Le Royal."

"When in Sixty-nine."

"Spring, we think."

"I'll see what I can learn."

They had started with the majestic central temple of Angkor Wat: a towering multi-layered wedding cake of gray stone surrounded by over two miles of moat, bridged east and west by stone causeways the length of two football fields. During the preparation to come to Cambodia, neither Davis nor Angie had taken time to learn anything about the ancient ruins, and Adam felt compelled as they crossed the stone bridge toward the central temple to serve as tour guide. He explained that *Angkor* meant "city," or "capital city," and *wat* meant temple. The main temple was the largest religious monument in the world, built in the 12$^{th}$ century by a Khmer king.

"Khmer?" they said, almost in unison. "Like in Khmer Rouge?"

He backed up and explained that the Khmer were the predominant ethnic group in Cambodia, distinguished, in part, by adherence to a unique mixture of Buddhist, Hindu and animist beliefs.

"You can see some of that influence reflected in the architect-ture," he said, waving toward the towers in front of them. "The successive layers of the central temple. The five pinecone-shaped crowns...." From the couple's reactions, if they cared one whit about the history they disguised it completely. The pair climbed ahead of him up the steep stone sides to the upper temple room, steps so high and narrow they were forced to climb at an angle with their inside hand on the upper steps for balance. Angie followed Davis with her other hand looped over the back of his belt.

They met breathlessly at the top and surveyed the lotus-covered moat and jungle landscape that stretched below. To the west, the complex of Angkor Thom rose above the palms and banyans, its own central temple a smaller jumble of stone that seemed to have been planned as the builders worked: random stacks of chiseled rock, embellished on every face by panoramic carvings of animals, battles, and domestic scenes from early Khmer life. Most of its thirty-seven towers displayed four carved stone Buddha faces, gazing with blank eyes and serene smiles in the four cardinal directions.

Overhead, the golden globe of a hot air balloon drifted on the cooling afternoon breeze, a donut-shaped basket, large enough to carry a dozen tourists, suspended beneath it by cabled spokes. On the road leading north to Angkor Thom, a line of brightly draped elephants swayed their way toward the entrance to the monument, pairs of excited visitors clinging to their wide, bench saddles.

"Oh my God!" Angie sputtered, watching the balloon drift lazily overhead. "I mean, this is just totally beyond anything I could have imagined! It's all so...so...*Hindu* or something."

"Or something," Adam muttered.

"Pretty cool," Davis said. "But I want to see the temple where *Tomb Raider* was filmed. Let's head up there before it gets dark."

They walked quickly through the temples at Angkor Thom, exiting the east gate and crossing the river to enter the jungle temples of Ta Phrom. Thick, smooth-barked trees, their roots strangling and fracturing the massive stone walls, cast leafy shadows over the tangled courtyards and narrow corridors, bathing the late afternoon air in pale green light. In the central sanctuary, Angie posed beside the roots of the *Tomb Raider* tree where Lara Croft had picked a flower and been sucked into the earth. Its tentacled roots, some as thick as Angie's waist, poured over the stone beside her like gray lava, gradually crushing the lichen-covered stone. She raised her hands beside her head and burst her fingers outward like exploding fireworks.

"*Waaay* too much!" she exclaimed, then darted through an intricately carved stone doorway and disappeared into the ruins.

Adam followed Davis down a long arched corridor of blue-tinted sandstone and into a second courtyard where piles of broken blocks and columns littered the mossy ground, leaving ragged gaps in the two-story walls that rose unevenly on every side. Davis planted himself on a massive block and looked up at a treetop that towered another eighty feet above the enclosure.

"Gotta be a great article in this somewhere," he said, glancing back at Adam who was examining a relief carving of what looked like two lions crouching beneath a bower of leafy vines.

"Maybe you could write something about...." Adam turned as he spoke, then sprinted toward Davis at a dead run, reacting to a red point of light that was tracing across the pile of stones beside him. Adam threw himself into Davis's side and knocked him sprawling onto the moss-covered ground, wrapping him with arms and legs and tumbling toward a broken section of column as a bullet shattered a block inches behind them. They continued to roll until shielded by a section of column, tucking tightly in behind it. The shot had been a muffled "thump," suppressed by a silencer, but of heavy caliber. No one else was in the courtyard and Adam feared that if they waited where they were, so would the attacker until they tried to move from cover.

"Shout!" he ordered Davis. "Yell for help as loud as you can." With heads pressed against the carved rock, they bellowed across the courtyard until two older couples rushed down the high arched corridor toward them.

One of the men hurried to the broken column and leaned over them.

"*Avez-vous été blessé?*"

Adam rose slowly, scanning the walls for the shooter.

"No. Not injured. Some men tried to rob us," he replied in French.

"Ah," the man said, surprised to hear French coming from a man who had been calling for help in English. "We must find the police!"

"Yes, we will. When we called out, the men ran. Thank you!"

Through another arched door at the other end of the courtyard, Angie Robb burst into the rubble-strewn square.

"Did I hear you shouting?" she asked breathlessly.

Adam walked to her and without invitation, unzipped the fanny pack strapped across her belly. It held only a pair of sunglasses in a teal green case, a packet of tissues, and some lip balm.

"What the hell's this all about?" she said, swiping his hand away from the pack.

"Just checking," he said. "But we need to get the hell out of here – now!"

. . .

Telluride, Colorado, sits in a deep box canyon with steep, pine-covered mountains rising in every direction. Those who settle in the narrow valley in the San Juan Mountains find that living among the peaks has one of two effects: the soaring cliffs that rise abruptly for 5,000 feet from the valley floor give them a sense of security and protection; or they feel a smothering claustrophobia at seeing high, rocky walls wherever they turn.

When Nine first moved into the home hugging the banks of the San Miguel River, he had reveled in the secure embrace of the valley: an extra degree of protection from a government far away on the east coast that was committed around the clock to discovering where he was and what he was doing. But for the past two weeks, his feelings had shifted toward claustrophobic. Now, the slope that rose so abruptly behind his home to barren rock cliffs seemed ready to thunder down the mountainside and bury him and his forty years of work beneath tons of granite rubble.

He had feared from the beginning that *Seres* might never be activated during his lifetime. In fact, it had been designed for a set of circumstances that Nine knew his country hoped would never develop – a crisis of such proportion that China was willing to sacrifice its mammoth investment in American debt by completely crippling the U.S. economy. He and the other Weavers had committed their lives to perfectly positioning themselves for something their leaders hoped would never happen. But the plan was so *elegant*! So perfectly woven. Each thread of the warp and weft matching so precisely that he often marveled at both his own genius and the group's ability to design and weave such an intricate tapestry. They had called it *Seres* after the Greco-Roman name for the ancient Chinese: "the people who make silk."

All of the Weavers had fulfilled their responsibilities with distinction.

All, that is, but Helen. Number Two. She had been seduced by the creature comforts their necessary successes had provided and had decided she could not be part of *Seres*. But they had reached her before she could reveal or dismantle her piece of the fabric, and Nine now controlled it. *Seres* was completely in place, and he was the man with his finger on the button.

There was a time, as his sleeper cell matured and the nature of the plan became more clearly defined, that he had questioned that it could be done. This wasn't China where a small cadre of elite leaders could insure that the right people ended up in the right positions: both in government and in industry. This was the great American free enterprise system where in the business world, merit, talent and productivity trumped nepotism and connection. But Nine had learned quickly that this wasn't entirely true: just true enough that it had turned out to be the genius of the plan. As members of his team demonstrated that they were smart enough, savvy enough, hard-working and ingenious enough, they were able to write their own tickets. So few Americans had the unwavering dedication required to learn what needed to be learned, and the work ethic to work as hard as needed to be worked. Those who did, prospered. And after their early village education in Cambodia, the Weavers had been integrated into an American system of education that, despite itself, was the best in the world. It provided them with everything the Chinese system lacked: great connections to the world's information resources; teachers who encouraged students to think, challenge, and explore; and universities where those who took advantage of the system had almost endless support. All the American system lacked was the best students. And the Weavers provided ten to meet that shortage.

For the first twenty years the plan had been only loosely defined, assuming that the future would be shaped by emerging technologies and that those who guided that future would be those most familiar with technological development. The key would be mathematics and the sciences, so the team remained thoroughly grounded in both, ready to move in any direction application demanded. It was Nine's responsibility to determine what became ubiquitous – so much a part of the business, governmental, and social structure that to disrupt it would cripple society as a whole. The answer had emerged in the "network of things:" the vast national and global infrastructure that had initially evolved as a network of ideas – the internet – then morphed into one that connected sophisticated machines, all programmed to do their master's bidding. At the most basic level, this network could turn on the ignition and heater as a driver walked to his car on a cold morning, check to see if an iron had been left on or a tap running at home. It could remotely adjust thermostats, arm the security system, or remind a parent that milk was running low in the refrigerator: to stop at the store on the way back from picking up the kids at school. As control of these systems became a small icon on every person's smartphone, each life began to depend on all of these networks working in harmony and working as they should.

But at the most sophisticated levels, the machines controlled cutting checks for the federal payroll, sequencing aircraft as they departed from and arrived at major airports, routing electrical power from one part of the national grid to another, and maintaining the vast satellite and tower-based telecommunications network that kept the country in touch with itself. The most sophisticated members of the public were no longer hard-wired or hand-tabulated. Their lives were completely under the control of the network of things, and the Weavers were in control of vast segments of that network.

Five served as Nine's backup. Since Five had developed the programs that managed some of the most critical national networks, he shared the needed passwords and accesses. But one of the boulders that now seemed to be precariously teetering on a cliff above Nine's secluded mountain home was this woman who was searching through Five's computer. Another was the self-appointed journalist kid who was running amuck in Cambodia. Four's call earlier in the day sent a tremor through the mounds of granite high on the slopes of the mountains above Telluride, and Nine could feel the earth beginning to shake.

"I wasn't able to stop him at the temple," Four said without apology. "And I'm worried about this man who's with him. He presents himself as another traveling writer, but he's too alert. Too aware of what's going on around him. I think he may be the person who got to the hotel room before I did – and may have rescued Eckerson at the bar."

"Do you think he has the letter?"

"We're past the point that the letter matters. They know about the Weavers and spoke to Phyllis Morin. She told them we had all been adopted into Chinese-American families."

"What did you do with Ms. Morin?"

"Nothing. She didn't even recognize me and I didn't tell her who I was. She's confused about all this sudden interest but doesn't connect it to anything other than families trying to trace their roots. She was good to us and is best left alone."

"Where are the others now?" Nine asked.

"I'm not certain. They may be headed back to the Thai border, but I know they would expect me to be watching there."

"I need you here," he said. "We have another issue that needs immediate attention, and may be more serious. I think I know how we can stop them there. Leave that to me."

Nine *wasn't* certain he could catch Eckerson and his protector before they crossed the border, but his only chance was to get north to Montrose where he could place an encrypted international call to the last dependable contact he had in China: a man who had himself been forgotten by the state but through his wealth, continued to have great influence. Nine selected a prepaid phone that he hadn't used before, walked quickly through the house to the garage, and drove through the city to where the road turned north to Montrose. If for some reason his call were flagged and traced, it would originate sixty miles from his home.

. . .

Nita pushed back from her console and stretched restlessly, looking over at Fisher who dozed in his chair, his head lolling heavily to the side. He had been doing that more regularly lately: dropping off in the early afternoon, then jerking back awake and stealing a glance at her to see if she had noticed. Mentally, he was as quick and alert as ever, but his body continued to waste away, taking his energy with it.

"Bud," she called in a loud whisper, then turned back to her screens as he blinked awake. She waited until he was fully conscious, then turned back to him as if just continuing a conversation that had never been interrupted.

"I haven't been able to turn up evidence of ten Chinese couples leaving here for Cambodia in the spring of Sixty-nine to pick up children. Or of any adoption records in the U.S. that year that would show the children coming here."

"As we guessed," Fisher said. "I suspect the children just showed up in the families and no one checked to see if the adoptions were legal. What about couples of Chinese descent traveling into Asia that year?"

"There were hundreds," Nita said. "But none going directly into Cambodia that I could find. This was the height of the Vietnam War, and relations with China were strained. Laos was off limits, and South Vietnam hardly a tourist destination."

"These little history lessons are usually a preface to your telling me you've figured this out," Fisher said dryly. "So, what do we know?"

"This was one of those projects I really love," Nita said, settling her round body comfortably into her chair. "Designed from the beginning to be difficult to trace, so fun to figure out."

Fisher nodded, smiling faintly. "I'm not getting any younger here...."

"*Okay, Okay*! I assumed a man would not go by himself to pick up a child. A woman, maybe – but probably a couple. And Phyllis Morin said it was couples that came for the children in Phnom Penh."

She shifted in her chair to face her partner. "Since none seemed to have entered Cambodia directly, I assumed they came in through South Vietnam or from Thailand. Not Laos. But they could have reached Saigon or Bangkok from almost anywhere. Arrivals in Saigon at the time were being tracked and recorded by the U.S. military and have now been digitized. No Chinese couples."

Fisher nodded in anticipation. Even when he pressured her, it wasn't in Nita's nature to just give him the bottom line. She had to provide the full backstory.

"But the Thai records are still all on paper. Fortunately, Langley has an asset in Thai Intelligence who was able to get a quick review of American arrivals in Bangkok between April and June of Sixty-nine. Tourism was down because of Vietnam, but twenty-seven couples on American passports with Chinese surnames arrived in Bangkok during that three month span. And that's where they got too clever."

Fisher raised an inquiring brow. "Don't tell me.... Ten of them later left Bangkok with children."

"Better than that," she said. "Ten had never left the U.S. Aside from this arrival information in Thailand, I can't find that they ever left this country. And when they do show up again back home, they're in different cities. Most in different states."

"So while moving from one community to another, they leave the U.S. through Canada or Mexico, return the same way, and show up in the new town with a child," Fisher reasoned.

Nita nodded. "They arrived in Bangkok from all over the world. Most went through Europe, flying into Thailand from Amsterdam, Paris, and Munich, but with stops in Delhi and even Tehran. Looks like they came back about the same way. We lose them when they get back to Europe, but they all made it to their new homes without crossing our borders where a passport was recorded."

"Well, we'd better find out what they've been up to the past forty-five years," Fisher muttered. "Where those ten children are…and what they're doing."

"Is it time to turn this over to Langley?" Nita wondered.

"Not on your life," Fisher said more energetically. "They didn't feel like it was worth their attention to begin with, and like you, I'm enjoying this one too much."

## TWENTY-TWO

They had picked up a second motorcycle and three helmets at a Honda shop on National Highway 6, a mile from the Siem Reap airport. Adam vaguely recalled reading that Cambodia had one of the highest traffic fatality rates in Asia, and driving the highway between Siem Reap and Phnom Penh without helmets was inviting more trouble than they already had. The new cycle was a silver SL 230, and the kid bought it with a Visa card for $1800. Adam hated to be leaving a card transaction, but using plastic in Siem Reap didn't tell those who were following them anything they didn't already know. And they needed transportation with no hired drivers. Adam had volunteered to make the purchase, but Davis objected. His card went through without a hitch.

"I've got lots of money," he said matter-of-factly. "And it looks like whoever's shooting at people is after me. I better have my own wheels."

Adam gathered their passports, made a ten minute call to Fisher, and within an hour of the near miss at the jungle temple the trio was cruising south in tandem toward Phnom Penh. Angie now rode wrapped tightly around Davis, with Adam bringing up the rear. If they stuck to the schedule he had shared with Fisher, they would reach the Cambodian capital well after dark, pick up Angie's things, and find another place to spend the night. He planned to head for the border with Vietnam at daybreak.

The brief status call to Fisher had arranged for an Agency jet to meet them in Ho Chi Minh City and, with luck, have them on their way back to the U.S. by late tomorrow. Someone didn't want them poking around in this Weaver business, and he hoped that 'someone' was waiting for them to cross back into Thailand.

The road south was again across flat fields of rice: two lanes bordered by coconut palms, ragged, thorn-covered trees that arched over the highway, and long stretches of stagnant canals that filled the heavy, evening air with the pungent scent of rotting vegetation and buffalo dung. A few miles to the west, the long shallow basin of Tonle Sap Lake stretched half the distance to Phnom Penh, its reed-choked surface dotted with the floating villages of Vietnamese refugees and their elaborate, stick-framed fish traps. The wetlands incubated swarms of mosquitoes that splattered like tiny red and yellow balloons against their arms and visors, adding additional wisdom to the helmet decision. In the occasional palm-thatched village, the riders stopped to scrape their visors clean and pull their bikes out of sight long enough to watch other traffic on the highway. There were no signs of a tail.

As night fell, low clouds trapped the damp heat against the sweating earth and shuttered any light from the sky, turning the narrow strip of asphalt into a black ribbon that disappeared in front of their headlights into an inky distance, with nothing separating land and sky. Points of light on the horizon grew into the blinding high beams of speeding trucks that tracked the highway's centerline like a homing beacon, sending the cycles fish-tailing onto the slippery dirt shoulder. They learned quickly that they were merely nuisances to the trucks and had to slow and pull aside as the lights approached, letting them barrel past.

They rolled into the Cambodian capital of two million people just before midnight, crossing the Tonle Sap River into the old city across a broad, four-lane bridge. A crush of late-night traffic surging into the city paid no attention to lanes, weaving from one side of the bridge to the other as drivers saw small breaks in the sea of vehicles. Adam had taken the lead and a quarter mile into the city swung around a wide roundabout, centered by a statue of what looked like a giant Colt 45, standing on the tip of its butt and pointing skyward with a metal knot tied midway along its barrel.

The Hotel Le Royal, a sprawling white, French Colonial edifice roofed with faded orange terra cotta tile, was half a mile south of the pistol monument along the brightly lit Boulevard Prah Monivong. They cruised between rows of modern concrete buildings that had been erected among the remnants of the old French city. The street reminded Adam of some of Bangkok's major thoroughfares, but operating at half speed. Fewer cars. Hundreds of motor scooters. Fewer girls walking the streets, and less chaotic noise and lights.

They had agreed that Angie would leave most of her clothes in the hotel, bringing only what was essential. While Davis sat with the bikes in a shadowed corner of the arched drive and monitored movement across the front of the hotel, Adam followed the girl into the sumptuous lobby and picked up a package from the night clerk at the desk. He slipped into a side alcove where he could watch activity in the foyer and looked quickly through his small box. Angie seemed to have been sobered by the attack at Angkor Wat and by Adam's open suspicion, and was in and out of the hotel in twenty minutes carrying a fabric shopping bag with extra clothes.

"I left some pretty nice things in there for the maid," she mumbled as the pair returned to the bikes. "And I'm going to look pretty grody 'til we get somewhere with a shower and hair dryer."

"I'll buy you what you need," Davis said. "And we're all going to look pretty grody."

They rode south again through the city, the visored helmets turning them into three of the thousands of anonymous night riders. On Preah Sihanouk Boulevard, they swung left past the sweeping gold roof of the Wat Lanka pagoda and joined three loosely defined lanes of traffic that circled the brightly lit dome of the Independence Monument. Adam was again in the lead and steered them toward the south end of the city. Ten kilometers from the Independence circle, he turned again onto a side street and a block later, into a quiet residential district, pulling his cycle to a halt in front of a white, arched gate that passed through a vine-covered wall. The arch was painted with twining leaves, with "The Little Garden" written in green script above the open gate.

He lifted off his helmet as the pair pulled up beside him.

"We'll get a few hours sleep here if they have rooms, then head downriver at first light and cross at the Pha Neak Loeng ferry in the morning. You two check into one room and pay with cash. See if you can get one with two beds. I'll get a second, but we're all staying together. They'll probably take either dollars or riels – just don't charge this. And they'll want to keep your passports." He handed the documents back to the pair. "Tell them you have some calls to make tonight and need information from them – that you'll bring them back to the desk later."

Davis swung from the bike and stretched beside Angie, looking suspiciously at Adam. "How did you find this place?"

Adam lifted his phone and shrugged. "Google."

"While we were riding?"

"Mainly while we were waiting for Angie at Le Royal. I've just been following the map."

"And why do we need to keep our passports?"

Adam opened the storage box behind his bike's seat and lifted out the package he had retrieved at Le Royale. "We need Vietnam visas before we cross the border tomorrow."

"I've already got one," Davis said, looking sideways at Angie, who didn't seem to be cluing in to what this conversation was all about. "And you picked up some visas while Angie was getting her clothes?"

"It's a service some of the more exclusive hotels provide," Adam said without expression. "That's why I needed your passports."

"I'll bet," Davis frowned. "And why are we all staying in the same room?"

"In case you hadn't noticed, someone's trying to keep us from getting out of the country."

"And you, Mr. Freelance Travel Writer, are going to keep that from happening?"

This time Angie did cast a puzzled look between the men.

Adam snapped the storage box shut and pushed the small package into the front pocket of his shorts. "Let's see if we can get rooms, and we can talk about this later. Just be sure to pay with cash and keep Angie's passport."

Davis nodded slowly and pushed Angie ahead of him through the gate while Adam locked and chained the bikes.

"What was that all about?" she said as they followed a short, palm-lined path to the hotel's entrance.

"My guess," Davis said, glancing back at the man who was securing the bikes, "is that it was about your mother."

. . .

The flashing eye on the bottom corner of Dreu's screen couldn't have blinked more than once before she clicked the red X in the upper right corner and closed the file. Within two more seconds she had backed out of the program and hit the "Shut Down" command, at the same time jabbing her finger onto the computer's "off" button. As the screen blackened, she stood rigidly at the tall desk and listened to the smothering silence of the building. Though almost 2:30 a.m., a few headlights still moved on the street below but there was no sound. The building seemed to join her in holding its breath and she froze beside the computer for a full five minutes, turning only her head to watch the smoked-glass panel in her office door. An exit sign at the end of the short corridor leading to the front reception area cast a pale red glow against the window and seemed to dim as she waited, as if someone had moved into the hallway.

Dreu slipped off her shoes and eased away from the desk, moving silently to the door where she paused to listen. Nothing moved in the corridor and she silently eased the chair away from the handle and released the lock, keeping her thumb over the button to keep it from popping out with a metallic "click." She pulled the door inward a few inches and peered down the section of hallway to her left, then eased it farther open and looked cautiously around the frame to her right. The hall was empty.

She returned to her main desk and retrieved her handbag from the drawer where she kept it with the Glock, tucking the pistol into the purse. With shoes in one hand and her bag over her shoulder, right hand inside the purse and wrapped tightly around the grip of the gun, Dreu crept down the hallway through the reception area to the elevator and punched the button for the basement garage. It took an eternity for the car to arrive and twice that long for the gray doors to slide open, then shut. Though the car descended quickly, she watched alertly as each floor passed without stopping, then slipped on her shoes and pressed against the front side of the elevator as it slowed to a stop at the B level. As the door slid open, she racked a round into the chamber and gripped the pistol up beside her cheek with two hands as Adam had taught her, then eased out of the elevator and scanned the brightly lit garage from left to right.

"I'm being paranoid," she muttered as she walked quickly toward her car: one of four that were scattered around the otherwise empty garage. Her heels rapped sharply on the bare concrete and echoed against the cavernous walls, and she continued to clutch the Glock in firing position and turn in half circles, left and right, until able to click the car open, toss her handbag onto the passenger seat, and slip behind the wheel. She slouched low in the seat and locked the doors.

Two of the cars she recognized: left by colleagues who were on the road visiting clients. The third was unfamiliar but wasn't Marshall Ding's black BMW. She gave the garage a final 360 before placing the weapon on the seat beside her purse, steered out of the garage, and headed toward the ramp onto the Dallas North Tollway.

There was only a smattering of traffic on the tollway at 2:45 in the morning and Dreu studied everything that moved, front and back, to see if she was being followed. The two cars she could see behind her continued on the Dallas North past her turn as she merged right onto the Sam Rayburn, and she pulled her purse onto her lap and fished into it for the keys to Adam's apartment. She would stay there tonight – try to connect through another text – and see what he thought she should do about Ding. With the weekend ahead, she had some time to sleep on it. If she couldn't reach Adam, she would call in sick Monday morning and go to the FBI. End of job at FedTegrity. But Marshall Ding was up to his eyeballs in something seriously dangerous, and she needed to make it clear to the authorities that she had nothing to do with it. But the computer genius from Stanford was suffering from one of the common shortcomings of being a candidate for Mensa: overlooking the obvious. In the new world of the network of things, she didn't need to see headlights in the rearview mirror to be followed.

. . .

He had watched her arrive at the building two days before and knew she was only leaving for lunch, then locking herself in her office and spending the night. He had been able to identify the office: the only one where a light burned until nine or ten o'clock and a shadowy figure stood at the dark window during the early morning hours. He recognized the figure. Knew it was his Dreu. But early the third morning, just as he was thinking of sleeping for a few hours, she left the underground lot.

He was parked in the surface visitors' area and though the car had been there for three nights, no one had bothered him. He followed her onto the tollway and north out of the city, remaining half a mile behind with headlights out. When she exited I-75 onto Virginia Parkway, he turned his lights on again but remained behind a white panel truck until she turned south on Custer Road. A blue pickup coming in the opposite direction turned right behind her, shielding him as he followed until she turned into a housing area. By the time he reached the turn, she had passed an open field and was into the subdivision, but he could see her lights disappear down a street to his left. As he passed the end of an alley that gave access to the rear garages of two rows of expensive-looking brick homes, the lights turned toward him and swung into a drive halfway along the block. He turned where she had turned on a street called Stonewood, again dousing his lights. The alley ran between Stonewood and Hunter Chase Drive and she had pulled into a driveway behind one of the homes on Hunter Chase. It was a nice neighborhood. They could be happy here.

# TWENTY-THREE

Dreu's 3:00 a.m. text seeking Adam's advice failed to find him in Cambodia. He and his two Gen X refugees had managed to book two rooms at The Little Garden without giving up their passports, and he had tried to persuade them to get some sleep in the larger of the two while he doctored their documents in the other. But Davis was having none of it. He sat cross-legged on the bed in Adam's room and refused to leave until shown what was in the package: three very official-looking, full-page C-1 visa stickers, authorizing them to enter Vietnam for thirty days. The box also held two equally official-looking authorization stamps with red and purple inkpads.

"So, Rand – how did you get those so quickly?" Davis asked as Adam spread the contents of the box out on a small writing desk. "I saw you call when we were buying the motorcycle, and by the time we get to the city, they're waiting for you. We were on the road for less than five hours." Angie entered from the next room and sat beside Davis: less curious, but knowing this was a conversation she should be part of.

"There's more to these Weavers than any of us know," Adam offered, sticking one of the visas onto an empty page in his own passport and stamping a red circular seal in the bottom left corner. "What do you know about industrial espionage?"

"You mean like stealing technology? That kind of thing?" Angie asked.

"Not so much the equipment as the ideas," Adam said. "Passing along R and D breakthroughs as soon as they happen."

"I know what it is," Davis said sharply.

"Well, it appears these Weavers are now involved in it. I was sent to see what I could learn about them."

"Who by?" Davis demanded.

"A group of American business interests that are trying to protect their intellectual property."

"And they can get visas in five hours…?"

"These are big businesses with lots of connections. I do investigative work for them."

"And who's trying to kill us?"

"I have no idea. But there's huge money involved in these technological breakthroughs. I mean hundreds of millions. It appears someone doesn't want you to know what happened to the ten Chinese children."

"What could have happened to them that would be worth shooting someone over?" Angie asked. "If one was my mother, they were just ordinary people."

Adam pressed a visa onto a blank page of Angie's passport and thumped the red stamp down onto the corner, making certain a portion of the stamp ran over onto the passport page. "Maybe not so ordinary. And as we get closer to discovering why, it's making people very nervous."

"I'd think I'd know if my mother wasn't just ordinary," Angie objected. "I lived with her for twenty years...."

"But you didn't know until she died that she spent six years of her early life in a Cambodian village. What else didn't you know?"

Angie was silent but Davis picked up the questioning.

"So what did your mother do? As a job...?"

"She worked for a power company."

"In Research and Development?"

"No. She just worked on power distribution."

Davis thought about that for a moment then turned to the man he knew as Rand.

"If you knew who they were, why did you have to come to Cambodia? Why not just stop them in the U.S.?"

"We only know who a couple are. We didn't even know there were ten. But we do know there's some kind of network that extends beyond those we've identified. I'm trying to track the group back to its roots to see who else is involved."

"So what do we do now?" Davis asked.

"We get some sleep. We can sleep 'til seven or eight, then head for Vietnam. By ten, our visa information will be in the Vietnamese database, so we should be able to cross without questions. We'll have transportation waiting in Ho Chi Minh City and can get you two back home where someone can keep an eye on you until we get this cleared up."

Davis sniffed cynically. "So these people you work for can get us visas and enter them into the Vietnamese immigration system within...

what? Ten or twelve hours?"

"As they say," Adam said. "Money talks."

"And how did you learn about these Weavers to begin with?"

"We had tracked the activities of three of them based on an anonymous tip. In fact, it may have come from Helen Robb," Adam said, knowing it may partly be true. "But we didn't know there were ten – or about the schooling in Cambodia. When Angie took off for Cambodia, I followed. As for whether my employers can get us through the border, tomorrow will tell. But I do want us to be in the same room tonight. I'm planning on coming in there in about ten minutes to get some sleep. You'd better get the bed before I do, or you'll be on the floor."

. . .

They were on the road by eight-thirty, crossing the Preah Monivong Bridge out of the city against the morning traffic and cruising south on National Highway 1 beside the broad, muddy sweep of the Mekong River. The road was lined for the first few miles by single story metal buildings, then passed through a stretch of expensive, gated residential communities before the buildings began to thin.

Ten kilometers beyond the city, the terrain turned to perfectly groomed orchards with the occasional village of three story, French-style stucco homes: open shops on the bottom floor, and living quarters with railed French balconies above. The day was again palpably hot, the shimmering air flavored by melting asphalt, stagnant water, and fertile black soil. They left the river for a few kilometers, then saw it again across the fields to their left: a flat expanse of olive-colored water that melted into the brighter green of the distant shoreline.

Adam had chosen to cross the Mekong at the Neak Loeung ferry, the best opportunity he could think of to insure they weren't being followed. He insisted they board last and by the time they wheeled their bikes from the pier onto the heavy plank deck of the rusty, over-loaded flatboat, it was jammed stem to stern with trucks, vans, and aging green buses, their tops piled high with rope-cinched cardboard boxes and bundles wrapped in brown paper and faded cloth. The trio squeezed the cycles along the rail beside a dented cream and pink van with what must have been twenty people crammed into its four-seat interior. Another ten balanced precariously on the overhead luggage rack. As the ferry labored away from the dock, the group atop the van clung to the bowed tubing of the rack, chattering in animated conversation with little notice of the boat's unsteady sway.

In front of the van, a dilapidated Toyota pick-up with two thick beams extending from the open bed to lengthen its hauling capacity, carried stacks of cylindrical bamboo baskets the size of fifty gallon drums, each filled with squealing pigs. Four young Khmer men sat atop the second tier of baskets in tattered jeans and baseball caps, smoking strong Cambodian cigarettes. They looked at Angie with open admiration, shouting back and forth above the thumping roar of the ferry's diesel engine, laughing and blowing blue smoke from their nostrils.

A light breeze from the river pushed the smoke back across the rear vehicles, partially masking the fetid odor of raw sewage that rose from the water and mixing with the plume of diesel fumes that poured from the ferry's single stack. Adam had watched intently as passengers and vehicles boarded and saw no other internationals. As the boat struggled into the current, he scanned the river bank where a line of corrugated metal shanties perched precariously above flood level on wooden poles, their crude plank walkways descending to the water's edge. Children splashed naked in the murky water, waving and shouting at the passengers as the boat churned away from the dock. But there was no sign of unwanted company.

As last to board, they were among the last off when the ferry nosed against the pier on the east shore of the Mekong. Adam again studied the faces of those waiting, watching for anyone who seemed intentionally disinterested in the three foreigners and their expensive motorcycles. Confident that they didn't have a reception party, he guided his charges out onto the main road through town, past a statue of two very intense-looking Cambodian soldiers with arms and weapons thrust skyward, then pulled over beside one of the crowded open-air cafes that lined the highway. They sat at a long table covered by an orange vinyl tablecloth and ordered Cokes and thin, sweet crepes. Rows of buses, trucks and scooters idled along the road waiting for the return ferry, draping the café in a thin, oily film. Most of the street vendors who were hawking wares to the waiting travelers wore cloth masks over their faces, their mouths marked behind the thin material by a damp streak of gray.

While Davis and Angie ate, Adam stepped out onto the side of the roadway and called Fisher.

"We're about two hours from the border," he said when his Control answered. "Are we in the system – and do we have transportation?"

"You're in. And I'll have someone waiting at the international terminal at Tan Son Nhat Airport. Just pull up to the front and he'll take you to the private aircraft terminal and get you cleared through."

"Any new information on our Weavers?"

"We've located five, including the girl's mother. They're scattered all over the country, and there are some common denominators that you'll find interesting. I'll have information waiting when you get Stateside. We might find more by then."

"Excellent. I'll be in touch when we're in the air."

There were fewer villages along the highway to the Vietnamese border. Most of the traffic was heading toward Phnom Phen, leaving long stretches of road where they could speed along side-by-side. Angie continued to ride behind Davis, her chin resting on his shoulder.

As they approached the border with Vietnam, it was difficult to distinguish the city from Piopet where they had crossed into the country from Thailand. On the outskirts of the city, metal shops and shanties first lined the street, then multi-storied houses in white stucco with shops below, and finally the garish casinos: The *King's Crown*, *Golden Palm*, and *Las Vegas Sun*. But here the official building housing passport control was more imposing: a structure resembling an elaborate Buddhist temple on the Cambodian side and in the distance in Vietnam, a modern white building with a sweeping, winged roof and pedestrian walk-over that spanned four lanes of highway. Between them, a metal fence marked the border, with guards stationed on each side of the gate. There was none of the fluid pass-through that Adam has seen on the Thai side of the country.

They chained their bikes together in front of the Cambodian passport station and joined the line, Angie fidgeting nervously as she studied the visa Adam had added to her passport.

"Relax," he muttered. "It's a regular visa and we're in the system. But the last thing you want is to look nervous. We're just three tourists headed for Ho Chi Minh City."

He was first to the control officer and stood calmly as the woman inspected his passport, studied his face, and made an entry into her computer. Adam thought he saw her jaw tighten almost imperceptibly as her eyes scanned the screen, then looked behind him at others in the line. Her left hand dropped below the counter for a moment, then returned to the passport.

"Are you traveling alone, Mr. Murch?"

"Yes. By myself," he said, sensing her uneasiness.

"And these two behind you? They are not traveling with you?"

"Not officially. We met in Siem Reap and decided to travel together since we're all headed to Vietnam."

"And what was your purpose for visiting Cambodia?"

"I'm a travel writer. And I wanted to visit Angkor Wat."

Two male officers in drab green uniforms stepped into the space that passed beside her booth.

"Please go with these men," she said. "And the two who are traveling with you…they will go also." She pointed back to where Angie and Davis watched nervously.

"What seems to be the problem?" Adam asked, trying to display the right balance of calm and irritation.

"Please go with these officers," the woman repeated. "You and your friends."

Adam nodded and beckoned for the others to follow. Another uniformed guard joined the pair behind the booth, and one stepped beside each of the Americans as they passed through the checkpoint, walking them down a short, dimly lit hallway. Their escorts paused beside a gray metal door and ushered them into a plain white room that held only a vinyl-topped table and four folding chairs. An officer of obviously higher rank sat behind the table: a thin young woman in black pants and a white, long-sleeved blouse standing beside him. Three of the chairs faced him across the table and he gestured for them to be seated. A wide mirror filled most of the wall opposite the door and Adam guessed others were standing behind it, watching what was about to transpire.

"Why are you in Cambodia?" the woman asked, dispensing with introductions.

"I'm a travel writer," Adam repeated. "Mr. Eckerson here is also a journalist and we were looking for stories about the silk weavers in villages near the Thai border. Two of us met in Paoy Snoul. Ms. Robb was there seeking information about her mother, who spent some time in the village when she was a young girl. We decided to travel together."

The woman did not translate for the officer who appeared to be following the conversation without help. "And you had not met before that time?" she asked.

"No. I met Ms. Robb at the village, and the two of us met Mr. Eckerson at the home of a teacher in Siem Reap – a woman who had taught Ms. Robb's mother."

"And where did you pick up the drugs?" the woman asked.

An audible gasp escaped Angie's lips, and Davis turned sharply in his chair to face Adam who was quickly piecing together their reason for being in the room. The senior officer and interpreter had been waiting for them. Three chairs were in place. The computer had informed the border officer to be watching for three Americans traveling together and had flagged their pictures. Whoever was trying to stop them couldn't watch every border crossing, so had enlisted Cambodian authorities to watch for them.

"We have no drugs and don't know anything about them," Adam said evenly.

"They were found in your motorcycles," the woman said without expression.

Adam shook his head. "No one had inspected our bikes before we were brought down here."

"They were inspected while you were waiting at the line," she said. The officer remained silent.

"And drugs were found in both?" Adam was having difficulty disguising his anger.

"Yes. In both." The interpreter's face showed the first sign of uneasiness.

"What kind of drugs?"

"Heroin. We believe it came into Cambodia with you from Thailand."

"I haven't even been in Thailand," Angie burst in. "And someone has been chasing us – and took a shot at Davis when we were at Angkor Wat."

Adam let her vent, knowing that nothing they said would make any difference. "Where are these drugs?" he asked, looking pointedly at the silent officer.

The man opened a center drawer in the table and extracted a brown leather pouch, tightened at the top by a draw string, and laid it in front of them.

Adam smiled thinly. "This was found in both of our motorcycles?"

"The rest has been taken as evidence," the woman said. "Your motorcycles have also been taken."

"I would like to make a call," Adam said. "I think we can get this cleared up."

"You are not in America," the officer said in clear English. "We will notify your government that you are being held."

"Our government will be very concerned when they learn you have held us on manufactured evidence," Adam said calmly. "You must realize that there are those in our country who are as influential as whoever instructed you to hold us."

"I only know that trafficking in drugs is a very serious offense in Cambodia," the officer said. "If you are found guilty, you may all be spending the rest of your lives in prison. And a Cambodian prison is not like your prisons in America."

They sat in silence for a moment while Davis and Angie looked desperately to Adam to do something.

Adam spoke finally. "The girl has never been in Thailand, as she said. You can't have any reason to hold her." If he could get Angie across into Vietnam, she could get someone working to get them out.

"We will let the court determine her involvement," the officer said. "I will need to collect your cell phones."

As Adam lifted his from his pocket and quickly pressed in a three number "purge" command, the phone buzzed loudly. Dreu's texts had finally caught up with him.

# TWENTY-FOUR

The woman the Weavers referred to as Four cruised past the home on Hunter Chase and noted that Dreu Sason's car was not parked along the street. But the signal on Four's locator showed the car to be at the house. The Sason woman must have parked in the garage.

Though in her mid-fifties, Four could easily have passed for twenty years younger. She had a slight, athletic body, and even as a child had demonstrated the keenest physical abilities of the children at Paoy Snoul. Her short hair was still a silky ebony and framed an attractive, oval face with pale skin, as smooth as the day she left Cambodia. Her adoptive parents had been instructed to turn her into a world-class gymnast, and although she had never quite reached the ranks of the world's elite, her skills as a collegian on the balance beam and in floor exercise had justified annual trips to train with one of China's leading coaches. Perhaps she had never reached the zenith of international rankings because much of that training time in China was spent mastering martial arts and becoming skilled with weaponry. At the national NCAA Division I gymnastics championship her senior year of college, a television announcer commented that what the lithe Chinese-American gymnast with the intense, dark eyes lacked in flawless execution, she made up for in killer instinct. It was this killer instinct that was in play as she drove by the home that held Dreu Sason.

Four realized that disposing of the computer analyst would require much greater finesse than a muffled shot among the tangle of stones and trees that formed the jungle temple in Siem Reap. The Dallas police didn't have the finest record in the country for solving homicides, but the murder of a beautiful ex-model who had been maimed by a stalker, then become a corporate success, was bound to merit priority status by the Dallas PD. And there would be intense media interest. Sason's death had to be a perfectly arranged accident – and soon. Five, who the target knew only as Marshall Ding, feared she might go to the authorities early Monday, leaving only tonight.

Four circled the block, then turned down a steeply crowned drive that separated the backs of the homes, providing access to the garages and a less public place for trash pick-up. The yards were fenced but she stopped briefly at a back gate and found it latched, but not locked. Through the gap in the gate she could see a gas meter hanging just above the recently mown lawn at one corner of the house. One of the useful bits of trivia Four kept in her "good things to know" memory file was that over 18,000 deaths occurred in the United States each year from household accidents, and that one of the major causes was fire. She also knew that fire marshals were among law enforcement's best trained investigators, and it was difficult to manufacture what looked like an accidental blaze. Plus, there might be collateral damage from a fire that would attract even more police and media attention.

She parked for ten minutes in front of a house at the end of the cul-de-sac with a realtor's sign on the lawn, appeared to take a few notes, then drove again slowly down the street, checking this time to see where underground power cabling surfaced and passed into the houses. The cables weren't visible from the street and must come in on the side of the garage. Perfect. Now, to wait until dark.

. . .

The provincial jail to which the three were taken was in a walled compound with rolls of razor wire topping the barricades, less than ten minutes from the Cambodian border crossing. When their phones were taken, they had not been permitted a call. Angie stayed with Adam and Davis until they entered the room where they were searched for personal items, then was steered tearfully away into another unit.

The men's cell was about the size of a tennis court: roughly constructed of unpainted cement block, with a bare concrete floor and no furnishings but a row of rolled mats that stood on end against one wall. In a front corner, three five-gallon buckets served as latrines, and the rancid smell of human excrement and seventy unwashed bodies assaulted them as they were pushed into the room.

"Oh, my God!" Davis murmured. The exclamation came out as a low sob and he edged closer to Adam, eyeing the ring of faces that turned toward them as the door clanged shut. The inmates were all dressed as they had been when arrested and their filthy clothes added to the stench that smothered Adam's lungs. Behind them, somewhere along the corridor, they heard women's voices, punctuated by the occasional cry of a baby. Adam wondered if Angie was packed into a women's cell like the one he now occupied.

Some of the men sat with their backs against the walls, their faces emotionless masks. But those who were standing had stopped a nervous pacing, their expressions reflecting the tension of over-crowding and the fear and anger of uncertainty. Adam turned to his left, keeping his peripheral vision toward the center of the room, and moved cautiously around the cell with Davis pressed against his left arm. Two young Caucasian men, a little older then Davis, sat along the back wall, their faces bruised and swollen and blood showing in purple splotches on their shirts and khaki shorts. Adam slid down beside them against the wall.

"Speak English?" he asked.

"Australian," one of the men said thickly through cracked lips.

"You okay? Looks like you got roughed up before they brought you in."

"Not before," the man said. "This lot did it. You'll get your turn. There's a bunch here who think they've got to let everyone know who's boss. They'll take most of your food when it comes and if you refuse, beat the bloody hell outta you."

Adam felt Davis shrink farther back into the wall. "Which ones?" he asked the Aussie.

"That mob over in the right corner that's watching us. You walked right past 'em."

Adam didn't look toward the men but could feel their eyes. "Anyone in here speak both English and Khmer?" he asked.

The Australian nodded toward a spot beside the door and licked his thick lips before he could speak again. "That old white bloke over there. I think he's in here for shaggin' little girls – or maybe little boys. But he speaks both."

Adam looked toward the old man. His ragged beard and hair covered a round, pallid face the color of vanilla pudding, and his pale blue eyes watched the newcomers intently.

"If these men come after us, when will it happen?" Adam asked.

"When they brought us food last night, the men came over and told us to give it to them. We said no, and this is what happened."

"When they bring the food tonight, stay by us," he told the Australians.

"Don't be thinkin' your being such a big bloke is going to scare them off," the other Australian muttered. "They'll come at you as a mob and before you know it, you're down with them kickin' at your face."

"I'm not asking you to do anything," Adam assured them. "Just take your food and stay close."

# TWENTY-FIVE

Shortly after 9:30 when the night had finally darkened and the high redwood fences cast shadows across the narrow lane, Four walked silently down the alley between Stonewood and Hunter Chase, carrying a small black case. She peered through the gap in the gate that led into the backyard of the home that held Dreu Sason. The house had a small breakfast area that opened through sliding glass doors onto a rear patio, and lights were on in both the breakfast room and the adjoining kitchen. Four had been watching throughout the afternoon and had seen movement on the lower floor, but no one enter or leave. The woman she wanted was alone in the house and spending most of her time in what appeared to be a study in the front right quarter of the lower floor.

The yard had been left with little landscaping: no trees and only a few artificial plants on the corners of the patio. It was the home of a person whose work schedule precluded yard work and who didn't see much value in paying a gardener to maintain plants that couldn't be appreciated. The light from the French doors stretched only halfway across the open lawn, leaving a strip of darkness along the inner side of the fence. Four slipped into the yard and skirted it to her right to the side of the garage where a rear door entered at the back corner: access to tools that might be used for yard work, should the house ever fall into the hands of someone interested in such things. The door was locked but not alarmed, a shortcoming of virtually every alarm system Four had encountered. Owners assumed that an alarmed door from the garage into the house was all the protection they needed. True, as long as an intruder didn't lure the occupant into the garage, which was exactly Four's intent.

She quickly picked the lock into the garage and flicked on a small penlight, locating the breaker box that hung beside the door that entered what Four guessed to be a laundry area or pantry adjoining the kitchen. She snapped the box cover open, finding what she had expected from a resident with a sense of order. Each breaker was labeled.

Four swept the narrow shaft of light around the garage and back to the breaker box. The door entering the house opened inward, but there was an area of open wall to the right as one stepped out into the garage. The light switch was on the left beneath the breaker box. A right-handed person stepping into the dark garage would turn and reach across to the left, leaving the area to the right of the door a blind spot. Sason was right handed. Before turning in, she would come into the kitchen to turn off the lights and find the circuit dead. The breaker for the kitchen lights was third down on the right side of the box and Four snapped it off, slipped across to the other side of the door, and waited. Waiting was another skill that came with competitive gymnastics and Four was very good at it.

A hundred feet away in a study lit only by a table lamp, Dreu thought she noticed a dimming in the light beyond the partially closed door and picked up her cell phone from the table beside the leather recliner. She had been sitting sideways with her legs draped over one arm, her back to the door, but felt, as much as saw, the subtle change in light. The last hour had been spent second guessing her actions since leaving the office: wondering if she should have gone to the police that morning or asked to meet with federal authorities over the weekend. But she wanted to talk through her suspicion with Adam first, not because she was uncertain about the seriousness of the backdoors she was finding in the FedTegrity programs, but because she was uncertain about her own culpability. Her limited experience with whistleblowers hadn't convinced her that they fared much better than those they accused, and she wanted to know exactly what she was getting herself into before she went to the police.

Every ten minutes she checked her phone for texts. An invitation to play racquetball in the morning from a couple with whom they occasionally played doubles. A note from the library that the digital copy of *Gone Girl* she was waiting for was now available. But nothing from Adam. Even when he was on the other side of the world, he rarely went more than twelve hours without a quick "ILY." His silence added to her anxiety.

She stretched back in the chair to look through the gap in the doorway and could see that the breakfast room light was still on. Had a bulb burned out in the kitchen? She sat completely still and listened to the quiet of the house, hearing only the hum of central air and the tick-tock of the antique Tambour clock on Adam's living room mantle.

She twisted from the chair and walked silently to the door, easing it open with senses probing the house. The curtains were drawn in the front, and she looked to her left to make certain she had snapped the deadbolt into place when she came in. The front door was locked. The combination living-dining room was cast in pale shadows from a single overhead light that seeped through from the breakfast nook. Dreu slipped sideways across the main entryway and flipped the switch for the four canned living room lights, feeling herself release a trapped breath as they instantly brightened the space. She skirted the room's mahogany baby grand and reached through the arch that opened from the dining area into the kitchen, groping around the edge of the partial wall for the switch. It was in the up position and she flipped it up and down without result. On the back of the range, a red digital clock indicated a few minutes after ten, so there was still power to the stove. The kitchen overhead fixture had three bulbs and she doubted all three had burned out at once. An electric kettle sat on the counter beside the door and she punched down its heating lever. Nothing. Something must have tripped a breaker.

She felt the comfort of light streaming into the darkened kitchen from either side and walked through into the laundry room, trying its switch and also finding it dead. The door to the garage was bolted and she punched the cancellation code into the alarm pad and flipped the deadbolt, pulling the door inward and reaching into the dark room for the light switch. With an involuntary shriek, she stumbled backward onto the floor of the laundry room as the small woman swung into her, a silenced pistol aimed at her chest.

Dreu crab-walked backward into the kitchen until she banged against the lower cupboards. The woman advanced with her, pushing the door closed behind her.

"Get up," the woman said in a voice that seemed completely without emotion.

Dreu started to say, "What do you want?" but knew exactly what the woman was there for.

"So...," she said instead, her heart pounding almost visibly beneath the navy sports bra that, with a loose pair of striped boxers, was all she had left on when she went into the study. "What do we do now?" She reached back for the edge of the counter, taking in the slim, Asian woman as her mind raced around the kitchen, trying to place objects that might serve as weapons.

"Hands in front where I can see them," the woman said in the same emotionless voice as Dreu struggled to her feet. She was at least eight inches shorter than Dreu and couldn't weigh more than a hundred pounds, but had the look of a loaded spring: all potential energy waiting to become kinetic if a sudden move tripped the release. She looked quickly left and right at the exits to the kitchen, then asked, "Where's the master bathroom?"

"Upstairs," Dreu answered, her thoughts leaping to the upper floor and sifting through what her attacker was planning.

"Take me up there... very slowly. Hands up where I can see them all the time. Any quick movements and I won't hesitate to kill you." Dreu knew she was telling the truth.

They moved slowly back through the living room to the stairs and Dreu ascended slowly, the woman far enough behind that her victim couldn't kick back suddenly. When the stairs turned back on themselves to climb to the second floor, the woman stayed against the far rail and out of reach.

The stairs ended in an open TV room with two small bedrooms to the left and the master bed and bath to the right. As she entered the large bedroom, Dreu thought fleetingly of throwing the door closed behind her but realized that if she wasn't shot instantly, she wouldn't be able to lock the door before the woman forced it open or shot her through the hollow core. Her best chance, she decided, was to get into the closer quarters of the bathroom and try to disarm her there.

The homes in this section of Virginia Hills had splurged on generous master baths, with a tiled walk-in shower on the right as she entered and a separate alcove beyond, with a slatted swinging door that held the toilet. His-and-hers sinks filled half the wall on the left, the mirrors separated by recessed shelving for toiletries. And beyond the sinks, a deep Jacuzzi tub. The gray-blue ceramic tile of the floor wrapped the walls of the shower and covered the tub's surround, giving the room a natural calm that completely escaped Dreu as the woman nudged her in with the end of the silencer.

"Over by the tub – and turn on the water," the woman ordered, glancing quickly around the bath. "Do you have some bath oils?"

Had she not known her assailant was somehow connected to Marshall Ding and FedTegrity, Dreu might have imagined that this was some kind of sexual fantasy being played out. But as she leaned over the Jacuzzi to twist on the nickel-plated faucet, she looked up into the black, almond eyes and saw no emotion at all.

"There are no bath beads," she said. "This is my boyfriend's place. In fact, he could be getting here any time. And the police are on their way. I called them about the FedTegrity files."

"Mr. Zak has been gone for a week," the woman said with a thin smile. "I don't think he'll be pulling up in the next hour. And I *am* the police. Now – close the drain and take off your clothes."

Dreu raised the lever on the drain and straightened to face the woman, but did nothing to remove her clothes. She guessed her assailant wasn't planning to shoot her unless Dreu attacked, but also knew she wasn't intended to leave the room alive. Drowning? The woman must know there would be a struggle and though she looked fit, Dreu had at least twenty years on her and thirty pounds. The only way she could get Dreu underwater without a fight would be to knock her out somehow – make it look like she slipped and fell getting into the water. The reason for the bath beads. If she didn't do something to resist within the next few seconds, she knew she would be sliding unconscious under the water and out of Adam's life. And Ding's programs, whatever their intent, would completely shut down a half dozen key federal agencies.

"Clothes off," the woman repeated, flicking the muzzle of the gun upward, signaling that Dreu should remove her top.

Dreu crossed her arms over her chest and grasped the bottom of the sports bra, pulling it upward over her head. With arms extended, she saw the woman glance instinctively at her scarred right breast – the split second Dreu had been waiting for. She swept her right arm with the tangled bra wrapped about the wrist downward and to the side, swiping the gun hand toward the wall above the tub. At the same moment, she surged forward, throwing her right knee upward into the woman's solar plexus just below the rib cage with every ounce of strength she could muster. The gun discharged with a heavy "thump" as the woman's muscles knotted, and tile shattered above the bath where the bullet tore into the wall.

Dreu's knee lifted the woman a foot off the floor and emptied her lungs with a rib-cracking explosion of air. As she gasped for breath, Dreu grasped the left arm that held the gun with both hands, slamming the wrist down over her knee and feeling the bones snap and twist as the gun tumbled into the rising water of the Jacuzzi. With the broken arm still locked in her grip, Dreu swung the woman over the edge of the tub after the weapon and bolted for the door.

She plunged down the stairs, vaulting the railing onto the lower stairs and tumbling to the bottom as her right knee, bruised by the pounding of the wrist bones, collapsed beneath her. She rolled into a crouch and hobbled toward the front door, hearing the slosh of water as the woman clambered from the tub. Dreu wondered if a gun that had been submerged could fire, and was answered by a bullet smashing into the door frame as she lurched out onto the front step. She stumbled across the small patch of lawn, hoping to see car lights turn onto the street in front of her. But even with the yellow glow of a dozen porch lamps, the night seemed oppressively dark and stone quiet. She thought about screaming: yelling for help at the top of her lungs. But her mind still reeled from the woman's declaration – "I *am* the police!" She gritted against the throbbing in her knee and began to run.

At the corner, she turned right along the high redwood fence that surrounded the back and sides of the last home on the block, looking desperately for a hiding place in the open expanse of street in front of her. Instinctively, she turned up the alley that backed the fenced properties. The first gate was unlatched and she slipped into the dark yard, praying there would be no dogs. A raised pool with a surrounding cedar deck filled most of the space, and she slid a bolt lock into place on the gate and stumbled into the darkest shadows between the pool and the fence, collapsing into a sitting position against the rough redwood slats.

Dreu clenched her jaw tightly, sucking air through her nose to stifle the gasps that echoed in the enclosed space. Through the fence, she heard the footsteps of her pursuer reach the corner, pause, then turn along the fence line and into the alley. The woman stopped at the gate and tried the lever, then moved on down the narrow lane. Dreu relaxed her breathing and closed her eyes, probing the sounds around her for any indication the woman was waiting beyond the gate. Then there seemed to be a second set of footsteps: muted, as if barefoot. They hesitated for a moment at the mouth of the alley, then continued past the gate to Dreu's hiding place and paused again. She froze in place and waited.

"Hey!" a male voice shouted beyond the gate, and the muted footsteps started running toward the far end of the alley. After another moment she heard an engine rumble to life in the cul-de-sac and a car speed the length of the block. The driver spun around the corner and accelerated down the street. Dreu sat without moving, listening to the night and massaging her throbbing knee, thinking again of the woman's claim to be with the police. She was probably lying: her way of letting Dreu know that her claim to have called the police was also a lie. But she had known who lived in the house – and this whole situation with Ding was so surreal. It was hard to know what to believe. Ding was such a passive, gentle man. She couldn't imagine him involved in some insidious plot to compromise the nation's security. Perhaps he was working *with* the government on something top secret that she was threatening to expose. Or with some rogue element within the government that had its own inside agents who could get to her before the sane people did. She had to talk to Adam before she went to anyone – if only he would call!

Crickets began to chirp beneath the raised pool and a car swung into the rear drive and nosed into one of the garages further down on the Stonewood side. Dreu struggled back to her feet and leaned against the side of the pool, realizing she was wearing only the baggy shorts. The blue top remained twisted about her right forearm and she untangled it and slipped it back over her head. She couldn't return to the house. Even when her wrist was being shattered, her attacker hadn't uttered a sound. Dreu knew she wouldn't hesitate to circle back on foot to the house and sit, cradling the broken arm, waiting for her prey to return. That meant no phone, no money, no clothes, and no car. She found that she felt as naked without the phone as without the bra, and instinctively patted the pockets of her loose shorts to make sure she hadn't slipped the cell into one of them. But she knew where it was. She had dropped it when the woman pushed her backward into the kitchen. It was lying on the floor somewhere by the cupboards.

There was an all-night pharmacy a quarter mile away at the corner of Custer and Virginia Parkway. She could cut through at the end of the cul-de-sac and across the open field behind the water tower, staying pretty much out of sight. She doubted the pharmacy had a pay phone – and even if it did, she didn't have a cent on her. A clerk might let her make a call…but call who? If they had the resources to find her at Adam's place and to know he'd been gone all week, they knew where she spent her time and who her friends were. She couldn't call anyone from work – or from the Y. Or any of her neighbors.

Then she thought of Sandi Cooperman.

. . .

He had been watching the house since he tailed her from the office, waiting for the right moment to step back into her life and let her know that this time it would be different. She didn't need to be afraid. He had no reason to be jealous, now that she wasn't publicly flaunting herself. "The Lord our God is merciful and forgiving, even though we have rebelled against him," the Lord God said to Daniel, and she would find mercy and forgiveness through His love.

He had parked his car at the community center on South Virginia Hills Drive, a lot often used by residents of the apartments across the street. Hunter Chase turned off of Wentworth, and the house on Wentworth immediately facing the cul-de-sac was empty and on the market. He had slipped into its backyard, finding that it backed against a golf course, and set up temporary quarters on the patio out of sight of the second floor windows of neighboring homes. If he heard a car coming toward him down the street, he could check to see if she was leaving. But she had remained inside the house the entire weekend.

At night, he had begun to carry a lawn chair onto the dark front porch and sit beneath the stone arch of the doorway in the deep shadows, shielded from the street by two short-needled pines that filled the front yard. A Bradford pear hid her own front porch, but he could see the end of her walk, and knew they were closer together than they had been for a long time. If she left the house – if she went for a walk in the evening – he would present himself to her again. And this time she would feel the strength of his love…and of God's love pouring through him like the balm of Gilead.

He was on the porch on Sunday night when he heard the distant splintering of wood and saw the figure running toward him down the walk. As she approached through the glow cast by porch lights, he knew that it was his Dreu. He started to rise but saw that she was naked above the waist, her dark, lovely face twisted in fear. She reached the corner and turned along Wentworth, then back down the alley that backed the homes on Hunter Chase. Moments later another figure followed: a smaller women dressed in black, her left arm clutched against her chest.

In her right hand she held a silenced handgun. The woman in black also turned right along the fence and into the alley, and this time he followed. His Dreu was in danger.

When he reached the entrance to the alley, the smaller woman was already halfway to the other end, stopping intermittently to check behind a dumpster, open a back gate, and look furtively into a dark yard. He moved into the shadows of the fence and followed until she turned at the far end and began to make her way back toward him, re-checking each gate. In the darkness of the narrow lane she was no more than an apparition: a black shadow drifting from one side of the alley to the other. He stepped into the middle of the space between fences where she could clearly see his own dark form, back-lighted by the street behind him.

"*Hey!*" he shouted, and she looked up with a start, paused for a brief moment as if considering his level of threat, then turned and ran from the alley. He sprinted after her but as he reached the turnabout at the end of Hunter Chase, she had climbed into a dark Jeep and gunned it back toward Wentworth. He ran after her on foot, then stood at the corner to see that she didn't return.

Dreu, he knew, was somewhere in the alley. She had not had time to reach the other end before the smaller women followed. The house directly across Wentworth from the alley was lighted only by a yellow porch lamp, its glow blocked from the street by a head-high clump of pampas grass. He backed into the long, dark whiskers of grass and waited.

She emerged ten minutes later from the first gate on the right, looked furtively in both directions, then walked away from him toward the back of her own house. When she passed it and continued down the lane, he slipped out of the shadows of the grass clump and followed. She left the cul-de-sac and crossed the street, then cut across a lot behind the dark silhouette of a water tower where the city had constructed a shallow runoff basin. For a brief moment he thought this would be the time to catch her – to ask why she was running and offer his help. She would know then that she could trust him...that he could be her salvation. But she would see him coming across the field and be frightened. Run from him. Instead he stayed in the shadows until she crossed Custer Road and entered a CVS pharmacy. He stood on the corner behind a traffic control box and watched the store's entrance, wondering if he should go in and tell her he was there to protect her. Twice, she came to the window and searched the dark street, then disappeared back among the rows of shelving. She may have gone in to call the police and if they came and found him, they wouldn't understand.

He watched for nearly an hour, pacing fifty steps along the walk in each direction, then returning to the control box. A red Ford pickup sped toward him down the parkway and swung into the lot. Before it had rolled to a complete stop, she hurried from the store and climbed into the passenger seat. As the truck left the pharmacy, he saw the lettering on the driver's door and committed it to memory.

# TWENTY-SIX

The evening meal arrived on four, double-layered carts with eight bowls of thin, dishwater-brown soup on each level, a stack of empty bowls, and a woven basket hanging from the end mounded high with heavy boiled rice. Four elderly women dressed in black pajama suits pushed the carts into the cell, took the honey buckets from the corner, and left quickly, replaced by three guards in olive drab. Each carried what Adam judged to be a Chinese-made QBZ-95 assault rifle slung loosely over his shoulder. One of the guards shouted something in Khmer and the men slouched back to line up against the back wall. The guards hastily scanned the row of prisoners, then backed silently out of the room, leaving the carts beside the locked door. Adam began to step forward but one of the Australians grabbed his arm.

"Wait!" he whispered loudly, and the line shuffled silently as the five men the Aussies had identified as the prison bullies walked to the carts, casting Adam a warning glare. They used other bowls of soup to fill those they had selected to the brim, mounded five of the empty bowls with rice, and returned to their back corner, menacingly walking the line to stare down any man who showed irritation at their liberties. As they passed Adam, he held their gaze but kept his face passive. The leader stopped in front of him and scoffed, muttered something in Khmer, then continued to his corner.

When the five were comfortably crouched over their bowls, the others crowded around the carts until the soup was dispersed and what was left of the rice divided among the remaining inmates. Adam carried his portion to the corner opposite the gang and sat cross-legged against the wall, keeping them on his right where they fell within his peripheral vision. Davis and the Australians huddled nervously beside him.

The broth smelled and tasted like *pho*, a bullion-flavored Vietnamese soup that Adam generally liked, but without the meat, vegetables, bean sprouts, and trace of lime that distinguished the Asian dish. As he dipped sticky balls of rice into the broth, the gang in the opposite corner rose and moved in his direction. The drone of quiet conversation and slurping of soup ceased on cue. Adam directed his gaze into his bowl until the five pairs of legs were directly in front of him. Without looking up, he placed his soup bowl beside the rice on the floor and pushed himself upright, keeping an attentive eye on the men's feet. He towered above them by nearly a foot and looking down directly into the eyes of the one he took to be the leader, his face firm but unthreatening.

The Cambodian held his ground and took a half-step forward, pointing at the bowls and barking something in Khmer. Without shifting his eyes or raising his voice, Adam called to the pedophile who squatted beside the cell door.

"Could you come over here a minute?"

The old man's pale face flushed a shade of pink and he glanced about nervously, then rose and shuffled to the center of the cell.

"What does this man want?" Adam asked.

The old man looked nervously at the gang leader who ignored him with his back. "He wants your food," he muttered.

"Come over here – where I can hear you," Adam instructed, and the doughy little man took two steps closer. Adam continued to look directly into the eyes of the prison bully.

"Now, tell him I don't want to cause any trouble and don't want anyone to get hurt. But if they try to take my food or anyone else's while I'm in here, I'll beat the hell out of them 'til they can't eat anything."

The pedophile's heavily lidded eyes opened to twice their normal size and he retreated the two steps.

"*Tell them*," Adam repeated sharply.

The old man spoke into the floor. As he repeated Adam's words in Khmer, the hush that had fallen over the room turned ominous: a silence of fearful expectation.

The bronze face of the gang leader turned an orange shade of copper and he moved another half-step closer, beckoning for his henchmen to tighten the front. He repeated his demand, pointing to the bowl.

"Stand up," Adam said evenly to Davis. "You don't want to be on the ground when this starts. Once I move, if that guy in front of you so much as blinks, punch him in the face as hard as you can."

Though short, the ringleader was as thick as a teak log, and Adam could see the veins begin to bulge under his jaw. Adam shifted his weight slightly onto his left foot and trusted that the man would understand at least one word of English.

"No," he said, shaking his head slightly for emphasis. He expected the man to move quickly and wasn't disappointed. The Cambodian stepped in with his left foot and shot a sweeping roundhouse kick with his right toward Adam's side. Adam turned into the kick, blocking it with his left arm as his right elbow shot up and forward like a pile driver, pounding hard into the bridge of the man's nose and shooting him backward in a crimson spray.

The man to Adam's right had also stepped into a kick, aiming at the small of Adam's back as he turned to ward off the first blow. Adam threw his right arm back, blunting the strike, then thrust his arm upward beneath the man's extended leg, lifting him from his feet and dropping the back of his head hard against the concrete floor. As the man sprawled backward in a daze, Adam dropped a knee hard onto his exposed stomach and swung his right elbow down toward the Cambodian's extended throat, stopping just before crushing his windpipe.

He glanced at the scuffle behind him to find a third Cambodian seated backward on the floor, clutching what looked to be a dislocated jaw. Davis stood over him, grimacing and rubbing his right fist. The gang leader lay unconscious in the middle of the cell floor, blood still streaming from his flattened nose.

"Watch out!" one of the Aussies shouted as Adam rose, and he turned to see the two remaining gang members firing kicks toward his groin and kidneys. He thrust his left arm downward to block the blow to his groin and shot his right hand, palm first, into the face of the fourth attacker, then steeled himself for the blow to his back. The foot landed, but with little force. One of the Australians had thrown a chop block under the fifth man's braced leg, toppling him backward. The second Aussie was on the fallen man in an instant, pounding his face with both fists.

Adam looked down at the man he had just knocked to the floor, who now stared up at him with wide, resigned eyes, expecting the big westerner to drop a knee onto his chest and crush the life out of him. Instead, Adam waved them away with the back of his hand, and the three who could move scooted backward across the floor.

"That's enough," Adam said to the Australian who continued to pummel the fifth attacker. The Aussie held a final blow poised above the man's battered face, then lowered his arm and staggered back from the unconscious Cambodian. The Australian was shaking uncontrollably, tears of rage staining his red face. His friend wrapped him in his arms to ease the trembling, and guided him back to a seat against the wall.

Adam waited for the other prisoners to react – for some swell of shouting or applause – but the room remained silent as a tomb and the inmates shrank back to their customary places. In their eyes, he realized, one menace had simply replaced another.

He turned again to the ragged old pedophile who had simply stepped aside as the gang leader stumbled backward onto the floor. He now stood beside the unconscious man, watching Adam with the same detached skepticism.

"Tell the men they can collect the rice over there and pass it around," Adam said, pointing to the mounded bowls in the gang's corner. The old man translated without enthusiasm and without response.

The door clanged loudly and the old women entered to retrieve the carts and return the buckets, followed by the guards. The armed men scanned the cell and did a quick assessment of the damage, then shouted instructions to one of the women who scurried out and returned with a mop and bucket of water, while the others wheeled the carts from the room. Without moving the unconscious men, the woman with the mop attacked the pools of blood. The guards watched in disinterested silence and when she had spread the stains enough to keep them from being tracked around the cell, ordered her out and followed, leaving the fallen leader and his beaten henchman where they lay. Adam motioned for the remaining gang members to drag them back to their corner.

"We'll need to sleep in shifts," he said to Davis and the Australians. "If anyone even gets to their feet and isn't headed toward one of the buckets, wake us all up. We may have to go through this a few more times before everyone's convinced."

They nodded in unison.

"And thanks," he said, nodding to each of the young men. "We were a good team." He squatted beside them against the wall.

"Now…," he said, turning to Davis, "tell me about your money."

. . .

Four had driven 63 miles north to Durant, Oklahoma, before checking into the emergency room at the Southeast Oklahoma Medical Center. The night admitting attendant accepted her story that she had tripped on the door sill of her motel room and fallen against a planter and was satisfied with her insurance. Four had the distinct impression that if the insurance was right, the hospital wasn't too worried about how she'd been injured. The single physician on duty was busy with the victims of an automobile accident and the attendant, an anorexic-looking girl with stringy blonde hair and a mouth full of gum, seemed to feel the need to give Four the details while she checked her in under the name Marion Chan.

"I know both of them," she said between smacks of the gum. "They were both freshmen when I graduated. From what I hear, Ashley didn't make it. That's the girl. Jared – that's the guy – rolled his Mustang coming off 75 onto North Washington. Convertible. No seat belts. Kids can be sooo stupid!"

The girl passed her along to an aging nurse with henna-colored hair who doubled as the night radiologist. She stabilized the arm and took pictures, gave her something for the pain and applied an ice pack.

"It may be awhile," she said as she ushered Four into a tiny, white examination room and sat her on the paper-covered table. "Weekend in Durant. And that means no rest for the weary."

When alone in the room, Four placed a call to a pre-set number in Telluride, Colorado.

When Nine answered, she said without explanation, "The woman evaded me. She knows we're after her and has disappeared."

"You're having a little trouble with your assignments." Nine's voice oozed disapproval.

"I would say none of us is doing too well," Four said acidly. "We tell ourselves we've been preparing for this possibility for a long time, but I don't think we really expected anything to happen. We're all rusty."

"I don't think our superiors will find that an acceptable excuse," Nine snapped. The other Weavers believed there were still superiors with whom Nine worked closely. "This is all we were trained for, and now we are not handling it well," he said.

Four sniffed. "But the systems are in place and so far, they have not been compromised. That's the important thing."

"But if she gets to the right people...."

"Change the execution passwords. If you can execute the kill orders, surely you can change the commands."

"Five would have to do that and he may be under surveillance. I don't know enough about how to modify the codes."

"I don't think she's been to the authorities, but she could go in the morning. Contact him now."

"It may be time to execute *Seres*...."

"We aren't authorized to execute without specific instructions from above. We just put the program in place."

"But for what purpose?" he argued. "If she exposes us, all of this work of fifty years is for nothing."

"That's not our decision."

"I may have to make it mine," he said.

Four was silent for a moment, then said. "Don't overstep your authority, Lawrence. We need to find the Sason woman and eliminate the threat."

"That was your assignment. And you are beginning to sound like an American," he said. "And as for my authority, I have been given all I need." The line clicked dead.

She sat on the end of the examination table with her arm draped in her lap, considering her failures. She didn't know how Eckerson had survived Soi Cowboy. She seemed so 'on her game' when in Bangkok. But when she discovered that he had lived – that he had been to the village and knew about Phyllis Morin – she suspected the Thai whores had simply robbed him of his money and passport, taken her money, and let him go. Failing to check to make sure he was dead should have been her first clue that she was not combat-ready. And when she missed the shot at the Jungle Temple because the other man reacted so quickly, she realized she had become too complacent: too expectant that everything would always go according to plan. That was not the way she was trained. Maybe she *was* becoming too American.

She shifted on the table to adjust the ice pack, thinking how typical this was of what she had heard about emergency rooms. Her thoughts moved back to the tall figure who had thrown Eckerson out of the way of her shot. She knew she had seen him before – not from the completely shaven face and head, but from the alert awareness with which he spotted the laser sight before she could execute, and the smooth, fluid motion with which the long body crossed the twenty feet that separated him from her target and swept him aside. Eckerson wasn't being followed by the bearded, one-eyed man at the airport – he was being protected by him. Her third mistake. And one that added to her clean-up list. But first-things-first. She needed to find and eliminate Dreu Sason.

While she had been watching the house, she ran a query on the address and learned the place was being rented by an Adam Zak. She had been able to get a cell number for him, but little else. She pulled the phone again from her pocket and punched in the auto-dial for Seven at NSA. When he failed to answer, she recited Zak's number into the phone and asked for any texts or phone messages to the number. "We have a loose end, and Zak might be our link to her," she ended. As she hung up, the nurse pushed back into the room.

"The boy didn't make it either," she said with the resigned weariness of one who spends her life dealing with tragedy. "The doctor is with the family. He'll be with you in a few minutes."

Wonderful, Four thought. Two people getting together who have both had a terrible night.

# TWENTY-SEVEN

Sandi Cooperman was the image of the East Texas cowgirl: flaxen, shoulder-length hair pulled back behind her ears; a buff-colored, pinch-front cowboy hat worn low over pale blue eyes that were direct to the point of being challenging; and a pert, sun-freckled face. Her standard uniform was a plain sleeveless or long sleeved shirt that matched her eyes, and faded denim jeans worn over scuffed, square-toed boots.

Sandi's father had been a cattleman, running polled Herefords on two sections of rolling grassland a mile east of Bonham, Texas, sandwiched between highways 82 and 56. Her mother was a rancher's wife: a woman who could bake, can vegetables, load round hay bales with a tractor spear as ably as any ranch hand, and help pull a calf in a blizzard when an extra pair of hands was needed. When her husband was crushed against the side of a stock pen while trying to help a neighbor load 1600 pounds of enraged Angus bull into a trailer, Sandi's mother quite willingly gave up ranch life and moved into town to live with her son, who had no interest in taking over his father's cattle operation.

Sandi did – but not to raise polled Herefords. She sold the herd and invested in her greatest passion: quarter horses. The other ranchers around Bonham initially called it Cooperman's Folly, claiming there was no money to be made in horses anymore unless you could breed good rodeo or racing stock. Sandi did both, producing a horse that was hailed as the top sprinter of the year by the American Quarter Horse Association, bringing home nearly a million and a half in winnings before becoming a breed mare. Her rodeo stock was prized throughout the southwest as roping, bull-dogging, and barrel racing horses. But Sandi derived her greatest satisfaction from exposing others to the joys of riding.

As suburban Dallas expanded east and north, some of the new rural subdivisions divided into three acre "ranchettes," complete with community riding trails. Sandi's stables couldn't keep up with the demand to train new riders. Soccer moms were becoming saddle moms, bringing their kids to Sandi to learn to ride and signing up for lessons themselves.

Behind the sprawling red brick ranch house that her father had built in the early 1970s when he returned from Vietnam, Sandi added a spacious indoor arena and two outdoor rings the size of standard rodeo grounds. One she used for basic instruction, with advanced students who wanted to ride competitively moving into the second arena to practice barrel racing, roping, or show jumping. For the suburbanites with a hankering to ride, but without the three acres, Sandi boarded horses and kept almost thirty for riding enthusiasts who drove from as far as Sherman and Dallas for a weekend canter across the Cooperman Ranch.

As much as she had been tempted, Dreu decided against buying her own horse. She had been on horseback only twice in her life before discovering Sandi: once when her family took a summer trip to Rocky Mountain National Park and had gone trail riding; and once for a perfume commercial. The photographer shooting the ad had draped her in a gauzy black gown and seated her backward on a very patient white stallion that stood like carved marble while she leaned against his powerful neck, holding a bottle of something called "Damsel." On both occasions she had been so intrigued by the huge animals that she promised that someday – that someday you expect will never happen – she would learn to ride. Moving to McKinney, Texas, made someday a possibility.

She found Sandi on the internet and drove out to Bonham on a Monday: the slow day at the ranch when saddle moms get the kids back to school and catch up on their own to-do lists. Sandi spent the afternoon showing her around the stables and introduced Dreu to what had become the other love in her life: a spirited chestnut mare named Summer Breeze, with liquid brown eyes that seemed to find in the willowy model-turned-computer geek a kindred spirit. So did the mare's owner, and when Dreu was able to put together a few vacation days or needed to decompress on a weekend, she left town without letting anyone know where she was going and worked the stables and horses with Sandi Cooperman. The rancher offered her a spare bedroom when she wanted to stay overnight and Dreu worked the next morning, then took the mare out into the pastures in the afternoon and let her run. Freedom, to Dreu, was releasing her own black hair and stretching forward along the neck of Summer Breeze, letting the wind lift both of their manes into ribbons of flowing silk.

When she began to see Adam, she refused to give up her time with

Breeze. He knew she loved to ride and that there were times when she needed to get away to Sandi's: somewhere up near Bonham. After she made him watch *The Man from Snowy River* for the second time, he began to call her "Jess" when she needed to escape to the ranch and would say, "Guess you'll be goin' out after the brumbies." They each had their secrets. But she had shared just enough of this one with him that the ranch would be the perfect escape. He could find her if he needed to, but no one else knew about her retreat.

Dreu called Sandi's landline an hour before midnight from the pharmacy on Custer Road, using the night clerk's cell. She knew Sandi wouldn't recognize the number and would let it ring until she heard Dreu's voice on the answering machine.

"Sandi – it's me," she whispered loudly, close enough to the clerk to reassure the girl she wasn't taking off with the phone, but far enough away to keep the conversation private. "I need your help!" She started to ask if she could stay for a few days, but the rancher was immediately on the line.

"What's going on? You okay?"

"Yeah, I'm okay. Can I come stay for a few days?"

"Sure… you know you don't need to ask. Come on out."

"I…I need to have you come get me if you can."

"Dreu, what's going on? Are you where you can't talk? Do I need to ask questions and you just say 'Yeah, that's right,' or whatever?"

"No. I'll tell you all about it when you get here. Can you come?"

"On my way. Where are you?"

"In McKinney at a CVS pharmacy at the corner of Virginia Hills Parkway and Custer Road. I'll be inside but will be watching for you."

"That's near your boyfriend's house, isn't it? Has he done something to you…?"

"No, he's gone. I was staying at his place. I'll tell you about it when you get here."

"It'll probably be forty-five minutes. I'll be in the red pickup."

"Don't let anyone know you're coming…."

"Dreu, you're sounding weird…."

"Weird doesn't begin to describe it. I'll be watching for you."

Before the red F-150 rolled to a stop, Dreu slipped from the pharmacy and pulled open the passenger door.

"Drive a ways down the Parkway and make sure no one's following us," she said, scrunching down in the seat.

Sandi wheeled out of the parking lot and headed east. "Is some-one after you?"

"Someone was... and I've still had this creepy feeling I'm being watched. Anyone behind us?"

Sandi watched the mirrors, turning north on the first major cross street and cruising for another three blocks before assuring her they were in the clear.

"There's a Walmart on Redbud Boulevard, just off 121," Dreu said. "Do you mind stopping so I can get a cheap phone?"

"You've lost your car *and* your phone?" Sandi looked suspiciously at Dreu's outfit as she turned again west toward Redbud, then added, "You don't look like you have any money either. Maybe I'd better do the shopping...."

"Until I can get to some cash," Dreu said, wondering exactly how she was going to do that.

After the Walmart stop, Dreu started at the beginning with what she had discovered at FedTegrity and her suspicion about Marshall Ding, ending with the encounter in Adam's home with the Asian woman.

"*Christ Almighty*... pardon my French..." Sandi said, then muttered, "...but with both these people being Chinese, do you think that's got something to do with it?"

Dreu shook her head. "No idea. Neither has an accent. Ding grew up here, and I think the woman did too."

"And this happened at your boyfriend's house? How did they know you were there?"

"I think they must have put some tracking device on my car. Or tracked my cell. Stupid me, for not thinking about that. I drove there from the office at about 2:00 a.m. Saturday morning. I'm sure no one followed me. Sometimes there wasn't a single car in sight."

"Why don't you just go to the cops?" Sandi asked bluntly.

"She said she *was* the cops. I'm not sure what she meant. Dallas PD? Federal? Maybe neither. But I don't dare go to the police until I talk to Adam. He'll have some idea...."

"But you haven't heard back from him?" They were passing the small town of Trenton and Sandi pulled into an all-night filling station to gas up the truck. "I don't care what they say. This thing drinks gas," she muttered as she swiped her card and talked to Dreu through the window while she watched the numbers spin on the pump display.

Dreu was defending Adam's silence. "He goes on these long overseas trips for his work and sometimes it's a few days before he can send or receive messages."

"Didn't think there were such places anymore," Sandi said, cradling the nozzle and waiting for her receipt.

"He ends up in some pretty backwater spots," Dreu said prophetically. "But I'll send a message from this phone and he'll call when he gets a chance."

"If the people following you are government and know whose house you were in, they'll be monitoring *his* phone. Won't matter what phone you use to send the message." Sandi climbed back into the truck and eased it out onto the access road to 121.

"Yeah, you're right. I've been so rattled I'm not thinking straight." Dreu sat for a moment in silence considering Sandi's warning as they sped across dark, open farmland.

"They may be watching, but they won't know what they're looking at," she said finally, pulling out the phone and squeezing it to life. "But Adam will know."

# TWENTY-EIGHT

"Greed," Adam said simply. "They haven't taken us to Phnom Penh, and I think the officer who had us arrested is working some side deal with the people who want us out of the way. That would be a lot simpler than paying off a bunch of people higher up."

"So...?" Davis muttered.

"So we do the same."

"What kind of money we talking about?"

"I'd start with an offer of eighty-five thousand – twenty-five to the head man for each of us, and another ten to the interpreter. Then she's complicit and will keep quiet."

"What about the Australians?" Davis asked.

"What about them?"

"They tipped us off to the guys trying to beat us up and helped with the fight. If they stay, I think they'll really get pounded. Maybe killed."

"I'm fine with including them, but it's your money we're talking about."

"There are still two problems, anyway," Davis said. "We've got to be able to get to the man who had us arrested – privately. And then I need to get to my money." He glanced around the bare concrete room at the men who paced restlessly or leaned in resignation against the block walls. "I don't see either of those things happening."

Adam signaled the pedophile who ambled over from his spot beside the door. "You got some kind of new proclamation for everyone?" he grinned through yellow, tobacco-stained teeth.

"Not for everyone. But when they bring the soup tonight, tell the guards I want to speak to the man in charge. I have some important information for him."

"Oh, they'll be impressed with that!" he smirked.

"The head man will be impressed. I guarantee it."

"What kind of information?"

"You just tell them."

"It won't make any difference."

"*Make* it make a difference," Adam said in a tone that silenced the old man. The pedophile shrugged and shuffled back to his spot.

Adam turned again to Davis. "You feel alright about trying to spring the two Aussies when there are probably forty other men in here who may not have done anything but upset the wrong official?"

"No one else helped us," Davis said. "And when I asked them why they were here, the Aussies said they'd just bought this little bag of stuff as sort of a joke. Weren't even sure what it was."

Adam smiled cynically. "Did they describe it to you? This bag they bought?"

Davis realized what he was thinking and nodded. "Yeah. They said it was a little leather bag. Like they carried old coins in."

"Our drug bust," Adam murmured.

For the next two nights the four slept in rotation, each watching for any signs of movement toward their corner from elsewhere in the cell. Since they had no way to judge time, each stood watch for as long as he could stay alert, then woke the man with the next shift. The gang leader and the man the Aussie had beaten were suffering enough that Adam was almost regretting injuring them so badly. But the five men stayed in their corner. With each meal, the old man passed along Adam's message to their captors. The first time, the guards cast Adam a suspicious glance but did nothing. From then on, they simply pushed the messenger aside as if they hadn't heard him.

The morning of the third day, Adam stood beside the pedophile as he delivered the message, looking menacingly at the three guards as the man spoke. When he finished, Adam said; "Tell them that if they don't arrange the meeting with their superior and he finds out later that they didn't pass along this request, they can count on being in here with us. And I don't think this lot will be very good to them."

The old man sighed. "Don't you get it? Once you're in here, no one gives a shit what happens to you."

"Give them the message," Adam ordered.

As the man spoke, Adam watched the soldiers, his expression reinforcing the seriousness of the request. They exchanged glances but left the prisoners with their food without comment. When they returned for the cart, none would make eye contact.

The following morning a fourth guard came with the soup cart. He signaled for Adam to follow and with another falling in behind, marched him back along the corridor that separated what appeared to be four cells like the one he was in. Through the door of the cell at the end of the corridor on the opposite side, he again heard the soprano voices of children and the muted murmur of women's conversation.

They passed through a heavy steel door into the area where they had initially been searched and stripped of belts, shoes, and anything they had in their pockets. Smaller rooms opened on both sides, and Adam was ushered into a replica of their initial interrogation room – complete with officer seated behind a bare metal table and thin female interpreter standing attentively beside him.

"Sit!" the officer ordered without the woman's assistance.

Adam settled into one of two plastic chairs and let the officer initiate the exchange.

The interpreter spoke first. "The Colonel would like to know what you have to say to him."

"Is the Colonel in charge here?"

"Yes. He is in charge of this border station."

"Was he the man who ordered us detained?"

"The Colonel is in charge here," the woman repeated.

Adam straightened in his chair. "I know my friends and I were arrested because someone made it worth your while to stop us," he said directly. "We wish to make it worth your while to allow us to leave."

The young woman paused, as if deciding how to phrase the translation, then spoke in Khmer without expression. The Colonel sat for several minutes, studying his prisoner.

"You are mistaken about someone making it worth our while to detain you," he said finally through the interpreter. "You were carrying drugs."

Adam locked eyes with the Cambodian officer, who seemed to notice for the first time that one of Adam's might be prosthetic. The realization seemed to unnerve him.

"We were pulled aside immediately when they checked our names," Adam said, aware that the man fully understood what he was saying without translation. The interpreter was simply serving to give the Colonel time to formulate answers. "I could see our motorcycles from the passport counter when I was told to go with the guard. No one had inspected them yet."

"We had been warned that you would be arriving at the border with drugs," the woman said, conveying the officer's response. "When your motorcycles were inspected, the drugs were found."

"I see," Adam said, unable to keep a cynical smile from curling his lips. "Drugs that looked suspiciously like the ones that were taken from the Australians the day before. Well, whatever the reason you detained us, I think you know we are not drug smugglers and have done nothing damaging to your country or your people. And we are in a position to make it personally worthwhile for you to allow us to cross safely into Vietnam."

The interpreter spoke back to him in English. "I don't understand the meaning of 'personally worthwhile.'"

"I mean we will pay you a very large amount of money if you will allow us to leave."

The interpreter hesitated, but the Colonel answered directly.

"You are offering me a bribe," he said.

"Let's call it a settlement," Adam corrected. "If you will permit me a phone call, I will have delivered to you twenty-five thousand dollars for each of us: myself and both of my traveling companions. If you will release the two Australians with us, we will pay another twenty-five for each of them. And we will give your able assistant here ten thousand dollars as well." He nodded toward the interpreter, who flushed visibly.

The Colonel leaned back comfortably in his chair and steepled his fingers in front of his heavily decorated chest.

"Bribery is a very serious crime in my country," he said solemnly.

"I have no desire to offer you a bribe," Adam said evenly. "I am trying to correct a wrong that was made when we were mistakenly detained. I know that it would be an embarrassment to admit to your superiors, if they are even aware that we are here, that a mistake was made. We just want to make it worthwhile to you to bear the burden of that error."

The Colonel flexed the steepled fingers against each other and worked his gaze systematically over Adam's face, returning to stare at his left eye. Finally he turned to the young woman who stood beside him.

"This man wishes to give us both money to correct an unfortunate error," he said in clear, but heavily accented English. "What do you think of that?"

The woman's face darkened another shade and she bowed slightly, in no particular direction.

"I am here only to serve you," she murmured.

The Colonel smiled thinly and turned again to Adam. "My error, should it turn out to be one, would indeed be an embarrassment to myself and a barrier to future opportunities. I am not certain that twenty-five thousand for each of you would allow me to endure the stain that such an admission would place on my name – and on my record. Plus, the Australians are guilty – without question."

It was Adam's turn to examine the creased, brown face of the Cambodian officer. He had known when they were arrested that the man had his price. That was never the question. They were now negotiating how much it was worth to have to explain, to whomever had asked him to detain the Americans, that the prisoners had been released.

"I can understand your concern," he said after a moment's pause. "This could indeed be a source of some embarrassment. I think I may be able to arrange for as much as forty thousand for each of us. That would be two hundred thousand dollars for five prisoners, when safely into Vietnam. And I will provide twenty thousand to your assistant." The interpreter swallowed hard but remained silent, staring ahead into the wall. Adam guessed that this would be close to three year's salary for the woman.

"Perhaps if we could make it two hundred fifty thousand, the damage to my reputation and career could be endured," the Colonel said. "I am certain my interpreter would be satisfied with the twenty thousand you offer."

"I'm not sure I can make that happen," Adam said, not wanting the Colonel to think he had settled for too little.

The officer shrugged and tilted his head to one side while his assistant held her breath.

"Honor can be priceless in my society," he said. "And prison can be most unpleasant."

Adam nodded. "Let me make a call and see if I can arrange it."

"Do you want to add the other American for an additional fifty thousand dollars" the Colonel offered.

"The old sex offender?"

The Colonel nodded.

"Is he here for sex with children?" Adam asked.

"Yes. He bought two young girls and kept them in his apartment in

Svay Riang."

"Let him rot in hell," Adam said.

The Colonel nodded grimly. "If you can make this call and if you can arrange for this amount, how will the transfer be made?"

"I will have an embassy official from Phnom Penh bring the money here tomorrow morning – very confidentially. Only you, he, and your assistant will know the transfer has occurred. He will hold it until we are safely in Ho Chi Minh City. Then he will give you the money."

"An officer from the Embassy?" The Colonel raised a surprised brow. "You are someone who can get this amount of money from the Embassy in one day?"

"It will be sent overnight to the Embassy. Let's just say I am someone who can make that happen."

"And once you are in Vietnam, if your courier chooses not to give me the money, knowing that one cannot accept bribes in this country?"

"He will know that arrangements of this kind are a way of doing business in this country," Adam said with a smile. "And he will also be carrying two hundred and seventy thousand dollars in cash. I'm certain that if he tries to keep it from you, you can find a small bag of drugs somewhere to place in the back of his automobile."

"But he would have diplomatic immunity...."

"Only if others know what happened to him," Adam said.

"I see that you are a very clever man," the Colonel said.

"If I were clever, I would have anticipated being stopped by you at the border. But I can tell you this. The people I work for know I made it to this border crossing. And within a few weeks, they would have figured out what happened to me. We're making this arrangement because I can't wait that long to get back to America. But if you choose to keep us here until they have to find us – or if you decide to dispose of us in some other way – I can assure you, Colonel, that all of the influence of your government won't be able to save you. Remember that, if you think about changing your mind."

The Colonel's expression didn't change, but Adam noted a hard swallow.

"I am not a man who goes back on his word," the officer said defensively.

"Good. If I can call now, the money can be here in the morning.

When we are released, I would like our motorcycles, phones, and passports returned."

This time the officer's face fell visibly. "I am afraid I cannot recover all of your belongings," he said nervously. "Your passports, yes. But as prisoners, your other belongings were disposed of."

"That just cost you that extra fifty thousand dollars," Adam said. "Now... let's make the phone call."

# TWENTY-NINE

In the electronic beehive near Ashburn, Virginia, that served as the nerve center for Unit I, Nita pushed away from one of the data consoles and grinned broadly at Fisher.

"Here we thought we may have lost Zak, and then he calls with a request that we unload someone else's bank account to get him out of jail. How much is he asking for?"

"Two hundred twenty thousand," Fisher said with the same amusement. "That must have been some negotiation – both with this Eckerson kid and with the Cambodian colonel!"

"And he asked for the money to come from Eckerson's personal account?"

"Always concerned about the budget. He had all the account numbers and passwords. We're to get a secure courier in Phnom Penh to take it to a Colonel Chey at the provincial prison in Svay Rieng Province....all but twenty thousand. He wants that delivered directly into the hands of the Colonel's interpreter."

"But hold the money until Zak, Eckerson, the Robb woman, and two Australians have lifted off from Tan Son Nhut...?"

Fisher nodded. "Zak wants the group in the air before the exchange is made. He apparently doesn't have a great deal of faith in this Colonel Chey."

"Our plane's still on the ground in Vietnam. I'll get a van to the border to bring them into Saigon and arrange to include the two Aussies on the manifest. What do we do with them when they get here?"

"It's no longer Saigon," Fisher chuckled. "Someday I'll get you to say Ho Chi Minh City,"

"Not in this lifetime," Nita said. "So, what do we do with the Aussies?"

"We'll bring them into Seattle, give them a little money, and turn them loose. They don't know anything and aren't likely to want to make a media splash in the U.S. after having been picked up for drug trafficking. Eckerson and Robb can talk to anyone they wish. Let's get all four names on a commercial manifest so if they start telling some story about being whisked out of Southeast Asia on a secret flight, they'll just look like publicity hounds. And I'm sure for their own safety's sake, Zak will impress on them the need to keep quiet. We need to get him back out of sight and on the trail of our Weavers."

Nita scooted forward until her round belly creased against the counter that held her keyboards.

"Anything else he wants?

"They took his phone at the border. Before they got it, he activated the buttons that fried its memory, but wants to know if there were any texts or calls in the last seventy-two hours."

"I'll get a recovery request in and see what's there," she said. "But first, let me get this money moving."

. . .

Nine had been in touch with Five, the man the world knew as Marshall Ding, on a twice-daily basis since the Sason woman evaded Four and disappeared. Ding had gone back into every security program and changed the access passwords: his own and the one Nine could use to trigger *Seres*.

After discovering that Dreu had hacked his programs, Ding spent most of the first night fretting over how she did it. He knew his superstitions about passwords were a potential vulnerability, but only if someone knew about them. Somehow Dreu had discovered the pattern, and she was definitely bright enough to develop an algorithm that could tease out the passwords. And he knew she had created the dummy account. What troubled him was that he couldn't figure out how she had been able to test thousands of passwords without triggering a shutdown alert. But the new passwords he had created were completely randomized, twenty character selections of letters, numbers and symbols in any order. Even if she tried to explain to the authorities what she had discovered, she could never get into the programs again to show them the hidden code.

Since discovering the breach, Ding had also issued new versions of the security programs to each of his clients, including those serviced by Sason and Anthony, with a personal call to the head of system security at each agency. One of FedTegrity's senior programmers, he told them apologetically, had gone rogue. Though there was no evidence she had compromised any of their systems, the woman had knowledge that could potentially allow her to do so. The new program versions were completely secure and clients had no reason for concern. FedTegrity had identified the potential problem before it could become one, and Dreu Sason was no longer with the company. If she should attempt to contact anyone within a client organization, they were to notify the Dallas office of the Federal Bureau of Investigation. Then Ding called the FBI himself to let them know there could be an imminent cyber-terrorist threat in the Dallas area.

# THIRTY

At 33,000 feet over the Pacific, Adam sat alone in a small office compartment in the rear of one of the CIA's Embraer Legacy 650s: a Brazilian-made aircraft used by Central Intelligence because it attracted less attention in foreign ports than an American-made plane, and because it had the qualities the Agency liked in an intercontinental business jet. It was designed with a range of 3,800 nautical miles when carrying eight passengers, allowing trans-oceanic flight from either coast at airspeed above 500 knots. Riding the jet stream, the flight back to Seattle had scheduled refueling stops in Tokyo and Anchorage, but the eight seats in the main cabin reclined into comfortable beds and all but Adam were now making up for lost sleep.

He was exhausted – almost to the point of being beyond sleep – and was seated beside the fax, waiting for a printout from Fisher of phone messages left on his cell since it was confiscated at the Cambodian border. There would be nothing job-critical – an admission that made his anxiety seem a little unprofessional. He just wanted to hear from Dreu. And his attempts to reach her using the secure on-board phones had been unsuccessful.

He and the other detainees had showered and been given a change of clothes at a VIP terminal at Tan Son Nhut, then boarded the plane and slept during the first leg into Japan's Norita International Airport. When the Legacy touched down and rolled to a stop beside a fuel truck at a remote hangar in the freight portion of the sprawling airfield, the Australians and Davis Eckerson didn't stir in their seats, desperately making up for hours lost keeping watch in the chaotic prison.

As the descent began into Norita, Adam had opened his eyes to see Angie staring at him from across the aisle. Since the group reassembled at the border for the transfer to Vietnam, she had been completely mute, watching every action and following each instruction with dark, furtive eyes, her lips a hard, immovable line. Though dirty and unkempt, something else had changed.

Adam straightened in his seat, watched her for a few moments while her eyes stayed connected to his, then stood and beckoned for her to follow him into the rear office. Two white leather lounge chairs, separated by a low table, sat against a sloping wall opposite the desk, and he invited her into one and took the other. They sat in silence for several minutes with Angie gazing intently at a spot on the table between them.

"What?" she finally spat at him, raising her eyes and twisting her mouth into a quivering pucker.

"Rough few days," Adam said softly, leaving it as a statement rather than a question.

The quiver in her lips spread across her face and she leaned forward onto her hands, her body shuddering with deep, anguished sobs. He pushed forward onto his knees and wrapped her in his arms, pressing his cheek against her black hair. When the sobs subsided, he continued to hold her silently until she straightened, then pushed back onto his heels but remained kneeling. She glanced at the door and he reached up and twisted the lock closed.

"It was horrible," she said finally, her voice barely audible. She shook her head slowly from side-to-side struggling for a place to begin.

"There were fifty women in there – all together in one big room with no running water and nothing but buckets for toilets, just…just sitting out in front of God and everybody."

Adam waited without moving. This was a horror she would have recovered from as soon as she was released and had a chance to clean up. He knew there was more.

Angie leaned forward again, gazing at her hands. "Lots of the women had children... most of them babies," she murmured. "No one spoke any English so we sort of used sign language. I asked if they were able to bring their babies with them when they were sent to prison…."

Adam felt a tightness rise in his throat, knowing where this was going.

"The women said no… and when the guards came with our food, pointed at them and then at the babies." She glanced up at Adam to see if there was any trace of judgment in his face. Seeing none, she drew a slow breath.

"The first evening when they came with the soup, they looked at me and laughed, and one came over and grabbed my breast and I slapped him. I thought he'd hit me, but it just made the three of them laugh all the harder – and one sort of humped at me with his hips. When they left, they pointed back at me like I'd better watch out."

She paused and twisted nervously in the chair, glancing up again to read Adam's face. He thought of taking her hand or of slipping back into the chair to give her more space, but decided to stay where he was. She straightened even more in her seat and lifted her chin, a new look of resolve in her dark eyes.

"Then they came back that night – when everyone was lying on their mats trying to get the children to go to sleep. It was black as pitch in there and I was curled up against the back wall, trying not to be sick from how bad the place smelled and how close everyone was to me.... And then they came back."

She tucked her hands in against her stomach and leaned into them as if she were going to retch on the floor.

"As soon as they heard the door, the other women moved away from me – and none of them tried to do anything," she whispered. "I fought and screamed and no one did anything. The babies were all crying, and no one came. One of the men pulled my arms up above my head while I was on the floor and knelt across them, grabbing my hair and holding it down against the floor on both sides of my head. And they pulled my clothes off, and another one stood with his boots on my ankles... and they raped me. All of them. And...no one did anything."

She looked up and laid her head to one side, her face a resigned 'so, now you know.' He reached forward and took her hands in both of his, squeezing them gently.

"I'm so sorry," he whispered. "Sorry you had to be part of this." He wanted to say, "Did they hurt you in other ways?" but knew how insensitive that would sound.

She understood his unspoken question and pulled her hands free, reaching down to raise the hems of her jeans. Deep purple bruises ringed her shins and ankles, with places where the skin was raw and broken by the heavy-soled boots that had clamped her against the concrete.

"Just this. They didn't hit me or anything."

"I'll have a doctor waiting when we get to Seattle." He paused, then quietly said again, "I'm so sorry. I should have left you in the village and gone to see Phyllis Morin on my own."

"I won't get pregnant," she said, telling him her immediate thoughts hadn't yet moved beyond the assault. "I had my pills in my purse and told them they were for my heart. They let me keep them." She gave him a wry smile. "Guess they don't want you to have a heart attack when you're in there."

"We'll still have you checked, and get you some antibiotics when we land to make sure...."

She silenced him with a shake of her head. "I don't want to think about it," she said.

Adam backed up into his chair. "This remains between us," he said. "You can choose to tell who you wish, but no one will hear anything from me."

"I don't know...," Angie murmured, as if speaking to herself. "I have some friends who were raped.... It never goes away. But a couple of them got married... and I know one told her husband."

Adam rose quietly and kissed her on the top of the head. "Stay in here as long as you want," and he left her to her thoughts.

She was back in the main cabin before the others awoke, still somber but communicative.

"It's amazing what a little sleep can do," she said to one of the Australians as he plopped beside her and asked how she was feeling. "You two look like you had a rough time."

"They beat the bloody hell out of us," he grinned, then grimaced as a split in his lower lip opened again.

"A place out of hell," she said.

Adam returned to the office compartment, waiting for the transmission from Fisher. In addition to the phone messages, his Control had promised information about the Weavers they had been able to track down. As he worked through next steps in his head, the machine beside the desktop whirred with the uneven buzz of ink jets spitting out type.

The first sheet contained voice and text messages that had gone to his phone over the past three days. All but one were from Dreu's phone. A voice message insisted that she needed to talk to him as soon as he could call. "I need your advice on a pretty serious matter," she said without explanation. The final text was from a number he didn't recognize, but he knew it was related and that whatever Dreu's 'matter' was, it had become worse.

"Hey," the text said. "This is Jess. Major storms in the area. Almost got struck by lightning. Just be riding the breeze 'til it blows through."

# THIRTY-ONE

The wiry Asian who met Art Dempsey in an overly neat, third story office of the FedTegrity Building was wiping beads of perspiration from his high forehead despite an air-conditioning system that had ambient temperatures in the room hovering in the upper sixties. The head of the FBI's Dallas field office shook Ding's moist hand and introduced Special Agent Brandon Hatch who had been assigned to be lead investigator, once the Bureau knew what it was dealing with. In the next office, two analysts from the Bureau's cybercrime division in Washington were already at work on Dreu Sason's computer with a set of carefully prepared, hand-written instructions from Marshall Ding, handed to them when the team came through the door.

Arthur Dempsey was an imposing African-American with short-cropped salt and pepper hair and a deeply-pitted complexion that made shaving a frustrating and painful part of his daily morning ritual to look the part of Special Agent in Charge. But to those who met him, there was no question that he had succeeded completely. He had the body and presence of an NFL linebacker scanning a formation the moment before the snap. Though he had been a high school standout athlete in two sports, he had chosen to fully commit his undergraduate education to getting into a first-tier law school, graduating third in his law class at Georgetown and working for five years as a prosecutor in D.C. before joining the Bureau. The agents in the Dallas office worshipped the man, but cautioned visitors to be wary of his powerful grip.

"When you shake his hand," they advised, "push yours in as far as you can, so he doesn't have you across the knuckles. The man has no sense of his own strength."

Marshall Ding was massaging his own right palm as Dempsey began the questioning.

"Go over with us again the concerns that led you initially to suspect this woman," the Agent in Charge said as the three settled around Ding's desk. "We've run what background we could on her in the time we've had, and she seems to be a model citizen." He smiled to himself, catching the unintended pun that apparently escaped the others.

Ding wiped at his forehead and adjusted a pad of notes that sat in front of him on the desk. "It started several weeks ago – perhaps months now – when she began to express concerns about our own internal security protocols. You know our business, so you know how imperative it is for us to have absolute security *within* our own organization. We have made it policy to limit access to our most sensitive client programs only to the lead designer. That way we can assure those we serve that their system information is available to as few people as possible. My personal motto is 'People compromise security. Limit people: maximize security.'"

"And she disagreed with that philosophy?" Dempsey prompted. His voice was a deep baritone that seemed to add to Ding's uneasiness.

"She came to me and said she thought all three senior designers should be able to fully access each other's work – so we could check on each other, if you will."

"In some ways, that's a very reasonable recommendation," Dempsey observed. "Though I understand the logic of your motto, one could argue that the more limited access is to a very few, the more it empowers those few to manipulate the system unobserved. Plus, what if something happens to one of the senior designers?"

"We have what we call the 'City Bus' protocol," Ding chuckled nervously. "Named after the old saying 'What if one of us should get run over by a city bus…?' All of the key passwords are locked in a safe here in my office, and only I and my assistant have the combination. If we need to, we can get into anyone's files using those passwords."

"Which compromises your motto to some degree already," Dempsey said, "…with you as the exception."

Ding nodded hesitantly. "Someone has to be," he said.

"And I assume that's why you were able to give us Sason's passwords," Hatch guessed.

"Right. As I said on the phone, we have an alert built into all of our computers that lets us know if someone is trying to access programs we've developed or are working on. I hadn't received any alerts, but noticed when I logged in one morning that there had been activity with some of my accounts during the night. Dreu was beginning to spend a lot of late nights in the office, so I stayed one night as well. About 1:00 a.m. someone entered my accounts and I was able to trace the activity to a computer with an account name I didn't recognize. But Dreu was the only other person in the building."

"And did you confront her?" Dempsey asked.

"She shut down immediately and it didn't seem wise for me to confront her in an empty building in the middle of the night."

"But you have twenty-four hour building security…."

"True. But I wanted others in the office to be here when I asked her about it – so it would be more than a 'he said-she said' kind of thing."

'And that was last Friday night?"

"Yes. Well…early Saturday morning."

"And she didn't come in this morning."

Ding nodded, dabbing at his forehead. "And we couldn't reach her by phone. So I sent someone by her apartment and no one was there."

"All this checking before calling us?"

"Yes. For obvious reasons, I wanted to see if we could resolve this internally."

"So you got her passwords, went into her computer, and found that she had authorized this other account under the name Tanvi."

"Yes. Exactly."

"And what makes you think this is more than a stubborn attempt on her part to provide that redundancy she was arguing for?"

Ding nodded as if he had anticipated the question. "But how did she get *my* passwords without setting off our internal intrusion alert? Hacking into parts of our own system that she didn't have normal access to is bad enough, but intentionally developing programs to search out a colleague's passwords while bypassing our own security – well, that's more than an ethical breach. It shows intent to do damage." He again patted his hairline with a wadded handkerchief.

"What she was doing seems to prove her point," Dempsey said. "Your systems aren't foolproof."

"Not if you're one of the developers," Ding muttered.

"Her point exactly."

Ding's thin lips began to quiver. "That may be. But rather than coming to me, she disappeared. That's what really got my attention."

"Given the nature of your work and clients, you did right to report it – and to us," Dempsey said, looking up as there was a sharp warning rap on the door and one of the analysts from Bureau Headquarters entered the office. At the same moment, Hatch's cell buzzed loudly and he moved past his entering colleague to take the call in the hallway.

The Washington agent was a woman in her late twenties, dressed in the traditional dark skirt and jacket. She had chocolate brown skin and her thin, serious face was framed by short-cropped black hair, with deep brown eyes that were all business. She nodded perfunctorily at Ding but spoke to Dempsey.

"Some interesting stuff here," she said without formalities. "And this is one smart lady, by the way." She dropped a yellow legal pad on the desk in front of the Dallas agent.

"She's been working at this all last week, entering the system in the wee hours of the morning through this bogus account she set up. She developed a very elaborate algorithm that ran potential password combinations for Mr. Ding here, and came up with all of them for the programs she wanted to look at." The analyst looked critically across the desk at Ding.

"You must have a pattern you follow when creating your passwords that she somehow knew about. Not very smart, for a high security program developer."

Ding crinkled the handkerchief in his fist. "The pattern assists with memory and there's no risk in the pattern unless someone is aware of it," he defended.

"That's just what I said," the woman said unsympathetically. "Well, anyway, the real stroke of genius is that she designed the algorithm so that after every password attempt, it triggered a re-set command on the program that normally shuts down the computer if too many wrong passwords are entered. She was definitely systematically going through her boss's files – including his copies of some she had written herself. Logged into the system for only a short time very early Saturday morning, then shut down suddenly. As far as we can tell, she didn't alter anything. Just examined the programs."

"What do you think she was looking for?" Dempsey asked the senior designer.

"I have no idea. Perhaps she was looking for ways to alter them without being caught."

"I need Special Agent Fordyce here to look through one of the programs she accessed," Dempsey said. "I know they're top secret, but she has all the clearances. We need to see if we can tell what Sason was trying to do."

"Naturally, I'm re-writing them all right now," Ding said hastily. "I'll log her into one of the earlier versions that Dreu was looking at, and she can study it as much as she wants."

"I already have your passwords," Fordyce said. "Sason teased them all out."

Ding shook his head. "They've all been changed. I'll have to log you in with a new one. Come – I'll find you a station." He rose as Special Agent Hatch reentered the office.

"Here's an interesting little twist," he frowned, looking first at Fordyce, then toward his boss. "Our lady has a love interest. Fairly recent. A man named Adam Zak who she met about four months ago at the Lifetime Fitness Center just south of where she lives. One of our people went to Zak's home and, though no one was there, the doors were unlocked, the alarm system off, and it looked like there'd been some kind of struggle in an upstairs bathroom. Tub partially full, water all over the floor – and bullet holes in one bathroom wall and in the front doorframe."

"Any blood?"

"No, sir," Hatch said.

"What do we know about this Adam Zak?" Dempsey asked, rising to follow Ding from the office.

"That's just the thing," Hatch said. "He's renting the place and has a driver's license and cell phone through Verizon, but beyond that, the man doesn't exist."

. . .

The cryptic message from Dreu was the kind that drove Adam absolutely crazy. He was a man who hated unresolved situations that he couldn't do anything about: itches that couldn't be scratched. He knew from past experience that calling an unknown number, several days after the fact, to ask about circumstances he didn't understand, wasn't smart – even if he thought he knew who the message was from. But he was still at least a day away from being back in McKinney, and it was eating at him that he didn't know what was happening to Dreu.

The fax began to spit out a second sheet: the first line a one-word heading that simply said *Weavers*. One-by-one the machine sprayed out ten names, eight of them followed by a home address and occupation. Adam scanned the first line and felt the hairs rise on the back of his neck.

*Bradley Han     811 Laurel Crest Road, Severn, MD*
*National Security Agency*

Well, so much for figuring out how Han might relate to the Weavers! The NSA specialist was one of them. Little wonder this bunch always seemed to know who was going to be where, and what would happen next.

Adam let the thought play through his mind that the Weavers could formally be connected to the NSA in some legitimate way. He certainly hoped the hell not, if they were taking shots at innocent Americans in the jungles of Cambodia.

He ran his eye further down the list. Three entries below was the name of Helen Robb and beside it an asterisk. His eye dropped to the bottom of the sheet where a note indicated that she was deceased and giving the date of death. Adam ran the date backward through his mental calendar. It was two days after he had been asked to follow up on the anonymous note to the Director advising that someone should investigate a link between Han, Marshall Ding, and some group called the Weavers. Too close to be coincidental.

He looked quickly at the two names with no additional information, *Marion Chan* and *Lawrence Li*, then scanned down the rest of the page. The second to the last name brought Adam's senses to high alert.

*Marshall Ding     1663 N. Colbert Ave., Dallas, TX*
*FedTegrity Security Systems*

Ding was also one of them. So what did that mean about others at FedTegrity? Was he playing Dreu, or was Dreu playing the man who had been assigned to investigate the anonymous tip? Chance meeting at the gym? Sympathy story about a stalker-slasher? He didn't like what the thoughts said about him: that he could have a moment's doubt about the genuineness of Dreu's affection…and that it was his first concern when he saw Ding's name. But a man in his line of business had to think first about survival.

He looked again at Dreu's cryptic text, trying to work through the possibilities. *This is Jess. Major storms in the area. Almost got struck by lightning. Just be riding the breeze 'til it blows through.* Maybe it wasn't from Dreu at all, but was an attempt to draw him out through a return call. Only Dreu would know about "Jess" and "Breeze," so somehow she was connected to this message. But if she were trying to get him to reveal his location, she wouldn't have needed this clever charade – just a text that said "I had to change phones and need you to call me at this new number." He would have called immediately. No – Dreu was in trouble because she *wasn't* involved in whatever Ding and the Weavers were up to, and had gotten tangled up in the web – just as the Eckerson kid had. And like Eckerson, they were after her and she needed to be where only he could find her.

Now, the only real kicker was whether this Weaver bunch was connected in some legitimate way with the NSA. Adam scanned the list again. Most of them worked in positions that involved computers and programming. And God knew the NSA was all about gathering information about everything and everybody. It was remotely possible that while the CIA Director and Fisher had been developing the invisible Unit 1, some other arm of America's security apparatus that Jim Thompson was connected to had been cultivating these Weavers. Thompson's trips to Paoy Snoul may not have been to learn about the Weavers, but to check on their progress, should he disappear. And if Adam aided in blowing the cover off some friendly black-ops network that had taken fifty years to develop, as his Uncle Max used to say, "His ass would be grass." And so would Unit 1.

For the next ten minutes, Adam sat hunched in one of the cabin's white leather lounge chairs, chin propped on a thumb and fingers curled against his upper lip, sorting through the possibilities. The equation, he decided, yielded four permutations, derived from two oppositional possibilities: Dreu was complicit with Ding, or she wasn't involved with whatever he was up to; the Weavers were part of a U.S. intelligence operation, or they were enemies of the state. If one of those permutations was correct – that Dreu was not involved, and the Weavers were a threat to American security, he had to act. If any of the other combinations was true and he did what he was about to do, he was screwed. And so were

Fisher and his operation.

He knew communication links from the plane were as close as you could get to being untraceable. Without thinking of the time difference, he snatched the phone from the desktop and dialed the cell number in "Jess's" note. After the fourth ring, a sleep-thickened voice murmured "hello?"

"Dreu?"

"Oh, Adam!" Her voice was immediately sharp and focused. "I'm in such a mess! Where are you?"

"On a plane. But I finally got to where I could pick up your messages. Tell me what's going on."

For the next ten minutes, Dreu described her expedition into the programming world of Marshall Ding and her discovery of the backdoors and hidden suicide commands. She finished with her encounter with the woman in his upstairs bathroom.

"But you're alright?" he asked.

"Yes, but you've got a bullet hole in the wall above the tub," she concluded.

Adam was silent for a full minute, running Ding's programming intentions through his head while he looked over the list of Weavers and tried to fit what he had heard into his permutations.

"Are you still there?" Dreu interrupted.

"Yes. Thinking…. So Ding can take control of these major systems through their security software and shut them down in such a way that any attempt to install a backup will be unsuccessful."

"That's what it looks like. He's put himself and whoever has the other password in a position to essentially delete major operating systems – shut down Air Traffic Control, the Social Security Administration, Federal Payroll, and any other system with the termination order. I suspect he goes back into each of our programs and inserts the same information before we ship them to the clients. But the woman they sent after me said she was 'police.' I know I'm getting paranoid, but I don't have any idea who I can trust."

"So why are you trusting me with all this?"

She hesitated. "I don't know…. You just seem…trustworthy. Am I wrong about that?"

Adam closed his eyes and ran a cold hand over the top of his bristled scalp.

"No," he said without hesitation. "Describe the woman who attacked you. If she's Federal and in the Dallas area, I might know who she is."

"Asian. Probably Chinese descent, though I think born here. Petite. About 5'2" or 5'3". Short black hair and dark eyes. I might normally say she was pretty, but she was trying to kill me."

"Age?"

"Hard to say. I'd guess forty-five to fifty."

Adam paused again as the fax beside him began to zip through a new message from Fisher. He read it quickly and when he returned to his call, his voice had a new edge. Another of the permutations had reared its ugly head...the possibility that Dreu was innocent, but that the Weavers *were* somehow connected to U.S. intelligence.

"Dreu, you're in very serious danger. I know where you are. With Breeze, right?"

"Yes, I...."

"Just listen. Stay out of sight and don't call anyone. Don't even *talk* to anyone you don't have to. I'll be in the country in about seven hours and will come to you as soon as I can...."

"Adam, what's this all about?" He could hear the fear in her voice.

"I'm not sure, but I'm starting to get a better idea. I have friends who can help. Is there any way you can think of to override these programs, if we can't get to these people and stop them?"

"What do you mean, 'we'... and 'these people?' Are there more than just Ding? ...and are you involved in this somehow?"

"I'll explain when I see you and yes, I think there could be more than Ding. Any ideas about a solution?"

"There might be one possibility...."

"Can you work on it off-line?"

"If I can get some thumb drives. And I'd have to download a copy of 'C.'"

"C?"

Yes. It's the programming language we use."

"Is there anyone you can trust to get the drives for you?"

"I think so."

"I'm going to have someone send a copy of C to your host's computer. She'll need to have it on so they can access it."

"How will they know what computer?"

"I can't explain right now, but they'll find it. Work on solutions off-line to the degree you can without anyone knowing where you are. And I mean 'no risks!' Okay?"

"Adam...how are you involved in this?"

"I'll tell you when I see you. Just stay out of sight."

"Do you think they're still trying to find me?"

"I know they are – and they have lots of ways to look. So stay low," he said, looking again at the latest fax. The brief message from Fisher said:

> *One of your Weavers, Marshall Ding, has convinced the FBI to issue an APB on a Dreu Sason, one of his employees. Claims she is involved in cyber terrorism. They are also looking for a friend of hers and person of interest – an Adam Zak of McKinney, Tex. We need to talk.*

# THIRTY-TWO

Special Agent Hatch had Adam Zak's telephone messages displayed in inch-high letters on a projector screen with the final one from "Jess" highlighted in yellow. He was huddled in a small conference room in the Bureau's Dallas office on Justice Way with Dempsey and Special Agent Fordyce, who had remained in Dallas after the search of Dreu Sason's computers.

Hatch ran a red laser dot over the first set of messages. "These earlier ones are clearly from Sason and seem to be related to the case. On the Saturday morning Ding caught her in his files, she tells this Zak that she needs his advice about something important. Over the weekend there are two other very short messages asking him to call as soon as he can. Although nothing explicitly refers to her activity at FedTegrity, the tone and timing certainly suggest a connection to what was going on at work."

The other agents nodded in mute agreement.

"It seems unusual, given the nature of her responsibilities, that she would be seeking advice from a fairly new acquaintance, even if he is a love interest, unless...."

Fordyce completed the sentence for him. "...unless his involvement with her extends to work. It strikes me as more than coincidental that after being with FedTegrity for more than a year, she suddenly develops this concern about internal checks and balances shortly after Mr. Right steps into her life."

"From what I've read about her, she hardly seems like someone who could easily be swayed to get involved in cybercrime – no matter how persuasive Mr. Right might be," Dempsey cautioned. "She doesn't need money. Gave up a dream career that was making her richer than any of us will ever be, and invested well. Hasn't suffered from lack of attention or any need for personal affirmation. And nothing we can find in her history would suggest a motive to want to damage the United States. If she's collaborating with this guy for some reason, what's the motive?"

"Being an attractive woman doesn't mean you're emotionally secure," Fordyce said. "Look at all the celebrity meltdowns we see every week. Maybe she left the modeling profession because she was running away from something – like her own insecurities. And that Marchisio character carved her up pretty badly. She might be kind of desperate to have someone care about her."

Dempsey's nod was qualified. "It's possible, but the people who know her present her as being pretty well adjusted and self-assured. But we're getting off track here. I'm interested in knowing more about this Zak character."

Hatch reentered the conversation, firing his laser pointer at the bottom entry. "This last one – this text message from 'Jess' – is a great example of why Zak is such an enigma. When we try to track down his friends to see if we can locate a Jess, we have trouble locating any friends at all. He's renting the place he gave the fitness center as his address, and there are no neighbors or known associates named Jess. In fact, no neighbors who seem to know much about him at all. He travels a great deal and keeps pretty much to himself when he's home. There are some people at the gym who he works out with on occasion, though he's generally there to play racquetball with Sason. And the others there don't know anything about his background. One person thought he worked for the airlines, but if he does, we can't find the employment record. In fact, there really is no record of this man."

"Which makes him suspect just on the face of it," Dempsey said. "People who are this hard to find, are hard to find for a reason."

Fordyce studied the screen as if it might somehow reveal something they had overlooked. "Could recently be out of prison and changed his name," she suggested.

"We checked on releases for three months prior to his appearance in McKinney and couldn't find anyone who matched his description," Hatch said. "Plus, his house is full of one set of prints that must belong to him and there are no matches – nationally or through Interpol."

"Doesn't exist for a reason," Dempsey repeated. "And I think we all agree that this last message is probably from Sason. Her attempt at a code of some kind."

"Assuming that it is from Sason, he must somehow connect her with "Jess," and the first part isn't really too subtle," Hatch said. " *'Major storms in the area....'* The evening this was sent, there was no severe weather anywhere in Texas. So it's referring to some other kind of storm. And the *'Almost got struck by lightning'* could mean she'd almost been caught. We think this last sentence tells him where she is."

"*Jess* is the name of a programming language written in Java," Fordyce suggested. "It's what we call a 'rule engine,' and defines and executes some specific rule or policy. They may use it as a code name that signals that in a given situation, take some predetermined action. I think the key words here would be *'riding the breeze.'* Making any progress there?"

Hatch clicked the remote mouse and advanced his slides to one that showed a bicycle and a small, belt-mounted digital counter.

"Several possibilities. There's a maker of bikes, including a fairly popular mountain bike, called Breezer. This might be a signal that she's gone somewhere they take their mountain bikes. There's also a brand of pedometer called Breeze – so could refer to a place they walk or hike together."

He advanced to another slide that depicted two city transportation route diagrams. "*Breeze* is also the name of the fare pass used on MARTA: the Metropolitan Atlanta Rapid Transit Authority. The reference could be a clue that she's headed to Atlanta to some location they both know about. Same could be true of the bus service provided by the North County Transit Authority in Oceanside, California. They call it 'riding the Breeze.' But we don't know of any connection either has with Atlanta or Oceanside."

"She's from California," Dempsey reminded them.

"Yes. But the Bay area. A long way from Oceanside." Hatch clicked the mouse and the screen darkened. "There are two other possibilities that are more of a stretch. There's an all-inclusive resort in the Bahamas called Breezes Resort and Spa. We have people watching all arrivals into the Bahamas. And there was a filly a few years back called *Summer Breeze* that placed well on the quarter horse circuit. We're tracing her owner to see if, by some chance, she might be at a stable where she can be ridden. Or it could be something completely unrelated to any of these...."

"I'd rate the last two with the pedometer," Dempsey chuckled. "The transit systems seem most likely as a clue to a community location that means something to them both, even if we haven't found the connection. But let's put someone on every possibility. FedTegrity's clients are *very* nervous, and when they're nervous, *I'm* nervous."

Three sharp raps rattled the door of the conference room.

"Enter!" Dempsey said loudly, and a fortyish African-American woman with a stylish red wig cracked the door open and poked her head into the room.

"Yes, Lydia. What is it?" Dempsey asked.

"A call for you that I've transferred to line one."

"We're about to wrap this up. I'll be in the office in a moment."

"I think you may want to take it here," she said. "And now. It's the Director."

Dempsey raised a brow. "This is why I'm nervous," he said with an 'I told you so' smile and picked up the phone.

"This is Dempsey," he said officially, then listened in silence for several minutes, his face twisting into a puzzled frown.

"And did they say where this information came from?"

He listened again.

"Hmmm," he said finally. "Sounds like the kind of cooperation I would expect. But we'll respond accordingly, sir…. Yes, sir. We're on it."

He dropped the receiver into its cradle and looked at the other agents, the frown tightening his jaw. They sat expectantly.

"Change of plan," he said. "Our partners in the intelligence community have received information that convinces them Ding is the man we need to be watching. But we can't be too direct. They think he's part of a larger network that needs to be identified before any member can alert the others they're under surveillance. So… we start a very quiet investigation of Marshall Ding."

Special Agent Hatch placed the remote on the table. "And Sason's not part of this network?"

"They – whoever *they* is – don't believe so. She may have had legitimate reasons to be concerned about internal security."

"So someone else has been investigating this thing too," Hatch said.

Dempsey nodded. "People who are hard to find, are hard to find for a reason," he repeated.

. . .

Had the group meeting with Dempsey seen the report from the agents who searched Adam Zak's rental on Hunter Chase Drive, they would have found that it told them very little about Zak – no more than they already knew – but one important thing about Dreu Sason. She rode horses. Marion Chan (aka Four) also had all of Sason's phone records for the past three days but happened to know this little bit of information. While steering Dreu through the master bedroom into the upstairs bath, she had seen a photograph of her on a table beside the bathroom door – riding at full gallop on a large brown horse with a white, diamond-shaped blaze on its forehead.

When Sason ran from the house in Virginia Hills, Four had struggled from the tub and fished her gun from the water, then rushed to the main floor with her left arm pressed tightly against her stomach. She had missed Sason with the shot from the top of the stairs, still unsteady and firing with her right hand. By the time Four reached the front door, Sason was already across the lawn and hobbling down the street. Four thought momentarily about another shot but realized she would probably miss and even if she didn't, neighbors might now be at the windows. She was at the corner by the time Sason could have made it to the next street and knew she had turned down the rear alley. But a quick walkthrough search turned up nothing and some Neighborhood Watch vigilante had seen her. Four was certain Sason had hidden in one of the yards, but rather than risk an encounter with police, she left McKinney and headed north.

Setting the arm in Durant had required surgery to insert two metal plates, each holding a fractured bone in place using six titanium screws. She had awakened in a private room in the regional hospital, groggy and aching across her entire left side. An IV drip tethered her to a bag of clear fluid that hung beside the bed, and a call button was strapped to her right wrist. She pushed the button and, in less than a minute, a white-uniformed nurse with blond hair pulled back under her cap was standing beside the bed. She looked like she couldn't be older than eighteen.

"Good afternoon, Ms. Chan. How are we feeling?"

Four was just uncomfortable enough to want to be sarcastic – to say "Well, I can't speak for *both* of us, but I feel like hell." But she didn't. No sense becoming more memorable than necessary, so she simply said, "A little sore, but not too bad. When can I get out of here?"

"You had a pretty bad break," the teen nurse said. "Both the radius and the ulna were broken – one in two places. So they had to insert plates and screw the bones into place. It's really important for them to heal right so you can rotate your forearm."

Four wondered if this lecture was the girl's way of letting her know she was a teen nurse who knew her business.

"They need to make sure the swelling is down and there's no infection before putting on a cast," the girl said. "The doctor was by an hour ago and thought it looked pretty good. He'll be back tonight after dinner."

"So, when can I leave?"

"If they can get the cast on tomorrow, you may be able to leave then. But that's up to Doctor Franks."

Four's head was starting to clear. "Can I have my phone? And the little notebook I carry."

"They'll be in the drawer," the nurse said, indicating a nightstand. "I'll get them for you, but you need to keep that arm still until the cast is on and the doctor gives you permission to start using it."

"The other one still works," Four said, deciding there was no reason to be completely pleasant.

The nurse retrieved the phone and when the girl was out of the room, Four sent a request to Seven's secure private number asking for voice messages and texts sent by Dreu Sason or received by Adam Zak during the previous forty-eight hours. While she waited, she sucked on ice chips from a bowl on the bedside table and tinkered with the switches that adjusted the hospital bed.

In less than ten minutes, her phone buzzed with a return text. She scanned the 'sent' and 'received' messages for Sason and Zak, noting that they were identical except for the final text to Zak. The Weaver recognized immediately that it had come from Dreu, and she believed she knew what it meant. Sason's discovery at FedTegrity was the storm. Four had produced the lightning strike. And Sason was somewhere riding that brown horse – a horse called *Breeze*.

# THIRTY-THREE

"Remind me...," Fisher said to Nita, leaning forward in his mechanized chair to place a lightly whiskered chin on his hand. "Did we ask Zak to take this assignment or did he contact us?"

"You contacted him," she grinned. "But you're wondering the same thing I am. How does he happen to get mixed up with this Sason woman before he could have known about her involvement with these Weavers – and vice versa?"

"He was investigating Ding and I suspect saw her as an avenue – unless she knew about his involvement with us and saw *him* as an avenue...."

"Virtually no chance," Nita said. "A) No one knows he works with the Unit. B) If they did know, there would be no reason to think the Unit would get involved with the Weaver thing. And C), even if we did...which I guess we did...there is one chance in six that Zak would be assigned to follow Eckerson. The odds are way too small."

"I follow you," Fisher said, "but to begin with, I don't like the fact that he's become involved with *anyone*. That's an unnecessary compromise, just for starters."

"Our people are regularly 'getting involved with someone' to get information. That's part of this messy business we're in."

Fisher nodded. "But I can tell from listening to him on the phone that this has moved beyond just using the woman. He really cares for her. That's the compromise."

"You have a girlfriend." Nita smiled. "Are you feeling compromise-ed?"

"Not the same," Fisher said testily. "You know what I do. I know what you do."

"Maybe having a girlfriend is a pretty smart part of staying under the radar," Nita offered. "I've seen Zak. He's the kind of guy who would draw attention if he weren't socially involved in some way. You just have this antiquated idea of the lone wolf out there, staying in his reclusive den. Nowadays those are the people who draw attention."

"So what do you think she thinks he does?"

"Not my job to wonder," Nita said. "And you know we have deep cover agents all over the intelligence community whose spouses don't know exactly what they do."

"Not among our people," Fisher grumbled.

"The problem with trying to manage half a dozen mavericks is that they're mavericks," Nita said. "We check them out as thoroughly as we can and train them as well as we can, but they're still mavericks."

"I always worry that their independence is going to get the best of them."

"We pick them because of that independence," she reminded him. "And if one becomes *too* independent, I guess that's the price we pay for valuing those obsessively free spirits. But Adam hasn't jumped ship. He's just not being what you have in your head as a model member of the club."

"And this attraction to Dreu Sason is okay?"

"You've seen her picture. If you ran into her, even at your age you'd be impressed. And if I were Sason and met Zak. *I'd* be impressed! Chemistry!"

"It's his job *not* to be impressed."

"Like I say – you're too old school," Nita laughed. "But he's convinced she's not part of it and that the Weavers are trying to hunt her down – using the Bureau to find her. How confident are you of your assurance to Zak that the Weavers aren't on our side? Connected to someone we don't know about?"

"The Director assures me they are not…assuming he knows. But I'm mainly convinced by what Zak says about the effect Marshall Ding's program modifications will have. I can't see any friendly explanation for being able to do that to our own systems."

Nita nodded her agreement. "Zak thinks she might be the person who can prevent the Weaver plan from working."

"Yes – and I don't like involving her in that either."

"But you arranged to have what he asked for waiting in Vietnam…and had the Director contact the Bureau and call off the search for Sason…and start watching this Marshall Ding."

"Zak's still our man," Fisher said. "Our whole operation is based on complete trust. If we don't go with him, we've got nothing."

"Exactly," Nita said.

. . .

Two hundred miles north of the Washington State coastline over Vancouver Island, Adam called his troupe together for a final briefing. He handed each of the Australians a thousand dollars from an envelope the pilot had given to him when they boarded in Ho Chi Minh City.

"Australia has an honorary consulate in Seattle, but if I were you, I'd head for the one in San Francisco. I don't think the Seattle guy does much more than ceremonial stuff. And don't take too much time getting to San Francisco or it will add more questions to the bunch you're already going to be asked. When they do grill you, just tell them the truth. They know you were detained in Cambodia, so tell them you were sprung by an American company that also had a couple of people there. Flown to Seattle from Vietnam and here you are."

"And what company would that be... if we're asked?" one of the Aussies wondered.

"You don't know."

"You don't think they'll find that a bit odd?"

"They might – but probably not under these circumstances. And you really don't know. So it will be the truth."

"And you want us to tell them we came in on a commercial flight...."

"Yes. You're on the passenger manifest for Delta flight 580 from Tokyo, along with Davis and Angie. It arrived at 5:25 pm. I'll give you your boarding passes when we land."

"So – this plane isn't coming in...officially?"

"Let's just say it's arriving as an international business flight with restricted passenger limitations. It will just be cleaner for everyone if you show them your flight documents and leave it at that."

"Suits us," the Australian said with a shrug. "We're out, thanks to you. Good on ya!"

Adam turned to Davis and Angie who now snuggled in one of the white leather chairs, Angie's head tucked in against Davis's shoulder while he held her tightly with an arm about her waist. For the past two hours they had been talking quietly.

"You two seem to be bonding," Adam grinned. "What are your plans?"

Angie turned her head slightly but remained wrapped in her

comfortable hug. "We're thinking we'll head down to Los Gatos and spend a few days at my place. This turned out to be a whole lot more than either of us bargained for, and we hope they've lost track of us. But if they're looking for Davis, it will be in St. Louis."

Adam nodded. "You've learned as much as you want to know about your mother's years in Cambodia?"

She shrugged against Davis's shoulder. "What more is there to know? Maybe there was some plan to get them involved in passing industrial secrets back to the Chinese, but I know mom didn't ever get into that. I mean, what are you going to pass along from PG&E? She married dad, and that ended all that for her."

Adam shifted his gaze to Davis. "And the investigative reporter has given up on Jim Thompson and the Weavers? Aren't you still curious what happened to the man?"

"Given up?" Eckerson said cynically. "To be honest, I'd like to be running from it! But I'd be dead three times over if you hadn't been there to save my sorry ass. I don't figure we're ever going to know what happened to Thompson, and don't know what you're planning to do to stop this Weaver thing. Angie wants us out completely, but I'd feel a lot better if I knew this was all finished – that whoever's after me was out of the way."

"I think we may be able to do that," Adam said. "But would the two of you be willing to help me with a couple of final things?"

They separated, looking suspiciously at Adam, then at each other."

"Depends on what it is," Davis said, keeping a tight grip on Angie's hand. "She's had about as much of this as she can take."

"This shouldn't change your plans too much and shouldn't add any danger for you," Adam said directly to Angie. He handed her a prepaid cell phone from the pilot's packet and in three minutes, outlined his request.

Angie shrugged. "I don't see why I can't do that." She looked at Davis. "But if you stay in this, I'm afraid you'll get hurt – or worse."

He gave her a quick kiss on the cheek. "This is one of those 'we'd always be looking over our shoulder' kind of deals if we don't see it to the end." He turned back to Adam. "What do you want from me?"

"Your part's a bit more complicated…." Adam said, and for the next fifteen minutes walked Davis through his plan. When he finished, Davis thought for a long moment.

"Yeah, I think I can do that. We need to go over it a few more times."

"As many as you need to feel comfortable."

"Okay. Where do we start?"

Adam smiled grimly. "First, we need to go see a lady about a horse."

# THIRTY-FOUR

The brief article in *America's Horse* featured Texas ranchers, members of the American Quarter Horse Association, who were actively promoting riding and horsemanship across the state. Four found the article on her smart phone while waiting for her arm to get beyond the 'chance of infection' stage. Two-thirds of the way through the piece, the author noted that Sandi Cooperman of Bonham, Texas, one of the state's most ardent and outspoken proponents of teaching children to ride, had successfully converted her father's cattle operation into a lucrative breeding and riding stable. The paragraph about Cooperman contained just the information Four was looking for.

*Cooperman's success can largely be attributed to her astute purchase from the New Mexico Bar-L Ranch of a two-year-old filly named Summer Breeze who went on to be a two year recipient of AQHA's Supreme Racehorse honors – a designation given to horses who win over $500,000 in a single year, win two or more open Grade 1 stakes races, and win at least 10 AQHA approved events. Cooperman built an impressive breeding stable around Summer Breeze before retiring her two years ago, but now commits most of her time and energy to promoting riding in north Texas.*

When she left the hospital in Durant, Four decided to stay clear of the Dallas area until she knew more about what had happened to Dreu Sason. She caught U.S. Highway 70 east to Hugo, just north of the Red River that borders East Texas. There, she turned south across the river, picking up the ring road around the northern edge of the city of Paris, where she checked into a hotel, took a pill to help her sleep, and at 4:00 a.m. the next morning was driving west on Texas Highway 82 the forty miles to Bonham.

At first light when the ranch began to stir with morning chores, Four sat in her Jeep Cherokee beneath an ancient live oak that spread across the roadway from the neighbor's pasture, a hundred yards beyond the arched gate that led up to the Cooperman ranch house. As hands began the morning by throwing small bales of alfalfa hay into the back of a pickup from a barn loft and distributing them to the row of stalls that stretched east from the house, Four studied each of the workers through a set of binoculars. Her target stuck out like a fashion model on a horse ranch: as tall as any of the men, and wearing jeans like a full-page spread for Calvin Klein. Even before the sun broke the horizon to the east, she was sporting over-sized sunglasses, and the long black hair Four remembered from her encounter with Sason at the house was braided into a plait that fell midway down the woman's back. She worked as effortlessly as the others but had forgotten that if you want to hide, you'd better blend in.

Four watched through the morning as the crew fed and watered, then exercised each of the stable horses in an arena behind the barns. Just before 11:00 they appeared to complete their rounds and Sason disappeared into a stable that stood by itself, closer to the ranch house. Twenty minutes later she led out a sleek chestnut horse with the white diamond blaze on its forehead. She paused with the animal in front of the stable, checked the cinch strap on the saddle, then swung up easily onto the horse's back. They trotted back through the arena, crossed a field on its far side, and cantered into an open pasture that stretched to a distant tree line. Sason kept the horse at a canter until halfway across the field, then turned her mount to the west and broke into the gallop Four had seen in the photograph on Zak's bedroom table.

Four checked quickly for traffic and made a hard U-turn, gunning the jeep a half mile down the road to the first right while keeping the distant horse and rider in sight. She turned along the fence line and, another half-mile north, saw Sason rein the horse to a halt and dismount, walking the animal to a stream that formed the north edge of the pasture. The Weaver pulled the car onto the road's grassy verge behind a row of lacy evergreens and again watched through the field glasses. Sason sat for almost twenty minutes while the horse drank, ate something from her hand, and nuzzled at her shoulder, then mounted again and cantered back across the field. This outing with Summer Breeze, Four decided, was a daily ritual. Tomorrow she would become part of it.

. . .

He had started to climb from beneath the bridge when he heard the car come to a stop midway between the road that fronted the ranch and his hiding place, and he slid hastily back down the bank and ducked beneath the low, concrete span. There had been only one "Cooperman Ranch" on the internet, but it had taken him most of the day after trailing her to the pharmacy to collect the things he needed and reach the town of Bonham. He parked in a lot beside the Texas State Veterans home on the edge of the city just after 8:00 p.m., hefted a pack onto his back, and hiked east along Seven Oaks Road with the sun falling below the horizon behind him. He knew that a short hike to the east, the ranch filled most of the land on that side of the city.

After watching her drive away from him at the pharmacy, he had spent the rest of the morning wrestling with the Devil: with the dark, consuming presence of Beelzebub himself. And the demon had said to him, "You deserve her. You have given so much for her. Await your time and she will be yours." But by the time he returned to his camp behind the empty house, he knew that he must love her as God loved his own creation, willing to cast it off and cleanse the earth when it became mired in iniquity. Had not the Lord said that no unclean thing can dwell in the presence of God? And he was now himself a sinner, having turned from God enough to allow a belief that she could abandon the ways of the flesh. But then she had come running from the house nearly naked – wearing only a pair of some man's underwear. As he paced outside the pharmacy and saw her looking through the window, wearing only the shorts and a blue halter, he realized she had not been in danger at all, but that the dark figure that pursued her was an offended wife – the embodiment of one of the seven angels of the Apocalypse, crying out "Come hither, and I will show unto thee the judgment of the great whore." And by morning he knew what he needed to do.

From a custom knife maker in west Dallas he purchased a long, Corian-handled *chalef*, the square-ended sacrificial knife used by Rabbis for kosher slaughter. He found a bedroll, backpack and mess kit in a surplus store beside the North Stemmons Freeway and bought provisions for three days and a can of charcoal lighter fluid at a convenience store on the way to Bonham. That night he slept beneath a row of cedars he guessed to be the edge of the ranch, and watched the next morning until she came toward him across the field, riding the chestnut mare.

"And I saw a woman sit upon a scarlet colored beast, full of names of blasphemy," he murmured. "And upon her forehead was a name written: Mystery, Babylon the Great, The Mother of Harlots and Abomination of the Earth."

He watched her water the horse at the stream and in the late afternoon, after moving his bedroll to the dark cleft beneath the bridge, found enough dry brush and wood north of the stream to build a pyre. "How much she hath glorified herself, and lived deliciously," he recited as he piled the tinder into a long, low bed and doused it with the lighter fluid. "…so much torment and sorrow give her: for she saith in her heart, I sit a queen, and am no widow, and shall see no sorrow." He emptied the last of the liquid onto the brush pile and looked back across the stream toward the back of the ranch buildings. "Therefore shall her plagues come in one day, death, and mourning, and famine; and she shall be utterly burned with fire: for strong is the Lord God who judgeth her."

# THIRTY-FIVE

Beyond the outside arenas, through two gates of green pipe and a ten acre exercise paddock, the Cooperman Ranch stretched for nearly a mile over open grassland. This was where Sandi pastured her own horses and let her students take their mounts when they wanted to run them at full gallop. Dreu spent the morning exercising the boarded horses whose owners didn't get out on a regular basis: some in the arenas and some in the larger paddock. But by 11:00, chores were finished. If his flight was on schedule, Adam should arrive around noon, giving her time to take Breeze out to the pool by the bridge. She was now on the chestnut mare, leaning forward into a light morning wind from the southwest that carried a hint of rain.

When headed to the ranch for a weekend, Dreu usually drove north out of the city to stop at her condo to change. But when she felt like variety, she opted for Route 78 through Wylie and kept an outfit in the closet of Sandi's guestroom: comfortable jeans, a long-sleeved shirt in strawberry red, and tan Justin boots. Though she usually rode without a hat, Adam's warning to stay out of sight prompted her to wear one of Sandi's weather-beaten pinch-brims and an oversized pair of sunglasses. Dreu suspected she looked more like a commercial for Drysdale's Western Wear than a ranch hand, but none of the patrons seemed to connect her to the face that had flashed almost hourly on local network channels the Monday after she left FedTegrity.

At the pool near the bridge, she reined the mare in and swung from the saddle, letting the horse drink, and sat back on the fallen trunk of a large cottonwood that had once bordered the creek. She pulled off the hat, placed it beside her on the log, and leaned over onto one hand to search for the carrot in her pocket.

Across the stream to her left, a clump of red birch rustled and she glanced over, expecting to see one of the white-tail deer that roamed unmolested across the ranch.

An icy hand reached into Dreu's chest and squeezed her heart almost to a stop as the small, intense woman with the oval face who had forced her way into Adam's kitchen stepped through a screen of sumac out onto the creek bank. Everything about the woman was black – hair, eyes, a buckled sling that held her left arm tightly against her side, and the short-barreled pistol she pointed across the stream at Dreu's chest. She was again unsmiling but displayed less of the cold certainty she had shown when she pushed into Adam's home. The gun was less steady in her right hand, her eyes furtive as she scanned the field behind Dreu.

"Get up," she ordered.

Dreu pushed slowly forward with her hands. Aside from a few remaining cottonwoods, her side of the creek had been clear-cut and was without cover. She measured the depth of the stream that separated her from the woman, guessing her assailant was uneasy about the distance because she was forced to hold the gun in her off-hand. But with the shallow, sandy bottom, her attacker could splash through easily and have open shots if Dreu tried to run in any direction. The road to her left was fifty yards away, edged by a green pipe fence that bordered the pasture inside a line of cedars that ran beside the pavement. Summer Breeze snorted nervously and danced backward as the woman stepped closer to the edge of the creek.

"You are a hard woman to kill," the Chinese woman said, easing closer along the far bank. "But this time, I won't get close enough for you to touch me, and you have no place to run."

"People will hear the shot," Dreu said, thinking of flipping backward behind the log. But that would mean only a brief delay before she was executed lying on the ground.

"They may hear, but by the time they get here, I will be gone," the woman said and turned sideways to steady her arm as she raised the pistol.

There was a sharp cry from the cedars beside the bridge, and the woman turned to see a man vault the pipe fence and charge her along Dreu's side of the creek waving a long, blunt-ended knife.

"*No!*" he shouted again, and the Weaver swung her weapon in his direction and fired. He stopped and looked in bewilderment at the two women, then down at a crimson stain that spread across the right side of his stomach. A manic spark returned to his eyes and with a guttural growl, he rushed into the stream toward the dark woman. She fired again – two quick shots that pitched him forward onto the bank a dozen paces from where she stood. She pivoted again toward Dreu, who had turned with her and was gazing in horror at the charging figure. There was another sharp report and Dreu gasped and looked down at her own strawberry shirt, stumbling backward over the cottonwood log as the Chinese woman's knees buckled and, with a shrill cry, she tumbled sideways into the stream.

. . .

Timing, the saying goes, is everything. But for Adam it was much less a matter of timing than of doing everything possible to reach Dreu before the Weavers found her. Angie and the Australians were booked on a 6:00 a.m. flight to San Francisco. An hour and a half earlier, Adam and Davis lifted off the runway at Seattle-Tacoma International in the Embraer, bound for Dallas' Love Field. Adam spent thirty minutes of the flight in the rear cabin on the phone with Fisher, exchanging briefings on what was known about the Weavers, explaining his plan for Davis, and catching up on the FedTegrity investigation in Dallas.

"Is the Bureau looking for Dreu?" he asked.

"Very quietly. As you saw from your list, one of the Weavers has managed to work himself into the NSA – which explains how they knew everything as soon as we did. We suspect they got copies of your phone exchanges when the Bureau did and are trying to get to her too. Do you want to tell me where she is, so I can get someone to her?"

"I don't think so – unless you have one of our people who can be there within three hours. Like you say, they seem to be learning everything as quickly as we do."

"I assume she's still in the Dallas area since you're headed that way. I can't get anyone there that quickly."

"Then I think she's safest with no one knowing where she is. I'll be there in about four hours. This Dempsey. Is he trustworthy?"

"Very good, I think."

"You might get word to him to have some people standing by about noon to go pick her up. And you'll want to get the Director to assemble a team in Washington to meet with her. She knows more about how this is being done than anyone but Marshall Ding."

"And you're confident she's not part of it?"

"Absolutely."

"No undue influence happening here?" Fisher asked.

Adam sniffed. "I've been thinking that all through myself. My greater concern was that somehow she knew who I was, and that I was the one being played. But I'll swear by her, and she's going to be critical to stopping this."

"She's going to learn pretty soon that *she* was being played. Are you ready for that?"

"To be honest? No – I'm not. I wish she had been the woman with the heavy thighs and messy hair."

"You lost me there," Fisher said.

"A Maxian Brain Fart," Adam muttered.

Three hours later, Davis had rented a Jeep Liberty and the two were maneuvering through Dallas morning traffic to catch the tollway north. As they passed McKinney, Adam considered stopping in Virginia Hills to retrieve a couple of weapons from his stash behind a panel in the bedroom closet, but knew Dreu's encounter in the house made it a place of interest. Someone – possibly several people – would be watching it.

As they turned onto 121 toward Bonham, Davis shifted nervously behind the wheel.

"One more time," he said. "Let me just run through this with you to make sure I've got it all straight in my head."

"Don't over-complicate things," Adam said, but listened as Eckerson walked through what his role would be over the next forty-eight hours. They were finishing the second review when Davis steered the car off the paved road onto the long gravel drive leading to the Cooperman ranch house. Three young women, all in jeans, sleeveless shirts, and cowboy hats, were unsaddling horses in front of a row of stables to the right of the house.

"Don't think one of them's your computer lady," Davis said. "Too young."

Adam nodded. "Too young and too short. She's six feet tall."

"They're too young to be Cooperman too," Davis said. "But that might be her...."

A wiry woman with sun-bleached hair pulled back into a short ponytail and wearing work-worn jeans and boots strode quickly out of one of the stables closest to them, started toward the house, then stopped and looked suspiciously at the two men as they climbed from the Jeep.

"I think that's Cooperman," Adam agreed, walking to where the woman stood, with Davis scrambling to join him.

"Are you Sandi?" Adam asked.

She examined both men cautiously. "Depends on who's askin'. And you are…?"

"I'm a friend of Dreu Sason's," Adam said. "She should be expecting us."

The woman's eyes brightened with recognition. "Oh, yeah. She is…. But you're earlier than she expected and just missed her. She took one of the horses out into the back pasture."

Adam looked over Cooperman's head toward the fields that stretched beyond the back of the house "She's by herself?"

"Yeah. But she's been doing it every day. She'll be okay."

"How do we find her?"

"I'd suggest you go around the road." Sandi pointed to her right where the road ran up the west side of the ranch property. "She'll take Breeze to a pool up near where the creek goes under the road. You'll probably get there about the same time she does."

"You don't happen to have some kind of firearm," Adam asked. "I don't think she should be up there by herself."

Cooperman looked nervously over her shoulder in the direction Dreu had taken Summer Breeze. "Why? Is somebody coming?"

"Do you have a gun?"

Cooperman started toward the house. "Yeah – this is Texas. Of course I got guns. What do you need?"

"Rifle of some kind would be best," Adam said. He turned to Davis. "Why don't you pull the car around."

"I got a Remington 770 I use for coyotes. Two-seventy caliber with a scope."

"Perfect. Is it well sighted?"

"Dead on at twenty-five yards."

The woman disappeared into the house and returned two minutes later with the rifle. "It's got four rounds in it. Maybe I should be calling the police," she said as she handed it to him.

"Wait 'til we see if there's any reason. But call this man in Dallas. He's the Station Chief for the FBI field office there. Ask him to get some people up here as quickly as he can. Don't talk to anyone but him – and don't tell him we're here. Just that Dreu Sason is here and needs his help. I'll be back with her in a few minutes."

Davis drove west along the road that fronted the ranch, turning north at the first intersection. In the early days of the cattle ranch, Cooperman's father had planted junipers along the north and west fence lines as windbreaks: now a thick curtain of lacy green that gave Adam only fleeting glimpses into the field.

"Stop!" he said suddenly as they passed one of the breaks. Davis swung the Jeep to the side and Adam signaled for quiet as he eased out of the passenger door, carrying the Remington. He met Davis at the rear of the Jeep and waved him to the opening in the trees, edging toward the fence until they could peer through the branches toward the north end of the pasture. A hundred yards in front of them, a woman sat on a fallen log facing the creek, a large chestnut horse moving nervously to her right. Across the stream a few steps to her left, another woman – smaller, and dressed completely in black – stood facing the seated figure, gripping a pistol in her right hand.

Adam fell to one knee behind the screen of trees, threw the bolt on the rifle and raised it to his shoulder.

"I need to wound her" he muttered. "Not sure I can make the shot at this range…."

He felt Davis's hand on his back. "I can make it. Give me the gun." Eckerson dropped beside him and reached for the rifle.

"We only get this one shot..." Adam whispered.

"I've got it," Davis said, taking the rifle. There was no uncertainty in the kid's voice.

"Shoot one of her knees, and aim an inch high," Adam whispered.

Eckerson sat with his feet together and knees apart, propping his elbows against the insides of his knees. As he sighted on the small figure beside the creek, there was shouting from farther up the tree line and a man ran into view, rushing the women along the near stream bank. The armed woman swung toward him and fired, paused when the man hesitated, then fired twice more as he rushed at her through the water. The second shots pitched him forward onto the bank.

"Shoot!" Adam said in a sharp whisper. Davis released a deep breath in what sounded to Adam like a long "*Squeeeze.*" The sound of the rifle and the agonizing shriek of the woman as the bullet tore through her right kneecap were a single, extended explosion, and she twisted onto her back into the water. Adam rolled under the bottom bar of the pipe fence and grabbed the rifle from Davis.

"Helluva shot! Now, drive to the bridge," he ordered and sprinted across the field toward the two women: one who lay flat behind the fallen cottonwood and the other, half submerged in the crimson ripples of the creek.

# THIRTY-SIX

It was another gathering of Deputy Directors: Soren Lansaw from the NSA, Darrell Hagebusch from Central Intelligence, and Genaro Serna from the FBI. Davis jotted their names on a pad in front of him on the conference table to keep them straight, wondering if Directors ever came to meetings like this. He guessed that as political appointees they were the front men and PR figures, while the Deputies took care of operational matters.

Art Dempsey from the FBI's Dallas office was also present and seemed to be running the show, with the others lending an air of importance and asking questions when they felt the urge. Rather than haul Dreu and Davis to Washington, they had chosen to bring all of the heavies to Dallas and the six were meeting in a third floor conference room of the Bureau's home on Justice Way. From the tone of the questioning, Davis wasn't certain whether he was being interviewed or interrogated.

Dempsey had the Jim Thompson letter spread in front of him on the table.

"Eric Compton confirmed your story and the time of your visit with him in Remington. And we did find a record of your stay at the LIT Hotel in Bangkok, but not the Bumrungrad Hospital."

"They didn't know who I was at the hospital," Davis said, wondering if they had been paying any attention earlier when he was explaining the whole Bangkok fiasco.

"And you chose not to tell them...."

"I was starting to suspect someone might be after me, and didn't want to give them any help."

Dempsey looked at him thoughtfully, then said; "We do find a record of you crossing over into Cambodia – but nothing in their immigration system that shows you leaving."

"Like I said," Davis repeated, "once we got the money to the man at the prison, they took us to the border and almost pushed us across. They gave us back our passports, but we didn't have to go through any checkpoint or anything."

"You, this man Murch, and your friend Angela...."

"Right."

"Now, when we talked to Phyllis Morin in Siem Reap, she said Mr. Murch was with Ms. Robb when they met you at her house. That's where you first met him?"

"Right. He'd followed her to the village, trying to track down her mother and the other Weaver kids."

"And he thought the children had grown into a group that's involved in industrial espionage?" Lansaw from the CIA asked.

"That's what he said. And someone was obviously concerned about us tracking them – from the attempt on me at Angkor Wat."

"Why do you think the attempt was on you, and not on this Mr. Murch? He was tracking them too."

"Probably because they learned I'd found the letter and were following it. Didn't know about Murch."

"And how did they know about the letter?"

"Good question. I'd only talked to Eric Compton...."

The Deputies all shifted uncomfortably.

"And why did Ms. Robb go with you to the border?" Hagebusch asked, seeming to want the conversation to move in a different direction. "She had a return ticket from Phnom Penh."

Davis shrugged. "Rand – that's Mr. Murch – thought whoever was chasing me might be after her too and would be watching the places they expected us to try to leave the country. Plus, we'd sort of hit it off. It seemed to make sense for us to stay together."

Hagebusch again shifted direction. "You paid a pretty handsome sum to get the three of you out of jail."

"Ever been in a Cambodian jail?"

Hagebusch ignored the sarcasm as if he were used to dealing with smart asses. "Whose idea was the payoff?" he asked.

"Rand's idea. But I was the one who had the money. So it came out of my account."

Dempsey reentered the conversation. "We've confirmed that too. Why didn't Murch contact whatever businesses he was working for to get the money?"

"He said he would. But I had the money where we could get to it and get it transferred in a hurry. And we wanted out - fast."

"But he went through his people to get the money delivered overnight to Phnom Penh, and to arrange for someone there to bring it to the border."

"Yup. That's about how it worked."

"One of your people delivered it," Deputy Lansaw said to Hagebusch. The CIA man nodded his acknowledgement.

"I spoke to the Director about that. He said it was authorized."

"By whom?" Lansaw pressed, and Davis leaned back to let the Deputies go a few rounds.

"That's all I know," Hagebusch said. "It was authorized."

"And the plane was authorized too?"

Hagebusch again nodded, but remained tight-lipped.

"This Murch seems to have had a lot of pull," Lansaw said with a grim smile, turning his attention back to Davis. "Now, this is where it starts getting a little murky for me. You're telling us this man Murch left you in Ho Chi Minh City, but told you where to find Ms. Sason after you got back to the States: that she might be in danger and you should collect her and go to Special Agent Dempsey. Am I remembering this correctly?"

"And that he had information about these children that he'd be sending to your office," Davis added, turning toward Hagebusch.

"The information I've given to all of you," Hagebusch said to the group.

Lansaw still wasn't satisfied and turned to Dreu, who to this point had remained silent.

"How did he know where you were? You'd only sent your message to your friend, Zak – who hasn't turned up yet. How did this Murch know where you were?"

Davis jumped back in. "How did the Chinese woman and the guy who's been stalking Dreu know where she was? Where Dreu was didn't seem to be a much of a secret. Sort of like the letter…. They – whoever *they* is – were a step ahead of us all the time."

As the deputies again exchanged glances, Davis had to acknowledge that Rand had prepared them well. After the shooting of the Chinese woman at the creek, they had hauled her unconscious from the stream and while Davis held the rifle on her still figure, Rand checked the man who had rushed the women from the bridge. The second shots had hit him squarely in the chest. Dreu had followed Rand through the stream and was beside him when he rolled the man over.

"It's Lonnie Marchisio," she said in a choked whisper.

Rand looked up at her questioningly.

"The man who stabbed me." She said it as if Rand would know what she was talking about.

"Was he coming after you or the Chinese woman?" Rand asked.

"When I first saw him, I was sure it was me," she said. "But when she shot him, he seemed to change, and went for her."

Within minutes of the shootings, Sandi Cooperman's red pickup skidded to a halt beside the stream and while they waited for the authorities to arrive, Rand pulled Dreu and the rancher aside. From where Davis stood, it didn't look friendly. Dreu's face had flushed dark and she was spitting her words at him. Rand was stoic and tight-jawed, answering in slow, emphatic sentences. Sandi stood uncomfortably between the two, staying out of it by nodding as they finally seemed to reach some kind of agreement. When sirens sounded in the distance, Rand signaled Davis that it was his to handle, mounted Summer Breeze, and galloped back across the field in the direction of the house. By the time the police reached the bridge, Rand was gone and neither woman mentioned that he had ever been there.

"You're making my point exactly," Lansaw was saying as Davis's thoughts returned to the room. "There seem to have been some people – outside of those of us here – who understood this operation pretty completely. And were exchanging information on a regular basis...."

"Rand said the list of children and their current employment would explain that," Davis interrupted, and this time the other Deputies looked directly at their colleague from NSA. Lansaw shuffled the papers in a folder that sat in front of him on the table.

"That still doesn't explain how Murch knew where you were, Ms. Sason," he said to Dreu, directing the attention back to her. "You don't know this man Randall Murch?"

Dreu shook her head. "Never heard of him before I met Davis at the ranch."

Lansaw drew a photograph from the folder and placed it in front of her. It was a poor quality visa picture of a bald, clean-shaven man with dark, heavy-rimmed glasses. "We obtained this from Cambodian immigration. This man entered the country under the name Randall

Murch. Is this your friend Zak?"

Dreu looked down quickly at the picture, then pushed the photo back across the table.

"No. That's not Adam."

"You decided pretty quickly," Lansaw said.

"I don't mean to be rude," Dreu said, "but if I showed you a picture of someone who wasn't your wife, would it take you long to decide?" The other Deputies smiled faintly.

Lansaw looked more closely at the passport photo. "Well, somehow this Murch knew where you were and believed you could help us solve this problem." He turned to Deputy Director Serna. "Genaro, I think we just moved into your jurisdiction."

Serna deferred to his Dallas Special Agent in Charge. "Dempsey, I'll let you take it from here."

Dempsey spread open a folder of his own. "Ms. Sason, you've explained how you believe Marshall Ding has been inserting what you refer to as a 'suicide command' into the security programs your firm has developed for major clients – including a number of federal agencies. But when we've gone into the programs, we aren't able to find those instructions."

Dreu looked at him with the same note of irritation they were getting from Eckerson. "As I told you, they are designed so that unless you initially enter the program with one of two prescribed passwords, they are what we call 'obfuscated.' You can't see that they are there."

"And Ding has changed those passwords since you were able to look at the added code?"

"Apparently so. I wasn't able to get into the one you gave me to check. And it was a program I had developed."

"How does it work?"

"It?"

"The suicide command."

"Well, in simple terms, all of our programs have imbedded in them what are called IVKs – Integrity Verification Kernels. Normally these kernels, which are very heavily encrypted, exchange information that lets them know if any changes are being made to the program between them. And if they detect any, instantly order a repair. Picture the Great Wall of China. These IVKs are the sentries in towers along the wall. If they see any activity between their towers, they alert each other and immediately stop the incursion. If I'm right about what Ding has done, he's added into the IVKs additional instructions that, if triggered by one of the passwords imbedded into the code we can't see, essentially work in reverse. They destroy the program and give the computer instructions to block any attempts to reload a backup. The sentries become part of the invasion and help tear down the wall."

"Is there anything that can be done to stop their execution?"

"I believe so – but there is a bigger issue."

"And what would that be?"

"Ding was only one of ten. I need to see your list of the Chinese children and what they are doing now."

"We can't share that with you. But I can assure you that all are under careful surveillance."

"Their work is probably already done and has been for some time," Dreu said. "Surely it has occurred to you gentlemen that each of them has done something similar to what Mr. Ding did to our programs. I need to know where they work and what they do."

The Deputies exchanged glances and after a brief pause, each nodded his assent. Serna slid the list across the table to Dreu who systematically worked her way down the ten names.

"And this Marion Chan is the woman who tried to kill us?"

"We believe so. Yes."

"Bradley Han at NSA. Very convenient. That certainly explains some things, doesn't it?" she said, glancing up at Hagebusch, then back at the list. "Looks like we'd better include your programs in our fix." She paused, then said; "I see you've marked out Helen Robb."

"She's dead," Serna said.

Dreu frowned dismissively. "Her programs may still be alive. And she was in a key position with PG&E. It looks like power grids were a major target. Kenneth Zhou is with Con Edison. Nancy Lin Roberts with Southern California Edison, and Cynthia Han with Potomac Electric. They have the major power companies covered. And then there's this Henry Liu with the Stock Exchange...."

"How do you think they managed to position these people so strategically?" Dempsey asked, addressing the group in general.

Dreu answered before the others could offer an opinion. "My guess is that if you look at their credentials, they have backgrounds and resumes like mine. Top tier universities. Excellent experience. I get calls all the time from headhunters and could probably walk into the personnel office at any one of these companies and get a job tomorrow. If I were committed to it, within three to five years I could work my way into their positions." She paused, then added, "…but what about this Lawrence Li? No occupation and no address."

"We don't know where he is or what he does," Dempsey said. "The CIA researched the group before the list reached us, and we've been working on him since. So far, no joy."

"The CommittedWeaver," Dreu muttered.

"The what?"

Dreu looked up at the Dallas agent. "The second password Ding inserted into the program – the CommittedWeaver password – was for someone else. My guess is that each of these people has access to the programs they developed and so does someone else – a master controller. That would probably be Li."

"Can we keep him from triggering these suicide commands without finding him?"

"Depends," Dreu said. "But we'd better get to work. I suspect he knows we've identified the rest of the group."

# THIRTY-SEVEN

"I fully agree," Fisher rasped into the phone, "that when we move on them, it needs to be on all fronts at once. Marion Chan is in custody and unless she has some kind of scheduled reporting time, the others won't be aware she's being held. NSA is keeping all related information from Bradley Han. But for what it's worth, as disastrous as this would be if executed, I suspect it was initiated fifty years ago as a contingency plan – one they hoped they'd never need to use."

"It was viewed as important enough to eliminate Jim Thompson when he discovered the children," Adam observed.

"That's just conjecture. Who knows what really happened to Thompson. He may have just decided he'd had enough of all of the hassles with the Thai government and chose to disappear. Years later, someone claimed to have seen him in the South Pacific. But as for these Weavers, the Chinese may have had one thing in mind to begin with, and with leadership and technology changing so quickly over fifty years, it didn't work out. The mission changed or was lost…."

Adam was silent for enough time that Fisher continued.

"For one thing, with the frequency with which companies and agencies update their security systems, they can't expect to have someone in place all the time to keep a program like this active. Their planning can't include having a new generation of programmers waiting in the wings to fill each of these roles as the Weavers retire or die."

"I think you've just described what's dangerous about this situation," Adam said. "Suppose the Weavers were initially trained and placed to be available if needed, but became lost as a strategic asset with all the Party changes that have happened in China over the last half century. But this group – these Weavers – have some internal leader: some mastermind who's created this cyber-strategy and knows it depends on the people who're now in place. He may still see it as his responsibility to carry out the mission if he thinks it's being compromised."

"And you think Li might be the man…."

"I'm just saying that this plan was never scrapped – either because it's still viewed by Chinese intelligence as being viable or because Chinese intelligence isn't even aware it's there. If it's the first, I don't see China wanting to execute it now. The worldwide repercussions would be catastrophic. But if it's the second, the plan might be executed by a man who sees it as the only acceptable culmination of a life's work."

"Then we'd better find Mr. Li."

"Aren't all of the agencies doing just that?"

"They're where they are now in this investigation because we handed them every bit of information. If Li's getting desperate, do you want to trust the agencies to locate him in time?"

"They all know by now that someone else is out there tracking the Weavers," Adam said.

Fisher's raspy chuckle rattled through the phone. "They all suspect the mysterious Randall Murch works for one of the others. So whatever you have to do, do it very carefully."

. . .

High above the San Miguel River, above the tree line where slides of granite boulders scarred the faces of Chicago, Dallas and La Junta Peaks, the mountains were beginning to shake. Laurence Li could feel it as he hunched over his computer and studied the list of Weavers that sat beside him on the desk. Someone, he knew, was aware they existed. Possibly more than one person. One, Six and Ten believed they were being watched, and Five reported that the investigation of Dreu Sason had suddenly been dropped. Four hadn't reported in on her attempt to get to Sason in Texas, and requests for information by Seven, Bradley Han at NSA, were being delayed or were coming back "information not available." The shaking was keeping Nine awake. He hadn't slept for forty-eight hours.

As with all of the Weavers, Nine had designed his escape plan years ago. He would go north through Montrose and Grand Junction and over into Utah, picking up US 6 west of Green River. When he reached Provo, the interstate would take him north through Idaho Falls and Helena, Montana, all the way into Canada. He would cross the border with a U.S. passport as Matthew Xu, then disappear into Alberta. Surely a man of his talents could find work in Calgary or Edmonton.

The challenge was to determine where to execute *Seres*. It was exactly twelve hundred miles from Telluride to Lethbridge, Canada, and once the program was activated, it may be impossible to get gasoline. He had briefly considered Helena. From there it was 270 miles to Lethbridge and he could make that on a single tank of gas. There would be something satisfying about initiating the economic collapse of the United States from within its borders. But the government response might be to close those borders, and he couldn't afford to be caught on the American side. He would execute *Seres* from Lethbridge.

Nine glanced at his watch. Seven-fifteen in the evening. It was Thursday. If he left Saturday morning and drove as far as Idaho Falls, he could be on the road by seven on Sunday and in Canada by mid-afternoon. Returning to his laptop, Nine typed a brief email message to eight non-descript email accounts.

*Initiating Seres at 3:00 p.m. Sunday. Respond accordingly.*

# THIRTY-EIGHT

The call from Angie Robb was making its way through cyber-space at the same time Nine's email messages were being routed to the eight Weaver accounts. Adam had just picked up two tacos and a vanilla shake at a fast food place in Oklahoma City and was back in his room at a hotel, a quarter mile east of Will Rogers World Airport. He had picked Oklahoma City because he wanted to be outside of Art Dempsey's jurisdiction, but close enough to Dallas that he could get there quickly if needed. Angie began to speak the instant Adam said "hello."

"You know the FBI was here for half the day yesterday. And it was just like you said. Lots of questions about you. I just said you'd stayed in Vietnam." She sounded ten years older: Not aged, as much as matured.

"Are you on the phone I gave you?"

"Of course. I'm doing just what you told me." She paused for a moment. When she spoke again, her voice had quieted. "They said Davis shot a woman."

"The woman who tried to kill him at Angkor Wat. She was also after the computer programmer who was digging up information about the group. He just wounded her. And by the way…don't mention the name of the children's group during this call. They may be watching for references to it. So – how did you do with the authorities?"

Her voice regained strength. "Okay, I think. I told them everything pretty much as it happened – except that you didn't come on to Seattle with us."

"Good. Thank you. But you weren't supposed to use this phone unless you had something."

"I do have something. Like you asked, I went through everything I could find of mother's and found more pictures. One's pretty interesting."

Adam tucked the phone under his chin and reached for the pen and pad on the nightstand. "I could use something interesting right now. Go ahead."

"Well, I found a sketch I hadn't seen before that includes the whole group. All ten. And under each person she has names – like Bradley or Ken or Nancy. And then there's a number beside each. Like, mom was number two, and Bradley was seven. Like that."

"If I give you an email address, can you scan or photograph the sketch and send it to me? You're right. This could be very helpful."

"I think they're probably watching everything that goes out on my text and email. How do I get it to you?"

"Put it on a drive and go to the library or somewhere that has public computers. Set up a new email account under some name that isn't close to anything you use, and send it to this address. Or maybe you can take a picture with someone's phone that wouldn't be suspect." He gave her an address that would go directly to Fisher in Virginia. "This is good, Angie. Thanks. Anything else?"

"Well..." she paused, as if hesitant to pass it along. "...I did find something else. Mom had this studio room where she did her drawing. And it has a little work desk. In one of the drawers there was one of those cheap phones...like this one you gave me? There was only one entry in the phone's directory – a number listed for Nine."

Adam knew why she was hesitant. The phone meant Angie's mother had stayed involved.

"And from her sketch, who was Nine?" he asked.

"A boy named Lawrence."

"Hmmm," Adam murmured. "That *does* help. Were you able to get the number for the phone in the desk?"

"Yes... I have it."

"And were there any incoming or outgoing call records?"

"No – it looks like everything was deleted."

"Give me the number and the one listed for Nine. Then see if you can get the drawing sent sometime tonight. Could you do that?"

"I think so. One of my neighbors is coming over to be with me tonight – till Davis gets here. She brings her daughter's phone. I'll take a picture with it and send it. Will that work?"

"I think so...and thank you, Angie. You doing alright?"

The line was silent for a long moment. "I've been better," she said finally. "But Davis will be out here soon. We've talked...and he's been really good about it. Things will be okay."

"Anything I can do?"

"Leave us out of this from now on – and get it cleared up. Davis thinks it's not over yet."

"I'll do what I can," he said. "You take care."

He placed a call, but not to the number Angie had given him for Nine.

"We've come across a drawing of the Weavers when they were children that indicates each had a number," he said to Fisher. "They may use the numbers when communicating with each other. A copy of the drawing is on its way to you as an email attachment."

Fisher's voice sounded unusually tired. "May I ask where this drawing came from?"

"The Robb woman found it among her mother's things. I asked her to look through them again with the little additional knowledge she now has… and the email will be coming to the account you use for this kind of thing, from a phone that isn't connected to her in any way."

"I'd assume as much."

Adam wondered if the weariness and touch of irritation in the old man's voice was a reflection of advanced age, or if this Weaver thing was becoming more than he felt comfortable with. Fisher liked to keep other agencies out of his business. But the additional information Adam had may draw the investigation more firmly back under Fisher's wing.

"The sketch had Lawrence Li as number Nine," Adam said. "And in a desk drawer, Robb found a phone with a directory listing for Nine."

"Humph," Fisher grunted. "But the girl's mother's been out of the picture for four or five months."

"True. But at least we have a place to start."

"I think NSA stores calls made from those disposable phones longer than they do others," Fisher said. "It's harder for the public to complain about breaches of privacy when they're using a phone that isn't linked to them in some official way. And people use those things because they don't want the calls traced. I'll see what I can come up with."

"Just a thought," Adam suggested. "But I'd guess calls between the members aren't made very often. And this Nine might use different phones for each. If you can find a place of origin for a call to Helen Robb, or a community destination for a call she made to him, you might check on calls using these disposables to the same location from the places we know the other Weavers are living."

"There will be thousands of them…."

"That's why we have computers," Adam said. "They'll be able to sort through all that stuff to see if there's a high probability of a single recipient."

Fisher's tone didn't change. "Given enough time, you might get to be good at this. I'll see what I can get done tonight." He paused for a moment. "How was the girl?" he asked.

"She sounded pretty subdued. Like a different woman."

"Life can be a bitch," Fisher said.

A Maxian Brain Fart, Adam thought.

. . .

Within minutes of sending his notification message, Nine began to receive calls. The first was from Henry Liu.

"Nine, this can't be serious," he said.

"Dead serious. And you know the instructions are to go completely silent once an execution notification is sent out. Initiate your exit plan."

"But Lawrence, there's no reason for this! Both we and China have other challenges that are much bigger than we have with each other. And the Chinese economy is dependent on this one remaining strong. I watch this stuff every day – and they bought the Waldorf Astoria, for God's sake !"

"That's just your problem, Three. You say "we' – speaking of this country! Your time with the Stock Exchange has turned you into a capitalist! You've become too wealthy and comfortable."

"And you think the Party leadership isn't capitalist, for God's sake? Talk about wealth and comfort…!"

"Execution is at 3:00 p.m. Sunday. Initiate your exit plan or deal with the consequences."

"Lawrence, *this is insane*! I'm going back into my programs and deleting the *Seres* sequence."

"You can't, Three. Five modifies the programs when they come to us. We're the only ones who can access them now. Get out," Nine ordered, "while you still can."

Incoming calls buzzed irritably on two other phones: Seven at NSA and another from New York. He ignored Kenneth Zhou with Con Edison and took the call from Han.

Seven came directly to the point. "Has this instruction come from

Beijing?" he wanted to know.

"Beijing has left the decision to me," Li said testily.

"There is communication going back and forth with Beijing right now, and they are claiming to know nothing of a sleeper cell in the U.S. Other global security agencies have been alerted to watch for Chinese-Americans leaving the country. I've been quarantined here, so they may even have a list of names. Doing something now will trigger an outcry from the entire international community."

Li stiffened at mention of the list. "It is our time," he said firmly. "You must not try to contact me again," and he hung up with unanswered calls from One and Eight buzzing in his ears.

Li kept each prepaid phone for thirty days, then destroyed it. He carried the set out onto the rear deck that overlooked the river, placed them one at a time on the plank decking over a sturdy floor joist, and dropped the leg of a heavy Adirondack chair onto the plastic cases. Carefully gathering the pieces, he carried them to the railing and threw them into the river.

Back inside the house, Li went to a small floor safe in the corner of his bedroom and spun in the combination. He checked the contents of its only item: a thick blue bank deposit bag. Two hundred thousand dollars in fifty and one hundred dollar bills; a US passport and university transcripts from Beijing Normal University in the name of Matthew Xu; three letters of recommendation from U.S. companies with subsidiaries in China, providing glowing accounts of the work Mr. Xu had done in the data management field. Li pulled a mid-sized gray suitcase from his closet, placed the bank bag in a leather briefcase that already held a Lenovo tablet computer, and carried both to his small, single car garage. He needed a few hours' sleep. But not in this box canyon. He would find a place to stop when he reached Grand Junction.

# THIRTY-NINE

Fisher's voice resonated with new energy. "In some ways," he said, "this is a pretty amateurish bunch. The number you gave us was still on record as having received a call from Helen Robb's phone six months ago. In Telluride, Colorado. As ingenious as your idea was to try to trace other calls going into Telluride from pre-paid phones, it would have taken some time. But within the last few hours, calls have been placed to phones there at the same GPS coordinate from five of the Weaver locations. They're starting to panic and have no internal discipline."

"We shouldn't be surprised," Adam said. "Their assassin wasn't exactly a pro."

"What it does tell us though," Fisher said," is that something's up. The Chinese are claiming they have no knowledge of the Weavers, which may or may not be true. But they seem genuinely nervous. If the group's a forgotten sleeper cell gone rogue, they'll be unpredictable and may present an even greater danger."

"I'd guess they'll be predictable to the degree we'll see them begin to scatter, "Adam said. "Either disappear into Chinese communities in the U.S. or try to get out of the country."

Fisher grunted his agreement. "The FBI has someone on everyone but Li. If the Weavers try to leave the country, they'll be stopped – or if they look like they're closing up shop and changing locations."

Adam was silent for a moment, then asked, "Am I the only one who knows about Li and Telluride? We should get APB's on him to the borders and major airports. But he may just go underground. He could execute this shutdown order from almost anywhere."

"I'll get bulletins out but as of now, only you know where he is."

"Are we getting the security programs replaced on the systems they've targeted?"

"That's apparently more easily said than done," Fisher said. "They can remove them, of course. But the word I get back from Langley is that there are literally dozens of attempts to hack those systems every day, and removing the security programs without something pretty good to replace them may create exactly the disaster we're trying to prevent. And since none of these agency's internal analysts can find the 'shut down' instructions we're telling them are there, it's been a hard sell convincing them to move with haste."

"What about Dreu?"

"Apparently she's been willing – but not enthusiastic. The FBI has her working on something. It's been hard to get details."

"I thought you could get anything," Adam chided.

"I have one contact in one agency," Fisher said defensively. "He can get most anything we ask for, but sometimes inter-agency rivalries make it hard even for him to know everything."

"Well, let's get roadblocks on everything going out of Telluride. As I recall, there are only a couple of ways in and out of that valley. And stop all aircraft leaving the airport there. Can you have someone contact the police and ask if there's a Lawrence Li in the community? If they can identify him, have him picked up. Then we'll turn it over to the Bureau."

"If he's already out of Telluride?"

"We can't count on our APB, and I think a public nationwide manhunt would be a mistake right now. We don't want to panic him. But get me the make and model of his car. If he's not expect-ing us to be after him and is inexperienced at avoiding detection, he may stay with his own vehicle. I'll go after him myself."

"And how do you propose to find him – if he's already out of Telluride?"

"We can hope for a stupid mistake – cell phone call from a phone under his name. Watch all five of those numbers that made calls into Telluride. Credit card purchases. Keep a watch on all those things."

"They've been amateurish, but they're smart. I wouldn't expect that kind of mistake."

"Do you have the resources that can get a law enforcement officer to a person or business, anywhere in the country, within an hour?"

The question caused even Fisher to pause. "I can," he said finally, "but I need a reason."

"A nationwide manhunt that's being conducted as quietly as possible."

"Even then, resources aren't limitless, Zak. We'll still need to know where to look."

Adam glanced down at the live video he had called up on his iPad. It was a webcam showing real-time activity on the main street of Telluride,

Colorado. "Then we'll have to rely on our backup national surveillance system," he said. "A camera on every corner."

. . .

A mile south of Montrose, two state troopers sped past Nine with lights flashing but without sirens. At the intersection where the road from Telluride joins US 50, another trooper turned on his siren just long enough to run the light, also turning south toward the mountain resort town. Nine sucked in a deep breath and released it slowly as he waited for the light to change. Telluride was being sealed off and he needed to be far enough from it that the route options were too numerous to monitor.

He continued north past the Montrose airport and out into open country. A three-quarter moon bathed the landscape in pale yellow, shimmering off the spray of rolling irrigation sprinklers that stretched across full acres of alfalfa hay on either side of the highway. At the town of Delta, he crossed the Gunnison River and turned west, seeing in the muted moonlight the dark silhouette of Grand Mesa rising to the north. There was something about the openness and clean air of the high desert that began to lift the malaise that had settled over him, and Nine relaxed back into the seat of the Volvo and mentally worked his way north along the western slope of the Rockies into Canada.

By the time he intersected I-70 at Grand Junction, he was fighting to keep his eyes open and exited in the small town of Fruita where a motel sign glowed off to his left behind a fast food restaurant. The girl behind the desk was no more alert than he was, and when he said he would pay with cash, checked him in without asking for a credit card for incidentals. Thirty minutes later, Li was asleep.

In a room across the street from where the Weaver slept, another guest had checked into a motel and was also settling in for the night. Beside him on the nightstand, a small monitor the size of a cigarette pack would alert him if Li's Volvo moved before he awoke. But he had the alarm set for 5:00 a.m. He expected to be sitting in his own car watching as the man the Weavers called Nine got back on the road.

# FORTY

Fisher, Adam decided, had become so removed from the real action of the operations he coordinated that they were no more than games to him: data on screens and backstories whispered over the telephone in which people didn't really suffer or have their lives turned upside down by the actions he was directing. He was the ultimate drone pilot: spotting the target on the road; watching the missile streak toward its mark; seeing the battered pickup disappear in a ball of flame. But never feeling the ground shake, hearing the air thunder and sizzle with the heat of the explosion, or smelling the acrid stench of burning explosive, diesel fuel, and human flesh.

On occasion Adam resented it, not knowing that at one time the mangled body of his Control had been pulled from the wreckage of a downed aircraft and only half patched together. But more often, Adam feared that this separation depersonalized Fisher's involvement to the point of making it sport, rather than one of the more tragic forms of human activity.

He heard traces of this remoteness in Fisher's voice when the old man called two hours after their earlier conversation.

"Well, I have some good news and some bad news," the old man said lightly. "I'll start with the bad news. The police in Telluride didn't know about Li. But there was a man in the community who fit the profile. Name's Matthew Xu. He's been a quiet presence in the community for twenty years. But according to one of his neighbors, while she and her husband were sitting on their porch enjoying the evening, they saw him leave his place carrying a suitcase. That was about seven-thirty. He left his home completely dark, which surprised the neighbor since he's pretty conscientious about leaving a light on when he goes out."

"I'd guess that's our man. And you're right. Not good news. But about what we expected. They have to be very nervous. What's the good news?"

"He drives a gunmetal gray Volvo XC60 – a car that won't be hard to spot. And according to the same neighbor, he's a little obsessive-compulsive by nature and especially about this car. Thinks it's the safest thing ever built and doesn't like to ride in anything else. I doubt he'll give it up if he doesn't suspect he's being followed."

"Do you have people watching for it?"

"As much as we can. We're setting up surveillance on all roads from Durango and Cortez north to Grand Junction and Ouray. Beyond that perimeter, there are too many options to cover."

"He could be outside that perimeter already."

"Granted" Fisher said. "But the Director sent information back advising that we be especially careful about stopping him. Your friend Sason seems to think that with a tablet – or possibly even a smart phone – Li can send a single instruction that will activate all of these suicide commands. She suggests we try to take him by surprise."

"Then we'd better figure out where he's going and I'll intercept. Were you able to get the camera information I asked about?"

"Yes. Most local police now keep a database on all surveillance cameras that are covering public spaces in their communities: at least those they know about. What do you need?"

"The odds are pretty good that he went either north or south on Highway 145 from Telluride. There are other ways out of the valley, but they're not ones he'd choose. If he went north to Montrose, Mapquest tells me he would have reached the intersection with Highway 50 in about an hour and twenty minutes. And he sounds like a man who drives the speed limit – especially if he doesn't want to be stopped. At that intersection he would either continue north toward Grand Junction, or turn east toward Gunnison. I see on Google Earth that there are commercial enterprises on all four corners at that intersection – and two major parking lots. See if any has a camera or if there are cameras on the highways that catch traffic through the intersection. If you find something, ask local authorities to check from 8:45 to 9:30 p.m. for the Volvo. Can you do that?"

"You're using Mapquest and Google Earth with all the high tech support we have for you?" Fisher chuckled.

"I'm not sure you could give me better information," Adam said. "Can you check those locations for cameras?"

"I'm recording this," Fisher grumbled. "Too complicated for me to remember. But yes, we can do that."

"Okay, well, Cortez is even more complicated. Nothing obvious at the intersection of 145 and Route 160. But a couple of businesses in both directions on 160 might have parking lot cameras. Have them checked for the same timeframe to see if the Volvo went east or west."

Adam paused, waiting for Fisher to acknowledge the instruction, but got nothing.

"Durango will be easy," he continued. "Where the highway comes into town from the west, there's a DoubleTree hotel that has a river walk bordering the highway. I called them and they have a camera that monitors the walking path, but also shows traffic on the road coming into the city from the west. We can check the same time span and if Li shows up, we'll know he's headed either east toward Pagosa Springs or south to Albuquerque."

"Simple as that...," Fisher muttered.

"It won't be simple at all. It will take a lot of legwork by a lot of people, but that's what you're good at. I need to know which way he's going as quickly as you can get an ID on the car, so I can get out of here in the right direction in the morning."

"We're on it..." Fisher said, "...but just out of curiosity, how did you get the DoubleTree to tell you they had a camera watching the walking trail?"

"I could see the trail on Google Earth and called and asked if it had cameras," Adam said. "People love to cooperate with the FBI."

"You said you were FBI? We don't want the Bureau starting to look for some renegade who's impersonating an agent...."

"I didn't say I was FBI," Adam said. "I just told them the FBI was trying to track a fugitive who may have passed through that intersection and asked if they had a camera on the path that showed highway traffic – one we could send officers over to review."

Fisher muttered something under his breath that Adam didn't catch, then said, "One other interesting bit of information before we hang up. When they were looking for Li in Telluride, some officer knew there was another Chinese American living in the village – a younger guy who's a ski instructor in the winter and works construction in the summer. He lives in an apartment near the ski lodge and didn't fit the profile. But a woman friend in the apartment next to his said he also left this evening – right around seven-thirty."

. . .

Nine rose precisely at six, showered, dressed and ate a bowl of cold cereal at one of four tables in the motel's breakfast area. At 6:45 he was turning onto I-70 headed west, and at 7:05 crossed the state line into Utah. The "Welcome to Utah" sign greeted him with pictures of the famous red sandstone arch in Arches National Monument and of a skier leaping onto a snow-covered slope. But in every direction as far as Nine could see, there was nothing but rolling, scrub-covered desert. A green highway sign notified him that he was forty-three miles from Crescent Junction and sixty-four from Green River. He knew from having driven this stretch of road once before that there was nothing in between.

As he passed under an overpass, a Utah state trooper clocked him on radar from the bridge, a reminder that the state's new 80 mph speed limit and the straight, open expanse of highway in front of him wasn't an invitations to see if those upper numbers on the speedometer were just there for show. Nine wasn't concerned. His cruise control was pegged exactly on seventy. He saw no reason to drive eighty, even if Utah thought he could.

As he approached the junction where a road turned south toward Moab and the arches of the national monument, flat sand-colored mesas defined the horizon to the north, but the desert in front of him lost its undulations and flattened into a barren, blue-gray expanse of sagebrush. He couldn't remember having driven a more God-forsaken stretch of highway.

Green River, Utah, straddles the river of the same name and for half a mile on the west side of the river provides a brief respite from the seemingly endless landscape of sand, sage and coarse, yellow grass. Nine passed an empty city park where a white, Minute Man missile stood on its tail beside the highway, surrounded by a low chain link fence. Somewhere in the barren wasteland south of town there were still silos with missiles targeted at his homeland. In the briefcase on the seat beside him, Nine knew that he had much greater destructive power than all of those missiles. He could cripple the entire nation with one push of a button.

He pulled into a service station at the east end of town to gas up the Volvo and buy a bottle of water. The next stretch of road took him north for an hour through high desert to the city of Price, then over the

Wasatch Plateau into Provo – another hour and a half of rough, mountainous driving. He didn't like to let his tank get below the half mark, especially when this far from civilization.

He bought two under-ripe bananas and ate one in the car, watching the traffic. Though it was just after eight in the morning, few vehicles moved in either direction on the main street of Green River. The ever-present semis. A few assorted pickup trucks that looked local. A white Honda CRV headed west, followed by a state patrolman – the one who had been clocking traffic as he entered the state, Nine guessed. An eastbound Chevy Suburban pulled in beside him and off-loaded a family with six children, all appearing to be under the age of ten. He couldn't imagine traveling in the midst of all that chaos.

Nine was finding the tedium of desert driving more tiring than he expected and his immediate goal became Idaho Falls, just under four hundred miles north. He should be there between three and four in the afternoon. If not too exhausted, he might try to drive the additional four hours to Helena. He looked at the tablet on the seat beside him and wondered if the other Weavers were on their way to safety. They'd been given plenty of notice but he had told them Sunday. That was before he knew Telluride was being sealed off. He didn't have that much time. Tomorrow – Saturday – at three, he would execute *Seres*.

# FORTY-ONE

At the Transportation Center in the Salt Lake International Airport, Adam rented a nondescript gray Ford and headed into the city to pick up I-15 south. He had taken a gamble by catching the early flight to Salt Lake City. A security camera monitoring a park in Montrose, Colorado, had picked up the Volvo continuing north toward Grand Junction, where a camera recording activity in the parking lot of an auto salvage yard spotted Li as he looped west around the downtown area. But just across the state line, a Utah state trooper had been positioned to monitoring traffic headed west on I-70 and hadn't seen the Volvo. Either Li had doubled back and headed east, changed cars, or stopped for the night before crossing the state line. Since Li had reached Grand Junction after 9:00 p.m. and faced at least another hour of desert driving before reaching another town of any size, Adam bet on the overnight stop.

When he boarded the flight for Salt Lake, he knew he was still gambling. Even if Li continued west into Utah, he could stay on I-70 to Las Vegas, then on to LA. But Adam was certain the man was leaving the country, and that once Li turned north out of Telluride, his destination was Canada. If he had chosen LA, he would have gone through Albuquerque.

When his plane touched down in the Utah capital, a voice message from Fisher confirmed Adam's suspicion. The Utah patrolman's replacement, monitoring traffic east of Green River, picked up the Volvo just after 7:00 a.m., then passed it again at a service station in town. The trooper parked along the interstate just west of the junction north toward Price, and saw Li make the turn.

As he approached Salt Lake's city center, Adam could see the gray dome of the state capitol perched on the foothills of the Wasatch Mountains to the east. There were no cities in the country quite like these in the valleys of central Utah, with nothing defining where city ended and mountain began, and peaks rising steeply from the valley floor in every direction. When Salt Lake hosted the Winter Olympics in 2002, the entire interstate system through the valley had been re-engineered, expanding I-15 to ten lanes through much of the valley. During the flight from Oklahoma, Adam had studied the road system on a digital map and was now driving south to where two of the mountain valleys joined at a low pass the maps called "The Point of the Mountain." Here the interstate narrowed in each direction to two "general use" lanes and an inside "high occupancy" commuter lane. Both to avoid being stopped and out of his elevated sense of propriety, Li would stay in the outer lanes – probably to the far right. The Weaver had refueled in Green River and if he drove straight through, should reach the Point of the Mountain between 11:30 and noon.

Adam exited onto Bluffdale Road just north of the summit of the low pass, turned left back under the freeway and drove on past the entry ramp that rejoined the interstate heading north. He continued east toward the foothills until he could U-turn at what looked like a small industrial park, driving back to a wide place on the shoulder just before the on-ramp. To his left, I-15 descended from the Point with both north-bound lanes clearly visible for half a mile. Farther down the valley to Adam's right, the high-fenced compound of the Utah State Penitentiary was clearly visible: a fitting setting to begin a chase. He glanced at the dashboard clock of the Ford. Nine-fifteen a.m. Li wouldn't be crossing the Point for at least another two hours. Time to find something to eat and check in with Fisher.

. . .

Lawrence Li did not drive straight through. Much of Utah's Highway 6 between Green River and the town of Price is long stretches of straight gray pavement – so long and straight that Li was reminded of a travel game he and his parents played when he was a boy. As they drove across straight, flat expanses of highway where the road disappeared ahead into the shimmering distance, they would see who could come closest to guessing how far it was to some distant landmark that was the only disruption on an otherwise featureless horizon. He had been very good at it and, at least in his memory, usually won the game.

Along both sides of the highway north of Green River, mounds of bare, buff-colored sand covered the landscape, giving the impression of driving through the remnants of some ancient strip-mining operation. Even the sagebrush had become scarce, replaced by patches of the sun-yellowed grass. In front of him and behind, all Li could see was straight, featureless highway. Every ten to fifteen minutes a car flew up on his rear bumper, paused for a brief moment to check for the occasional oncoming truck, then zoomed past until it was no more than a dot on the gray ribbon ahead of him. All but one. A white car remained barely in sight, a constant mile or more behind.

As he rolled into the small town of Wellington, a few miles east of Price, Li checked his mirror and could not see the white vehicle. He turned quickly off the road into a church parking lot that circled the building, pulling to a spot in the rear where he could not be seen by approaching traffic, but could watch anything that passed. Three minutes later, the Honda CRV with heavily tinted windows that he had seen in Green River eased past the building like a white bloodhound, sniffing along for something it knew must be nearby. Li waited exactly ten minutes, then pulled back onto the highway and continued through Price without seeing the Honda.

Beyond the town, the road began to climb immediately into the mountains with cliffs so sheer and close that as he started up a sweeping incline, the rock face seemed to close behind him like the gates of some mountain fortress. Li thought again of the boulders that had begun to threaten him on the ragged slopes above Telluride and shivered against the leather seat.

Twenty-five miles above Price, just beyond a plain, vinyl-sided building that called itself "Colton Hilltop Country Service," the canyon widened and the road straightened again beside a shallow stream that meandered through a willow-choked meadow to Li's right. A road sign informed him that Soldiers' Summit lay two miles ahead at 7,440 feet and as he approached the small collection of buildings that marked the high point of the pass, he glanced into the rearview mirror at the stretch of road behind him. The CRV was just coming into view at the bottom of the grade.

There was only one road that anyone driving from Grand Junction to Salt Lake City could reasonably take – the one Li was traveling. It shouldn't be surprising to see the same vehicles at stops along the way or passing each other as the day went by. But he knew he was probably the most cautious driver on this stretch of highway and that everyone passed him. Everyone but the Honda with the tinted windows.

The descent from the summit into Utah Valley was a steep, forty-five miles of unnerving switchbacks and blind curves and Li had little time to see who was following him. At the bottom of the canyon, instead of continuing on toward the interstate he turned onto US 89 toward the town of Springville, knowing that anyone going north to Salt Lake would continue on to the freeway. At a pizza place on Main Street, he pulled into the lot and waited. Two minutes later, the Honda cruised past.

Li was certain the driver hadn't seen him turn onto Highway 89. Somewhere on his car was a tracking device. He thought momentarily about trying to locate it, but decided it would be well hidden and that getting rid of it may simply mean his pursuer would have to keep him more closely in sight. With the way Li felt compelled to drive, that wouldn't be difficult. Instead, he pulled his Lenovo tablet from the leather briefcase, plugged a small remote "hotspot" into a USB port, and activated it until he received confirmation that he was connected to the web. Li began to type.

Five minutes later, when a single key stroke away from activating *Seres*, he placed the tablet on the seat beside him and pulled back onto Springville's Main Street. His GPS signaled that a left turn at the next light would take him west to I-15.

# FORTY-TWO

Special Agent in Charge Art Dempsey stepped into the room and took a seat at the end of the table where Dreu Sason continued to work on one of the Bureau's laptops. He tried to look at ease but not relaxed, feeling that he should exude confidence, but not certainty.

"Everything sent out?" he asked.

"Only a few left," she said without looking up.

He paused, letting the confident façade slip for a moment. "Do you think this will work?"

Sason stopped tapping at the keyboard and met his gaze with a grim smile. "To be honest, I don't know. I didn't have enough time to study the construction of the obfuscated code well enough to know exactly what it would allow or prevent."

"If you had to place odds on it, what would you give it?"

"Fifty-fifty. I'm hoping they were anticipating that they wouldn't be discovered and didn't plan for something like I've tried to do here. The only way we'll know is if the program is executed. What progress are you making in getting that stopped?"

"I'd like to say I can't discuss our plan with you. But the truth is, I don't know what the plan is. There's a lot of inter-agency activity going on and for some reason, our role seems to be one of providing a liaison to Central Intelligence, who is mainly asking favors of local law enforcement units around the country. And I'm not even clear what those favors include."

Sason raised her head in mild acknowledgment, adding to Dempsey's conviction that she knew more about what was happening beyond the Bureau's Dallas offices than she admitted. He watched in silence as she sent out the last set of instructions to the list of companies and agencies that sat in front of her on the table. She leaned back and spread her fingers to stretch the tired joints.

"Are you confident they'll all incorporate these recommendations?" she asked.

"Their instructions have been clear and unequivocal, working directly through the various security directors and CEOs. They haven't all been happy, but they'll do it."

"Let's hope we don't have to test its effectiveness," she said. "From the look of this list, if it doesn't work, this country will grind to a halt – and for who knows how long."

"Apparently, that's the idea," Dempsey said, reassuming his air of confidence. "But I think we'll get it stopped." He paused and waited until Sason looked up again. "Tell me about your friend, Adam Zak," he said, watching her eyes.

They didn't waiver.

"What's to tell?"

"Well, to begin with, he's a man with a very interesting history – or should I say, lack of history. When we traced your phone messages to him, we naturally checked to see who he was. Aside from having a cell phone in his name and a driver's license, the man has no history. Not even a mortgage."

"And what do you mean by 'history?'" she asked.

Dempsey shrugged. "No military record, no registration for selective service, no college records, or even ancestry that we can find...."

"You seem to have spent a lot of time looking," Sason said, giving him the same grim smile.

"We were just curious about how you were found at the ranch, when the only message you sent telling anyone where you were, went to him."

"As Mr. Eckerson said, you'd be the first to know that those messages seemed to have been pretty widely available to all the national security agencies," she said. "And to a lot of others as well. Lonnie Marchisio and the woman who attacked me at Adam's home managed to find me. And I'm sure Adam didn't tip them off."

"You're certain?"

Dreu Sason scoffed. "You think he contacted both one of these Weavers *and* a mental case who was trying to track me down? Get serious!"

"How can you be positive if you haven't spoken to each other since this all began?"

Sason's glare spoke volumes. "I know him," she said.

"What do you know about him? Really?"

Dreu leaned forward against the table and cocked her head to one side. "Is this some kind of interrogation? I see you delayed asking all these questions until I finished trying to save you all from a national disaster...."

"Of course it's not an interrogation. Believe it or not, I'm thinking about you, Ms. Sason. I just wondered if you really know who you've established this relationship with."

"I know what I need to know," she said.

"You said Zak works in airline security," Dempsey pushed. "Would it surprise you to know that the TSA and none of the airlines want to claim him?"

"I've suspected that he's an air marshal, and I wouldn't think they would want that information public," Sason said dismissively.

"Even when *we* ask?"

"Maybe *especially* if you asked. You people seem to think you can snap your fingers and the world says, 'Oh, Yes sir! No, sir!' Well, not everyone thinks you need to know so damned much. I'd think that if he's private security for one of the airlines and not TSA, they wouldn't feel compelled to tell you, no matter what you people think of your ability to force information out of them."

"I'm sensing a trace of bitterness here...."

"*You're* the guys who put my picture on TV and wanted the country to hunt me down! *You* are part of the legal system that turned the guy who mutilated me loose after one year of a twenty-year sentence! That doesn't engender a high degree of confidence in you – and neither of those things had anything to do with Adam."

Dempsey nodded his acknowledgement. "Touché. But someone who knows a great deal about this Weaver deal appears to be out there directing this attempt to stop them. And your friend Zak hasn't reappeared since this began."

"What about this Randall Murch the Eckerson kid told you about? It sounds like he was pretty deeply involved in all of this."

"Right.... While your friend Zak was out of touch in Southeast Asia. Coincidence?"

"There are more coincidences in this mess than you can shake a stick at," Sason muttered.

"My thoughts exactly," Dempsey said.

. . .

The gunmetal gray Volvo crested the Point of the Mountain at 12:20 p.m. and began the gradual descent into the valley of the Great Salt Lake. Adam picked it up a quarter mile above the Bluffdale exit and was rolling up the access ramp onto I-15 when Li passed. He was three cars behind the Volvo when he blended into traffic and immediately recognized the challenge of following Lawrence Li. The man was clearly the slowest driver on the interstate.

A mile ahead the highway expanded to four, then five lanes in each direction and Adam moved on past the Volvo until a hundred yards in front, then slowed to match its speed. He reasoned that the man would pay less attention to a car driving slowly in front of him than to a tail, and that any driver as deliberate as Li would signal well in advance if he decided to leave the freeway.

His conversation with Fisher had been brief: letting him know that Li appeared to be bound for Canada, and learning that the other Weavers were also on the move. Four of the remaining seven had been taken into custody and three were under close surveillance. Henry Liu had started to talk and had told his interrogators that they had until 3:00 p.m. Sunday. But he didn't know where Li was going, or how to stop what he planned to do.

The cross streets south of Salt Lake City were numbered using some measuring system that counted down as a driver approached the center of the city. Adam crossed 10600 South, 9000 South, then 7800 South as he passed through the suburb of Midvale. As he approached 6400 South, I-215 separated, heading west to the airport and east along the foothills of the Wasatch Range to intersect the interstate to Denver. Adam slowed and watched for Li's signal, but the Volvo continued north through the suburbs of Murray and Mill Creek and on into south Salt Lake.

Traffic had become heavy and as they passed through the maze of ramps and overpasses that signaled the junction with Interstate 80, Adam eased into an inside lane, slowed until Li passed him, then again slipped in behind, four cars back. As they approached 400 South, Adam glimpsed the iconic gray granite spires of the Mormon Temple peeking through spaces between taller buildings that had grown around it, and a green sign indicated he could exit right to Temple Square. Three of the vehicles that separated him from Li followed the sign's direction onto the exit ramp and Adam slowed until another two filled the gap.

North of the city center, the mountains closed in against the highway on the right, and the left side of the freeway became metal industrial buildings and acres of white petroleum storage tanks that stretched west to the gray, lifeless edge of the Great Salt Lake. Thirty miles north, traffic began to thin as they approached Hill Air Force Base and Adam knew that beyond the city of Ogden, traffic would thin again as a major road through the mountains exited right to the city of Logan. Once past the exit and certain Li was remaining on I-15, Adam slipped back until the Volvo was barely distinguishable, following a white Honda with Colorado plates that seemed committed to the same cautious speed. Now, all he needed to do was watch to see if the Weaver exited the interstate.

At 2:30 they crossed into Idaho and seven miles into the state, the Volvo signaled a right turn into a north-bound welcome center. In front of Adam, the Honda slowed and also signaled, pulling onto the off ramp as Li eased into a parking space in front of the rustic stone and cedar building of the rest stop. For a quarter mile behind the center to the east, nothing but open, scrub-covered country separated them from the ochre slopes of Idaho's Bannock Mountains.

As the Honda approached the building, its driver swung into a parking area for picnickers where a small construction trailer blocked the view from the welcome center. Adam drove past to the front of the building and pulled into a space separated from the Volvo by a white and yellow Idaho Power utility truck.

Li had gone into the building and Adam followed, needing to take advantage of the restroom. The Chinese-American was at one of the urinals when Adam entered the men's room and didn't look up at the man who stepped up two stalls to his right. Li washed his hands meticulously and used the blow dryer, giving Adam time to wash and follow him from the building.

As Li reached the top of the concrete steps that descended to the parking lot, a younger Asian man hurried toward him from the direction of the picnic area. He was taller than Li and his snug blue T-shirt and worn jeans covered a well-conditioned body.

Li hesitated at the top of the steps and glanced at the approach-ing stranger with a glimmer of recognition, then looked about with what Adam recognized as sheer panic. The Volvo was parked to the left of the steps in the direction of the younger man, and Li suddenly jumped the stairs two at a time and rushed toward his car, fumbling in his pocket for the key fob. Adam heard the locks click open. The other man bolted forward in a race for the car, but Li reached the driver's door first, threw it open and flung himself forward across the seat. The young Asian reached the passenger door and yanked it open, ducking inside to pull a small computer tablet from the seat.

Li slid back out of the car and stood leaning against the roof of the Volvo, his face relaxed with relieved satisfaction.

"You're too late," he said, facing the man who stood with the computer on the other side of the car. "It's done."

The younger man walked slowly around the front of the car, holding the tablet out toward the Weaver. As he approached Li with the computer in his left hand, he reached up with his right and slapped him firmly on the side of the neck.

"I'm sorry," he said as Li winced, grabbing the Lenovo. The stranger turned quickly and walked back toward the picnic area.

Li checked the screen on the computer, rubbing absently at the side of his neck and nodding to himself. He turned and looked toward Adam and a man in an orange vest who had just exited the building and was approaching the steps. Li suddenly stiffened and dropped the computer, grasping at the door frame of the Volvo. His eyes widened and face contorted as a spasm knotted his entire body. He opened his mouth wide to suck in a desperate breath, but got only the strained rasp of a severe allergic attack. His hand went to his pants pocket and fumbled for an EpiPen, jamming the needle through his pant leg into his thigh. But the spasm continued.

Adam had been watching the exchange from the top of the steps and sprang forward, reaching Li as he collapsed onto the pavement.

"Call 911," he shouted at the man in the vest. "This guy's had some kind of attack."

The worker reached for his phone as Adam bent over the fallen Weaver, pumping rhythmically on his chest, then pinched his nose closed and tried to force air into the starving lungs. But the injection from the slap on the neck had paralyzed every system and Li lay rigid against the black asphalt.

On Adam's blind side, he heard a car speed across the lot reserved for tractor trailers at the rear of the welcome center, and straightened to see the white CRV exit the parking area, headed north. Adam followed it briefly but as the utility worker stepped up beside him, bent again over Li and resumed the CPR.

"First responders are on the way from Malad," the man said. "That's just a couple of miles up the road."

As he straightened again to pressure Li's chest, Adam noticed the copper bracelet about the Weaver's wrist and waved the utility worker down beside him.

"What does that bracelet say?" he asked, and the man lifted Li's wrist and read the engraved inscription.

"It says 'severe allergies, especially bee and wasp stings," the man said.

"I'm not getting any air into him. Can you maintain the heart pressure?"

The worker squatted beside him and took over the rhythmic pressure on Li's chest as Adam continued to try to force air into his lungs. Sirens sounded from the north, wailing down the south-bound lanes of the interstate. A young couple who had pulled into the rest stop watched nervously from the sidewalk.

"The man's had a severe allergic attack," Adam called to them. "Run inside and see if they have another EpiPen."

The woman looked confused, but the man sprinted toward the building.

A red fire department rescue truck swung down through the highway median and raced up the access ramp to the welcome center. The EMTs burst from both doors at once: a stocky young man with a dark, closely trimmed beard, and a spindly woman of about the same age whose white uniform shirt flapped loosely on her in the afternoon breeze off the mountains. Following a routine rehearsed through hours of practice, they threw open the rear doors of the truck and as the man slid out two black cases of emergency equipment, the woman grabbed a mask and oxygen bottle and hurried to the victim.

"He's wearing a medical alert bracelet," Adam told her. "Says he's highly allergic, especially to bee and wasp stings." The man who had run into the center returned, shaking his head.

"Epinephrine!" the woman shouted to her partner. "He's in severe anaphylaxis!"

A Malad City police car swerved down through the median and up the access road, screeching to a halt beside the emergency truck. An officer who looked even younger than the EMTs slid from the patrol car, straightened a wide black belt that Adam was certain held every enforcement device known to man, and strode officially to where the small group stood on the walk watching the emergency team. He glanced at Li lying beside the Volvo and turned his chin into a mic that was clipped against his shoulder on the epaulet of his uniform.

"I've got a Code 3 at the welcome center at the seven mile marker. EMT's are on the scene. Need an ambulance, stat!" Behind him on the interstate, the ambulance was already wailing south toward the rest stop.

"Now – who here saw what happened?" the officer asked. Adam left it to the utility worker to respond. He was pretty certain the man had come out of the building after the younger Asian walked away.

"We were coming down the walk here when this man collapsed," the utility man said. "He was just getting into his car and looked like he had a seizure of some kind, then just dropped over. Had this computer in his hand and dropped it on the drive." He handed the officer Li's Lenovo.

"And who called in the report?" the officer wanted to know, pulling a notepad from his breast pocket.

The utility man raised his hand. "I did. This guy started to give him CPR."

"Let me get names, addresses, and phones" the officer said, and the young couple backed away.

"We got here after it happened," the woman said.

The utility man stepped forward. "Howard Olsen. Eight Eleven, Pinehurst Drive, Pocatello." He gave the officer his phone number.

The officer scribbled the information and turned to Adam.

"Stan Paulson. Fourteen Seven-o-Four, Black Mesa Road, Tucumcari, New Mexico." Adam made up a fictitious phone number that he hoped was close to Tucumcari's area code.

"Just passing through?" the policeman asked.

"Headed up to Helena to see friends," Adam said. "Really sorry about the man there. Anything more we can do?"

The ambulance had pulled up and Li was being loaded into the back. Though a mask was strapped tightly across his face, it was clear to Adam that he was dead.

"I think we've got it from here," the officer said. "Thanks for your quick response. We'll be in touch if we need more information.

Adam nodded and shook the hand of the utility worker, then climbed in the Ford and eased back out onto I-15. When the welcome center had disappeared in the rearview mirror, he called Fisher.

"Li's dead," he said when his control answered. "I'll give you details later. But before he died, he said the attempt to stop him was too late."

"I know," Fisher rasped. "Twenty minutes ago, Seattle and Portland went black."

# FORTY-THREE

"The irony," said Special Agent Dempsey, "is that the damage was done by the one Weaver who seemed to have decided she wanted out – Helen Robb. Seattle City Lights and Pacific Power in Portland contracted with PG&E for their security programming, mainly because Robb had such a reputation as a talented designer. We didn't know she had done that out-of-state work when we sent the fixes out."

The three deputy directors again surrounded the table, joined by Dempsey and Dreu Sason. Davis Eckerson had gone to California to be with Angie Robb.

Soren Lansaw from NSA directed his question to Sason.

"You think these systems can be up within a couple of days? The outages are reaping havoc in the Northwest. These cities have come to a complete standstill. I can't imagine what would have happened had we lost the others that were targeted – and the federal agencies."

"The time consuming part is that they have to install completely new equipment," Sason said. "Without a 'fix' that we weren't able to prepare because we couldn't examine the actual programming, all of the hardware remains contaminated and will respond by rejecting installation of any backups. Both companies had backup programs, of course, and with the changes we sent, they should be safe to load, once the new equipment is in place."

"Might I ask how the fix worked?" Hagebusch from the CIA asked. "You seemed to have reservations...."

Dreu lifted her hands from the table and arched her brows, acknowledging that she hadn't been certain. "What I was unsure about was how the code we couldn't see instructed the IVKs. We hide the kernels in the code at FedTegrity so that hackers won't see them, but I knew where to look and essentially understood how Mr. Ding constructed his. I tried to take one of them apart, but he had encrypted it so well I couldn't deconstruct it. My guess was that they weren't counting on anyone ever discovering that the IVKs were there, so didn't take special steps to protect the kernels themselves. Are you following?"

The men nodded their heads uncertainly.

"The Message from Li, using one of the authorized passwords, was essentially a trigger instruction to a part of the IVK that wasn't active until he triggered it. It was some kind of 'go to' command. I just created a new set of IVKs using what I knew were Ding's typical coding techniques, and instructed each program to replace all of his IVKs with mine. Ding must have done something similar when he modified the programs Anthony and I sent to him. The Weaver programmers had designed their verification kernels to repair any tampering with the program, but not to repair themselves. When a 'replace all' instruction was given for them, the new ones popped into place and the old ones were trashed. The trigger instruction from Li had nothing to activate."

"Brilliant," Hagebusch murmured.

Deputy Director Serna from the FBI inserted himself, speaking to the group as a whole. "And it appears this execution command that knocked out Seattle and Portland came from Li just before he had a fatal allergic reaction of some kind. Interesting coincidence."

Dempsey glanced over at Dreu.

"Do we know there wasn't foul play?" he asked.

"The police in Malad City, Idaho, said he was wearing an alert bracelet, warning of severe allergies, especially to bees. He apparently was stung on the neck and though he had an epinephrine injector with him, it wasn't enough. The EMTs said he was dead before they could get anything else into him."

"Were there others there when he died?" Dempsey asked.

"Four others. A couple who got there after the attack started and two men who tried to help him. They weren't together, but both confirmed that Li was by himself when he had the attack. Plus, the ME in Pocatello said it looked like severe anaphylactic shock. He didn't feel an autopsy was warranted."

"And we didn't ask for one?" Dempsey pressed.

"Do we have reason to suspect foul play?" his boss asked.

Dempsey shrugged. "Someone has been after these Weavers since Eckerson and Robb came back from Cambodia. Do we have descriptions of the people who were around when Li had his attack – just out of curiosity?"

Serna flipped open a folder and checked some notes. "One of the men was a local lineman for Idaho Power who lives in Pocatello. So unless you think there's some kind of giant utility conspiracy, I think we can rule him out. The other was just some traveler from New Mexico."

"Name and description?"

Serna looked at his Dallas Field agent with mild irritation, but offered the information. "Stan Paulson. Described as Caucasian, six two or three, very short bristle hair."

Dempsey again looked at Dreu Sason who returned his glance without expression. "Did anyone check on this Stan Paulson?"

"We haven't had reason to," Serna said, the irritation now more than mild.

"You might want to have someone do that," Dempsey said. "My guess is, you won't find him."

# FORTY-FOUR

Nita nuzzled more closely against Fisher's stubbled neck and lifted her left leg to rest across his hips. He couldn't feel it, but she could, and she kissed his cheek and pressed her own hips more tightly against him as they lay uncovered on the large bed. Her brown left breast rested on his chest, accenting the pallor of his skin.

She nibbled on the lobe of his ear and he smiled, his mind still elsewhere.

"You have a theory about all this," she said.

"It's more than a theory. I think we've learned enough to know what happened with some certainty."

"They've been monitoring these Weavers all along, then?"

"When Jim Thompson discovered them in Cambodia, he was naturally suspicious of why the Chinese would send children somewhere else to learn the silk trade. The Chinese developed silk to begin with and had the finest processes in the world. So my guess is that they had to get rid of him before he alerted western authorities that the children were there, being schooled in English and western culture for some purpose."

"But why didn't they provide the Weavers with more direction? Once they became adults, they seem to have developed their plan pretty much on their own."

"I suspect in the early days, they did receive direction. They were instructed to get the best educations possible and watch to see where they could insert themselves into places where the U.S. had particular vulnerability. But then the Party leadership lost track of them, and their Number Nine assumed independent control. According to the Director, a Chinese source said Li continued to have a disaffected backer in the country with considerable wealth who feared China was becoming too capitalist. He continued to provide funding for them, but Li was the one who masterminded *Seres*."

"But *someone* was keeping track of them. They knew about the plan and knew about Li's allergy risks...."

"Chinese intelligence. It's always maintained a degree of independence, and they knew where the Weavers were. I suspect they thought *Seres* might be useful at some point, but couldn't have Li making independent decisions about when. So they had him monitored."

"The ski instructor in Telluride."

Fisher's left hand found the small of Nita's back and worked its way onto her hip, stroking its round softness.

"He was put there to watch Li, but we were the ones who alerted them that the Weavers had been discovered when we tried to get them to admit to having a sleeper cell in the country. And when Li got nervous, they got nervous. They had their man tighten his surveillance. I think they knew he was unstable and that executing *Seres* right now would be an international disaster. So they had to stop him. Fortunately, we didn't have to rely entirely on their intelligence to get this thing shut down."

"Our man and his friend did a good job," Nita said.

"He's one of our best," Fisher agreed. "And about the only one who seems like a really decent guy."

"Is there a place for a decent guy in our work?"

"If he continues to believe in it. But I'm worried about him right now. He cares for this woman."

"That's an interesting concern, coming from you!"

He turned his face toward her. "You think, after all this time, that I have no conscience?"

She smiled, but answered with a question. "What are you going to do about his request?"

Fisher kissed her gently on the forehead. "I think I'll worry about it in the morning."

. . .

The prepaid phone arrived in a small package through UPS – signature required. Dreu opened it at the kitchen table, looked it over carefully and unfolded the note that had been tucked beneath it.

*If you feel like you want to talk, find a public place a few miles from your home and give me a call at this number. Any time. I've missed you.*

She did a search on her smart phone for the 602 area code that was part of the number scribbled at the bottom of the note. Phoenix.

Twenty minutes later, she dialed from a secluded corner of a coffee shop on the Virginia Parkway. The phone rang only once before he answered.

"I wasn't sure you'd call," he said.

"I have a lot of unanswered questions."

"You were pretty upset at the ranch...."

"Upset doesn't begin to describe it."

"But you chose not to out me to Dempsey and the others… which I appreciate."

"We were in crisis – and I knew you were working to get us out of it. And I didn't know exactly who I might be 'outing'."

"I obviously didn't tell you everything – but for equally obvious reasons."

"No. You were using me. That's different than not telling me everything."

He was silent for a moment, then said;" You're right. When I arranged the introduction at the gym, I'd seen a file photo that led me to expected some frumpy woman with flabby thighs and messy hair. Not a beautiful, bright, fun, sexy woman I would completely fall for."

"Where did the picture come from?"

"No idea. It looked like a mug shot. Ever been arrested?"

"Ohhh," Dreu moaned. "Texas driver's license. It *is* pretty bad!" She paused, then said, "But does that mean you couldn't have loved me if I'd been frumpy and had flabby thighs…?"

"Maxian Brain Fart," he muttered. "Of course I could. I find myself loving Dreu Sason for all kinds of reasons – and would even if you had flabby thighs."

Dreu didn't want the conversation to turn light. "The thing that puzzles me," she said, "is that none of the agencies seemed to want to claim you – or even seemed certain who you were."

"As it should be."

"Can you tell me more about that?"

"That depends," he said. "I'm guessing that you're unemployed."

"I prefer to think that I'm 'between jobs.' But as a matter of fact, all three of the deputy directors I was working with on the computer solution offered me a position."

"I can imagine! And…?"

"I'm considering my options."

"Would you consider another?"

She paused and looked suspiciously around the coffee shop. "You aren't here watching me now, are you?"

He laughed. "No. I'm steering clear of McKinney – and Art Dempsey's Texas jurisdiction. He's been asking too many questions."

"So…. What's the option?"

"I need to know first if you could ever trust me – after our little 'true confession' session that wasn't all true. You have plenty of reasons not to."

She had to think about that for a moment. "The funny thing…," she said finally, "…is that I'd trust you with my life. I guess I already have. I'm just not sure I'd trust you with my love."

"Do you believe I really care about you?"

Again, she paused. "Yes…. I really do. Am I wrong?"

"Not in any way," he said.

Both were silent for another long moment. "Well," she said finally. "Just out of curiosity, what's the option?"

"That you work with me. I've been able to arrange a comfortable salary and the best computer equipment you could ever ask for."

"And what would I be doing, Mr. Disappears-for-weeks-at-a-time.?"

"The same things you've been doing to help with this case."

She considered this, then asked, "I assume I'd have to move. Are you in Phoenix?"

"Scottsdale," he said.

"It's hot there."

"That's the idea. I hate cold."

"Could it be San Francisco?"

"I thought about that – but I really do think the Bay Area's going to slide into the Pacific one of these days. Want to know the salary?"

"Not really. I'm very comfortable and can see that you've had what you need to get around. Cambodia. Vietnam. Private plane to the U.S. I guess what I need to think about is how alone I want to be when you're off doing whatever it is you do."

"An important thing to think about…."

"And if while you're away, you're lying to and seducing some other woman who can help you get done whatever it is you do."

"Another big question."

"And what I'd do if you didn't come back at all from one of these adventures. You worried me when you were gone this time."

"Also important to think about."

"Why do you want me to work with you?"

This time it was Adam's turn to pause. "Because," he said after a moment, "I can't imagine that there's anyone who's better at what *you* do than you are. But mainly, I don't want to be alone either. And when I'm home and think about who I want to be at home with, or away and think about who I'd like to come back to, it's always you."

"Good answer. Do they have stables in Scottsdale?"

"Very close to the apartment I'm leasing."

"I assume I couldn't tell anyone where I was moving. My family. Bri or Sandi – or anyone."

"I'm not sure that would be quite as critical in this position. You could just be working for your own computer solutions firm."

"There's another option," she said.

"And what would that be?"

"I actually *could* be working for my own computer solutions firm. When I was talking to the Deputies, I pointed out that they could really use someone to do what FedTegrity did. But someone they knew would be fully transparent with clients, completely trustworthy, and could do the job. They all agreed."

"And that could be you."

"Yes, that could be me."

"And you're considering that option?"

"Actually, I just decided on it. I think I'll set up shop in Phoenix. Hang onto that phone. I may be getting in touch."

# AUTHOR'S NOTE

Although this novel is a work of fiction, much of the information presented in *The Weavers of Meanchey* about Jim Thompson is true. He was an OSS agent at the end of World War II who ended up in Southeast Asia and is credited with having revitalized the Thai silk industry. He was a collector of Thai antiquities and his collection, much of which can be seen at the Jim Thompson house (or collection of houses) in Bangkok, is one of the finest in the country. If visiting the Thompson House, you can have your picture taken with a life-sized wax figure of Thompson, seated on a bench in the gift shop. Thompson did disappear during a vacation trip to Malaysia in 1967 and hasn't been heard from since. And his sister Katharine, nicknamed Kaa, was mysteriously murdered in her bed a few months later.

It is not known whether Thompson remained involved in intelligence gathering after he left the OSS. And though he did travel throughout Southeast Asia acquiring resources for his silk revitalization, we don't know that he visited the village of Paoy Snoul – though it is well known for its unique golden silk and might have been of interest to him. The letter from Thompson to his sister is a complete creation of this novel, as are the Chinese children of Paoy Snoul. No one really knows what happened to Thompson or why he disappeared.

During the past fifteen years, while traveling extensively in Southeast Asia, I have developed a great love and appreciation for the countries of the region and their peoples. As with any countries, they have their challenges and darker sides and some of those are depicted in this novel. I hope these depictions don't serve in any way to reflect poorly on Thailand or Cambodia, since I have found them two of the most enjoyable and hospitable places I have visited.

All other characters and circumstances presented in this book are fictional and any similarity to real persons or situations is purely coincidental and unintended.

Other novels by Allen Kent

*The Shield of Darius*

*Backwater*

*River of Light and Shadow*

*Guardians of the Second Son*

Excerpt from
# *The Shield of Darius*

"Reports that say that something hasn't happened are always interesting to me, because as we know, there are known knowns; there are things we know we know. We also know there are known unknowns; that is to say we know there are some things we do not know. But there are also unknown unknowns - - the ones we don't know we don't know. And if one looks throughout the history of our country and other free countries, it is the latter category that tend to be the difficult ones."

**Donald H. Rumsfeld, Department of Defense news briefing, February 12, 2002**

This is the story of one of the unknown unknowns.

# ONE

Nothing in the lush green countryside surrounding Ben Sager suggested his day would end so badly. It was unusually warm in England's County Dorset, with only a wisp of horse-tail clouds brushing the top of the gray stone tower that rose above him on the low, grassy hill.

Ben turned the brochure in his hand to orient the diagram to match the castle ruin, glanced from the page to the crumbling structure, then back to the drawing. The gate and keep were to his left, with a long section of toppled stone wall stretching across in front of him into an overgrown mound at his far right. The river was behind him and the small wood of thick pines to his left. He nodded with absent satisfaction, comfortable that he was properly oriented. Flipping the pamphlet to its back, Ben read the brief narrative, learning that Roger de Caen, Bishop of Sarum and Abbot of Sherborne, had built this hilltop fortress overlooking the River Yoe in the early twelfth century. The paragraph claimed that a succession of proud English noblemen had inhabited Sherborne Castle since, but as Ben scanned the ruin with sad amusement, he saw little to suggest its early grandeur.

"Whew," he thought. "These places must have been cold in the winter."

"Hellooo....Dad!"

A small dark figure appeared atop one of the crumpled battlements and swung an arm in long, exaggerated sweeps, then darted down the far side without waiting for a response. Though too distant to be seen clearly, the figure had been PJ. At ten, he was a carbon copy of his father – short and wiry with a shock of black hair that waved naturally over his forehead. Ben waved back at the empty wall and smiled at how much the boy reminded him of himself at that age.

Genetically, PJ seemed to have ignored the fact that he had a mother. He drew gene for gene from Ben's store of Roma ancestry, a line that after immigrating to American from the old Yugoslav Republic, had bred without compromise until Ben broke the chain, captured by the allure of an Irish beauty while a graduate student at the University of

Virginia. Kate's hair was as black as his own, but she had the creamy, flawless skin and deep green eyes of County Cork. And each time Ben shot baskets with PJ, he wished his son had picked up an inch or two of his mother's height. At 5'9" Kate was two inches taller than Ben, but none of it had gone to their son.

Ben turned and flopped onto the grassy slope beside the river, gazing across its mirrored surface at a manor house that stood surrounded by live oaks on a hill opposite the castle. He never ceased to marvel at how much England looked like it should. With the expansion of Sager Technologies into Leeds, he now visited the British Isles three or four times a year, always finding the countryside and villages to be calendar perfect. When he mentioned the observation to Kate, she laughed.

"You're just too used to big dirty cities," she said. "No place is that unspoiled anymore." But now that she was coming with him and they were taking an extra few weeks to get into the countryside, she admitted he was right.

On this outing they had rented a camper – what the British call a caravan – and driven north from London to Stratford and Coventry. Then southwest through the quaint stone villages of the Cotswolds; Chipping Campden, Stow-on-the-Wold, and Bourton-on-the-Waters. Constable landscapes with storybook names. Tidy thatched cottages surrounded by manicured gardens, nestled along narrow cobbled lanes that left the villages to wind into the countryside between neatly trimmed hedges and white stone walls.

At Trowbridge the evening before, PJ and his sister Jennifer had walked unattended through the campground, listening to soft English accents and feasting on McVitty's Jaffa Cakes and Cadbury's chocolate. Ben could very comfortably live here. If he could get the company through another ten profitable years, the kids would be in college and he just might be able to buy a place like the one across the river. Not quite that imposing, but one where he could settle down with Kate in peaceful country style and fish for trout in a stream like the River Yoe.

The warm softness of the grass and quiet ripple of the river soothed his travel-weary back and legs and tugged heavily at his eyelids. He dozed for a moment, then forced his lids open and glanced at his watch, jumping quickly to his feet. Four-fifteen! They wanted to make Seaton on the coast by dark and needed to move. He turned down the bank and started toward the stand of young pine and oak that stretched across the bottom of the hill to the small lot where he had parked the camper. Kate and Jenn might already be in the van, but PJ? Finding PJ could take some time.

Ben turned along a path that skirted the wood leading toward the front entrance to the fortress. At the edge of the trees in front of him, a man in khaki slacks and jacket with a bright yellow scarf tied about his neck stepped into view, then retreated back into the wood. Ben stopped and peered into the shadows, straining to follow the man. His movements had been too quick. Too conscious – as if he had been startled to see Ben and was dodging away. For a long moment Ben watched the spot where he had disappeared, then chuckled and shook his head. The poor guy probably had a son like PJ and was in the middle of some medieval war game, assigned by his son to storm the castle without being seen. Given the slow tourist day at Sherborne, it was a good time for hiding games. When the Sagers pulled into the parking area an hour earlier, their caravan had been the only vehicle in the lot.

As he entered the trees to head toward the parking area, Ben ducked low and peered between the thatched branches of the pines for the other tourist. The first glance had been fleeting, but the man looked Middle Eastern. Not swarthy enough to be East Indian, but darker than north Mediterranean. Arab or Persian, which added to Ben's curiosity. He did not share the aversion for that part of the world that had been conditioned into most Americans by a decade of Iraqi and Afghan conflicts and the on-going Palestinian debacle. Ben had spent all but one of his high school years in the Middle East where his father had been on a three year assignment with the U.S. Information Agency in the Iranian capital of Tehran. The years in Iran just before the Shah was deposed had affected him more profoundly than any other period in his life. He didn't admit it much. It wasn't stylish to speak kindly of Iran. But he loved the rugged country and its exuberant, passionate people, an affection he sustained by continuing to study the country and its language as something of a hobby. Someday he was going to get back, taking Kate and the kids with him.

He did not find the man in the castle wood. Instead, a young woman appeared suddenly among the trees to his right, dressed in blue jeans and a bulky sweatshirt, pushing toward him through the branches with an anxious face. She saw him and beckoned frantically for him to come. Ben jumped forward, feeling the blood course to his temples as he sensed her alarm.

"*Mr. Sager? Mr. Sager?*"

He nodded quickly.

"Please come. *You must hurry!*" Her voice carried the thick inflection that matched her black hair and olive skin and confirmed Ben's assessment of the origin of the man in the trees.

"What is it? What's happened?"

"Your son, sir. He has fallen from one of the towers and is hurt very badly. We must hurry!"

"Where is he? You haven't moved him...." Ben scrambled after her, thrashing through the pine boughs toward the parking lot, the pressure that had seized his chest at the sight of the woman growing to a frantic pounding.

"We have him in our van…to go to hospital," she gasped back over her shoulder. "My father and your wife are with him."

"My God, *you shouldn't have moved him!*"

The woman had reached the edge of the lot and was dashing toward a cream colored van that stood near the entrance to the drive, its sliding panel door half open. Across the lot, the Sager caravan still sat alone beside the ticket booth that faced away from him toward the iron-gated entrance to Sherborne Castle.

"Here! *Hurry please!*" She stopped breathlessly beside the door of the van.

Ben reached her and squinted into the dark interior. A small huddled figure lay motionless on the seat, covered with a faded brown blanket.

"PJ?" He leaned inward and reached for the boy's shoulder. From the rear of the vehicle to his left he sensed a faint blur of motion and the back of his head exploded in a numbing flash of colored spots – then blackness.

Made in the USA
Lexington, KY
02 December 2014